NON SANZ DROICT.

William Shakespeare

The Tragedy
of
KING LEAR

Edited by Russell Fraser

**With New Dramatic Criticism
and an Updated Bibliography**

The Signet Classic Shakespeare
GENERAL EDITOR: SYLVAN BARNET

A SIGNET CLASSIC

NEW AMERICAN LIBRARY

NEW YORK AND SCARBOROUGH, ONTARIO

This book is for Allan Macdonald
Requiescat a labore
Doloroso et amore

SIGNET, SIGNET CLASSIC, MENTOR, PLUME, MERIDIAN AND NAL
BOOKS are published *in the United States* by
New American Library,
1633 Broadway, New York, New York 10019,
in Canada by The New American Library of Canada Limited,
81 Mack Avenue, Scarborough, Ontario M1L 1M8

First Printing, May, 1963

24 25 26 27 28 29 30 31

PRINTED IN THE UNITED STATES OF AMERICA

Contents

Shakespeare: Prefatory Remarks

Between the record of his baptism in Stratford on 26 April 1564 and the record of his burial in Stratford on 25 April 1616, some forty documents name Shakespeare, and many others name his parents, his children, and his grandchildren. More facts are known about William Shakespeare than about any other playwright of the period except Ben Jonson. The facts should, however, be distinguished from the legends. The latter, inevitably more engaging and better known, tell us that the Stratford boy killed a calf in high style, poached deer and rabbits, and was forced to flee to London, where he held horses outside a playhouse. These traditions are only traditions; they may be true, but no evidence supports them, and it is well to stick to the facts.

Mary Arden, the dramatist's mother, was the daughter of a substantial landowner; about 1557 she married John Shakespeare, who was a glove-maker and trader in various farm commodities. In 1557 John Shakespeare was a member of the Council (the governing body of Stratford), in 1558 a constable of the borough, in 1561 one of the two town chamberlains, in 1565 an alderman (entitling him to the appellation "Mr."), in 1568 high bailiff—the town's highest political office, equivalent to mayor. After 1577, for an unknown reason he drops out of local politics. The birthday of William Shakespeare, the eldest son of this locally prominent man, is unrecorded; but the Stratford parish register records that the infant was baptized on 26 April 1564. (It is quite possible that he was born on 23 April, but this date has probably been assigned by tradition because it is the date on which, fifty-two years later, he died.) The attendance records of the Stratford grammar school of the period are not extant, but it is reasonable to assume that the son of a local official attended the school and received substantial training in Latin. The masters of the school from Shakespeare's seventh to fifteenth years held Oxford degrees; the Elizabethan curriculum excluded mathematics and the natural sciences but taught a good deal of Latin rhetoric, logic, and literature. On 27 November 1582 a marriage license was issued to Shakespeare and Anne Hathaway, eight years his senior. The couple had a child in May, 1583. Perhaps the marriage was necessary, but perhaps the couple had earlier engaged in a formal "troth-plight," which would render their children legitimate even if no further ceremony were performed. In 1585 Anne Hathaway bore Shakespeare twins.

That Shakespeare was born is excellent; that he married and had children is pleasant; but that we know nothing about his departure from Stratford to London, or about the beginning of his theatrical career, is lamentable and must be admitted. We would gladly sacrifice details about his children's baptism for details about his earliest days on the stage. Perhaps the poaching episode is true (but it is first reported almost a century after Shakespeare's death), or perhaps he first left Stratford to be a schoolteacher, as another tradition holds; perhaps he was moved by

Such wind as scatters young men through the world,
To seek their fortunes further than at home
Where small experience grows.

In 1592, thanks to the cantankerousness of Robert Greene, a rival playwright and a pamphleteer, we have our first reference, a snarling one, to Shakespeare as an actor and playwright. Greene warns those of his own

educated friends who wrote for the theater against an
actor who has presumed to turn playwright:

> There is an upstart crow, beautified with our feath-
> ers, that with his *tiger's heart wrapped in a player's*
> *hide* supposes he is as well able to bombast out a
> blank verse as the best of you, and being an absolute
> Johannes-factotum is in his own conceit the only
> Shake-scene in a country.

The reference to the player, as well as the allusion to
Aesop's crow (who strutted in borrowed plumage, as an
actor struts in fine words not his own), makes it clear
that by this date Shakespeare had both acted and written. That Shakespeare is meant is indicated not only by
"Shake-scene" but by the parody of a line from one of
Shakespeare's plays, *3 Henry VI*: "O, tiger's heart
wrapped in a woman's hide." If Shakespeare in 1592
was prominent enough to be attacked by an envious
dramatist, he probably had served an apprenticeship in
the theater for at least a few years.

In any case, by 1592 Shakespeare had acted and
written, and there are a number of subsequent references to him as an actor: documents indicate that in
1598 he is a "principal comedian," in 1603 a "principal
tragedian," in 1608 he is one of the "men players." The
profession of actor was not for a gentleman, and it occasionally drew the scorn of university men who resented writing speeches for persons less educated than
themselves, but it was respectable enough: players, if
prosperous, were in effect members of the bourgeoisie,
and there is nothing to suggest that Stratford considered
William Shakespeare lesse than a solid citizen. When, in
1596, the Shakespeares were granted a coat of arms, the
grant was made to Shakespeare's father, but probably
William Shakespeare (who the next year bought the
second-largest house in town) had arranged the matter
on his own behalf. In subsequent transactions he is occasionally styled a gentleman.

Although in 1593 and 1594 Shakespeare published

two narrative poems dedicated to the Earl of Southampton, *Venus and Adonis* and *The Rape of Lucrece,* and may well have written most or all of his sonnets in the middle nineties, Shakespeare's literary activity seems to have been almost entirely devoted to the theater. (It may be significant that the two narrative poems were written in years when the plague closed the theaters for several months.) In 1594 he was a charter member of a theatrical company called the Chamberlain's Men (which in 1603 changed its name to the King's Men); until he retired to Stratford (about 1611, apparently), he was with this remarkably stable company. From 1599 the company acted primarily at the Globe Theatre, in which Shakespeare held a one-tenth interest. Other Elizabethan dramatists are known to have acted, but no other is known also to have been entitled to a share in the profits of the playhouse.

Shakespeare's first eight published plays did not have his name on them, but this is not remarkable; the most popular play of the sixteenth century, Thomas Kyd's *The Spanish Tragedy,* went through many editions without naming Kyd, and Kyd's authorship is known only because a book on the profession of acting happens to quote (and attribute to Kyd) some lines on the interest of Roman emperors in the drama. What is remarkable is that after 1598 Shakespeare's name commonly appears on printed plays—some of which are not his. Another indication of his popularity comes from Francis Meres, author of *Palladis Tamia: Wit's Treasury* (1598): in this anthology of snippets accompanied by an essay on literature, many playwrights are mentioned, but Shakespeare's name occurs more often than any other, and Shakespeare is the only playwright whose plays are listed.

From his acting, playwriting, and share in a theater, Shakespeare seems to have made considerable money. He put it to work, making substantial investments in Stratford real estate. When he made his will (less than a month before he died), he sought to leave his property intact to his descendants. Of small bequests to relatives and to friends (including three actors, Richard Burbage,

John Heminges, and Henry Condell), that to his wife of the second-best bed has provoked the most comment; perhaps it was the bed the couple had slept in, the best being reserved for visitors. In any case, had Shakespeare not excepted it, the bed would have gone (with the rest of his household possessions) to his daughter and her husband. On 25 April 1616 he was buried within the chancel of the church at Stratford. An unattractive monument to his memory, placed on a wall near the grave, says he died on 23 April. Over the grave itself are the lines, perhaps by Shakespeare, that (more than his literary fame) have kept his bones undisturbed in the crowded burial ground where old bones were often dislodged to make way for new:

> Good friend, for Jesus' sake forbear
> To dig the dust enclosèd here.
> Blessed be the man that spares these stones
> And cursed be he that moves my bones.

Thirty-seven plays, as well as some nondramatic poems, are held to constitute the Shakespeare canon. The dates of composition of most of the works are highly uncertain, but there is often evidence of a *terminus a quo* (starting point) and/or a *terminus ad quem* (terminal point) that provides a framework for intelligent guessing. For example, *Richard II* cannot be earlier than 1595, the publication date of some material to which it is indebted; *The Merchant of Venice* cannot be later than 1598, the year Francis Meres mentioned it. Sometimes arguments for a date hang on an alleged topical allusion, such as the lines about the unseasonable weather in *A Midsummer Night's Dream,* II.i.81–117, but such an allusion (if indeed it is an allusion) can be variously interpreted, and in any case there is always the possibility that a topical allusion was inserted during a revision, years after the composition of a play. Dates are often attributed on the basis of style, and although conjectures about style usually rest on other conjectures, sooner or later one must rely on one's literary sense. There is no real proof, for example, that *Othello* is not as early as *Romeo and Juliet,* but one feels *Othello* is later, and because the first record of its performance is 1604, one is glad enough to set its composition at that date and not push it back into Shakespeare's early years. The following chronology, then, is as much indebted to informed guesswork and sensitivity as it is to fact. The dates, necessarily imprecise, indicate something like a scholarly consensus.

PLAYS

1588–93	*The Comedy of Errors*
1588–94	*Love's Labor's Lost*
1590–91	*2 Henry VI*
1590–91	*3 Henry VI*
1591–92	*1 Henry VI*
1592–93	*Richard III*
1592–94	*Titus Andronicus*
1593–94	*The Taming of the Shrew*
1593–95	*The Two Gentlemen of Verona*
1594–96	*Romeo and Juliet*
1595	*Richard II*
1594–96	*A Midsummer Night's Dream*
1596–97	*King John*
1596–97	*The Merchant of Venice*
1597	*1 Henry IV*
1597–98	*2 Henry IV*
1598–99	*Henry V*
1598–1600	*Much Ado About Nothing*
1599	*Julius Caesar*
1599–1600	*As You Like It*
1599–1600	*Twelfth Night*
1600–01	*Hamlet*
1597–1601	*The Merry Wives of Windsor*
1601–02	*Troilus and Cressida*
1602–04	*All's Well That Ends Well*
1603–04	*Othello*
1603–06	*King Lear*

1604	*Measure for Measure*
1605–06	*Macbeth*
1606–07	*Antony and Cleopatra*
1605–08	*Timon of Athens*
1607–09	*Coriolanus*
1608–09	*Pericles*
1609–10	*Cymbeline*
1610–11	*The Winter's Tale*
1611–12	*The Tempest*
1612–13	*Henry VIII*

POEMS

1592	*Venus and Adonis*
1593–94	*The Rape of Lucrece*
1593–1600	*Sonnets*
1600–01	*The Phoenix and the Turtle*

Shakespeare's Theater

In Shakespeare's infancy, Elizabethan actors performed wherever they could—in great halls, at court, in the courtyards of inns. The innyards must have made rather unsatisfactory theaters: on some days they were unavailable because carters bringing goods to London used them as depots; when available, they had to be rented from the innkeeper; perhaps most important, London inns were subject to the Common Council of London, which was not well disposed toward theatricals. In 1574 the Common Council required that plays and playing places in London be licensed. It asserted that

> sundry great disorders and inconveniences have been found to ensue to this city by the inordinate haunting of great multitudes of people, specially youth, to plays, interludes, and shows, namely occasion of frays and quarrels, evil practices of incontinency in great inns having chambers and secret places adjoining to their open stages and galleries,

and ordered that innkeepers who wished licenses to hold performances put up a bond and make contributions to the poor.

The requirement that plays and innyard theaters be licensed, along with the other drawbacks of playing at inns, probably drove James Burbage (a carpenter-turned-actor) to rent in 1576 a plot of land northeast of the city walls and to build here—on property outside the jurisdiction of the city—England's first permanent construction designed for plays. He called it simply the Theatre. About all that is known of its construction is that it was wood. It soon had imitators, the most famous being the Globe (1599), built across the Thames (again outside the city's jurisdiction), out of timbers of the Theatre, which had been dismantled when Burbage's lease ran out.

There are three important sources of information about the structure of Elizabethan playhouses—drawings, a contract, and stage directions in plays. Of drawings, only the so-called De Witt drawing (c. 1596) of the Swan—really a friend's copy of De Witt's drawing—is of much significance. It shows a building of three tiers, with a stage jutting from a wall into the yard or center of the building. The tiers are roofed, and part of the stage is covered by a roof that projects from the rear and is supported at its front on two posts, but the groundlings, who paid a penny to stand in front of the stage, were exposed to the sky. (Performances in such a playhouse were held only in the daytime; artificial illumination was not used.) At the rear of the stage are two doors; above the stage is a gallery. The second major source of information, the contract for the Fortune, specifies that although the Globe is to be the model, the Fortune is to be square, eighty feet outside and fifty-five inside. The stage is to be forty-three feet broad, and is to extend into the middle of the yard (i.e., it is twenty-seven and a half feet deep). For patrons willing to pay more than the general admission charged of the groundlings, there were to be three galleries provided with seats. From the third chief source, stage di-

rections, one learns that entrance to the stage was by
doors, presumably spaced widely apart at the rear
("Enter one citizen at one door, and another at the
other"), and that in addition to the platform stage there
was occasionally some sort of curtained booth or alcove
allowing for "discovery" scenes, and some sort of playing space "aloft" or "above" to represent (for example)
the top of a city's walls or a room above the street.
Doubtless each theater had its own peculiarities, but perhaps we can talk about a "typical" Elizabethan theater
if we realize that no theater need exactly have fit the
description, just as no father is the typical father with
3.7 children. This hypothetical theater is wooden, round
or polygonal (in *Henry V* Shakespeare calls it a
"wooden *O*"), capable of holding some eight hundred
spectators standing in the yard around the projecting
elevated stage and some fifteen hundred additional spectators seated in the three roofed galleries. The stage, protected by a "shadow" or "heavens" or roof, is entered by two doors; behind the doors is the "tiring
house" (attiring house, i.e., dressing room), and above
the doors is some sort of gallery that may sometimes
hold spectators but that can be used (for example) as
the bedroom from which Romeo—according to a stage
direction in one text—"goeth down." Some evidence suggests that a throne can be lowered on to the platform
stage, perhaps from the "shadow"; certainly characters
can descend from the stage through a trap or traps into
the cellar or "hell." Sometimes this space beneath the
platform accommodates a sound-effects man or musician
(in *Antony and Cleopatra* "music of the hautboys is
under the stage") or an actor (in *Hamlet* the "Ghost
cries under the stage"). Most characters simply walk on
and off, but because there is no curtain in front of the
platform, corpses will have to be carried off (Hamlet must
lug Polonius' guts into the neighbor room) or will have
to fall at the rear, where the curtain on the alcove or
booth can be drawn to conceal them.

Such may have been the so-called "public theater." Another kind of theater, called the "private theater" because

its much greater admission charge limited its audience to the wealthy or the prodigal, must be briefly mentioned. The private theater was basically a large room, entirely roofed, and therefore artificially illluminated, with a stage at one end. In 1576 one such theater was established in Blackfriars, a Dominican priory in London that had been suppressed in 1538 and confiscated by the Crown and thus was not under the city's jurisdiction. All the actors in the Blackfriars theater were boys about eight to thirteen years old (in the public theaters similar boys played female parts; a boy Lady Macbeth played to a man Macbeth). This private theater had a precarious existence, and ceased operations in 1584. In 1596 James Burbage, who had already made theatrical history by building the Theatre, began to construct a second Blackfriars theater. He died in 1597, and for several years this second Blackfriars theater was used by a troupe of boys, but in 1608 two of Burbage's sons and five other actors (including Shakespeare) became joint operators of the theater, using it in the winter when the open-air Globe was unsuitable. Perhaps such a smaller theater, roofed, artificially illuminated, and with a tradition of a courtly audience, exerted an influence on Shakespeare's late plays.

Performances in the private theaters may well have had intermissions during which music was played, but in the public theaters the action was probably uninterrupted, flowing from scene to scene almost without a break. Actors would enter, speak, exit, and others would immediately enter and establish (if necessary) the new locale by a few properties and by words and gestures. Here are some samples of Shakespeare's scene painting:

This is Illyria, lady.

Well, this is the Forest of Arden.

This castle hath a pleasant seat; the air
Nimbly and sweetly recommends itself
Unto our gentle senses.

On the other hand, it is a mistake to conceive of the Elizabethan stage as bare. Although Shakespeare's Chorus in *Henry V* calls the stage an "unworthy scaffold" and urges the spectators to "eke out our performance with your mind," there was considerable spectacle. The last act of *Macbeth,* for example, has five stage directions calling for "drum and colors," and another sort of appeal to the eye is indicated by the stage direction "Enter Macduff, with Macbeth's head." Some scenery and properties may have been substantial; doubtless a throne was used, and in one play of the period we encounter this direction: "Hector takes up a great piece of rock and casts at Ajax, who tears up a young tree by the roots and assails Hector." The matter is of some importance, and will be glanced at again in the next section.

The Texts of Shakespeare

Though eighteen of his plays were published during his lifetime, Shakespeare seems never to have supervised their publication. There is nothing unusual here; when a playwright sold a play to a theatrical company he surrendered his ownership of it. Normally a company would not publish the play, because to publish it meant to allow competitors to acquire the piece. Some plays, however, did get published: apparently treacherous actors sometimes pieced together a play for a publisher, sometimes a company in need of money sold a play, and sometimes a company allowed a play to be published that no longer drew audiences. That Shakespeare did not concern himself with publication, then, is scarcely remarkable; of his contemporaries only Ben Jonson carefully supervised the publication of his own plays. In 1623, seven years after Shakespeare's death, John Heminges and Henry Condell (two senior members of Shakespeare's company, who had performed with him for about twenty years) collected his plays—published and unpublished—into a large volume, commonly called the First Folio.

(A folio is a volume consisting of sheets that have been folded once, each sheet thus making two leaves, or four pages. The eighteen plays published during Shakespeare's lifetime had been issued one play per volume in small books called quartos. Each sheet in a quarto has been folded twice, making four leaves, or eight pages.) The First Folio contains thirty-six plays; a thirty-seventh, *Pericles,* though not in the Folio, is regarded as canonical. Heminges and Condell suggest in an address "To the great variety of readers" that the republished plays are presented in better form than in the quartos: "Before you were abused with diverse stolen and surreptitious copies, maimed and deformed by the frauds and stealths of injurious impostors that exposed them; even those, are now offered to your view cured and perfect of their limbs, and all the rest absolute in their numbers, as he [i.e., Shakespeare] conceived them."

Whoever was assigned to prepare the texts for publication in the First Folio seems to have taken his job seriously and yet not to have performed it with uniform care. The sources of the texts seem to have been, in general, good unpublished copies or the best published copies. The first play in the collection, *The Tempest,* is divided into acts and scenes, has unusually full stage directions and descriptions of spectacle, and concludes with a list of the characters, but the editor was not able (or willing) to present all of the succeeding texts so fully dressed. Later texts occasionally show signs of carelessness: in one scene of *Much Ado About Nothing* the names of actors, instead of characters, appear as speech prefixes, as they had in the quarto, which the Folio reprints; proofreading throughout the Folio is spotty and apparently was done without reference to the printer's copy; the pagination of *Hamlet* jumps from 156 to 257.

A modern editor of Shakespeare must first select his copy; no problem if the play exists only in the Folio, but a considerable problem if the relationship between a quarto and the Folio—or an early quarto and a later one—is unclear. When an editor has chosen what seems to him to be the most authoritative text or texts for his copy, he has not done with making decisions. First of all, he must reckon with Elizabethan spelling. If he is not producing a facsimile, he probably modernizes it, but ought he to preserve the old form of words that apparently were pronounced quite unlike their modern forms—"lanthorn," "alablaster"? If he preserves these forms, is he really preserving Shakespeare's forms or perhaps those of a compositor in the printing house? What is one to do when one finds "lanthorn" and "lantern" in adjacent lines? (The editors of this series in general, but not invariably, assume that words should be spelled in their modern form.) Elizabethan punctuation, too, presents problems. For example, in the First Folio, the only text for the play, Macbeth rejects his wife's idea that he can wash the blood from his hand:

> no: this my Hand will rather
> The multitudinous Seas incarnardine,
> Making the Greene one, Red.

Obviously an editor will remove the superfluous capitals, and he will probably alter the spelling to "incarnadine," but will he leave the comma before "red," letting Macbeth speak of the sea as "the green one," or will he (like most modern editors) remove the comma and thus have Macbeth say that his hand will make the ocean *uniformly* red?

An editor will sometimes have to change more than spelling or punctuation. Macbeth says to his wife:

> I dare do all that may become a man,
> Who dares no more, is none.

For two centuries editors have agreed that the second line is unsatisfactory, and have emended "no" to "do": "Who dares do more is none." But when in the same play Ross says that fearful persons

> floate vpon a wilde and violent Sea
> Each way, and moue,

need "move" be emended to "none," as it often is, on the
hunch that the compositor misread the manuscript? The
editors of the Signet Classic Shakespeare have restrained themselves from making abundant emendations.
In their minds they hear Dr. Johnson on the dangers of
emending: "I have adopted the Roman sentiment, that it
is more honorable to save a citizen than to kill an
enemy." Some departures (in addition to spelling, punctuation, and lineation) from the copy text have of course
been made, but the original readings are listed in a note
following the play, so that the reader can evaluate them
for himself.

The editors of the Signet Classic Shakespeare, following tradition, have added line numbers and in many
cases act and scene divisions as well as indications of
locale at the beginning of scenes. The Folio divided
most of the plays into acts and some into scenes. Early
eighteenth-century editors increased the divisions. These
divisions, which provide a convenient way of referring
to passages in the plays, have been retained, but when
not in the text chosen as the basis for the Signet Classic
text they are enclosed in square brackets [ ] to indicate
that they are editorial additions. Similarly, although no
play of Shakespeare's published during his lifetime was
equipped with indications of locale at the heads of
scene divisions, locales have here been added in square
brackets for the convenience of the reader, who lacks
the information afforded to spectators by costumes, properties, and gestures. The spectator can tell at a glance
he is in the throne room, but without an editorial indication the reader may be puzzled for a while. It should
be mentioned, incidentally, that there are a few authentic
stage directions—perhaps Shakespeare's, perhaps a
prompter's—that suggest locales: for example, "Enter
Brutus in his orchard," and "They go up into the Senate
house." It is hoped that the bracketed additions provide
the reader with the sort of help provided in these two
authentic directions, but it is equally hoped that the
reader will remember that the stage was not loaded with
scenery.

No editor during the course of his work can fail to recollect some words Heminges and Condell prefixed to the Folio:

> It had been a thing, we confess, worthy to have been wished, that the author himself had lived to have set forth and overseen his own writings. But since it hath been ordained otherwise, and he by death departed from that right, we pray you do not envy his friends the office of their care and pain to have collected and published them.

Nor can an editor, after he has done his best, forget Heminges and Condell's final words: "And so we leave you to other of his friends, whom if you need can be your guides. If you need them not, you can lead yourselves, and others. And such readers we wish him."

Sylvan Barnet
Tufts University

Introduction

In structure *Lear* differs significantly from the other tragedies of Shakespeare. It is like them in this. It dramatizes the fall of a hero who, assailed by the rebel passion, gives it sovereign sway and masterdom, and is in consequence destroyed. That is the case of Brutus, Othello, and Macbeth. But the resemblance is more ostensible than real. Ostensibly the play is one long denouement. In fact the declining action, which is the dogging of the hero to death, is complemented by a rising action, which is the hero's regeneration. Yeats's metaphor of the gyres is apposite. As the one wanes to nothing, the other, which lives within it, emerges. This emergent, or renascent, action is a condition of the hero's loss of the world. The play fools us. Its primary story is not the descent of the King into Hell, but the ascent of the King as he climbs the Mountain of Purgatory and is fulfilled. The suspense the play develops is a function of the ascending action, which is not material but spiritual. Battles and thrones are nugatory. What does it profit a man if he gain the whole world and suffer the loss of his soul?

The rising and falling curves, the hero tasting his folly, the hero triumphing over it, intersect in the center of the play, in the fourth scene of Act III. It is on the heath that Lear reaches his nadir. His characteristic utterance is the imperative mood: the wonted reversal follows: he is made less than the slave and sumpter to a detested groom. These are the injuries that he himself has procured. So far the parallel is precise to the action of the other tragedies.

But now the crucial difference. It is also on the heath that Lear is made pregnant to pity. That is another and an unexpected kind of reversal. "In boy, go first." These words, addressed to the Fool, who stands shivering in the rain before a hovel that is the refuge of a madman, constitute the real, as opposed to the apparent, hinge of the play. They do not signal the decay but the metamorphosis of the King: Lear in a red shirt. The great apostrophe to the poor follows at once. From this point, the action turns upward.

The structure of the subplot duplicates and so of course clarifies and confirms that of the central story. As the King is limed, and by his own folly, so are Gloucester and Edgar: "A credulous father, and a brother noble." The one is, initially, an unthinking sensualist. The other, the younger, is initially a kind of clown: "and pat he comes like the catastrophe of the old comedy." But the degradation of Gloucester is not ratified. He also undergoes a miraculous transformation. The critical point or pivot at which this transformation is announced is located, like Lear's, in the mathematical center of the play (III, iii), which is also, with a fit symmetry, the metaphysical center. The placatory man, who would have all well between the contending parties, is emboldened suddenly to choose. "If I die for it, as no less is threatened me, the King my old master must be relieved." In that decision is his death, but also his salvation.

The retrieving of Edgar is more spectacular, if not so abruptly achieved. Edgar is conceded the chance to grow and prosper. He seizes his chance; he makes himself over. "Bear free and patient thoughts." The dupe of the opening scenes is the philosopher who dominates in the close of the play.

This is not to pretend that the close is thereby made happy. "All's cheerless, dark, and deadly." Kent's somber valediction is approved. If the kindness of the one daughter hints at the redemption of Nature, it does not deprecate entirely the general curse which twain have brought her to. The implication is uneasy in Edgar's assertion (as of one who is saying "what we ought to say") that man must obey the weight of the time. His flawed heart, on the evidence of the play, is too weak to support it. His nature cannot carry the affliction or the fear.

> What ribs of oak, when mountains melt on them,
> Can hold the mortise?

Man endures until he expires, dying the pain of death every hour, in a night that pities neither wise man nor fool. What is more unsettling, to be wise is not to be provident. "Man may his fate foresee, but not prevent." And thus Webster's conclusion, in *The White Devil*: " 'Tis better to be fortunate than wise." Man is the natural fool of fortune. That is the title he is born with. It is the stars, and not our own endeavors, that govern. After all we are their tennis balls, struck and bandied which way please them. We do not get our deserts. The optimism is foolishness, to which we are prone.

> I would not take this from report. It is,
> And my heart breaks at it.

The wry conjunctions contrived by the playwright—who knows out of what bitterness or whimsy—attest to its fatuity. Edgar, in a sanguine mood, is sure that the worst returns to laughter. He is confronted at once with the bleeding visage of his father.

> The worst is not
> So long as we can say "This is the worst."

But Shakespeare is not done with him yet. "If ever I return to you again, I'll bring you comfort." That is Edgar's promise to Gloucester before the battle. It is a rash promise, and poor comfort attends on it. A hiatus ensues, filled up with alarums and excursions. Then Edgar reenters and speaks again: "Away, old man. . . . King Lear hath lost."

The optimism of Albany, as it is more eupeptic, is more sternly reproved.

All friends shall taste
The wages of their virtue, and all foes
The cup of their deservings.

In that cheerful saying his philosophy is embodied. But
the pentameter line wants its conclusion. Albany, rather
cruelly, is made to supply it: "O, see, see!" It is the last
agony of Lear to which his attention is directed.

Albany, as he presents the hopeful man who insists, a
little too suavely, that God's in His Heaven, is Shakespeare's particular butt. It is he who cries, of Cordelia:
"The gods defend her!" The stage direction follows,
enforcing the most monstrous conjunction in the play:
"Enter Lear with Cordelia in his arms." The gods do not
defend us. Perhaps they are unable to do so. "The gods
reward your kindness," says Kent to Gloucester. That
is the reading of the Folio, and surely it is the right
reading. But the reading of the Quarto provokes speculation: "The gods deserve your kindness." It is as if the
gods are weak, and require that man collaborate with
them in wielding the world (Shakespeare imitating Will
James). Lear, as his ardor for the right grows upon
him, shakes the superflux to the wretched. His intent is,
as he says, to show the heavens more just. It is at least
tenable to interpret: his intent is to justify their feckless
ways as he can.

Maybe the heavens are worse than insufficient. What
is said of the King,

If Fortune brag of two she loved and hated,
One of them we behold,

suggests not merely a lack of capacity in the ordering of
things, but a malevolent purpose, as if the gods had
marked us down for their sport. On this reading, Lear's
reference to himself and Cordelia as "God's spies" will
mean, as Warburton suggested long ago, "spies placed
over God Almighty, to watch his motions." Maybe there
is need of surveillance, if the human sacrifices on which
the gods themselves throw incense are offered up for

their delectation; if the brand of fire that parts the pre-
destined victims is handed down, and with an antique
malice, from Heaven. *Tantaene animis coelestibus irae!*
The chill that invades us as, huddled with the others
against the roaring wind and rain, we await the advent
of unaccommodated man: "What art thou that dost
grumble there i' th' straw?" is occasioned by the wild
surmise, so much more fearful because it is involuntary,
that the fiend is really walking up and down in the earth,
and with the sufferance and even the connivance of
Heaven. In the pitiless conclusion of *King Lear*,

> Thou'lt come no more,
> Never, never, never, never, never,

the dominion of the Prince of Darkness seems confirmed,
and his presence a substantial presence as, with his terrible vans, he enshadows and overwhelms the just and
the unjust alike.

That is, I daresay, only an apparition, the disnatured
child of night thoughts, and as such may be dispelled.
But it needs more than to rub one's eyes, or to mutter a
pious ejaculation. To such a degree is this true that even
critics so tough-minded as Dr. Johnson have averted
their eyes rather than acquiesce in the final horror with
which the dramatist confronts them. It is too literal, too
realistic for "dramatick exhibition." And yet it is remarkable that this play, in which Shakespeare's unremitting
fidelity to fact is almost an occasion for scandal, mani-
fests in its beginning a studied and a deliberate indif-
ference to fact. If subsequent scenes are so realistic as
hardly to be endured, the opening scenes have not to do
with realism but with ritual and romance. Their abiding
characteristic is a niggling formality. They do not wear
the aspect of life so much as the aspect of art. Kent,
lapsing into rude rhyme as he takes his departure,
catches and communicates that aspect. His language is
gnomic, admonitory, and simple—not naïvely but consciously simple: "artificial." He is not, for the moment, a
real (an eccentric) man who displaces air like Hamlet or

Parolles. He is, and by design, a flat character, highly conventionalized, who figures in a mumming or mystery. He would speak a prophecy before he goes.

The language of the other protagonists is of a piece with his. It does not evoke—not yet—the savage business of dragons of the prime (for all that the dragon is portentous in the comminatory speeches of the King), so much as the ceremonious (the otherworldly!) business of proceedings at law and finance. Legal and fiscal metaphors reverberate. Gloucester, treating of his sons, asserts that the elder is no more dear than the younger, in his account. Lear, enacting his intention to abdicate the throne, renounces interest of territory, or possession. In lieu of Kent's insistence that he reserve his state, he stipulates his troop of knights as reservation, explicitly a legalism, in which the action of retaining a privilege is denoted. He would extend his largest bounty where nature challenges merit, or makes title to it. Regan, whose tenders of affection aim at that title, finds that Goneril has anticipated her very deed of love. The King, in whose lexicon love is a commodity, urges his youngest daughter to discover what portion her protestations can draw. But Cordelia loves only according to her bond. Failing to please, her price is fallen. Goneril pleases, in that she is taken as permitting to her father twice the retinue permitted by Regan. Her devotion may therefore be measured. She is precisely twice her sister's love.

Lear is not easily persuaded of his error, that devotion—in his psychology, a ponderable thing—is to be assessed and ought to be requited in ponderable ways. The inadmissible equation is there still, in the crass appeal to Regan when his agony is upon him:

> Thy half o' th' kingdom hast thou not forgot,
> Wherein I thee endowed.

He is appropriately answered, since that respects of fortune are his love:

> Good sir, to the purpose.

This patina of the unreal and the ritualistic, overlaying the initial action of the play, is not peculiar to the love test. The characters themselves move in an air of unreality. There is about them a felt sense of disjunction, as between what they are and what they seem to be. Lear is not a king but the show of a king. It is an insubstantial pageant over which he presides, recalling, in its unreality, the specious parade with which an earlier tragedy of Shakespeare's commences, that of Richard II, the mockery king of snows. Kent's acumen is verified when, with a lack of respect that is intended to shock and thereby to quicken perception, he sees and salutes his master, not as a monarch but as an old man.

But if Lear is a simulacrum, so are the wicked daughters. Their essential vacuity, echoing to the touch, announces itself as it issues in their fulsome avowals of love. Kent points to it obliquely in his praise of Cordelia:

Nor are those empty-hearted whose low sounds
Reverb no hollowness.

Gloucester discerns it, magnified to cosmic proportions, in the disordered state of the macrocosm, riven by machinations, by the hollowness that is hypocrisy. All that glisters is taken for gold. The pretension of the hypocrite, who professes herself

an enemy to all other joys
Which the most precious square of sense professes,

weighs more than the practice of the candid and guileless retainer, who professes himself to be no less than he seems. The vizard is everything, and hence what is lifelike and vital is eclipsed. The characters are cut in alabaster. The same metaphor describes the fool and the knave and the paragon of virtue, divesting each of human personality. Gloucester, who seems a good old man, is brazed by self-indulgence, become like hard metal. Regan, in whom nature appears tender-hefted, is hardened to insensibility, made of that self metal as her

sister. Cordelia is, conversely, a little-seeming substance.
But Cordelia is rendered also in nonhuman terms: her
love, a precious metal, is more ponderous than her
tongue.

   Stylization of language and gesture is notable in such
a play as *The Tempest,* and for excellent and obvious
reasons. Shakespeare's resort to it in *King Lear* seems,
however, gratuitous, and even antipathetic to the spirit
of the play. *Lear* is not masquelike nor, certainly, romantic, in the harrowing story it tells. But observe that
The Tempest begins, not formally, but realistically, with
the faithful depicting of a ship driving on the rocks, a
wild and literal scene in which the blasphemy and execra-
tion of real and affrighted persons bass the throbbing
of the storm. And then the scene shifts abruptly.
The auditor or reader, whose belief is purchased at the
outset by a terrific glimpse of the real world, is brought
safe to shore: is induced to enter, and willingly, the world
of enchantment and romance. The fact of the transition,
and the implausibility attendant on it, elude him. The
tempest is still dinning in his ears.

   In *King Lear* the dramatic problem is exactly re-
versed. It is to ensure that those whose disenchantment
the playwright is already preparing, who are to be compelled to look on the Gorgon-features, will not evince incredulity or petrifaction. The problem is resolved by
emphasizing at the outset the elements of unreality and
romance. The impelling action of *Lear* is made to re-
semble a fairy tale, which is, I suppose, its ultimate
provenance. The auditor or reader is cozened. Before he
is aware, he has become a participant in the fierce and
excessively painful dispute between damnation and im-
passioned clay.

   But there is more than craft to Shakespeare's design
in thus introducing his drama. He makes his characters
unreal initially because he means them, at least in part,
to be symbolic. The stylized quality of the beginning, as
of a charade, its legalistic and ceremonious nature, the
exalting in it of appearance as against reality, all work
to the fulfilling of that primary intention. And though

Lear is essentially representational drama, though realism very quickly takes precedence over ritual, the element of the symbolic is never dissipated altogether but figures in important ways until the end. Just as in *Twelfth Night,* whose burden is mistaken identity and the hocus-pocus of identical twins, realism intrudes persistently to temper and give substance to romance—

> In nature there's no blemish but the mind;
> None can be called deformed but the unkind.
> Virtue is beauty, but the beauteous evil
> Are empty trunks o'erflourished by the devil

—so in *King Lear,* an anti-romantic play in that its burden is a relentless anatomizing of evil, the symbolic declines to yield entirely to the representational. It persists, not to give substance to the real, which is substantial enough—

> Out, vile jelly!
> Where is thy luster now?

—but to order the real and make it meaningful, to avoid a confounding of it with the merely sensational. Not to grasp this ordering function is, necessarily, to run counter, to smell a fault where no fault is. Thus the embarrassment of critics so estimable as Goethe (for whom the action of the play was a tissue of the improbable and absurd), and Coleridge (who saw the first scene as dispensable), and A. C. Bradley (who detected and enumerated in the whole, more and grosser inconsistencies than in any other of the great tragedies).

Misconstruction of the role and character of Cordelia typifies this failure to come to terms with the symbolic. Cordelia is, of old, a deeply disquieting figure. Why does she love, and yet remain silent? The question has engendered a little galaxy of answers. It is a question not to be asked. The first principle of good dramatic manners is to concede to the dramatist his given, so long as he is able to exploit it. Here, the given is the heroine's

fatal reserve. It is the lever or prise that starts the
play on its progress. As such, it may not be queried,
any more than the procedure that governs in chess or in
the writing of an Italian sonnet.

But "reserve" is after all the wrong word. It suggests
the wrong frame of reference. It leads to the rationaliza-
tion of conduct, on realistic grounds. To make the horrid
point, this judgment of a contemporary critic may be cited,
that Cordelia loved her father "less than she loved her
own way and hated her sisters." That is a fair sample
of the appeal to realism. It is at all costs to be avoided.
Cordelia does not betray, what Coleridge thought to perceive, "some little faulty admixture of pride and sullen-
ness." No faintest stain of guilt or responsibility at-
taches to her. She is not imperious, like the King, not
headstrong, not intractable. The appeal to heredity is a
variation of the appeal to realism, and is, in this con-
text, equally and altogether inapposite. Shakespeare's
characters, unlike Eugene O'Neill's, have no antecedents. It is of no use to say that Cordelia is her father's
daughter. The reason she will not speak is because she
cannot speak; and she cannot because the heart of a
fool is in his mouth but the mouth of the wise is in his
heart.

This is to say that the muteness of Cordelia (like the
fantastic credulity of Gloucester) is not so much a reflection of character as it is the embodiment of an idea.
Less real than symbolic, her affinity is more to a creature of fairy tale like Cinderella than to a heroine of
the realistic drama like Blanche DuBois. In delineating
her behavior the playwright may be, psychologically, so
penetrating and exact as really to catch the manners living as they rise: that is partly a gratuity. More important is his intention, not to portray a veritable woman,
but to dramatize the proposition that plainness is more
than eloquence, that beauty is to be purchased by the
weight, that meager lead, which rather threatens than
promises aught, buys more than silver and gold. The
agitation of those who worry the details of the love test
in an attempt to make it credible, which means to make

it conformable to the canons of the realistic theater, is founded on their misapprehension of symbolic action.

When Cordelia is depicted as the last and least, it is not her slightness of stature that the dramatist is glancing at—or not that, decisively. He is preparing an ironic and a pregnant echo, to amplify Kent's assertion, a little later:

> Thy youngest daughter does not love thee least.

But more than that, he is invoking the promise of Scripture, unspoken in the play, and yet close to the theme, which is the heart (but not the moral!) of the play: The first shall be last and the last shall be first. When Cordelia herself exclaims, as she prepares to engage the British powers,

> O dear father,
> It is thy business that I go about,

it is not altogether the realistic business of an imminent battle to which she is adverting. (Certainly that business does not much preoccupy Shakespeare.) And therefore we are not to wonder why the King of France was, so inopportunely, called back to his kingdom, nor whether Shakespeare's allegiance or circumspection dictated the victory of the English. We want to catch in what is said an anterior saying, the sentence of the Evangelist, so much more than a literary reminiscence, and estimate accordingly the symbolic role the speaker plays: "Knew ye not that I must go about my father's business." It may be that Cordelia is that quintessence of womanhood celebrated reverentially (and with an appropriate taciturnity as to particulars) by critics like A. W. Schlegel: "Of Cordelia's heavenly beauty of soul, I do not dare to speak." But it is not after all the literal woman to whom Shakespeare is holding up the mirror. Compare Beatrice in *Much Ado,* or Rosalind in *As You Like It.*

It is a nice but an indispensable point to adjudicate, just when the dramatist intends that the canons of ordi-

nary realism are to be set aside or, better, transcended.
Pretty clearly he wishes to transcend them when, in
Act II, Kent is made to sleep in the stocks, and Edgar,
unmindful of him, to step forward and tell of his purposed transformation. Bradley is bemused: "One cannot
help asking . . . whether Edgar is mad that he should return from his hollow tree . . . to his father's castle in
order to soliloquize." But Shakespeare, in juxtaposing
the two characters, is not concerned with motivation
or, certainly, with locale. No doubt the Bedlam is understood to remain on the heath. But precisely where he
is, is not a question that ought to detain us. Neither are
we to ask why he fails to perceive that someone else is
up there with him on stage, in full view of the audience,
and so, presumably, of himself; nor how Kent, for all
his travails, can sleep undisturbed through twenty lines
of blank verse. In the bringing together of the two good
men, each of whom has been driven to the lowest
and most dejected point of fortune, a dramatic emblem
is achieved, a speaking picture, whose purport is not
realistic but symbolic. What Shakespeare is after is this
dark collocation, or sequence:

A good man's fortune may grow out at heels.

Edgar I nothing am.

In the same way the symbolic overtops the conven-
tionally real when, in the final act, Edgar issues his
challenge to Edmund. One is not to belabor the improbability of Edmund's failure to recognize his brother,
though, in point of fact, the failure is itself symbolic:
the villain is indeed cozened and beguiled, and not for
reasons of dramatic exigency but by virtue of his own
willful behavior. But what is central to the scene is the
intimation one hears, in the blast of the trumpet that announces the combat, of that final trump that vindicates
the right and summons the perpetrator of wrong to the
Judgment. When—another illustration—Edgar, opposing
Oswald, assumes the character of a rustic, the clown-

ish dialect he speaks is, realistically, absurd: what is its occasion? Symbolically, however, it is deeply congruous. The power of truth is attested to, however ludicrous its aspect, and the frailty which is falsehood exposed, in this meeting of the ragged fellow, whose West Country accent gives him out to be a bumpkin, but who intrinsically merits and possesses all honors, and the gilded courtier, whose extrinsic show and sophistication betoken all honors and are as paste and cover to none.

> The Prince of Darkness is a gentleman.

In Edgar's vanquishing of Oswald, which is the triumph of the lowly and the unprepossessing over the world of robes and furred gowns, Lear's great social speeches are enacted and answered.

A similar intention, to effect on stage a symbolic tableau, dictates the grouping of the protagonists at the end of the play. All are there in the resolution, occupying, I think, the same positions they assumed at first, and not least the wicked sisters, whose dead bodies are brought on, no doubt to exemplify this judgment of the heavens, but more, to direct the attention of the audience back and back, over all the dreadful ground that has been traced, to the opening scene. In their beginning is their ending. Perhaps the great wheel of the play, now come full circle, is impelled in its progress by something more than mechanical law.

What this other law may be is the central question Shakespeare poses and endeavors to answer. Lear, as is fitting, is made to enunciate it: "Who is it that can tell me who I am?" But the question is not peculiar to Lear but is implicit in the utterance and conduct of all those who inhabit the darkness with him. Kent as Caius is interrogated by the King:

> What art thou?
> A man, sir.

But what is it, to be a man? What is man to profess?

To what law are his services bound? Gloucester in-
terrogates Edgar: "Now, good sir, what are you?" and is
answered:

> A most poor man, made tame to fortune's blows,
> Who, by the art of known and feeling sorrows,
> Am pregnant to good pity.

Cornwall, whose disposition will not be rubbed or
stopped, does not manifest that pity. It is ascendant,
though tardily, in Gloucester, who, if he dies for it, must
relieve his master. Why is that? And why had Kent
rather break his own heart than the King's? How does
one construe that fitness to which Albany appeals, in
declining to let his hands obey his blood; or that pleasure, a more intriguing word, which inclines the Old Man
to succor the blinded Gloucester, "Come on't what will"?
What point inheres in Albany's characterization of Oswald, as Oswald reports it:

> he called me sot,
> And told me I had turned the wrong side out;

and in what manner does it comment on the Captain's
decision to collaborate in the killing of the King and
Cordelia:

> If it be man's work, I'll do it.

There ought here to ensue a brief though perceptible
silence, in token of the irony and expectation with which
these laconic words are charged. The dramatist is bidding
us essay a definition of the nature of man's work and,
concomitantly, of the nature of man. Edmund, with his
customary *sang-froid*, addresses himself to the task:

> men
> Are as the time is.

Kent speaks to it, describing Oswald:

A tailor made thee.

So in whimsical ways does the Fool, begging pardon of Goneril:

Cry you mercy, I took you for a joint stool;

and also the King, whose confusion is at once real and assumed:

Your name, fair gentlewoman?

and, in sterner ways, the Servant, drawing his sword against Cornwall:

Nay, then, come on, and take the chance of anger.

To divine the way in which these lines reticulate is to resolve at least a corner of the mystery which is the play.

RUSSELL FRASER
University of Michigan

The Tragedy of
KING LEAR

[DRAMATIS PERSONAE

Lear, King of Britain
King of France
Duke of Burgundy
Duke of Cornwall, husband to Regan
Duke of Albany, husband to Goneril
Earl of Kent
Earl of Gloucester
Edgar, son to Gloucester
Edmund, bastard son to Gloucester
Curan, a courtier
Oswald, steward to Goneril
Old Man, tenant to Gloucester
Doctor
Lear's Fool
A Captain, subordinate to Edmund
Gentlemen, attending on Cordelia
A Herald
Servants to Cornwall
Goneril ⎫
Regan ⎬ daughters to Lear
Cordelia ⎭
Knights attending on Lear, Officers,
    Messengers, Soldiers, Attendants

Scene: Britain]

The Tragedy of King Lear

ACT I

Scene I. [*King Lear's palace*.]

Enter Kent, Gloucester, and Edmund.

Kent. I thought the King had more affected°[1] the Duke of Albany° than Cornwall.

Gloucester. It did always seem so to us; but now, in the division of the kingdom, it appears not which of the dukes he values most, for equalities are so   5
weighed that curiosity in neither can make choice of either's moiety.°

Kent. Is not this your son, my lord?

Gloucester. His breeding,° sir, hath been at my charge. I have so often blushed to acknowledge   10
him that now I am brazed° to't.

Kent. I cannot conceive° you.

Gloucester. Sir, this young fellow's mother could; whereupon she grew round-wombed, and had indeed, sir, a son for her cradle ere she had a hus-   15
band for her bed. Do you smell a fault?

---

[1] The degree sign (°) indicates a footnote, which is keyed to the text by line number. Text references are printed in *italic* type; the annotation follows in roman type.
I.i. 1 *affected* loved   2 *Albany* Albanacte, whose domain extended "from the river Humber to the point of Caithness" (Holinshed)   5-7 *equalities . . . moiety* i.e., shares are so balanced against one another that careful examination by neither can make him wish the other's portion   9 *breeding* upbringing   11 *brazed* made brazen, hardened   12 *conceive* understand (pun follows)

Kent. I cannot wish the fault undone, the issue° of it
being so proper.°

20 *Gloucester.* But I have a son, sir, by order of law,
some year elder than this, who yet is no dearer
in my account:° though this knave° came something saucily° to the world before he was sent
for, yet was his mother fair, there was good sport
at his making, and the whoreson° must be acknowl-
25 edged. Do you know this noble gentleman, Edmund?

Edmund. No, my lord.

Gloucester. My Lord of Kent. Remember him here-
after as my honorable friend.

30 *Edmund.* My services to your lordship.

Kent. I must love you, and sue° to know you better.

Edmund. Sir, I shall study deserving.

Gloucester. He hath been out° nine years, and away
he shall again. The King is coming.

*Sound a sennet.° Enter one bearing a coronet,°
then King Lear, then the Dukes of Cornwall and
Albany, next Goneril, Regan, Cordelia, and Attendants.*

35 *Lear.* Attend the lords of France and Burgundy,
Gloucester.

Gloucester. I shall, my lord.   *Exit [with Edmund].*

Lear. Meantime we shall express our darker purpose.°
Give me the map there. Know that we have divided
40 In three our kingdom; and 'tis our fast° intent
To shake all cares and business from our age,
Conferring them on younger strengths, while we

---

17 *issue* result (child) 18 *proper* handsome 21 *account* estimation
21 *knave* fellow (without disapproval) 22 *saucily* (1) insolently (2)
lasciviously 24 *whoreson* fellow (lit., son of a whore) 31 *sue* entreat
33 *out* away, abroad 34 s.d. *sennet* set of notes played on a trumpet,
signalizing the entrance or departure of a procession 34 s.d. *coronet*
small crown, intended for Cordelia 38 *darker purpose* hidden intention 40 *fast* fixed

Unburthened crawl toward death. Our son of
    Cornwall,
And you our no less loving son of Albany,
We have this hour a constant will to publish°   *45*
Our daughters' several° dowers, that future strife
May be prevented° now. The Princes, France and
    Burgundy,
Great rivals in our youngest daughter's love,
Long in our court have made their amorous sojourn,
And here are to be answered. Tell me, my daughters   *50*
(Since now we will divest us both of rule,
Interest° of territory, cares of state),
Which of you shall we say doth love us most,
That we our largest bounty may extend
Where nature doth with merit challenge.° Goneril,   *55*
Our eldest-born, speak first.

Goneril. Sir, I love you more than word can wield°
    the matter;
Dearer than eyesight, space° and liberty;
Beyond what can be valued, rich or rare;
No less than life, with grace, health, beauty, honor;   *60*
As much as child e'er loved, or father found;
A love that makes breath° poor, and speech
    unable:
Beyond all manner of so much° I love you.

Cordelia. [*Aside*] What shall Cordelia speak? Love,
    and be silent.

Lear. Of all these bounds, even from this line to this,   *65*
With shadowy forests, and with champains riched,°
With plenteous rivers, and wide-skirted meads,°
We make thee lady. To thine and Albany's issues°
Be this perpetual.° What says our second daughter,

---

45 *constant will to publish* fixed intention to proclaim   **46** *several* separate   **47** *prevented* forestalled   **52** *Interest* legal right   **55** *nature . . . challenge* i.e., natural affection contends with desert for (or lays claim to) bounty   **57** *wield* handle   **58** *space* scope   **62** *breath* language   **62** *unable* impotent   **63** *Beyond . . . much* beyond all these comparisons   **66** *champains riched* enriched plains   **67** *wide-skirted meads* extensive grasslands   **68** *issues* descendants   **69** *perpetual* in perpetuity

70   Our dearest Regan, wife of Cornwall? Speak.

Regan. I am made of that self mettle° as my sister,
        And prize me at her worth.° In my true heart
        I find she names my very deed of love;°
        Only she comes too short, that° I profess
75   Myself an enemy to all other joys
        Which the most precious square of sense
            professes,°
        And find I am alone felicitate°
        In your dear Highness' love.

Cordelia.   [*Aside*] Then poor Cordelia!
        And yet not so, since I am sure my love's
80   More ponderous° than my tongue.

Lear. To thee and thine hereditary ever
        Remain this ample third of our fair kingdom,
        No less in space, validity,° and pleasure
        Than that conferred on Goneril. Now, our joy,
85   Although our last and least;° to whose young love
        The vines of France and milk° of Burgundy
        Strive to be interest;° what can you say to draw
        A third more opulent than your sisters? Speak.

Cordelia. Nothing, my lord.

90 *Lear.* Nothing?

Cordelia. Nothing.

Lear. Nothing will come of nothing. Speak again.

Cordelia. Unhappy that I am, I cannot heave
        My heart into my mouth. I love your Majesty
95   According to my bond,° no more nor less.

Lear. How, how, Cordelia? Mend your speech a little,
        Lest you may mar your fortunes.

---

71 *self mettle* same material or temperament   72 *prize . . . worth* value
me the same (imperative)   73 *my . . . love* what my love really is (a
legalism)   74 *that* in that   76 *Which . . . professes* which the choicest
estimate of sense avows   77 *felicitate* made happy   80 *ponderous* weighty
83 *validity* value   85 *least* youngest, smallest   86 *milk* i.e., pastures
87 *interest* closely connected, as interested parties   95 *bond* i.e., filial
obligation

Cordelia.   Good my lord,
    You have begot me, bred me, loved me. I
    Return those duties back as are right fit,°
    Obey you, love you, and most honor you.   *100*
    Why have my sisters husbands, if they say
    They love you all? Haply,° when I shall wed,
    That lord whose hand must take my plight° shall
      carry
    Half my love with him, half my care and duty.
    Sure I shall never marry like my sisters,   *105*
    To love my father all.

Lear. But goes thy heart with this?

Cordelia.   Ay, my good lord.

Lear. So young, and so untender?

Cordelia. So young, my lord, and true.

Lear. Let it be so, thy truth then be thy dower!   *110*
    For, by the sacred radiance of the sun,
    The mysteries of Hecate° and the night,
    By all the operation of the orbs°
    From whom we do exist and cease to be,
    Here I disclaim all my paternal care,   *115*
    Propinquity and property of blood,°
    And as a stranger to my heart and me
    Hold thee from this for ever. The barbarous
      Scythian,°
    Or he that makes his generation messes°
    To gorge his appetite, shall to my bosom   *120*
    Be as well neighbored, pitied, and relieved,
    As thou my sometime° daughter.

Kent.   Good my liege——

Lear. Peace, Kent!

---

99 *Return . . . fit* i.e., am correspondingly dutiful   102 *Haply* perhaps
103 *plight* troth plight   112 *mysteries of Hecate* secret rites of Hecate
(goddess of the infernal world, and of witchcraft)   113 *operation of
the orbs* astrological influence   116 *Propinquity and property of blood*
relationship and common blood   118 *Scythian* (type of the savage)
119 *makes his generation messes* eats his own offspring   122 *sometime*
former

Come not between the Dragon° and his wrath.
125 I loved her most, and thought to set my rest°
On her kind nursery.° Hence and avoid my sight!
So be my grave my peace, as here I give
Her father's heart from her! Call France. Who stirs?
Call Burgundy. Cornwall and Albany,
130 With my two daughters' dowers digest° the third;
Let pride, which she calls plainness, marry her.°
I do invest you jointly with my power,
Pre-eminence, and all the large effects
That troop with majesty.° Ourself,° by monthly
course,
135 With reservation° of an hundred knights,
By you to be sustained, shall our abode
Make with you by due turn. Only we shall retain
The name, and all th' addition° to a king. The sway,
Revènue, execution of the rest,
140 Belovèd sons, be yours; which to confirm,
This coronet° part between you.

Kent.   Royal Lear,
Whom I have ever honored as my king,
Loved as my father, as my master followed,
As my great patron thought on in my prayers——

Lear. The bow is bent and drawn; make from the
145   shaft.°

Kent. Let it fall° rather, though the fork° invade
The region of my heart. Be Kent unmannerly
When Lear is mad. What wouldst thou do, old
man?
Think'st thou that duty shall have dread to speak

---

124 *Dragon* (1) heraldic device of Britain (2) emblem of ferocity
125 *set my rest* (1) stake my all (a term from the card game of primero)
(2) find my rest   126 *nursery* care, nursing   130 *digest* absorb
131 *Let . . . her* i.e., let her pride be her dowry and gain her a husband   133-34 *effects/That troop with majesty* accompaniments that go with
kingship   134 *Ourself* (the royal "we")   135 *reservation* the action of
reserving a privilege (a legalism)   138 *addition* titles and honors   141 *coronet* (the crown which was to have been Cordelia's)   145 *make from
the shaft* avoid the arrow   146 *fall* strike   146 *fork* forked head of the
arrow

When power to flattery bows? To plainness honor's
　　bound   150
When majesty falls to folly. Reserve thy state,°
And in thy best consideration° check
This hideous rashness. Answer my life my
　　judgment,°
Thy youngest daughter does not love thee least,
Nor are those empty-hearted whose low sounds   155
Reverb° no hollowness.°

Lear.   Kent, on thy life, no more!

Kent. My life I never held but as a pawn°
　　To wage° against thine enemies; nor fear to lose it,
　　Thy safety being motive.°

Lear.   Out of my sight!

Kent. See better, Lear, and let me still° remain   160
　　The true blank° of thine eye.

Lear. Now by Apollo——

Kent.   Now by Apollo, King,
　　Thou swear'st thy gods in vain.

Lear.   O vassal! Miscreant!°
                          [*Laying his hand on his sword.*]

Albany, Cornwall. Dear sir, forbear!

Kent. Kill thy physician, and the fee bestow   165
　　Upon the foul disease. Revoke thy gift,
　　Or, whilst I can vent clamor° from my throat,
　　I'll tell thee thou dost evil.

Lear.   Hear me, recreant!°
　　On thine allegiance,° hear me!
　　That thou hast sought to make us break our vows,   170

---

151 *Reserve thy state* retain your kingly authority 152 *best consideration* most careful reflection 153 *Answer . . . judgment* I will stake my
life on my opinion 156 *Reverb* reverberate 156 *hollowness* (1) empti-
ness (2) insincerity 157 *pawn* stake in a wager 158 *wage* (1) wager
(2) carry on war 159 *motive* moving cause 160 *still* always 161 *blank*
the white spot in the center of the target (at which Lear should aim)
163 *vassal! Miscreant!* base wretch! Misbeliever! 167 *vent clamor* utter
a cry 168 *recreant* traitor 169 *On thine allegiance* (to forswear, which
is to commit high treason)

Which we durst never yet, and with strained° pride
To come betwixt our sentence° and our power,
Which nor our nature nor our place can bear,
Our potency made good,° take thy reward.
175 Five days we do allot thee for provision°
To shield thee from diseases° of the world,
And on the sixth to turn thy hated back
Upon our kingdom. If, on the tenth day following,
Thy banished trunk° be found in our dominions,
180 The moment is thy death. Away! By Jupiter,
This shall not be revoked.

Kent. Fare thee well, King. Sith° thus thou wilt appear,
Freedom lives hence, and banishment is here.
[*To Cordelia*] The gods to their dear shelter take
thee, maid,
185 That justly think'st, and hast most rightly said.
[*To Regan and Goneril*] And your large speeches
may your deeds approve,°
That good effects° may spring from words of love.
Thus Kent, O Princes, bids you all adieu;
He'll shape his old course° in a country new.   *Exit.*

*Flourish.° Enter Gloucester, with France and
Burgundy; Attendants.*

190 *Gloucester.* Here's France and Burgundy, my noble
lord.

Lear. My Lord of Burgundy,
We first address toward you, who with this king
Hath rivaled for our daughter. What in the least
Will you require in present° dower with her,
Or cease your quest of love?

195 *Burgundy.*   Most royal Majesty,
I crave no more than hath your Highness offered,

---

171 *strained* forced (and so excessive)   172 *sentence* judgment, decree
174 *Our potency made good* my royal authority being now asserted
175 *for provision* for making preparation   176 *diseases* troubles
179 *trunk* body   182 *Sith* since   186*approve* prove true   187 *effects* results
189 *shape . . . course* pursue his customary way   189 s.d. *Flourish* trumpet
fanfare   194 *present* immediate

Nor will you tender° less.

Lear.   Right noble Burgundy,
When she was dear° to us, we did hold her so;
But now her price is fallen. Sir, there she stands.
If aught within that little seeming substance,°   200
Or all of it, with our displeasure pieced,°
And nothing more, may fitly like° your Grace,
She's there, and she is yours.

Burgundy.   I know no answer.

Lear. Will you, with those infirmities she owes,°
Unfriended, new adopted to our hate,   205
Dow'red with our curse, and strangered° with our
    oath,
Take her, or leave her?

Burgundy.   Pardon me, royal sir.
Election makes not up° on such conditions.

Lear. Then leave her, sir; for, by the pow'r that made
    me,
I tell you all her wealth. [*To France*.] For you,
    great King,   210
I would not from your love make such a stray
To° match you where I hate; therefore beseech°
    you
T' avert your liking a more worthier way°
Than on a wretch whom nature is ashamed
Almost t' acknowledge hers.

France.   This is most strange,   215
That she whom even but now was your best object,°
The argument° of your praise, balm of your age,
The best, the dearest, should in this trice of time
Commit a thing so monstrous to dismantle°

---

197 *tender* offer   198 *dear* (1) beloved (2) valued at a high price
200 *little seeming substance* person who is (1) inconsiderable (2) out-
spoken   201 *pieced* added to it   202 *fitly like* please by its fitness
204 *owes* possesses   206 *strangered* made a stranger   208 *Election makes
not up* no one can choose   211-12 *make such a stray/To* stray so far as to
212 *beseech* I beseech   213 *avert . . . way* turn your affections from her
and bestow them on a better person   216 *best object* i.e., the one you
loved most   217 *argument* subject   219 *dismantle* strip off

220   So many folds of favor. Sure her offense
       Must be of such unnatural degree
       That monsters it,° or your fore-vouched° affection
       Fall into taint;° which to believe of her
       Must be a faith that reason without miracle
       Should never plant in me.°

225 *Cordelia.*   I yet beseech your Majesty,
       If for° I want that glib and oily art
       To speak and purpose not,° since what I well intend
       I'll do't before I speak, that you make known
       It is no vicious blot, murder, or foulness,
230   No unchaste action or dishonored step,
       That hath deprived me of your grace and favor;
       But even for want of that for which I am richer,
       A still-soliciting° eye, and such a tongue
       That I am glad I have not, though not to have it
       Hath lost° me in your liking.

235 *Lear.*   Better thou
       Hadst not been born than not t' have pleased me
          better.

     France. Is it but this? A tardiness in nature°
       Which often leaves the history unspoke°
       That it intends to do. My Lord of Burgundy,
240   What say you° to the lady? Love's not love
       When it is mingled with regards° that stands
       Aloof from th' entire point.° Will you have her?
       She is herself a dowry.

     Burgundy.   Royal King,
       Give but that portion which yourself proposed,
245   And here I take Cordelia by the hand,
       Duchess of Burgundy.

---

222 *That monsters it* as makes it monstrous, unnatural   222 *fore-vouched* previously sworn   223 *Fall into taint* must be taken as having been unjustified all along i.e., Cordelia was unworthy of your love from the first   224-25 *reason . . . me* my reason would have to be supported by a miracle to make me believe   226 *for* because   227 *purpose not* not mean to do what I promise   233 *still-soliciting* always begging   235 *lost* ruined   237 *tardiness in nature* natural reticence   238 *leaves the history unspoke* does not announce the action   240 *What say you* i.e., will you have   241 *regards* considerations (the dowry)   241-42 *stands . . . point* have nothing to do with the essential question (love)

Lear. Nothing. I have sworn. I am firm.

Burgundy. I am sorry then you have so lost a father
   That you must lose a husband.

Cordelia.   Peace be with Burgundy.
   Since that respects of fortune° are his love,   250
   I shall not be his wife.

France. Fairest Cordelia, that art most rich being
     poor,
   Most choice forsaken, and most loved despised,
   Thee and thy virtues here I seize upon.
   Be it lawful I take up what's cast away.   255
   Gods, gods! 'Tis strange that from their cold'st
     neglect
   My love should kindle to inflamed respect.°
   Thy dow'rless daughter, King, thrown to my
     chance,°
   Is Queen of us, of ours, and our fair France.
   Not all the dukes of wat'rish° Burgundy   260
   Can buy this unprized precious° maid of me.
   Bid them farewell, Cordelia, though unkind.
   Thou losest here, a better where° to find.

Lear. Thou hast her, France; let her be thine, for we
   Have no such daughter, nor shall ever see   265
   That face of hers again. Therefore be gone,
   Without our grace, our love, our benison.°
   Come, noble Burgundy.

     *Flourish. Exeunt [Lear, Burgundy, Cornwall,
      Albany, Gloucester, and Attendants].*

France. Bid farewell to your sisters.

Cordelia. The jewels of our father,° with washed°
     eyes   270
   Cordelia leaves you. I know you what you are,

---

250 *respects of fortune* mercenary considerations 257 *inflamed respect*
more ardent affection 258 *chance* lot 260 *wat'rish* (1) with many
rivers (2) weak, diluted 261 *unprized precious* unappreciated by others, and yet precious 263 *here . . . where* in this place, in another
place 267 *benison* blessing 270 *The jewels of our father* you creatures
prized by our father 270 *washed* (1) weeping (2) clear-sighted

And, like a sister,° am most loath to call
Your faults as they are named.° Love well our
    father.
To your professèd° bosoms I commit him.
275 But yet, alas, stood I within his grace,
I would prefer° him to a better place.
So farewell to you both.

Regan. Prescribe not us our duty.

Goneril.   Let your study
Be to content your lord, who hath received you
280 At Fortune's alms.° You have obedience scanted,°
And well are worth the want that you have wanted.°

Cordelia. Time shall unfold what plighted° cunning
    hides,
Who covers faults, at last shame them derides.°
Well may you prosper.

France.   Come, my fair Cordelia.
           Exit France and Cordelia.

285 *Goneril.* Sister, it is not little I have to say of what
most nearly appertains to us both. I think our
father will hence tonight.

Regan. That's most certain, and with you; next month
with us.

290 *Goneril.* You see how full of changes his age is. The
observation we have made of it hath not been little. He always loved our sister most, and with
what poor judgment he hath now cast her off appears too grossly.°

295 *Regan.* 'Tis the infirmity of his age; yet he hath ever
but slenderly known himself.

---

272 *like a sister* because I am a sister i.e., loyal, affectionate   273 *as
they are named* i.e., by their right and ugly names   274 *professèd*
pretending to love   276 *prefer* recommend   280 *At Fortune's alms* as
a charitable bequest from Fortune (and so, by extension, as one beggared or cast down by Fortune)   280 *scanted* stinted   281 *worth . . .
wanted* deserve to be denied, even as you have denied   282 *plighted*
pleated, enfolded   283 *Who . . . derides* those who hide their evil are
finally exposed and shamed ("He that hideth his sins, shall not prosper")   294 *grossly* obviously

Goneril. The best and soundest of his time° hath
   been but rash; then must we look from his age to
   receive not alone the imperfections of long-in-
   grafted° condition,° but therewithal° the unruly 300
   waywardness that infirm and choleric years bring
   with them.

Regan. Such unconstant starts° are we like to have
   from him as this of Kent's banishment.

Goneril. There is further compliment° of leave-taking 305
   between France and him. Pray you, let's hit° together; if our father carry authority with such disposition as he bears,° this last surrender° of his
   will but offend° us.

Regan. We shall further think of it.   810

Goneril. We must do something, and i' th' heat.°
                                        Exeunt.

Scene II.   [*The Earl of Gloucester's castle.*]

Enter Edmund [*with a letter*].

Edmund. Thou, Nature,° art my goddess; to thy law
   My services are bound. Wherefore should I
   Stand in the plague of custom,° and permit
   The curiosity° of nations to deprive me,
   For that° I am some twelve or fourteen
      moonshines °   3

297 *of his time* period of his life up to now   299-300 *long-ingrafted* im-
planted for a long time   300 *condition* disposition   300 *therewithal*
with them   303 *unconstant starts* impulsive whims   305 *compliment*
formal courtesy   306 *hit* agree   307-8 *carry . . . bears* continues, and
in such frame of mind, to wield the sovereign power   308 *last surren-*
der recent abdication   309 *offend* vex   811 *i' th' heat* while the iron is
hot   I.ii. 1 *Nature* (Edmund's conception of Nature accords with our
description of a bastard as a natural child)   3 *Stand . . . custom*
respect hateful convention   4 *curiosity* nice distinctions   5 *For that*
because   5 *moonshines* months

Lag of° a brother? Why bastard? Wherefore base?
When my dimensions are as well compact,°
My mind as generous,° and my shape as true,
As honest° madam's issue? Why brand they us
10   With base? With baseness? Bastardy? Base? Base?
Who, in the lusty stealth of nature, take
More composition° and fierce° quality
Than doth, within a dull, stale, tired bed,
Go to th' creating a whole tribe of fops°
15   Got° 'tween asleep and wake? Well then,
Legitimate Edgar, I must have your land.
Our father's love is to the bastard Edmund
As to th' legitimate. Fine word, "legitimate."
Well, my legitimate, if this letter speed,°
20   And my invention° thrive, Edmund the base
Shall top th' legitimate. I grow, I prosper.
Now, gods, stand up for bastards.

Enter Gloucester.

Gloucester. Kent banished thus? and France in choler
      parted?
      And the King gone tonight? prescribed° his pow'r?
25   Confined to exhibition?° All this done
      Upon the gad?° Edmund, how now? What news?

Edmund. So please your lordship, none.

Gloucester. Why so earnestly seek you to put up°
      that letter?

30   *Edmund.* I know no news, my lord.

Gloucester. What paper were you reading?

Edmund. Nothing, my lord.

Gloucester. No? What needed then that terrible dis-
      patch° of it into your pocket? The quality of noth-

---

6 *Lag of* short of being (in age)   7 *compact* framed   8 *generous* gal-
lant   9 *honest* chaste   12 *composition* completeness   12 *fierce* energetic
14 *fops* fools   15 *Got* begot   19 *speed* prosper   20 *invention* plan
24 *prescribed* limited   25 *exhibition* an allowance or pension   26 *Upon
the gad* on the spur of the moment (as if pricked by a gad or goad)
28 *put up* put away, conceal   33-34 *terrible dispatch* hasty putting away

ing hath not such need to hide itself. Let's see. 35
Come, if it be nothing, I shall not need spectacles.

Edmund. I beseech you, sir, pardon me. It is a letter
from my brother that I have not all o'er-read; and
for so much as I have perused, I find it not fit
for your o'erlooking.°   40

Gloucester. Give me the letter, sir.

Edmund. I shall offend, either to detain or give it.
The contents, as in part I understand them, are
to blame.°

Gloucester. Let's see, let's see.   45

Edmund. I hope, for my brother's justification, he
wrote this but as an essay or taste° of my virtue.

Gloucester. (*Reads*) "This policy and reverence° of
age makes the world bitter to the best of our
times;° keeps our fortunes from us till our oldness 50
cannot relish° them. I begin to find an idle and
fond° bondage in the oppression of aged tyranny,
who sways, not as it hath power, but as it is suffered.° Come to me, that of this I may speak more.
If our father would sleep till I waked him, you   55
should enjoy half his revenue° for ever, and live
the beloved of your brother,   EDGAR."
Hum! Conspiracy? "Sleep till I waked him, you
should enjoy half his revenue." My son Edgar! Had
he a hand to write this? A heart and brain to   60
breed it in? When came you to this? Who brought
it?

Edmund. It was not brought me, my lord; there's the
cunning of it. I found it thrown in at the casement of my closet.°   65

---

40 *o'erlooking* inspection 44 *to blame* blameworthy 47 *essay or taste*
test 48 *policy and reverence* policy of reverencing (hendiadys)
49-50 *best of our times* best years of our lives (i.e., our youth) 51 *relish*
enjoy 51-52 *idle and fond* foolish 53-54 *who . . . suffered* which rules,
not from its own strength, but from our allowance 56 *revenue* income
64-65 *casement of my closet* window of my room

Gloucester. You know the character° to be your
     brother's?

Edmund. If the matter were good, my lord, I durst
     swear it were his; but in respect of that,° I would
70   fain° think it were not.

Gloucester. It is his.

Edmund. It is his hand, my lord; but I hope his
     heart is not in the contents.

Gloucester. Has he never before sounded° you in this
75   business?

Edmund. Never, my lord. But I have heard him
     oft maintain it to be fit that, sons at perfect° age,
     and fathers declined, the father should be as ward
     to the son, and the son manage his revenue.

80 *Gloucester.* O villain, villain! His very opinion in the
     letter. Abhorred villain, unnatural, detested,° brut-
     ish villain; worse than brutish! Go, sirrah,° seek
     him. I'll apprehend him. Abominable villain! Where
     is he?

85 *Edmund.* I do not well know, my lord. If it shall
     please you to suspend your indignation against my
     brother till you can derive from him better testi-
     mony of his intent, you should run a certain
     course;° where, if you violently proceed against
90   him, mistaking his purpose, it would make a great
     gap° in your own honor and shake in pieces the
     heart of his obedience. I dare pawn down° my life
     for him that he hath writ this to feel° my affec-
     tion to your honor, and to no other pretense of
95   danger.°

Gloucester. Think you so?

---

66 *character* handwriting   69 *in respect of that* in view of what it is
70 *fain* prefer to   74 *sounded* sounded you out   77 *perfect* mature
81 *detested* detestable   82 *sirrah* sir (familiar form of address)   88-89 *run a certain course* i.e., proceed safely, know where you are going   91 *gap* breach   92 *pawn down* stake   93 *feel* test   94-95 *pretense of danger* dangerous purpose

Edmund. If your honor judge it meet,° I will place
you where you shall hear us confer of this, and
by an auricular assurance° have your satisfaction,
and that without any further delay than this very *100*
evening.

Gloucester. He cannot be such a monster.

Edmund. Nor is not, sure.

Gloucester. To his father, that so tenderly and entirely loves him. Heaven and earth! Edmund, seek *105*
him out; wind me into him,° I pray you; frame°
the business after your own wisdom. I would unstate myself to be in a due resolution.°

Edmund. I will seek him, sir, presently;° convey° the
business as I shall find means, and acquaint you *110*
withal.°

Gloucester. These late° eclipses in the sun and moon
portend no good to us. Though the wisdom of Na-
ture° can reason° it thus and thus, yet Nature
finds itself scourged by the sequent effects.° Love *115*
cools, friendship falls off,° brothers divide. In
cities, mutinies;° in countries, discord; in palaces,
treason; and the bond cracked 'twixt son and
father. This villain of mine comes under the prediction,° there's son against father; the King falls *120*
from bias of nature,° there's father against child.
We have seen the best of our time.° Machinations,
hollowness,° treachery, and all ruinous disorders
follow us disquietly° to our graves. Find out this

---

97 *meet* fit   99 *auricular assurance* proof heard with your own ears
106 *wind me into him* insinuate yourself into his confidence for me
106 *frame* manage   107-08 *unstate . . . resolution* forfeit my earldom
to know the truth   109 *presently* at once   109 *convey* manage   111 *withal*
with it   112 *late* recent   113-14 *wisdom of Nature* scientific learning   114 *reason* explain   114-15 *yet . . . effects* nonetheless our world
is punished with subsequent disasters   116 *falls off* revolts   117 *mutinies*
riots   119-20 *This . . . prediction* i.e., my son's villainous behavior is
included in these portents, and bears them out   121 *bias of nature*
natural inclination (the metaphor is from the game of bowls)   122 *best
of our time* our best days   123 *hollowness* insincerity   124 *disquietly*
unquietly

125 villain, Edmund; it shall lose thee nothing.° Do it
carefully. And the noble and true-hearted Kent
banished; his offense, honesty. 'Tis strange.

Exit.

Edmund. This is the excellent foppery° of the world,
that when we are sick in fortune, often the surfeits
130 of our own behavior,° we make guilty of our disasters the sun, the moon, and stars; as if we were
villains on° necessity; fools by heavenly compulsion; knaves, thieves, and treachers by spherical
predominance;° drunkards, liars, and adulterers by
135 an enforced obedience of planetary influence;° and
all that we are evil in, by a divine thrusting on.°
An admirable evasion of whoremaster° man, to
lay his goatish° disposition on the charge of a
star. My father compounded° with my mother
140 under the Dragon's Tail,° and my nativity° was
under Ursa Major,° so that it follows I am rough
and lecherous. Fut!° I should have been that° I
am, had the maidenliest star in the firmament twin-
kled on my bastardizing. Edgar——

Enter Edgar.

145 and pat he comes, like the catastrophe° of the old
comedy. My cue is villainous melancholy, with a
sigh like Tom o' Bedlam.°—O, these eclipses do
portend these divisions. Fa, sol, la, mi.°

Edgar. How now, brother Edmund; what serious con-
150 templation are you in?

125 *it . . . nothing* you will not lose by it   128 *foppery* folly
129-30 *often . . . behavior* often caused by our own excesses   132 *on* of
133-34 *treachers . . . predominance* traitors because of the ascen-
dancy of a particular star at our birth   134-35 *by . . . influence* because
we had to submit to the influence of our star   136 *divine thrusting on*
supernatural compulsion   137 *whoremaster* lecherous   138 *goatish* las-
civious   139 *compounded* (1) made terms (2) formed (a child)
140 *Dragon's Tail* the constellation Draco   140 *nativity* birthday
141 *Ursa Major* the Great Bear   142 *Fut!* 's foot (an impatient oath)
142 *that* what   145 *catastrophe* conclusion   146-47 *My . . . Bedlam* I must
be doleful, like a lunatic beggar out of Bethlehem (Bedlam) Hospital, the
London madhouse   148 *Fa, sol, la, mi* (Edmund's humming of the
musical notes is perhaps prompted by his use of the word "division,"
which describes a musical variation)

Edmund. I am thinking, brother, of a prediction I
read this other day, what should follow these
eclipses.

Edgar. Do you busy yourself with that?

Edmund. I promise you, the effects he writes of suc- 155
ceed° unhappily: as of unnaturalness° between the
child and the parent, death, dearth, dissolutions of
ancient amities,° divisions in state, menaces and
maledictions against King and nobles, needless diffidences,° banishment of friends, dissipation of co- 160
horts,° nuptial breaches, and I know not what.

Edgar. How long have you been a sectary astronomical?°

Edmund. Come, come, when saw you my father last?

Edgar. Why, the night gone by. 165

Edmund. Spake you with him?

Edgar. Ay, two hours together.

Edmund. Parted you in good terms? Found you no
displeasure in him by word nor countenance?°

Edgar. None at all. 170

Edmund. Bethink yourself wherein you may have offended him; and at my entreaty forbear his pres-
ence° until some little time hath qualified° the heat
of his displeasure, which at this instant so rageth
in him that with the mischief of your person it 175
would scarcely allay.°

Edgar. Some villain hath done me wrong.

Edmund. That's my fear, brother I pray you have a
continent forbearance° till the speed of his rage
goes slower; and, as I say, retire with me to my 180

155-56 *succeed* follow   157 *unnaturalness* unkindness   158 *amities* friend-
ships   159-60 *diffidences* distrusts   160-61 *dissipation of cohorts* falling
away of supporters   162-63 *sectary astronomical* believer in astrology
169 *countenance* expression   172-73 *forbear his presence* keep away from
him   173 *qualified* lessened   175-76 *with . . . allay* even an injury to you
would not appease his anger   178-79 *have a continent forbearance* be restrained and keep yourself withdrawn

lodging, from whence I will fitly° bring you to hear
my lord speak. Pray ye, go; there's my key. If
you do stir abroad, go armed.

Edgar. Armed, brother?

185 *Edmund.* Brother, I advise you to the best. Go armed.
I am no honest man if there be any good meaning
toward you. I have told you what I have seen and
heard; but faintly, nothing like the image and hor-
ror° of it. Pray you, away.

190 *Edgar.* Shall I hear from you anon?°

Edmund. I do serve you in this business.

                           Exit Edgar.

A credulous father, and a brother noble,
Whose nature is so far from doing harms
That he suspects none; on whose foolish honesty
195 My practices° ride easy. I see the business.
Let me, if not by birth, have lands by wit.
All with me's meet° that I can fashion fit.°   *Exit.*

Scene III.   [*The Duke of Albany's palace.*]

Enter Goneril, and [Oswald, her] Steward.

Goneril. Did my father strike my gentleman for chid-
ing of his Fool?°

Oswald. Ay, madam.

Goneril. By day and night he wrongs me. Every hour
5   He flashes into one gross crime° or other

---

181 *fitly* at a fit time   188-89 *image and horror* true horrible picture
190 *anon* in a little while   195 *practices* plots   197 *meet* proper   197 *fashion
fit* shape to my purpose   I.iii. 2 *Fool* court jester   5 *crime* offense

That sets us all at odds. I'll not endure it.
His knights grow riotous,° and himself upbraids us
On every trifle. When he returns from hunting,
I will not speak with him. Say I am sick.
If you come slack of former services,°   10
You shall do well; the fault of it I'll answer.°

                              [*Horns within.*]

Oswald. He's coming, madam; I hear him.

Goneril. Put on what weary negligence you please,
You and your fellows. I'd have it come to question.°
If he distaste° it, let him to my sister,   15
Whose mind and mine I know in that are one,
Not to be overruled. Idle° old man,
That still would manage those authorities
That he hath given away. Now, by my life,
Old fools are babes again, and must be used   20
With checks as flatteries, when they are seen
    abused.°
Remember what I have said.

Oswald.   Well, madam.

Goneril. And let his knights have colder looks among
    you.
What grows of it, no matter; advise your fellows so.
I would breed from hence occasions, and I shall,   25
That I may speak.° I'll write straight° to my sister
To hold my course. Go, prepare for dinner.

                                   Exeunt.

7 *riotous* dissolute   10 *come . . . services* are less serviceable to him
than formerly   11 *answer* answer for   14 *come to question* be discussed
openly   15 *distaste* dislike   17 *Idle* foolish   21 *With . . . abused*
with restraints as well as soothing words when they are misguided
25-26 *breed . . . speak* find in this opportunities for speaking out
26 *straight* at once

Scene IV.   [*A hall in the same.*]

Enter Kent [disguised].

Kent. If but as well I other accents borrow
That can my speech defuse,° my good intent
May carry through itself to that full issue°
For which I razed my likeness.° Now, banished
          Kent,
If thou canst serve where thou dost stand
          condemned,
So may it come,° thy master whom thou lov'st
Shall find thee full of labors.

*Horns within.° Enter Lear, [Knights] and
          Attendants.*

Lear. Let me not stay° a jot for dinner; go, get it
ready. [*Exit an Attendant.*] How now, what art
thou?

Kent. A man, sir.

Lear. What dost thou profess?° What wouldst thou
with us?

Kent. I do profess° to be no less than I seem, to
serve him truly that will put me in trust, to love
him that is honest, to converse with him that is
wise and says little, to fear judgment,° to fight
when I cannot choose, and to eat no fish.°

I.iv. 2 *defuse* disguise   3 *full issue* perfect result   4 *razed my likeness*
shaved off, disguised my natural appearance   6 *So may it come* so may
it fall out   7 s.d. *within* offstage   8 *stay* wait   12 *What dost thou profess* what do you do   14 *profess* claim   17 *judgment* (by a heavenly or
earthly judge)   18 *eat no fish* i.e., (1) I am no Catholic, but a loyal
Protestant (2) I am no weakling (3) I use no prostitutes

Lear. What art thou?

Kent. A very honest-hearted fellow, and as poor as ²⁰
the King.

Lear. If thou be'st as poor for a subject as he's for a
king, thou art poor enough. What wouldst thou?

Kent. Service.

Lear. Who wouldst thou serve?   25

Kent. You.

Lear. Dost thou know me, fellow?

Kent. No, sir, but you have that in your countenance°
which I would fain° call master.

Lear. What's that?   30

Kent. Authority.

Lear. What services canst thou do?

Kent. I can keep honest counsel,° ride, run, mar a
curious tale in telling it,° and deliver a plain message bluntly. That which ordinary men are fit for, I ³⁵
am qualified in, and the best of me is diligence.

Lear. How old art thou?

Kent. Not so young, sir, to love a woman for singing, nor so old to dote on her for anything. I have
years on my back forty-eight.   40

Lear. Follow me; thou shalt serve me. If I like thee
no worse after dinner, I will not part from thee
yet. Dinner, ho, dinner! Where's my knave?° my
Fool? Go you and call my Fool hither.

[Exit an Attendant.]

Enter Oswald.

You, you, sirrah, where's my daughter?   45

Oswald. So please you——   *Exit.*

---

²⁸ *countenance* bearing ²⁹ *fain* like to ³³ *honest counsel* honorable
secrets ³³⁻³⁴ *mar . . . it* i.e., I cannot speak like an affected courtier
("curious" = "elaborate," as against "plain") ⁴³ *knave* boy

Lear. What says the fellow there? Call the clotpoll°
back. [*Exit a Knight.*] Where's my Fool? Ho, I
think the world's asleep.

[*Re-enter Knight.*]

50   How now? Where's that mongrel?

Knight. He says, my lord, your daughter is not well.

Lear. Why came not the slave back to me when I
called him?

Knight. Sir, he answered me in the roundest° manner,
55   he would not.

Lear. He would not?

Knight. My lord, I know not what the matter is;
but to my judgment your Highness is not enter-
tained° with that ceremonious affection as you
60   were wont. There's a great abatement of kindness
appears as well in the general dependants° as in the
Duke himself also and your daughter.

Lear. Ha? Say'st thou so?

Knight. I beseech you pardon me, my lord, if I be
65   mistaken; for my duty cannot be silent when I
think your Highness wronged.

Lear. Thou but rememb'rest° me of mine own conception.° I have perceived a most faint neglect°
of late, which I have rather blamed as mine own
70   jealous curiosity° than as a very pretense° and
purpose of unkindness. I will look further into't.
But where's my Fool? I have not seen him this two
days.

Knight. Since my young lady's going into France, sir,
75   the Fool hath much pined away.

Lear. No more of that; I have noted it well. Go you

---

47 *clotpoll* clodpoll, blockhead   **54** *roundest* rudest   **58-59** *entertained*
treated   **61** *dependants* servants   **67** *rememb'rest* remindest   **67-68** *conception* idea   **68** *faint neglect* i.e., "weary negligence" (I.iii.13)
69-70 *mine own jealous curiosity* suspicious concern for my own dignity
70 *very pretense* actual intention

and tell my daughter I would speak with her. Go
you, call hither my Fool. [*Exit an Attendant.*]

Enter Oswald.

O, you, sir, you! Come you hither, sir. Who am I,
sir? 80

Oswald. My lady's father.

Lear. "My lady's father"? My lord's knave, you
whoreson dog, you slave, you cur!

Oswald. I am none of these, my lord; I beseech your
pardon. 85

Lear. Do you bandy° looks with me, you rascal?
[*Striking him.*]

Oswald. I'll not be strucken,° my lord.

Kent. Nor tripped neither, you base football° player.
[*Tripping up his heels.*]

Lear. I thank thee, fellow. Thou serv'st me, and I'll
love thee. 90

Kent. Come, sir, arise, away. I'll teach you differences.° Away, away. If you will measure your lubber's° length again, tarry; but away. Go to!° Have
you wisdom?° So.° [*Pushes Oswald out.*]

Lear. Now, my friendly knave, I thank thee. There's 95
earnest° of thy service. [*Giving Kent money.*]

Enter Fool.

Fool. Let me hire him too. Here's my coxcomb.°
[*Offering Kent his cap.*]

Lear. How now, my pretty knave? How dost thou?

Fool. Sirrah, you were best° take my coxcomb.

Kent. Why, Fool? 100

---

86 *bandy* exchange insolently (metaphor from tennis) 87 *strucken*
struck 88 *football* (a low game played by idle boys to the scandal of
sensible men) 91-92 *differences* (of rank) 92-93 *lubber's* lout's 93 *Go
to* (expression of derisive incredulity) 93-94 *Have you wisdom* i.e., do
you know what's good for you 94 *So* good 96 *earnest* money for services rendered 97 *coxcomb* professional fool's cap, shaped like a coxcomb 99 *you were best* you had better

Fool. Why? For taking one's part that's out of favor.
Nay, an° thou canst not smile as the wind sits,°
thou'lt catch cold shortly. There, take my coxcomb.
Why, this fellow has banished° two on's daughters,
105 and did the third a blessing against his will. If thou
follow him, thou must needs wear my coxcomb.
—How now, Nuncle?° Would I had two coxcombs
and two daughters.

Lear. Why, my boy?

110 *Fool.* If I gave them all my living,° I'd keep my coxcombs myself. There's mine; beg another of thy
daughters.

Lear. Take heed, sirrah—the whip.

Fool. Truth's a dog must to kennel; he must be
115 whipped out, when Lady the Brach° may stand by
th' fire and stink.

Lear. A pestilent gall° to me.

Fool. Sirrah, I'll teach thee a speech.

Lear. Do.

120 *Fool.* Mark it, Nuncle.
        Have more than thou showest,
        Speak less than thou knowest,
        Lend less than thou owest,°
        Ride more than thou goest,°
125   Learn more than thou trowest,°
        Set less than thou throwest;°
        Leave thy drink and thy whore,
        And keep in-a-door,
        And thou shalt have more
130   Than two tens to a score.°

Kent. This is nothing, Fool.

---

102 *an* if 102 *smile . . . sits* ingratiate yourself with those in power
104 *banished* alienated (by making them independent) 107 *Nuncle*
(contraction of "mine uncle") 110 *living* property 115 *Brach* bitch
117 *gall* sore 123 *owest* ownest 124 *goest* walkest 125 *trowest* knowest
126 *Set . . . throwest* bet less than you play for (get odds from your
opponent) 129-30 *have . . . score* i.e., come away with more than you
had (two tens, or twenty shillings, make a score, or one pound)

Fool. Then 'tis like the breath of an unfeed° lawyer
  —you gave me nothing for't. Can you make no use
  of nothing, Nuncle?

Lear. Why, no, boy Nothing can be made out of   *135*
  nothing.

Fool. [*To Kent*] Prithee tell him, so much the
  rent of his land comes to; he will not believe a
  Fool.

Lear. A bitter° Fool.   *140*

Fool. Dost thou know the difference, my boy, between
  a bitter Fool and a sweet one?

Lear. No, lad; teach me.

Fool.

> That lord that counseled thee
>   To give away thy land,   *145*
> Come place him here by me,
>   Do thou for him stand.
> The sweet and bitter fool
>   Will presently appear;
> The one in motley° here,   *150*
>   The other found out° there.°

Lear. Dost thou call me fool, boy?

Fool. All thy other titles thou hast given away; that
  thou wast born with.

Kent. This is not altogether fool, my lord.   *155*

Fool. No, faith; lords and great men will not let me.°
  If I had a monopoly° out, they would have part
  on't. And ladies too, they will not let me have all
  the fool to myself; they'll be snatching. Nuncle,
  give me an egg, and I'll give thee two crowns.   *160*

---

132 *unfeed* unpaid for   140 *bitter* satirical   150 *motley* the drab costume
of the professional jester   151 *found out* revealed   151 *there* (the Fool
points at Lear, as a fool in the grain)   156 *let me* (have all the folly to
myself)   157 *monopoly* (James I gave great scandal by granting to his
"snatching" courtiers royal patents to deal exclusively in some commodity)

Lear. What two crowns shall they be?

Fool. Why, after I have cut the egg i' th' middle
and eat up the meat, the two crowns of the egg.
When thou clovest thy crown i' th' middle and
165   gav'st away both parts, thou bor'st thine ass on
thy back o'er the dirt.° Thou hadst little wit in thy
bald crown when thou gav'st thy golden one away.
If I speak like myself° in this, let him be whipped°
that first finds it so.
170   [*Singing*] Fools had ne'er less grace in a year,
         For wise men are grown foppish,
      And know not how their wits to wear,
         Their manners are so apish.°

Lear. When were you wont to be so full of songs,
175   sirrah?

Fool. I have used° it, Nuncle, e'er since thou mad'st
thy daughters thy mothers; for when thou gav'st
them the rod, and put'st down thine own breeches,
[*Singing*] Then they for sudden joy did weep,
180   And I for sorrow sung,
      That such a king should play bo-peep°
         And go the fools among.
Prithee, Nuncle, keep a schoolmaster that can teach
thy Fool to lie. I would fain learn to lie.

185   *Lear.* And° you lie, sirrah, we'll have you whipped.

Fool. I marvel what kin thou and thy daughters are.
They'll have me whipped for speaking true; thou'lt
have me whipped for lying; and sometimes I am
whipped for holding my peace. I had rather be any
190   kind o' thing than a Fool, and yet I would not be

165–66 *bor'st . . . dirt* (like the foolish and unnatural countryman in
Aesop's fable)   168 *like myself* like a Fool   168 *let him be whipped* i.e.,
let the man be whipped for a Fool who thinks my true saying to be
foolish   170–73 *Fools . . . apish* i.e., fools were never in less favor than
now, and the reason is that wise men, turning foolish, and not knowing
how to use their intelligence, imitate the professional fools and so make
them unnecessary   176 *used* practiced   181 *play bo-peep* (1) act like a
child (2) blind himself   185 *And* if

thee, Nuncle: thou hast pared thy wit o' both sides
and left nothing i' th' middle. Here comes one o'
the parings.

Enter Goneril.

Lear. How now, daughter? What makes that frontlet°
    on? Methinks you are too much of late i' th'   *195*
    frown.

Fool. Thou wast a pretty fellow when thou hadst no
    need to care for her frowning. Now thou art an O
    without a figure.° I am better than thou art now: I
    am a Fool, thou art nothing. [*To Goneril.*] Yes,   *200*
    forsooth, I will hold my tongue. So your face bids
    me, though you say nothing. Mum, mum,
        He that keeps nor crust nor crum,°
        Weary of all, shall want° some.

    [*Pointing to Lear*] That's a shealed peascod.°   *205*

Goneril. Not only, sir, this your all-licensed° Fool,
    But other° of your insolent retinue
    Do hourly carp and quarrel, breaking forth
    In rank° and not-to-be-endurèd riots. Sir,
    I had thought by making this well known unto you   *210*
    To have found a safe° redress, but now grow
        fearful,
    By what yourself too late° have spoke and done,
    That you protect this course, and put it on
    By your allowance;° which if you should, the fault
    Would not 'scape censure, nor the redresses sleep,°   *215*
    Which, in the tender of° a wholesome weal,°
    Might in their working do you that offense,
    Which else were shame, that then necessity
    Will call discreet proceeding.°

---

194 *frontlet* frown (lit., ornamental band)   199 *figure* digit, to give
value to the cipher (Lear is a nought)   203 *crum* soft bread inside
the loaf   204 *want* lack   205 *shealed peascod* empty pea pod   206 *all-
licensed* privileged to take any liberties   207 *other* others   209 *rank*
gross   211 *safe* sure   212 *too late* lately   213-14 *put . . . allowance*
promote it by your approval   214 *allowance* approval   215 *redresses
sleep* correction fail to follow   216 *tender of* desire for   216 *weal* state
217-19 *Might . . . proceeding* as I apply it, the correction might humiliate you; but the need to take action cancels what would otherwise be
unfilial conduct in me

²²⁰ *Fool.* For you know, Nuncle,
　　　　The hedge-sparrow fed the cuckoo° so long
　　　　That it had it head bit off by it° young.
　　　So out went the candle, and we were left darkling.°

Lear. Are you our daughter?

²²⁵ *Goneril.* Come, sir,
　　　I would you would make use of your good wisdom
　　　Whereof I know you are fraught° and put away
　　　These dispositions° which of late transport you
　　　From what you rightly are.

²³⁰ *Fool.* May not an ass know when the cart draws the
　　　horse? Whoop, Jug,° I love thee!

Lear. Does any here know me? This is not Lear.
　　　Does Lear walk thus? Speak thus? Where are his
　　　　eyes?
　　　Either his notion° weakens, or his discernings°
²³⁵　Are lethargied°—Ha! Waking? 'Tis not so.
　　　Who is it that can tell me who I am?

Fool. Lear's shadow.

Lear. I would learn that; for, by the marks of sover-
　　　eignty,° knowledge, and reason, I should be false°
²⁴⁰　persuaded I had daughters.

Fool. Which° they will make an obedient father.

Lear. Your name, fair gentlewoman?

Goneril. This admiration,° sir, is much o' th' savor°
　　　Of other your° new pranks. I do beseech you
²⁴⁵　To understand my purposes aright.
　　　As you are old and reverend, should be wise.
　　　Here do you keep a hundred knights and squires,

---

²²¹ *cuckoo* (who lays its eggs in the nests of other birds)　²²² *it* its
²²³ *darkling* in the dark　²²⁷ *fraught* endowed　²²⁸ *dispositions* moods
²³¹ *Jug* Joan (? a quotation from a popular song)　²³⁴ *notion* under-
standing　²³⁴ *discernings* faculties　²³⁵ *lethargied* paralyzed　²³⁸⁻³⁹ *marks
of sovereignty* i.e., tokens that Lear is king, and hence father to his
daughters　²³⁹ *false* falsely　²⁴¹ *Which* whom (Lear)　²⁴³ *admiration*
(affected) wonderment　²⁴³ *is much o' th' savor* smacks much
²⁴⁴ *other your* others of your

Men so disordered, so deboshed,° and bold,
That this our court, infected with their manners,
Shows° like a riotous inn. Epicurism° and lust   *250*
Makes it more like a tavern or a brothel
Than a graced° palace. The shame itself doth speak
For instant remedy. Be then desired°
By her, that else will take the thing she begs,
A little to disquantity your train,°   *255*
And the remainders° that shall still depend,°
To be such men as may besort° your age,
Which know themselves, and you.

Lear.   Darkness and devils!
Saddle my horses; call my train together.
Degenerate° bastard, I'll not trouble thee: *260*
Yet have I left a daughter.

Goneril. You strike my people, and your disordered
rabble
Make servants of their betters.

Enter Albany.

Lear. Woe, that too late repents. O, sir, are you
come?
Is it your will? Speak, sir. Prepare my horses.   *265*
Ingratitude! thou marble-hearted fiend,
More hideous when thou show'st thee in a child
Than the sea-monster.

Albany.   Pray, sir, be patient

Lear. Detested kite,° thou liest.
My train are men of choice and rarest parts,°   *270*
That all particulars of duty know,
And, in the most exact regard,° support
The worships° of their name. O most small fault,

---

248 *deboshed* debauched   250 *Shows* appears   250 *Epicurism* riotous living   252 *graced* dignified   253 *desired* requested   255 *disquantity your
train* reduce the number of your dependents   256 *remainders* those who
remain   256 *depend* attend on you   257 *besort* befit   260 *Degenerate*
unnatural   269 *kite* scavenging bird of prey   270 *parts* accomplishments
272 *exact regard* strict attention to detail   273 *worships* honor

How ugly didst thou in Cordelia show!
Which, like an engine,° wrenched my frame of
275   nature
From the fixed place;° drew from my heart all love,
And added to the gall.° O Lear, Lear, Lear!
Beat at this gate that let thy folly in [*Striking
    his head.*]
And thy dear judgment out. Go, go, my people.

280 *Albany.* My lord, I am guiltless, as I am ignorant
Of what hath moved you.

Lear.   It may be so, my lord.
Hear, Nature, hear; dear Goddess, hear:
Suspend thy purpose if thou didst intend
To make this creature fruitful.
285 Into her womb convey sterility,
Dry up in her the organs of increase,°
And from her derogate° body never spring
A babe to honor her. If she must teem,°
Create her child of spleen,° that it may live
290 And be a thwart disnatured° torment to her.
Let it stamp wrinkles in her brow of youth,
With cadent° tears fret° channels in her cheeks,
Turn all her mother's pains and benefits°
To laughter and contempt, that she may feel
295 How sharper than a serpent's tooth it is
To have a thankless child. Away, away!   *Exit.*

Albany. Now, gods that we adore, whereof comes
    this?

Goneril. Never afflict yourself to know the cause,
But let his disposition° have that scope
300 As° dotage gives it.

Enter Lear.

Lear. What, fifty of my followers at a clap?°

---

275 *engine* destructive contrivance 274-76 *wrenched . . . place* i.e.,
disordered my natural self 277 *gall* bitterness 286 *increase* childbear-
ing 287 *derogate* degraded 288 *teem* conceive 289 *spleen* ill humor
290 *thwart disnatured* perverse unnatural 292 *cadent* falling 292 *fret*
wear 293 *benefits* the mother's beneficent care of her child 299 *disposition* mood 300 *As* that 301 *at a clap* at one stroke

Within a fortnight?

Albany. What's the matter, sir?

Lear. I'll tell thee. [*To Goneril*] Life and death,
  I am ashamed
That thou hast power to shake my manhood°
  thus!
That these hot tears, which break from me
  perforce,° 305
Should make thee worth them. Blasts and fogs
  upon thee!
Th' untented woundings° of a father's curse
Pierce every sense about thee! Old fond° eyes,
Beweep° this cause again, I'll pluck ye out
And cast you, with the waters that you loose,° 310
To temper° clay. Yea, is it come to this?
Ha! Let it be so. I have another daughter,
Who I am sure is kind and comfortable.°
When she shall hear this of thee, with her nails
She'll flay thy wolvish visage. Thou shalt find 315
That I'll resume the shape° which thou dost think
I have cast off for ever.
                Exit [*Lear with Kent and Attendants*].

Goneril. Do you mark that?

Albany. I cannot be so partial, Goneril,
  To the great love I bear you°——

Goneril. Pray you, content. What, Oswald, ho! 320
  [*To the Fool*] You, sir, more knave than fool,
    after your master!

Fool. Nuncle Lear, Nuncle Lear, tarry. Take the Fool°
  with thee.

---

304 *shake my manhood* i.e., with tears 305 *perforce* involuntarily, against my will 307 *untented woundings* wounds too deep to be probed with a tent (a roll of lint) 308 *fond* foolish 309 *Beweep* if you weep over 310 *loose* (1) let loose (2) lose, as of no avail 311 *temper* mix with and soften 313 *comfortable* ready to comfort 316 *shape* i.e., kingly role 318-19 *I cannot . . . you* i.e., even though my love inclines me to you, I must protest 322 *Fool* (1) the Fool himself (2) the epithet or character of "fool"

325
A fox, when one has caught her,
And such a daughter,
Should sure to the slaughter,
If my cap would buy a halter.°
So the Fool follows after.°   *Exit.*

Goneril. This man hath had good counsel. A hundred knights!
330
'Tis politic° and safe to let him keep
At point° a hundred knights: yes, that on every dream,
Each buzz,° each fancy, each complaint, dislike,
He may enguard° his dotage with their pow'rs
And hold our lives in mercy.° Oswald, I say!

Albany. Well, you may fear too far.

335 *Goneril.*   Safer than trust too far.
Let me still take away the harms I fear,
Not fear still to be taken.° I know his heart.
What he hath uttered I have writ my sister.
If she sustain him and his hundred knights,
When I have showed th' unfitness——

Enter Oswald.
340
                    How now, Oswald?
What, have you writ that letter to my sister?

Oswald. Ay, madam.

Goneril. Take you some company,° and away to horse.
Inform her full of my particular° fear,
345
And thereto add such reasons of your own
As may compact° it more. Get you gone,
And hasten your return. [*Exit Oswald.*] No, no, my lord,
This milky gentleness and course° of yours,
Though I condemn not,° yet under pardon,

327-28 *halter, after* pronounced "hauter," "auter"   **330** *politic* good policy   **331** *At point* armed   **332** *buzz* rumor   **333** *enguard* protect   **334** *in mercy* at his mercy   **337** *Not . . . taken* rather than remain fearful of being overtaken by them   **343** *company* escort   **344** *particular* own   **346** *compact* strengthen   **348** *milky . . . course* mild and gentle way (hendiadys)   **349** *condemn not* condemn it not

You are much more attasked° for want of wisdom   350
Than praised for harmful mildness.°

Albany. How far your eyes may pierce I cannot tell;
Striving to better, oft we mar what's well.

Goneril. Nay then——

Albany. Well, well, th' event.°   *Exeunt.* 355

Scene V.   [*Court before the same.*]

Enter Lear, Kent, and Fool.

Lear. Go you before to Gloucester with these letters.
Acquaint my daughter no further with anything
you know than comes from her demand out of
the letter.° If your diligence be not speedy, I shall
be there afore you.   5

Kent. I will not sleep, my lord, till I have delivered
your letter.   *Exit.*

Fool. If a man's brains were in's heels, were't° not
in danger of kibes?°

Lear. Ay, boy.   10

Fool. Then I prithee be merry. Thy wit shall not go
slipshod.°

Lear. Ha, ha, ha.

Fool. Shalt° see thy other daughter will use thee
kindly;° for though she's as like this as a crab's°   15
like an apple, yet I can tell what I can tell.

350 *attasked* taken to task, blamed 351 *harmful mildness* dangerous in-
dulgence 355 *th' event* i.e., we'll see what happens I.v. 3-4 *than . . .
letter* than her reading of the letter brings her to ask 8 *were't* i.e., the
brains 9 *kibes* chilblains 11-12 *Thy . . . slipshod* your brains shall not
go in slippers (because you have no brains to be protected from chilblains) 14 *Shalt* thou shalt 15 *kindly* (1) affectionately (2) after her
kind or nature 15 *crab* crab apple

Lear. Why, what canst thou tell, my boy?

Fool. She will taste as like this as a crab does to a
crab. Thou canst tell why one's nose stands i' th'
20   middle on's° face?

Lear. No.

Fool. Why, to keep one's eyes of° either side's nose,
that what a man cannot smell out, he may spy
into.

25   *Lear.* I did her wrong.

Fool. Canst tell how an oyster makes his shell?

Lear. No.

Fool. Nor I neither; but I can tell why a snail has a
house.

30   *Lear.* Why?

Fool. Why, to put 's head in; not to give it away to
his daughters, and leave his horns° without a case.

Lear. I will forget my nature.° So kind a father! Be
my horses ready?

35   *Fool.* Thy asses are gone about 'em. The reason why
the seven stars° are no moe° than seven is a pretty°
reason.

Lear. Because they are not eight.

Fool. Yes indeed. Thou wouldst make a good Fool.

40   *Lear.* To take't again perforce!° Monster ingratitude!

Fool. If thou wert my Fool, Nuncle, I'd have thee
beaten for being old before thy time.

Lear. How's that?

Fool. Thou shouldst not have been old till thou hadst
45   been wise.

---

20 *on's* of his   22 *of* on   32 *horns* (1) snail's horns (2) cuckold's
horns   33 *nature* paternal instincts   36 *seven stars* the Pleiades   36 *moe*
more   36 *pretty* apt   40 *To . . . perforce* (1) of Goneril, who has
forcibly taken away Lear's privileges; or (2) of Lear, who meditates
a forcible resumption of authority

Lear. O, let me not be mad, not mad, sweet heaven!
   Keep me in temper;° I would not be mad!

                        [*Enter Gentleman.*]

   How now, are the horses ready?

Gentleman. Ready, my lord.

Lear. Come, boy.   50

Fool. She that's a maid now, and laughs at my
      departure,
   Shall not be a maid long, unless things be cut
      shorter.°   *Exeunt.*

---

⁴⁷ *in temper* sane   ⁵¹⁻⁵² *She . . . shorter* the maid who laughs, missing
the tragic implications of this quarrel, will not have sense enough to
preserve her virginity ("things" = penises)

ACT II

Scene I. [*The Earl of Gloucester's castle.*]

Enter Edmund and Curan, severally.°

Edmund. Save° thee, Curan.

Curan. And you, sir. I have been with your father, and given him notice that the Duke of Cornwall and Regan his duchess will be here with him this night.

Edmund. How comes that?

Curan. Nay, I know not. You have heard of the news abroad? I mean the whispered ones, for they are yet but ear-kissing arguments.°

Edmund. Not I. Pray you, what are they?

Curan. Have you heard of no likely° wars toward,° 'twixt the Dukes of Cornwall and Albany?

Edmund. Not a word.

Curan. You may do, then, in time. Fare you well, sir.   *Exit.*

Edmund. The Duke be here tonight? The better!° best!

II.i. ¹ s.d. *severally* separately (from different entrances on stage) ¹ *Save* God save ⁹ *ear-kissing arguments* subjects whispered in the ear ¹¹ *likely* probable ¹¹ *toward* impending ¹⁶ *The better* so much the better

This weaves itself perforce° into my business.
My father hath set guard to take my brother,
And I have one thing of a queasy question°
Which I must act. Briefness° and Fortune, work!   20
Brother, a word; descend. Brother, I say!

Enter Edgar.

My father watches. O sir, fly this place.
Intelligence° is given where you are hid.
You have now the good advantage of the night.
Have you not spoken 'gainst the Duke of Cornwall?   25
He's coming hither, now i' th' night, i' th' haste,°
And Regan with him. Have you nothing said
Upon his party° 'gainst the Duke of Albany?
Advise yourself.°

Edgar.   I am sure on't,° not a word.

Edmund. I hear my father coming. Pardon me: 30
In cunning° I must draw my sword upon you.
Draw, seem to defend yourself; now quit you° well.
Yield! Come before my father! Light ho, here!
Fly, brother. Torches, torches! —So farewell.

Exit Edgar.

Some blood drawn on me would beget opinion°   35
                    [*Wounds his arm*]
Of my more fierce endeavor. I have seen drunkards
Do more than this in sport. Father, father!
Stop, stop! No help?

Enter Gloucester, and Servants with torches.

Gloucester. Now, Edmund, where's the villain?

Edmund. Here stood he in the dark, his sharp sword
          out,   40
Mumbling of wicked charms, conjuring the moon
To stand auspicious mistress.

Gloucester.   But where is he?

---

17 *perforce* necessarily   19 *of a queasy question* that requires delicate
handling (to be "queasy" is to be on the point of vomiting)   20 *Brief-
ness* speed   23 *Intelligence* information   26 *i' th' haste* in great haste
28 *Upon his party* censuring his enmity   29 *Advise yourself* reflect
29 *on't* of it   31 *In cunning* as a pretense   32 *quit you* acquit yourself
35 *beget opinion* create the impression

Edmund. Look, sir, I bleed.

Gloucester.   Where is the villain, Edmund?

Edmund. Fled this way, sir, when by no means he
   could——

Gloucester. Pursue him, ho! Go after.

                         [*Exeunt some Servants.*]

45   By no means what?

Edmund. Persuade me to the murder of your lordship;
   But that I told him the revenging gods
   'Gainst parricides did all the thunder bend;°
   Spoke with how manifold and strong a bond
50   The child was bound to th' father. Sir, in fine,°
   Seeing how loathly opposite° I stood
   To his unnatural purpose, in fell° motion°
   With his preparèd sword he charges home
   My unprovided° body, latched° mine arm;
55   But when he saw my best alarumed° spirits
   Bold in the quarrel's right,° roused to th'
        encounter,
   Or whether gasted° by the noise I made,
   Full suddenly he fled.

Gloucester.   Let him fly far.
   Not in this land shall he remain uncaught;
60   And found—dispatch.° The noble Duke my master,
   My worthy arch° and patron, comes tonight.
   By his authority I will proclaim it,
   That he which finds him shall deserve our thanks,
   Bringing the murderous coward to the stake.
65   He that conceals him, death.°

Edmund. When I dissuaded him from his intent,
   And found him pight° to do it, with curst° speech
   I threatened to discover° him. He replied,

---

48 *bend* aim   50 *in fine* finally   51 *loathly opposite* bitterly opposed
52 *fell* deadly   52 *motion* thrust (a term from fencing)   54 *unprovided*
unprotected   54 *latched* wounded (lanced)   55 *best alarumed* wholly
aroused   56 *Bold . . . right* confident in the rightness of my cause
57 *gasted* struck aghast   60 *dispatch* i.e., he will be killed   61 *arch* chief
65 *death* (the same elliptical form that characterizes "dispatch," 1.60)
67 *pight* determined   67 *curst* angry   68 *discover* expose

"Thou unpossessing° bastard, dost thou think,
If I would stand against thee, would the reposal°   70
Of any trust, virtue, or worth in thee
Make thy words faithed?° No. What I should
    deny—
As this I would, ay, though thou didst produce
My very character°—I'd turn it all
To thy suggestion,° plot, and damnèd practice.°   75
And thou must make a dullard of the world,°
If they not thought° the profits of my death
Were very pregnant° and potential spirits°
To make thee seek it."

Gloucester.   O strange and fastened° villain!
Would he deny his letter, said he? I never got° him.   80

                    Tucket° within.

Hark, the Duke's trumpets. I know not why he
    comes.
All ports° I'll bar; the villain shall not 'scape;
The Duke must grant me that. Besides, his picture
I will send far and near, that all the kingdom
May have due note of him; and of my land,   85
Loyal and natural° boy, I'll work the means·
To make thee capable.°

Enter Cornwall, Regan, and Attendants.

Cornwall. How now, my noble friend! Since I came
    hither,
Which I can call but now, I have heard strange
    news.

Regan. If it be true, all vengeance comes too short   90
Which can pursue th' offender. How dost, my lord?

Gloucester. O madam, my old heart is cracked, it's
    cracked.

---

⁶⁹ *unpossessing* beggarly (landless) ⁷⁰ *reposal* placing ⁷² *faithed* believed ⁷⁴ *character* handwriting ⁷⁵ *suggestion* instigation ⁷⁵ *practice* device ⁷⁶ *make . . . world* think everyone stupid ⁷⁷ *not thought* did not think ⁷⁸ *pregnant* teeming with incitement ⁷⁸ *potential spirits* powerful evil spirits ⁷⁹ *fastened* hardened ⁸⁰ *got* begot ⁸⁰ s.d. *Tucket* (Cornwall's special trumpet call) ⁸² *ports* exits, of whatever sort ⁸⁶ *natural* (1) kind (filial) (2) illegitimate ⁸⁷ *capable* able to inherit

Regan. What, did my father's godson seek your life?
　　He whom my father named, your Edgar?

95　*Gloucester.* O lady, lady, shame would have it hid.

Regan. Was he not companion with the riotous knights
　　That tended upon my father?

Gloucester. I know not, madam. 'Tis too bad, too bad.

Edmund. Yes, madam, he was of that consort.°

100　*Regan.* No marvel then, though he were ill affected.°
　　'Tis they have put° him on the old man's death,
　　To have th' expense and waste° of his revenues.
　　I have this present evening from my sister
　　Been well informed of them, and with such cautions
105　That, if they come to sojourn at my house,
　　I'll not be there.

Cornwall.　　　　　　Nor I, assure thee, Regan.
　　Edmund, I hear that you have shown your father
　　A childlike° office.

Edmund. It was my duty, sir.

110　*Gloucester.* He did bewray his practice,° and received
　　This hurt you see, striving to apprehend him.

Cornwall. Is he pursued?

Gloucester.　　　　　　　　Ay, my good lord.

Cornwall. If he be taken, he shall never more
　　Be feared of doing° harm. Make your own purpose,
115　How in my strength you please.° For you, Edmund,
　　Whose virtue and obedience° doth this instant
　　So much commend itself, you shall be ours.
　　Natures of such deep trust we shall much need;
　　You we first seize on.

Edmund.　　　　　　I shall serve you, sir,
　　Truly, however else.

120　*Gloucester.*　　　　　For him I thank your Grace.

---

99 *consort* company　100 *ill affected* disposed to evil　101 *put* set
102 *expense and waste* squandering　108 *childlike* filial　110 *bewray his
practice* disclose his plot　114 *of doing* because he might do
114-15 *Make . . . please* use my power freely, in carrying out your plans
for his capture　116 *virtue and obedience* virtuous obedience

Cornwall. You know not why we came to visit you?

Regan. Thus out of season, threading dark-eyed night.
   Occasions, noble Gloucester, of some prize,°
   Wherein we must have use of your advice.
   Our father he hath writ, so hath our sister,   125
   Of differences,° which° I best thought it fit
   To answer from° our home. The several
     messengers
   From hence attend dispatch.° Our good old friend,
   Lay comforts to your bosom,° and bestow
   Your needful° counsel to our businesses,   130
   Which craves the instant use.°

Gloucester.   I serve you, madam.
   Your Graces are right welcome.

                      Exeunt. Flourish.

Scene II.   [*Before Gloucester's castle.*]

Enter Kent and Oswald, severally.

Oswald. Good dawning° to thee, friend. Art of this
   house?°

Kent. Ay.

Oswald. Where may we set our horses?

Kent. I' th' mire.   5

Oswald. Prithee, if thou lov'st me, tell me.

Kent. I love thee not.

---

122 *prize* importance   125 *differences* quarrels   125 *which* (referring not
to "differences," but to the letter Lear has written)   126 *from* away
from   127 *attend dispatch* are waiting to be sent off   128 *Lay . . .
bosom* console yourself (about Edgar's supposed treason)   129 *needful*
needed   131 *craves the instant use* demands immediate transaction
II.ii. 1 *dawning* (dawn is impending, but not yet arrived)   1-2 *Art of
this house* i.e., do you live here

Oswald. Why then, I care not for thee.

Kent. If I had thee in Lipsbury Pinfold,° I would make
10   thee care for me.

Oswald. Why dost thou use me thus? I know thee not.

Kent. Fellow, I know thee.

Oswald. What dost thou know me for?

Kent. A knave, a rascal, an eater of broken meats;°
15   a base, proud, shallow, beggarly, three-suited,°
      hundred-pound,° filthy worsted-stocking° knave;
      a lily-livered, action-taking,° whoreson, glass-gaz-
      ing,° superserviceable,° finical° rogue; one-trunk-
      inheriting° slave; one that wouldst be a bawd in
20   way of good service,° and art nothing but the com-
      position° of a knave, beggar, coward, pander, and
      the son and heir of a mongrel bitch; one whom I
      will beat into clamorous whining if thou deniest the
      least syllable of thy addition.°

25 *Oswald.* Why, what a monstrous fellow art thou, thus
      to rail on one that is neither known of thee nor
      knows thee!

Kent. What a brazen-faced varlet art thou to deny
      thou knowest me! Is it two days since I
30   tripped up thy heels and beat thee before the
      King? [*Drawing his sword*] Draw, you rogue,
      for though it be night, yet the moon shines. I'll
      make a sop o' th' moonshine° of you. You whore-
      son cullionly barbermonger,° draw!

9 *Lipsbury Pinfold* a pound or pen in which strayed animals are enclosed ("Lipsbury" may denote a particular place, or may be slang for
"between my teeth")   14 *broken meats* scraps of food   15 *three-suited*
(the wardrobe permitted to a servant or "knave")   16 *hundred-pound*
(the extent of Oswald's wealth, and thus a sneer at his aspiring to
gentility)   16 *worsted-stocking* (worn by servants)   17 *action-taking*
one who refuses a fight and goes to law instead   17-18 *glass-gazing*
conceited   18 *superserviceable* sycophantic, serving without principle.
18 *finical* overfastidious   18-19 *one-trunk-inheriting* possessing only a
trunkful of goods   19-20 *bawd . . . service* pimp, to please his master
20-21 *composition* compound   24 *addition* titles   33 *sop o' th' moonshine*
i.e., Oswald will admit the moonlight, and so sop it up, through the
open wounds Kent is preparing to give him   34 *cullionly barbermonger*
base patron of hairdressers (effeminate man)

Oswald. Away, I have nothing to do with thee.   35

Kent. Draw, you rascal. You come with letters
against the King, and take Vanity the puppet's° part
against the royalty of her father. Draw, you rogue,
or I'll so carbonado° your shanks. Draw, you rascal. Come your ways!°   40

Oswald. Help, ho! Murder! Help!

Kent. Strike, you slave! Stand, rogue! Stand, you neat°
slave! Strike! [*Beating him*]

Oswald. Help, ho! Murder, murder!

    Enter Edmund, with his rapier drawn, Cornwall,
        Regan, Gloucester, Servants.

Edmund. How now? What's the matter? Part!   45

Kent. With you,° goodman boy,° if you please! Come,
I'll flesh° ye, come on, young master.

Gloucester. Weapons? Arms? What's the matter here?

Cornwall. Keep peace, upon your lives.
He dies that strikes again. What is the matter?   50

Regan. The messengers from our sister and the King.

Cornwall. What is your difference?° Speak.

Oswald. I am scarce in breath, my lord.

Kent. No marvel, you have so bestirred° your valor.
You cowardly rascal, nature disclaims in thee.° A   55
tailor made thee.°

Cornwall. Thou art a strange fellow. A tailor make a
man?

Kent. A tailor, sir. A stonecutter or a painter could

---

37 *Vanity the puppet's* Goneril, here identified with one of the personified characters in the morality plays, which were sometimes put
on as puppet shows   **39** *carbonado* cut across, like a piece of meat
before cooking   **40** *Come your ways* get along   **42** *neat* (1) foppish
(2) unmixed, as in "neat wine"   **46** *With you* i.e., the quarrel is with
you   **46** *goodman boy* young man (peasants are "goodmen"; "boy" is
a term of contempt)   **47** *flesh* introduce to blood (term from hunting)
52 *difference* quarrel   **54** *bestirred* exercised   **55** *nature disclaims in thee*
nature renounces any part in you   **55-56** *A tailor made thee* (from the
proverb "The tailor makes the man")

60   not have made him so ill, though they had been
        but two years o' th' trade.

Cornwall. Speak yet, how grew your quarrel?

Oswald. This ancient ruffian, sir, whose life I have
        spared at suit of° his gray beard——

65 *Kent.* Thou whoreson zed,° thou unnecessary letter!
        My lord, if you will give me leave, I will tread this
        unbolted° villain into mortar and daub the wall of
        a jakes° with him. Spare my gray beard, you wag-
        tail!°

70 *Cornwall.* Peace, sirrah!
        You beastly° knave, know you no reverence?

Kent. Yes, sir, but anger hath a privilege.

Cornwall. Why art thou angry?

Kent. That such a slave as this should wear a sword,
        Who wears no honesty. Such smiling rogues as
75   these,
        Like rats, oft bite the holy cords° atwain
        Which are too intrince° t' unloose; smooth°
            every passion
        That in the natures of their lords rebel,
        Being oil to fire, snow to the colder moods;
80   Renege,° affirm, and turn their halcyon beaks°
        With every gale and vary° of their masters,
        Knowing naught, like dogs, but following.
        A plague upon your epileptic° visage!
        Smile you° my speeches, as I were a fool?

---

⁶⁴ *at suit of* out of pity for   ⁶⁵ *zed* the letter Z, generally omitted in
contemporary dictionaries   ⁶⁷ *unbolted* unsifted, i.e., altogether a villain   ⁶⁸ *jakes* privy   ⁶⁸⁻⁶⁹ *wagtail* a bird that bobs its tail up and down,
and thus suggests obsequiousness   ⁷¹ *beastly* irrational   ⁷⁶ *holy cords*
sacred bonds of affection (as between husbands and wives, parents and children)   ⁷⁷ *intrince* entangled, intricate   ⁷⁷ *smooth* appease
⁸⁰ *Renege* deny   ⁸⁰ *halcyon beaks* (the halcyon or kingfisher serves
here as a type of the opportunist because, when hung up by the tail or
neck, it was supposed to turn with the wind, like a weathervane)
⁸¹ *gale and vary* varying gale (hendiadys)   ⁸³ *epileptic* distorted by
grinning   ⁸⁴ *Smile you* do you smile at

Goose, if I had you upon Sarum Plain,°
    I'd drive ye cackling home to Camelot.°

Cornwall. What, art thou mad, old fellow?

Gloucester. How fell you out? Say that.

Kent. No contraries° hold more antipathy
    Than I and such a knave.   90

Cornwall. Why dost thou call him knave? What is his
    fault?

Kent. His countenance likes° me not.

Cornwall. No more perchance does mine, nor his, nor
    hers.

Kent. Sir, 'tis my occupation to be plain:
    I have seen better faces in my time   95
    Than stands on any shoulder that I see
    Before me at this instant.

Cornwall.   This is some fellow
    Who, having been praised for bluntness, doth
        affect
    A saucy roughness, and constrains the garb
    Quite from his nature.° He cannot flatter, he;   100
    An honest mind and plain, he must speak truth.
    And° they will take it, so; if not, he's plain.
    These kind of knaves I know, which in this
        plainness
    Harbor more craft and more corrupter ends
    Than twenty silly-ducking observants°   105
    That stretch their duties nicely.°

Kent. Sir, in good faith, in sincere verity,
    Under th' allowance° of your great aspect,°
    Whose influence,° like the wreath of radiant fire

---

85 *Sarum Plain* Salisbury Plain   86 *Camelot* the residence of King
Arthur (presumably a particular point, now lost, is intended here)
89 *contraries* opposites   92 *likes* pleases   99-100 *constrains . . . nature*
forces the manner of candid speech to be a cloak, not for candor but
for craft   102 *And* if   105 *silly-ducking observants* ridiculously obsequious attendants   106 *nicely* punctiliously   108 *allowance* approval
108 *aspect* (1) appearance (2) position of the heavenly bodies   109 *influence* astrological power

On flick'ring Phoebus' front°——

110 *Cornwall.* What mean'st by this?

Kent. To go out of my dialect,° which you discommend
so much. I know, sir, I am no flatterer. He° that
beguiled you in a plain accent was a plain knave,
which, for my part, I will not be, though I should
115 win your displeasure to entreat me to't.°

Cornwall. What was th' offense you gave him?

Oswald. I never gave him any.
It pleased the King his master very late°
To strike at me, upon his misconstruction;°
120 When he, compact,° and flattering his displeasure,
Tripped me behind; being down, insulted, railed,
And put upon him such a deal of man°
That worthied him,° got praises of the King
For him attempting who was self-subdued;°
125 And, in the fleshment° of this dread exploit,
Drew on me here again.

Kent. None of these rogues and cowards
But Ajax is their fool.°

Cornwall. Fetch forth the stocks!
You stubborn° ancient knave, you reverent°
    braggart,
We'll teach you.

Kent. Sir, I am too old to learn.

110 *Phoebus' front* forehead of the sun 111 *dialect* customary manner
of speaking 112 *He* i.e., the sort of candid-crafty man Cornwall has
been describing 114-15 *though . . . to't* even if I were to succeed in
bringing your graceless person ("displeasure" personified, and in lieu
of the expected form, "your grace") to beg me to be a plain knave
118 *very late* recently 119 *misconstruction* misunderstanding 120 *compact* in league with the king 122 *put . . . man* pretended such manly
behavior 123 *worthied him* made him seem heroic 124 *For . . . self-
subdued* for attacking a man (Oswald) who offered no resistance
125 *fleshment* the bloodthirstiness excited by his first success or "flesh-
ing" 126-27 *None . . . fool* i.e., cowardly rogues like Oswald always
impose on fools like Cornwall (who is likened to Ajax: [1] the brag-
gart Greek warrior [2] a jakes or privy) 128 *stubborn* rude 128 *rev-
erent* old

Call not your stocks for me, I serve the King,   *130*
On whose employment I was sent to you.
You shall do small respect, show too bold malice
Against the grace and person° of my master,
Stocking his messenger.

Cornwall. Fetch forth the stocks. As I have life and   *135*
   honor,
There shall he sit till noon.

Regan. Till noon? Till night, my lord, and all night
   too.

Kent. Why, madam, if I were your father's dog,
You should not use me so.

Regan.   Sir, being his knave, I will.

Cornwall. This is a fellow of the selfsame color°   *140*
Our sister speaks of. Come, bring away° the stocks.
                    Stocks brought out.

Gloucester. Let me beseech your Grace not to do so.
His fault is much, and the good King his master
Will check° him for't. Your purposed° low
   correction
Is such as basest and contemnèd'st° wretches   *145*
For pilf'rings and most common trespasses
Are punished with.
The King his master needs must take it ill
That he, so slightly valued in° his messenger,
Should have him thus restrained.

Cornwall.   I'll answer° that.   *150*

Regan. My sister may receive it much more worse,
To have her gentleman abused, assaulted,
For following her affairs. Put in his legs.
                    [*Kent is put in the stocks.*]
Come, my good lord, away!
                    [*Exeunt all but Gloucester and Kent.*]

---

133 *grace and person* i.e., Lear as sovereign and in his personal character 140 *color* kind 141 *away* out 144 *check* correct 144 *purposed* intended 145 *contemnèd'st* most despised 149 *slightly valued in* little honored in the person of 150 *answer* answer for

Gloucester. I am sorry for thee, friend. 'Tis the Duke's
155   pleasure,
Whose disposition° all the world well knows
Will not be rubbed° nor stopped. I'll entreat for
thee.

Kent. Pray do not, sir. I have watched° and traveled
hard.
Some time I shall sleep out, the rest I'll whistle.
160   A good man's fortune may grow out at heels.°
Give° you good morrow.

Gloucester. The Duke's to blame in this. 'Twill be
ill taken.°   *Exit.*

Kent. Good King, that must approve° the common
saw,°
Thou out of Heaven's benediction com'st
165   To the warm sun.°
Approach, thou beacon to this under globe,°
That by thy comfortable° beams I may
Peruse this letter. Nothing almost sees miracles
But misery.° I know 'tis from Cordelia,
170   Who hath most fortunately been informed
Of my obscurèd° course. And shall find time
From this enormous state, seeking to give
Losses their remedies.° All weary and o'erwatched,
Take vantage,° heavy eyes, not to behold
175   This shameful lodging. Fortune, good night;
Smile once more, turn thy wheel.°

Sleeps.

---

156 *disposition* inclination   157 *rubbed* diverted (metaphor from the
game of bowls)   158 *watched* gone without sleep   160 *A . . . heels*
even a good man may have bad fortune   161 *Give* God give   162 *taken*
received   163 *approve* confirm   163 *saw* proverb   164-65 *Thou . . . sun*
i.e., Lear goes from better to worse, from Heaven's blessing or shelter
to lack of shelter   166 *beacon . . . globe* i.e., the sun, whose rising
Kent anticipates   167 *comfortable* comforting   168-69 *Nothing . . .
misery* i.e., true perception belongs only to the wretched   171 *obscurèd*
disguised   171-73 *shall . . . remedies* (a possible reading: Cordelia,
away from this monstrous state of things, will find occasion to right
the wrongs we suffer)   174 *vantage* advantage (of sleep)   176 *turn thy
wheel* i.e., so that Kent, who is at the bottom, may climb upward

[Scene III.   *A wood.*]

Enter Edgar.

Edgar. I heard myself proclaimed,
And by the happy° hollow of a tree
Escaped the hunt. No port is free, no place
That guard and most unusual vigilance
Does not attend my taking.° Whiles I may 'scape,   5
I will preserve myself; and am bethought°
To take the basest and most poorest shape
That ever penury, in contempt of man,
Brought near to beast;° my face I'll grime with filth,
Blanket° my loins, elf° all my hairs in knots,   10
And with presented° nakedness outface°
The winds and persecutions of the sky.
The country gives me proof° and precedent
Of Bedlam° beggars, who, with roaring voices,
Strike° in their numbed and mortified° bare arms   15
Pins, wooden pricks,° nails, sprigs of rosemary;
And with this horrible object,° from low° farms,
Poor pelting° villages, sheepcotes, and mills,
Sometimes with lunatic bans,° sometime with
     prayers,
Enforce their charity. Poor Turlygod, Poor Tom,°   20
That's something yet: Edgar I nothing am.° *Exit.*

II.iii.   ² *happy* lucky   ⁵ *attend my taking* watch to capture me   ⁶ *am
bethought* have decided   ⁸⁻⁹ *penury . . . beast* poverty, to show how
contemptible man is, reduced to the level of a beast   ¹⁰ *Blanket* cover
only with a blanket   ¹⁰ *elf* tangle (into "elflocks," supposed to be caused
by elves)   ¹¹ *presented* the show of   ¹¹ *outface* brave   ¹³ *proof* example
¹⁴ *Bedlam* (see I.ii.r. ¹⁴⁶⁻⁴⁷)   ¹⁵ *strike* stick   ¹⁵ *mortified* not alive to pain
¹⁶ *pricks* skewers   ¹⁷ *object* spectacle   ¹⁷ *low* humble   ¹⁸ *pelting* paltry
¹⁹ *bans* curses   ²⁰ *Poor . . . Tom* (Edgar recites the names a Bedlam
beggar gives himself)   ²¹ *That's . . . am* there's a chance for me in that
I am no longer known for myself

[Scene IV.   *Before Gloucester's castle. Kent in the stocks.*]

Enter Lear, Fool, and Gentleman.

Lear. 'Tis strange that they should so depart from
      home,
   And not send back my messenger.

Gentleman.   As I learned,
   The night before there was no purpose° in them
   Of this remove.°

Kent.   Hail to thee, noble master.

5 *Lear.* Ha!
   Mak'st thou this shame thy pastime?°

Kent.   No, my lord.

Fool. Ha, ha, he wears cruel° garters. Horses are tied
   by the heads, dogs and bears by th' neck, monkeys
   by th' loins, and men by th' legs. When a man's over-
10 lusty at legs,° then he wears wooden netherstocks.°

Lear. What's he that hath so much thy place mistook
   To set thee here?

Kent.   It is both he and she,
   Your son and daughter.

Lear. No.

15 *Kent.* Yes.

Lear. No, I say.

Kent. I say yea.

II.iv. 8 *purpose* intention   4 *remove* removal   6 *Mak'st . . . pastime* i.e.,
are you doing this to amuse yourself   7 *cruel* (1) painful (2)
"crewel," a worsted yarn used in garters   9-10 *overlusty at legs* (1) a
vagabond (2) ? sexually promiscuous   10 *netherstocks* stockings (as
opposed to knee breeches or upperstocks)

Lear. No, no, they would not.

Kent. Yes, they have.

Lear. By Jupiter, I swear no!   20

Kent. By Juno, I swear ay!

Lear.   They durst not do't;
They could not, would not do't. 'Tis worse than
    murder
To do upon respect° such violent outrage.
Resolve° me with all modest° haste which way
Thou mightst deserve or they impose this usage,   25
Coming from us.

Kent.   My lord, when at their home
I did commend° your Highness' letters to them,
Ere I was risen from the place that showed
My duty kneeling, came there a reeking post,°
Stewed° in his haste, half breathless, panting forth   30
From Goneril his mistress salutations,
Delivered letters, spite of intermission,°
Which presently° they read; on° whose contents
They summoned up their meiny,° straight took
    horse,
Commanded me to follow and attend   35
The leisure of their answer, gave me cold looks,
And meeting here the other messenger,
Whose welcome I perceived had poisoned mine,
Being the very fellow which of late
Displayed° so saucily against your Highness,   40
Having more man than wit° about me, drew;
He raised° the house, with loud and coward cries.
Your son and daughter found this trespass worth°
The shame which here it suffers.

23 *upon respect* (1) on the respect due to the King (2) deliberately
24 *Resolve* inform   24 *modest* becoming   27 *commend* deliver   29 *reeking post* sweating messenger   30 *stewed* steaming   32 *spite of intermission* in spite of the interrupting of my business   33 *presently* at once
33 *on* on the strength of   34 *meiny* retinue   40 *Displayed* showed off
41 *more man than wit* more manhood than sense   42 *raised* aroused
43 *worth* deserving

45 *Fool*. Winter's not gone yet, if the wild geese fly that
          way.°

                    Fathers that wear rags
                         Do make their children blind,°
                    But fathers that bear bags°
50   Shall see their children kind.
                    Fortune, that arrant whore,
                         Ne'er turns the key° to th' poor.
          But for all this, thou shalt have as many dolors° for
          thy daughters as thou canst tell° in a year.

55 *Lear*. O, how this mother° swells up toward my heart!
          Hysterica passio,° down, thou climbing sorrow,
          Thy element's° below. Where is this daughter?

Kent. With the Earl, sir, here within.

Lear.   Follow me not;
          Stay here.   *Exit*.

Gentleman. Made you no more offense but what you
60   speak of?

Kent. None.
          How chance° the King comes with so small a
               number?

Fool. And° thou hadst been set i' th' stocks for that
          question, thou'dst well deserved it.

65 *Kent*. Why, Fool?

Fool. We'll set thee to school to an ant, to teach thee
          there's no laboring i' th' winter.° All that follow

---

45-46 *Winter's . . . way* i.e., more trouble is to come, since Cornwall
and Regan act so ("geese" is used contemptuously, as in Kent's quarrel with Oswald, II.ii. 85-6)   48 *blind* i.e., indifferent   49 *bags* money-
bags   52 *turns the key* i.e., opens the door   53 *dolors* (1) sorrows (2)
dollars (English name for Spanish and German coins)   54 *tell* (1) tell
about (2) count   55-56 *mother . . . Hysterica passio* hysteria, causing
suffocation or choking   57 *element* proper place   62 *How chance* how
does it happen that   63 *And* if   66-67 *We'll . . . winter* (in the popular
fable the ant, unlike the improvident grasshopper, anticipates the winter
when none can labor by laying up provisions in the summer. Lear,
trusting foolishly to summer days, finds himself unprovided for, and
unable to provide, now that "winter" has come)

their noses are led by their eyes but blind men,
and there's not a nose among twenty but can smell
him that's stinking.° Let go thy hold when a great   70
wheel runs down a hill, lest it break thy neck with
following. But the great one that goes upward,
let him draw thee after. When a wise man gives
thee better counsel, give me mine again. I would
have none but knaves follow it since a Fool gives   75
it.

 That sir, which serves and seeks for gain,
  And follows but for form,°
 Will pack,° when it begins to rain,
  And leave thee in the storm.   80
 But I will tarry; the Fool will stay,
  And let the wise man fly.
 The knave turns Fool that runs away,
  The Fool no knave,° perdy.°

Kent. Where learned you this, Fool?   85

Fool. Not i' th' stocks, fool.

   Enter Lear and Gloucester.

Lear. Deny° to speak with me? They are sick, they
 are weary,
They have traveled all the night? Mere fetches,°
The images° of revolt and flying off!°
Fetch me a better answer.

Gloucester.   My dear lord,   90
You know the fiery quality° of the Duke,
How unremovable and fixed he is
In his own course.

Lear.   Vengeance, plague, death, confusion!
Fiery? What quality? Why, Gloucester, Gloucester,
I'd speak with the Duke of Cornwall and his wife.   95

67-70 *All . . . stinking* i.e., all can smell out the decay of Lear's fortunes 78 *form* show 79 *pack* be off 83-84 *The . . . knave* i.e., the
faithless man is the true fool, for wisdom requires fidelity. Lear's Fool,
who remains faithful, is at least no knave 84 *perdy* by God (Fr. *par
Dieu*) 87 *Deny* refuse 88 *fetches* subterfuges, acts of tacking (nautical
metaphor) 89 *images* exact likenesses 89 *flying off* desertion 91 *quality* temperament

Gloucester. Well, my good lord, I have informed them so.

Lear. Informed them? Dost thou understand me, man?

Gloucester. Ay, my good lord.

Lear. The King would speak with Cornwall. The dear father

100   Would with his daughter speak, commands—tends°
   —service.

Are they informed of this? My breath and blood!
Fiery? The fiery Duke, tell the hot Duke that—
No, but not yet. May be he is not well.
Infirmity doth still neglect all office

105   Whereto our health is bound.° We are not ourselves

When nature, being oppressed, commands the mind
To suffer with the body. I'll forbear;
And am fallen out° with my more headier will°
To take the indisposed and sickly fit

110   For the sound man. [*Looking on Kent*] Death on my state!° Wherefore

Should he sit here? This act persuades me
That this remotion° of the Duke and her
Is practice° only. Give me my servant forth.°
Go tell the Duke and's wife I'd speak with them!

115   Now, presently!° Bid them come forth and hear me,

Or at their chamber door I'll beat the drum
Till it cry sleep to death.°

  Gloucester. I would have all well betwixt you.

Exit.

---

100 *tends* attends (i.e., awaits); with, possibly, an ironic second meaning, "tenders," or "offers" 105 *Whereto . . . bound* duties which we are required to perform, when in health 108 *fallen out* angry 108 *headier will* headlong inclination 110 *state* royal condition 112 *remotion* (1) removal (2) remaining aloof 113 *practice* pretense 113 *forth* i.e., out of the stocks 115 *presently* at once 117 *cry . . . death* follow sleep, like a cry or pack of hounds, until it kills it

Lear. O me, my heart, my rising heart! But down!

Fool. Cry to it, Nuncle, as the cockney° did to   120
the eels when she put 'em i' th' paste° alive. She
knapped° 'em o' th' coxcombs° with a stick and
cried, "Down, wantons,° down!" 'Twas her brother
that, in pure kindness to his horse, buttered his
hay.°   125

Enter Cornwall, Regan, Gloucester, Servants.

Lear. Good morrow to you both.

Cornwall.   Hail to your Grace.

Kent here set at liberty.

Regan. I am glad to see your Highness.

Lear. Regan, I think you are. I know what reason
I have to think so. If thou shouldst not be glad,
I would divorce me from thy mother's tomb,   130
Sepulchring an adultress.° [*To Kent*] O, are you
    free?
Some other time for that. Beloved Regan,
Thy sister's naught.° O Regan, she hath tied
Sharp-toothed unkindness, like a vulture, here.

                 [*Points to his heart.*]

I can scarce speak to thee. Thou'lt not believe   135
With how depraved a quality°—O Regan!

Regan. I pray you, sir, take patience. I have hope
You less know how to value her desert
Than she to scant her duty.°

Lear.   Say? how is that?

---

120 *cockney* Londoner (ignorant city dweller)   121 *paste* pastry pie
122 *knapped* rapped   122 *coxcombs* heads   123 *wantons* i.e., playful
things (with a sexual implication)   125 *buttered his hay* i.e., the city
dweller does from ignorance what the dishonest ostler does from craft:
greases the hay the traveler has paid for, so that the horse will not
eat   130-31 *divorce . . . adultress* i.e., repudiate your dead mother as
having conceived you by another man   133 *naught* wicked   136 *quality*
nature   137-39 *I . . . duty* (despite the double negative, the passage
means, "I believe that you fail to give Goneril her due, rather than
that she fails to fulfill her duty")

140 *Regan.* I cannot think my sister in the least
     Would fail her obligation. If, sir, perchance
     She have restrained the riots of your followers,
     'Tis on such ground, and to such wholesome end,
     As clears her from all blame.

Lear. My curses on her!

145 *Regan.*   O, sir, you are old,
     Nature in you stands on the very verge
     Of his confine.° You should be ruled, and led
     By some discretion that discerns your state
     Better than you yourself.° Therefore I pray you
150 That to our sister you do make return,
     Say you have wronged her.

Lear.   Ask her forgiveness?
     Do you but mark how this becomes the house:°
     "Dear daughter, I confess that I am old.

                              [*Kneeling.*]

     Age is unnecessary. On my knees I beg
155 That you'll vouchsafe me raiment, bed, and food."

Regan. Good sir, no more. These are unsightly tricks.
     Return you to my sister.

Lear.   [*Rising*] Never, Regan.
     She hath abated° me of half my train,
     Looked black upon me, struck me with her tongue,
160 Most serpentlike, upon the very heart.
     All the stored vengeances of heaven fall
     On her ingrateful top!° Strike her young bones,°
     You taking° airs, with lameness.

Cornwall.   Fie, sir, fie!

Lear. You nimble lightnings, dart your blinding flames
165 Into her scornful eyes! Infect her beauty,

146-47 *Nature . . . confine* i.e., you are nearing the end of your life
148-49 *some . . . yourself* some discreet person who understands your
condition more than you do   152 *becomes the house* suits my royal and
paternal position   158 *abated* curtailed   162 *top* head   162 *young bones*
(the reference may be to unborn children, rather than to Goneril herself)   163 *taking* infecting

You fen-sucked° fogs, drawn by the pow'rful sun,
To fall and blister° her pride.

Regan.   O the blest gods!
So will you wish on me when the rash mood is on.

Lear. No, Regan, thou shalt never have my curse.
Thy tender-hefted° nature shall not give   170
Thee o'er to harshness. Her eyes are fierce, but thine
Do comfort, and not burn. 'Tis not in thee
To grudge my pleasures, to cut off my train,
To bandy° hasty words, to scant my sizes,°
And, in conclusion, to oppose the bolt°   175
Against my coming in. Thou better know'st
The offices of nature, bond of childhood,°
Effects° of courtesy, dues of gratitude.
Thy half o' th' kingdom hast thou not forgot,
Wherein I thee endowed.

Regan.   Good sir, to th' purpose.°   180

Tucket within.

Lear. Who put my man i' th' stocks?

Cornwall.   What trumpet's that?

Regan. I know't—my sister's. This approves° her
    letter,
That she would soon be here.

Enter Oswald.

                     Is your lady come?

Lear. This is a slave, whose easy borrowed° pride
Dwells in the fickle grace° of her he follows.   185
Out, varlet,° from my sight.

Cornwall.   What means your Grace?

---

166 *fen-sucked* drawn up from swamps by the sun   167 *fall and blister*
fall upon and raise blisters   170 *tender-hefted* gently framed   174 *bandy*
volley (metaphor from tennis)   174 *scant my sizes* reduce my allow-
ances   175 *oppose the bolt* i.e., bar the door   177 *offices . . . childhood*
natural duties, a child's duty to its parent   178 *Effects* manifestations
180 *to th' purpose* come to the point   182 *approves* confirms   184 *easy
borrowed* (1) facile and taken from another (2) acquired without anything to back it up (like money borrowed without security)   185 *grace*
favor   186 *varlet* base fellow

Lear. Who stocked my servant? Regan, I have good
hope
  Thou didst not know on't.

Enter Goneril.

                    Who comes here? O heavens!
  If you do love old men, if your sweet sway
190 Allow° obedience, if you yourselves are old,
  Make it° your cause. Send down, and take my part.
  [*To Goneril*] Art not ashamed to look upon
      this beard?
  O Regan, will you take her by the hand?

Goneril. Why not by th' hand, sir? How have I
      offended?
195 All's not offense that indiscretion finds°
  And dotage terms so.

Lear.   O sides,° you are too tough!
  Will you yet hold? How came my man i' th' stocks?

Cornwall. I set him there, sir; but his own disorders°
  Deserved much less advancement.°

Lear.   You? Did you?

200 *Regan.* I pray you, father, being weak, seem so.°
  If till the expiration of your month
  You will return and sojourn with my sister,
  Dismissing half your train, come then to me.
  I am now from home, and out of that provision
205 Which shall be needful for your entertainment.°

Lear. Return to her, and fifty men dismissed?
  No, rather I abjure all roofs, and choose
  To wage° against the enmity o' th' air,
  To be a comrade with the wolf and owl,
210 Necessity's sharp pinch.° Return with her?
  Why, the hot-blooded° France, that dowerless
      took

---

190 *Allow* approve of   191 *it* i.e., my cause   195 *finds* judges   196 *sides*
breast   198 *disorders* misconduct   199 *advancement* promotion   200 *seem
so* i.e., act weak   205 *entertainment* maintenance   208 *wage* fight
210 *Necessity's sharp pinch* (a summing up of the hard choice he has
just announced)   211 *hot-blooded* passionate

Our youngest born, I could as well be brought
To knee° his throne, and, squirelike,° pension beg
To keep base life afoot. Return with her?
Persuade me rather to be slave and sumpter°   215
To this detested groom. [*Pointing at Oswald.*]

Goneril.   At your choice, sir.

Lear. I prithee, daughter, do not make me mad.
I will not trouble thee, my child; farewell.
We'll no more meet, no more see one another.
But yet thou art my flesh, my blood, my daughter,   220
Or rather a disease that's in my flesh,
Which I must needs call mine. Thou art a boil,
A plague-sore, or embossèd carbuncle°
In my corrupted blood. But I'll not chide thee.
Let shame come when it will, I do not call it.   225
I do not bid the Thunder-bearer° shoot,
Nor tell tales of thee to high-judging° Jove.
Mend when thou canst, be better at thy leisure,
I can be patient, I can stay with Regan,
I and my hundred knights.

Regan.   Not altogether so.   230
I looked not for you yet, nor am provided
For your fit welcome. Give ear, sir, to my sister,
For those that mingle reason with your passion°
Must be content to think you old, and so—
But she knows what she does.

Lear.   Is this well spoken?   235

Regan. I dare avouch° it, sir. What, fifty followers?
Is it not well? What should you need of more?
Yea, or so many, sith that° both charge° and
      danger
Speak 'gainst so great a number? How in one house

---

²¹³ *knee* kneel before ²¹³ *squirelike* like a retainer ²¹⁵ *sumpter* pack
horse ²²³ *embossèd carbuncle* swollen boil ²²⁶ *Thunder-bearer* i.e.,
Jupiter ²²⁷ *high-judging* (1) supreme (2) judging from heaven
²³³ *mingle . . . passion* i.e., consider your turbulent behavior coolly
and reasonably ²³⁶ *avouch* swear by ²³⁸ *sith that* since ²³⁸ *charge*
expense

240 Should many people, under two commands,
Hold° amity? 'Tis hard, almost impossible.

Goneril. Why might not you, my lord, receive
    attendance
From those that she calls servants, or from mine?

Regan. Why not, my lord? If then they chanced to
    slack° ye,
245 We could control them. If you will come to me
(For now I spy a danger), I entreat you
To bring but five-and-twenty. To no more
Will I give place or notice.°

Lear. I gave you all.

Regan.   And in good time you gave it.

250 *Lear.* Made you my guardians, my depositaries,°
But kept a reservation° to be followed
With such a number. What, must I come to you
With five-and-twenty? Regan, said you so?

Regan. And speak't again, my lord. No more with me.

Lear. Those wicked creatures yet do look well-
255   favored°
When others are more wicked; not being the worst
Stands in some rank of praise.° [*To Goneril*] I'll
    go with thee.
Thy fifty yet doth double five-and-twenty,
And thou art twice her love.°

Goneril.   Hear me, my lord.
260 What need you five-and-twenty? ten? or five?
To follow° in a house where twice so many
Have a command to tend you?

Regan.   What need one?

Lear. O reason° not the need! Our basest beggars

241 *hold* preserve   244 *slack* neglect   248 *notice* recognition   250 *depositaries* trustees   251 *reservation* condition   255 *well-favored* handsome
256-57 *not . . . praise* i.e., that Goneril is not so bad as Regan is one
thing in her favor   259 *her love* i.e., as loving as she   261 *follow* attend
on you   263 *reason* scrutinize

Are in the poorest thing superfluous.°
Allow not nature more than nature needs,°   265
Man's life is cheap as beast's. Thou art a lady:
If only to go warm were gorgeous,
Why, nature needs not what thou gorgeous wear'st,
Which scarcely keeps thee warm.° But, for true
    need—
You heavens, give me that patience, patience I
    need.   270
You see me here, you gods, a poor old man,
As full of grief as age, wretched in both.
If it be you that stirs these daughters' hearts
Against their father, fool° me not so much
To bear° it tamely; touch me with noble anger,   275
And let not women's weapons, water drops,
Stain my man's cheeks. No, you unnatural hags!
I will have such revenges on you both
That all the world shall—I will do such things—
What they are, yet I know not; but they shall be   280
The terrors of the earth. You think I'll weep.
No, I'll not weep.

> *Storm and tempest.*

I have full cause of weeping, but this heart
Shall break into a hundred thousand flaws°
Or ere° I'll weep. O Fool, I shall go mad!   285

> *Exeunt Lear, Gloucester, Kent, and Fool.*

Cornwall. Let us withdraw, 'twill be a storm.

Regan. This house is little; the old man and's people
    Cannot be well bestowed.°

Goneril. 'Tis his own blame; hath° put himself from
    rest°
    And must needs taste his folly.   290

---

²⁶⁴ *Are . . . superfluous* i.e., have some trifle not absolutely necessary
²⁶⁵ *needs* i.e., to sustain life ²⁶⁷⁻⁶⁹ *If . . . warm* i.e., if to satisfy the
need for warmth were to be gorgeous, you would not need the clothing you wear, which is worn more for beauty than warmth ²⁷⁴ *fool*
humiliate ²⁷⁵ *To bear* as to make me bear ²⁸⁴ *flaws* (1) pieces (2)
cracks (3) gusts of passion ²⁸⁵ *Or ere* before ²⁸⁸ *bestowed* lodged
²⁸⁹ *hath* he hath ²⁸⁹ *rest* (1) place of residence (2) repose of mind

Regan. For his particular,° I'll receive him gladly,
But not one follower.

Goneril.   So am I purposed.°
Where is my Lord of Gloucester?

Cornwall. Followed the old man forth.

Enter Gloucester.

                              He is returned.

Gloucester. The King is in high rage.

295 *Cornwall.*   Whither is he going?

Gloucester. He calls to horse, but will I know not
whither.

Cornwall. 'Tis best to give him way, he leads himself.°

Goneril. My lord, entreat him by no means to stay.

Gloucester. Alack, the night comes on, and the high
winds
800   Do sorely ruffle.° For many miles about
There's scarce a bush.

Regan.   O, sir, to willful men
The injuries that they themselves procure
Must be their schoolmasters. Shut up your doors.
He is attended with a desperate train,
805   And what they may incense° him to, being apt
To have his ear abused,° wisdom bids fear.

Cornwall. Shut up your doors, my lord; 'tis a wild
night.
My Regan counsels well. Come out o' th' storm.

                              Exeunt.

---

291 *his particular* himself personally   292 *purposed* determined   297 *give
. . . himself* let him go; he insists on his own way   300 *ruffle* rage
305 *incense* incite   305-06 *being . . . abused* he being inclined to harken
to bad counsel

ACT III

Scene I. [*A heath.*]

Storm still.° *Enter Kent and a Gentleman*
severally.

Kent. Who's there besides foul weather?

Gentleman. One minded like the weather most
    unquietly.°

Kent. I know you. Where's the King?

Gentleman. Contending with the fretful elements;
    Bids the wind blow the earth into the sea,
    Or swell the curlèd waters 'bove the main,°   *5*
    That things might change,° or cease; tears his white
      hair,
    Which the impetuous blasts, with eyeless° rage,
    Catch in their fury, and make nothing of;
    Strives in his little world of man° to outscorn   *10*
    The to-and-fro-conflicting wind and rain.
    This night, wherein the cub-drawn° bear would
      couch,°
    The lion, and the belly-pinchèd° wolf
    Keep their fur dry, unbonneted° he runs,

III.i.s.d. *still* continually 2 *minded . . . unquietly* disturbed in mind,
like the weather 6 *main* land 7 *change* (1) be destroyed (2) be exchanged (i.e., turned upside down) (3) change for the better 8 *eyeless* (1) blind (2) invisible 10 *little world of man* (the microcosm, as
opposed to the universe or macrocosm, which it copies in little)
12 *cub-drawn* sucked dry by her cubs, and so ravenously hungry
12 *couch* take shelter in its lair 13 *belly-pinchèd* starved 14 *unbonneted*
hatless

And bids what will take all.°

15 Kent.   But who is with him?
    Gentleman. None but the Fool, who labors to outjest
        His heart-struck injuries.

    Kent.   Sir, I do know you,
        And dare upon the warrant of my note°
        Commend a dear thing° to you. There is division,
20   Although as yet the face of it is covered
        With mutual cunning, 'twixt Albany and Cornwall;
        Who have—as who have not, that° their great
            stars
        Throned° and set high?—servants, who seem no
            less,°
        Which are to France the spies and speculations
25   Intelligent° of our state. What hath been seen,
        Either in snuffs and packings° of the Dukes,
        Or the hard rein which both of them hath borne°
        Against the old kind King, or something deeper,
        Whereof, perchance, these are but furnishings°—
30   But, true it is, from France there comes a power°
        Into this scattered° kingdom, who already,
        Wise in our negligence, have secret feet
        In some of our best ports, and are at point°
        To show their open banner. Now to you:
35   If on my credit you dare build° so far
        To make your speed to Dover, you shall find
        Some that will thank you, making° just° report
        Of how unnatural and bemadding° sorrow
        The King hath cause to plain.°
40   I am a gentleman of blood and breeding,°

---

¹⁵ *take all* (like the reckless gambler, staking all he has left)   ¹⁸ *warrant of my note* strength of what I have taken note (of you)   ¹⁹ *Commend . . . thing* entrust important business   ²² *that* whom   ²²⁻²³ *stars /Throned* destinies have throned   ²³ *seem no less* seem to be so   ²⁴⁻²⁵ *speculations/Intelligent* giving intelligence   ²⁶ *snuffs and packings* quarrels and plots   ²⁷ *hard . . . borne* close and cruel control they have exercised   ²⁹ *furnishings* excuses   ³⁰ *power* army   ³¹ *scattered* disunited   ³³ *at point* ready   ³⁵ *If . . . build* if you can trust me, proceed   ³⁶ *To* as to   ³⁷ *making* for making   ³⁷ *just* accurate   ³⁸ *bemadding* maddening   ³⁹ *plain* complain of   ⁴⁰ *blood and breeding* noble family

And from some knowledge and assurance° offer
This office° to you.

Gentleman. I will talk further with you.

Kent.   No, do not.
For confirmation that I am much more
Than my out-wall,° open this purse and take   45
What it contains. If you shall see Cordelia,
As fear not but you shall, show her this ring,
And she will tell you who that fellow° is
That yet you do not know. Fie on this storm!
I will go seek the King.   50

Gentleman. Give me your hand. Have you no more to
    say?

Kent. Few words, but, to effect,° more than all yet:
That when we have found the King—in which your
    pain°
That way, I'll this—he that first lights on him,
Holla the other.   *Exeunt [severally].* 55

Scene II.   [*Another part of the heath.*]
              Storm still.

              Enter Lear and Fool.

Lear. Blow, winds, and crack your cheeks. Rage, blow!
    You cataracts and hurricanoes,° spout
    Till you have drenched our steeples, drowned the
        cocks.°

---

41 *knowledge and assurance* sure and trustworthy information   42 *office*
service (i.e., the trip to Dover)   45 *out-wall* superficial appearance
48 *fellow* companion   52 *to effect* in their importance   53 *pain* labor
III.ii. 2 *hurricanoes* waterspouts   3 *cocks* weathercocks

You sulph'rous and thought-executing° fires,

5 Vaunt-couriers° of oak-cleaving thunderbolts,
Singe my white head. And thou, all-shaking thunder,
Strike flat the thick rotundity° o' th' world,
Crack Nature's molds,° all germains spill° at once,
That makes ingrateful° man.

10 *Fool.* O Nuncle, court holy-water° in a dry house is
better than this rain water out o' door. Good
Nuncle, in; ask thy daughters blessing. Here's a
night pities neither wise man nor fools.

Lear. Rumble thy bellyful. Spit, fire. Spout, rain!

15 Nor rain, wind, thunder, fire are my daughters.
I tax° not you, you elements, with unkindness.
I never gave you kingdom, called you children,
You owe me no subscription.° Then let fall
Your horrible pleasure.° Here I stand your slave,

20 A poor, infirm, weak, and despised old man.
But yet I call you servile ministers,°
That will with two pernicious daughters join
Your high-engendered battles° 'gainst a head
So old and white as this. O, ho! 'tis foul.

25 *Fool.* He that has a house to put 's head in has a good
headpiece.°
                 The codpiece° that will house
                 Before the head has any,
                 The head and he° shall louse:
30   So beggars marry many.°
                 The man that makes his toe

---

4 *thought-executing* (1) doing execution as quick as thought (2) exe-
cuting or carrying out the thought of him who hurls the lightning
5 *Vaunt-couriers* heralds, scouts who range before the main body of the
army 7 *rotundity* i.e., not only the sphere of the globe, but the round-
ness of gestation (Delius) 8 *Nature's molds* the molds or forms in
which men are made 8 *all germains spill* destroy the basic seeds of
life 9 *ingrateful* ungrateful 10 *court holy-water* flattery 16 *tax* accuse
18 *subscription* allegiance, submission 19 *pleasure* will 21 *ministers*
agents 23 *high-engendered battles* armies formed in the heavens
26 *headpiece* (1) helmet (2) brain 27 *codpiece* penis (lit., padding
worn at the crotch of a man's hose) 29 *he* it 30 *many* i.e., lice
27-30 *The . . . many* i.e., the man who gratifies his sexual appetites
before he has a roof over his head will end up a lousy beggar

       What he his heart should make
    Shall of a corn cry woe,
       And turn his sleep to wake.°
For there was never yet fair woman but she made   *35*
mouths in a glass.°

Enter Kent.

Lear. No, I will be the pattern of all patience,
  I will say nothing.

Kent. Who's there?

Fool. Marry,° here's grace and a codpiece; that's a   *40*
wise man and a fool.°

Kent. Alas, sir, are you here? Things that love night
  Love not such nights as these. The wrathful skies
  Gallow° the very wanderers of the dark
  And make them keep° their caves. Since I was man,   *45*
  Such sheets of fire, such bursts of horrid° thunder,
  Such groans of roaring wind and rain, I never
  Remember to have heard. Man's nature cannot
    carry°
  Th' affliction nor the fear.

Lear.   Let the great gods
  That keep this dreadful pudder° o'er our heads   *50*
  Find out their enemies now.° Tremble, thou wretch,
  That hast within thee undivulgèd crimes
  Unwhipped of justice. Hide thee, thou bloody
    hand,
  Thou perjured,° and thou simular° of virtue

31-34 *The . . . wake* i.e., the man who, ignoring the fit order of things,
elevates what is base above what is noble, will suffer for it as Lear
has, in banishing Cordelia and enriching her sisters 35-36 *made mouths
in a glass* posed before a mirror (irrelevant nonsense, except that it
calls to mind the general theme of vanity and folly) 40 *Marry* by the
Virgin Mary 40-41 *here's . . . fool* (Kent's question is answered: The
King ("grace") is here, and the Fool—who customarily wears an ex-
aggerated codpiece. But which is which is left ambiguous, since Lear
has previously been called a codpiece) 44 *Gallow* frighten 45 *keep*
remain inside 46 *horrid* horrible 48 *carry* endure 50 *pudder* turmoil
51 *Find . . . now* i.e., discover sinners by the terror they reveal
54 *perjured* perjurer 54 *simular* counterfeiter

55   That art incestuous. Caitiff,° to pieces shake,
        That under covert and convenient seeming°
        Has practiced on° man's life. Close° pent-up guilts,
        Rive° your concealing continents° and cry
        These dreadful summoners grace.° I am a man
        More sinned against than sinning.

60 *Kent.*   Alack, bareheaded?
        Gracious my lord,° hard by here is a hovel;
        Some friendship will it lend you 'gainst the
            tempest.
        Repose you there, while I to this hard house
        (More harder than the stones whereof 'tis raised,
65   Which even but now, demanding after° you,
        Denied me to come in) return, and force
        Their scanted° courtesy.

    Lear.   My wits begin to turn.
        Come on, my boy. How dost, my boy? Art cold?
        I am cold myself. Where is this straw, my fellow?
70   The art° of our necessities is strange,
        That can make vile things precious. Come, your
            hovel.
        Poor Fool and knave, I have one part in my heart
        That's sorry yet for thee.

    Fool. [*Singing*]
            He that has and a little tiny wit,
75   With heigh-ho, the wind and the rain,
            Must make content with his fortunes fit,°
            Though the rain it raineth every day.

    Lear. True, my good boy. Come, bring us to this hovel.
                                            Exit [*with Kent*].

---

55 *Caitiff* wretch   56 *seeming* hypocrisy   57 *practiced on* plotted against
57 *Close* hidden   58 *Rive* split open   58 *continents* containers   58-59 *cry
. . . grace* beg mercy from the vengeful gods (here figured as officers
who summoned a man charged with immorality before the ecclesiastical
court)   61 *Gracious my lord* my gracious lord   65 *demanding after*
asking for   67 *scanted* stinted   70 *art* magic powers of the alchemists,
who sought to transmute base metals into precious   76 *Must . . . fit*
must be satisfied with a fortune as tiny as his wit

Fool. This is a brave° night to cool a courtesan. I'll   80
speak a prophecy ere I go:

When priests are more in word than matter;
When brewers mar their malt with water;
When nobles are their tailors' tutors,
No heretics burned, but wenches' suitors;°   85
When every case in law is right,
No squire in debt nor no poor knight;
When slanders do not live in tongues;
Nor cutpurses come not to throngs;
When usurers tell their gold i' th' field,°
And bawds and whores do churches build,°   90
Then shall the realm of Albion°
Come to great confusion.
Then comes the time, who lives to see't,
That going shall be used with feet.°

This prophecy Merlin° shall make, for I live before   95
his time.   *Exit.*

Scene III.   [*Gloucester's castle.*]

Enter Gloucester and Edmund.

Gloucester. Alack, alack, Edmund, I like not this unnatural dealing. When I desired their leave that I
might pity° him, they took from me the use of mine

---

79 *brave* fine   81-84 *When . . . suitors* (the first four prophecies are
fulfilled already, and hence "confusion" has come to England. The
priest does not suit his action to his words. The brewer adulterates
his beer. The nobleman is subservient to his tailor [i.e., cares only for
fashion]. Religious heretics escape, and only those burn [i.e., suffer]
who are afflicted with venereal disease)   89 *tell . . . field* count their
money in the open   85-90 *When . . . build* (the last six prophecies, as
they are Utopian, are meant ironically. They will never be fulfilled)
91 *Albion* England   94 *going . . . feet* people will walk on their feet
95 *Merlin* King Arthur's great magician who, according to Holinshed's
Chronicles, lived later than Lear III.iii.   3 *pity* show pity to

own house, charged me on pain of perpetual dis-
5　pleasure neither to speak of him, entreat for him,
or any way sustain° him.

Edmund. Most savage and unnatural.

Gloucester. Go to; say you nothing. There is division°
between the Dukes, and a worse° matter than that.
10　I have received a letter this night—'tis dangerous
to be spoken°—I have locked the letter in my
closet.° These injuries the King now bears will be
revenged home;° there is part of a power° already
footed;° we must incline to° the King. I will look°
15　him and privily° relieve him. Go you and maintain
talk with the Duke, that my charity be not of° him
perceived. If he ask for me, I am ill and gone to
bed. If I die for it, as no less is threatened me, the
King my old master must be relieved. There is
20　strange things toward,° Edmund; pray you be careful.　　　　　　　　　　　　　　　　　*Exit.*

Edmund. This courtesy forbid° thee shall the Duke
Instantly know, and of that letter too.
This seems a fair deserving,° and must draw me
25　That which my father loses—no less than all.
The younger rises when the old doth fall.

　　　　　　　　　　　　　　　　　　　Exit.

III.iii. 6 *sustain* care for　8 *division* falling out　9 *worse* more serious
(i.e., the French invasion)　11 *spoken* spoken of　12 *closet* room
13 *home* to the utmost　13 *power* army　14 *footed* landed　14 *incline to*
take the side of　14 *look* search for　15 *privily* secretly　16 *of* by
20 *toward* impending　22 *courtesy forbid* kindness forbidden (i.e., to
Lear)　24 *fair deserving* an action deserving reward

Scene IV.   [*The heath. Before a hovel.*]

Enter Lear, Kent, and Fool.

Kent. Here is the place, my lord. Good my lord,
    enter.
  The tyranny of the open night's too rough
  For nature to endure.

                              Storm still.

Lear.   Let me alone.

Kent. Good my lord, enter here.

Lear.   Wilt break my heart?°

Kent. I had rather break mine own. Good my lord,
    enter.   *5*

Lear. Thou think'st 'tis much that this contentious
    storm
  Invades us to the skin: so 'tis to thee;
  But where the greater malady is fixed,°
  The lesser is scarce felt. Thou'dst shun a bear;
  But if thy flight lay toward the roaring sea,   *10*
  Thou'dst meet the bear i' th' mouth.° When the
    mind's free,°
  The body's delicate. The tempest in my mind
  Doth from my senses take all feeling else,
  Save what beats there. Filial ingratitude,
  Is it not as° this mouth should tear this hand   *15*
  For lifting food to't? But I will punish home.°
  No, I will weep no more. In such a night
  To shut me out! Pour on, I will endure.

III.iv. 4 *break my heart* i.e., by shutting out the storm which distracts
me from thinking   8 *fixed* lodged (in the mind)   11 *i' th' mouth* in the
teeth   11 *free* i.e., from care   15 *as* as if   16 *home* to the utmost

In such a night as this! O Regan, Goneril,
Your old kind father, whose frank° heart gave
20   all—
O, that way madness lies; let me shun that.
No more of that.

Kent.   Good my lord, enter here.

Lear. Prithee go in thyself; seek thine own ease.
This tempest will not give me leave to ponder
25 On things would hurt me more, but I'll go in.
[*To the Fool*] In, boy; go first. You houseless
    poverty°—
Nay, get thee in. I'll pray, and then I'll sleep.

                        Exit [*Fool*].

Poor naked wretches, wheresoe'er you are,
That bide° the pelting of this pitiless storm,
30 How shall your houseless heads and unfed sides,
Your looped and windowed° raggedness, defend
    you
From seasons such as these? O, I have ta'en
Too little care of this! Take physic, pomp;°
Expose thyself to feel what wretches feel,
85 That thou mayst shake the superflux° to them,
And show the heavens more just.

Edgar. [*Within*] Fathom and half, fathom and half!°
Poor Tom!

                   Enter Fool.

Fool. Come not in here, Nuncle, here's a spirit. Help
40 me, help me!

Kent. Give me thy hand. Who's there?

Fool. A spirit, a spirit. He says his name's Poor Tom.

Kent. What art thou that dost grumble there i' th'
    straw?
Come forth.

---

20 *frank* liberal (magnanimous)   26 *houseless poverty* (the unsheltered
poor, abstracted)   29 *bide* endure   31 *looped and windowed* full of
holes   33 *Take physic, pomp* take medicine to cure yourselves, you
great men   35 *superflux* superfluity   37 *Fathom and half* (Edgar, because of the downpour, pretends to take soundings)

Enter Edgar [disguised as a madman].

Edgar. Away! the foul fiend follows me. Through the   *45*
    sharp hawthorn blows the cold wind.° Humh! Go
    to thy cold bed, and warm thee.°

Lear. Didst thou give all to thy daughters? And art
    thou come to this?

Edgar. Who gives anything to Poor Tom? Whom the   *50*
    foul fiend hath led through fire and through flame,
    through ford and whirlpool, o'er bog and quag-
    mire; that hath laid knives under his pillow and
    halters in his pew,° set ratsbane° by his porridge,°
    made him proud of heart, to ride on a bay trotting   *55*
    horse over four-inched bridges,° to course° his
    own shadow for° a traitor. Bless thy five wits,°
    Tom's a-cold. O, do, de, do, de, do, de. Bless thee
    from whirlwinds, star-blasting,° and taking.° Do
    Poor Tom some charity, whom the foul fiend vexes.   *60*
    There could I have him now—and there—and
    there again—and there.

                                            Storm still.

Lear. What, has his daughters brought him to this
    pass?°
    Couldst thou save nothing? Wouldst thou give 'em
    all?

Fool. Nay, he reserved a blanket,° else we had been   *65*
    all shamed.

Lear. Now all the plagues that in the pendulous° air
    Hang fated o'er° men's faults light on thy
    daughters!

45-46 *Through . . . wind* (a line from the ballad of "The Friar of
Orders Gray") 46-47 *go . . . thee* (a reminiscence of *The Taming of
the Shrew*, Induction, 1.10) 53-54 *knives . . . halters . . . ratsbane* (the
fiend tempts Poor Tom to suicide) 54 *pew* gallery or balcony outside
a window 54 *porridge* broth 55-56 *ride . . . bridges* i.e., risk his life
56 *course* chase 57 *for* as 57 *five wits* i.e., common wit, imagination,
fantasy, estimation, memory 59 *star-blasting* the evil caused by malignant stars 59 *taking* pernicious influences 63 *pass* wretched condition
65 *blanket* i.e., to cover his nakedness 67 *pendulous* overhanging
68 *fated o'er* destined to punish

Kent. He hath no daughters, sir.

70 *Lear.* Death, traitor; nothing could have subdued°
        nature
        To such a lowness but his unkind daughters.
        Is it the fashion that discarded fathers
        Should have thus little mercy on° their flesh?
        Judicious punishment—'twas this flesh begot
75   Those pelican° daughters.

Edgar. Pillicock sat on Pillicock Hill.° Alow, alow,
        loo, loo!°

Fool. This cold night will turn us all to fools and
        madmen.

80 *Edgar.* Take heed o' th' foul fiend; obey thy parents;
        keep thy word's justice;° swear not; commit not°
        with man's sworn spouse; set not thy sweet heart
        on proud array. Tom's a-cold.

Lear. What hast thou been?

85 *Edgar.* A servingman, proud in heart and mind; that
        curled my hair, wore gloves in my cap;° served the
        lust of my mistress' heart, and did the act of dark-
        ness with her; swore as many oaths as I spake
        words, and broke them in the sweet face of
90   heaven. One that slept in the contriving of lust,
        and waked to do it. Wine loved I deeply, dice
        dearly; and in woman out-paramoured the Turk.°
        False of heart, light of ear,° bloody of hand; hog
        in sloth, fox in stealth, wolf in greediness, dog in
95   madness, lion in prey.° Let not the creaking° of
        shoes nor the rustling of silks betray thy poor

---

70 *subdued* reduced   73 *on* i.e., shown to   75 *pelican* (supposed to feed
on its parent's blood)   76 *Pillicock . . . Hill* (probably quoted from a
nursery rhyme, and suggested by "pelican." *Pillicock* is a term of
endearment and the phallus)   76-77 *Alow . . . loo* (? a hunting call,
or the refrain of the song)   81 *keep . . . justice* i.e., do not break thy
word   81 *commit not* i.e., adultery   86 *gloves in my cap* i.e., as a pledge
from his mistress   92 *out-paramoured the Turk* had more concubines
than the Sultan   93 *light of ear* ready to hear flattery and slander
95 *prey* preying   95 *creaking* (deliberately cultivated, as fashionable)

heart to woman. Keep thy foot out of brothels,
thy hand out of plackets,° thy pen from lenders'
books,° and defy the foul fiend. Still through the
hawthorn blows the cold wind; says suum, mun, 100
nonny.° Dolphin° my boy, boy, sessa!° let him trot
by.

Storm still.

Lear. Thou wert better in a grave than to answer°
with thy uncovered body this extremity° of the
skies. Is man no more than this? Consider him 105
well. Thou ow'st° the worm no silk, the beast no
hide, the sheep no wool, the cat° no perfume. Ha!
here's three on's° are sophisticated.° Thou art the
thing itself; unaccommodated° man is no more
but such a poor, bare, forked° animal as thou art. 110
Off, off, you lendings!° Come, unbutton here.

[*Tearing off his clothes.*]

Fool. Prithee, Nuncle, be contented, 'tis a naughty°
night to swim in. Now a little fire in a wild° field
were like an old lecher's heart—a small spark, all
the rest on's body, cold. Look, here comes a walk- 115
ing fire.

Enter Gloucester, with a torch.

Edgar. This is the foul fiend Flibbertigibbet.° He begins at curfew,° and walks till the first cock.° He
gives the web and the pin,° squints° the eye, and
makes the harelip; mildews the white° wheat, and 120
hurts the poor creature of earth.

---

⁹⁸ *plackets* openings in skirts   ⁹⁸⁻⁹⁹ *pen . . . books* i.e., do not enter
your name in the moneylender's account book   ¹⁰⁰⁻⁰¹ *suum, mun, nonny*
the noise of the wind   ¹⁰¹ *Dolphin* the French Dauphin (identified by
the English with the devil. Poor Tom is presumably quoting from a
ballad)   ¹⁰¹ *sessa* an interjection: "Go on!"   ¹⁰³ *answer* confront, bear
the brunt of   ¹⁰⁴ *extremity* extreme severity   ¹⁰⁶ *ow'st* have taken from
¹⁰⁷ *cat* civet cat, whose glands yield perfume   ¹⁰⁸ *on's* of us   ¹⁰⁸ *sophisticated* adulterated, made artificial   ¹⁰⁹ *unaccommodated* uncivilized
¹¹⁰ *forked* i.e., two-legged   ¹¹¹ *lendings* borrowed garments   ¹¹² *naughty*
wicked   ¹¹³ *wild* barren   ¹¹⁷ *Flibbertigibbet* (a figure from Elizabethan
demonology)   ¹¹⁸ *curfew:* 9 P.M.   ¹¹⁸ *first cock* midnight   ¹¹⁹ *web and
the pin* cataract   ¹¹⁹ *squints* crosses   ¹²⁰ *white* ripening

Swithold footed thrice the old;°
He met the nightmare,° and her nine fold;°
    Bid her alight°
125   And her troth plight,°
And aroint° thee, witch, aroint thee!

Kent. How fares your Grace?

Lear. What's he?

Kent. Who's there? What is't you seek?

130 *Gloucester.* What are you there? Your names?

Edgar. Poor Tom, that eats the swimming frog, the
toad, the todpole, the wall-newt and the water;°
that in the fury of his heart, when the foul fiend
rages, eats cow-dung for sallets,° swallows the old
135 rat and the ditch-dog,° drinks the green mantle°
of the standing° pool; who is whipped from tithing°
to tithing, and stocked, punished, and imprisoned;
who hath had three suits to his back, six shirts to
his body,
140   Horse to ride, and weapon to wear,
      But mice and rats, and such small deer,°
      Have been Tom's food for seven long year.°
Beware my follower!° Peace, Smulkin,° peace,
thou fiend!

Gloucester. What, hath your Grace no better com-
145 pany?

Edgar. The Prince of Darkness is a gentleman.
Modo° he's called, and Mahu.°

---

122 *Swithold . . . old* Withold (an Anglo-Saxon saint who subdued
demons) walked three times across the open country   123 *nightmare*
demon   123 *fold* offspring   124 *alight* i.e., from the horse she had
possessed   125 *her troth plight* pledge her word   126 *aroint* be gone
132 *todpole . . . water* tadpole, wall lizard, water newt   134 *sallets*
salads   135 *ditch-dog* dead dog in a ditch   135 *mantle* scum   136 *stand-*
ing stagnant   136 *tithing* a district comprising ten families   141-42 *But*
. . . year (adapted from a popular romance, "Bevis of Hampton")
141 *deer* game   143 *follower* familiar   143, 147 *Smulkin, Modo, Mahu*
(Elizabethan devils, from Samuel Harsnett's *Declaration* of 1603)

Gloucester. Our flesh and blood, my Lord, is grown
    so vile
  That it doth hate what gets° it.

Edgar. Poor Tom's a-cold.   150

Gloucester. Go in with me. My duty cannot suffer°
  T' obey in all your daughters' hard commands.
  Though their injunction be to bar my doors
  And let this tyrannous night take hold upon you,
  Yet have I ventured to come seek you out   155
  And bring you where both fire and food is ready.

Lear. First let me talk with this philosopher.
  What is the cause of thunder?

Kent. Good my lord, take his offer; go into th' house.

Lear. I'll talk a word with this same learnèd Theban.°   160
  What is your study?°

Edgar. How to prevent° the fiend, and to kill vermin.

Lear. Let me ask you one word in private.

Kent. Importune him once more to go, my lord.
  His wits begin t' unsettle.

Gloucester.   Canst thou blame him?   165

                        Storm still.

  His daughters seek his death. Ah, that good Kent,
  He said it would be thus, poor banished man!
  Thou say'st the King grows mad—I'll tell thee,
    friend,
  I am almost mad myself. I had a son,
  Now outlawed from my blood;° he sought my life   170
  But lately, very late.° I loved him, friend,
  No father his son dearer. True to tell thee,
  The grief hath crazed my wits. What a night's this!

---

149 *gets* begets   151 *suffer* permit me   160 *Theban* i.e., Greek philosopher   161 *study* particular scientific study   162 *prevent* balk   170 *outlawed from my blood* disowned and tainted, like a carbuncle in the
corrupted blood   171 *late* recently

I do beseech your Grace——

Lear.   O, cry you mercy,° sir.
175   Noble philosopher, your company.

Edgar. Tom's a-cold.

Gloucester. In, fellow, there, into th' hovel; keep thee
    warm.

Lear. Come, let's in all.

Kent.   This way, my lord.

Lear.   With him!
    I will keep still with my philosopher.

Kent. Good my lord, soothe° him; let him take the
180   fellow.

Gloucester. Take him you on.°

Kent. Sirrah, come on; go along with us.

Lear. Come, good Athenian.°

Gloucester. No words, no words! Hush.

185 *Edgar*. Child Rowland to the dark tower came;°
    His word was still,° "Fie, foh, and fum,
    I smell the blood of a British man."°   *Exeunt.*

---

174 *cry you mercy* I beg your pardon   180 *soothe* humor   181 *you on*
with you   183 *Athenian* i.e., philosopher (like "Theban")   185 *Child
. . . came* (? from a lost ballad; "child"＝a candidate for knighthood;
Rowland was Charlemagne's nephew, the hero of *The Song of Roland*)
186 *His . . . still* his motto was always   186-87 *Fie . . . man* (a deliberately absurd linking of the chivalric hero with the nursery tale of
Jack the Giant-Killer)

Scene V.   [*Gloucester's castle.*]

Enter Cornwall and Edmund.

Cornwall. I will have my revenge ere I depart his house.

Edmund. How, my lord, I may be censured,° that nature thus gives way to loyalty, something fears° me to think of.   3

Cornwall. I now perceive it was not altogether your brother's evil disposition made him seek his death; but a provoking merit, set a-work by a reprovable badness in himself.°

Edmund. How malicious is my fortune that I must   10 repent to be just! This is the letter which he spoke of, which approves° him an intelligent party° to the advantages° of France. O heavens, that his treason were not! or not I the detector!

Cornwall. Go with me to the Duchess.   15

Edmund. If the matter of this paper be certain, you have mighty business in hand.

Cornwall. True or false, it hath made thee Earl of Gloucester. Seek out where thy father is, that he may be ready for our apprehension.°   20

Edmund. [*Aside*] If I find him comforting° the King, it will stuff his suspicion more fully.—I will persever° in my course of loyalty, though the conflict be sore between that and my blood.°

III.v.   3 *censured* judged   4 *something fears* somewhat frightens   8-9 *a provoking . . . himself* a stimulating goodness in Edgar, brought into play by a blamable badness in Gloucester   12 *approves* proves   12 *intelligent party* (1) spy (2) well-informed person   13 *to the advantages* on behalf of   20 *apprehension* arrest   21 *comforting* supporting (a legalism)   23 *persever* persevere   24 *blood* natural feelings

25   *Cornwall*. I will lay trust upon° thee, and thou
          shalt find a dearer father in my love.   *Exeunt*.

Scene VI.   [*A chamber in a farmhouse
adjoining the castle.*]

Enter Kent and Gloucester.

Gloucester. Here is better than the open air; take it
     thankfully. I will piece out the comfort with what
     addition I can. I will not be long from you.

Kent. All the power of his wits have given way to his
5   impatience.° The gods reward your kindness.
                              Exit [Gloucester].

Enter Lear, Edgar, and Fool.

Edgar. Frateretto° calls me, and tells me Nero° is
     an angler in the lake of darkness. Pray, innocent,°
     and beware the foul fiend.

Fool. Prithee, Nuncle, tell me whether a madman be a
10   gentleman or a yeoman.°

Lear. A king, a king.

Fool. No, he's a yeoman that has a gentleman to his
     son; for he's a mad yeoman that sees his son a gen-
     tleman before him.

15   *Lear*. To have a thousand with red burning spits
          Come hizzing° in upon 'em——

---

25 *lay trust upon* (1) trust (2) advance III.vi. 5 *impatience* raging
6 *Frateretto* Elizabethan devil, from Harsnett's *Declaration* 6 *Nero*
(who is mentioned by Harsnett, and whose angling is reported by
Chaucer in "The Monk's Tale") 7 *innocent* fool 10 *yeoman* farmer
(just below a gentleman in rank. The Fool asks what class of man has
most indulged his children, and thus been driven mad) 16 *hizzing*
hissing

Edgar. The foul fiend bites my back.

Fool. He's mad that trusts in the tameness of a wolf,
a horse's health, a boy's love, or a whore's oath.

Lear. It shall be done; I will arraign° them straight.°   20
  [*To Edgar*] Come, sit thou here, most learned
    justice.°
  [*To the Fool*] Thou, sapient° sir, sit here. Now,
    you she-foxes——

Edgar. Look, where he° stands and glares. Want'st
  thou eyes at trial, madam?°
  Come o'er the bourn,° Bessy, to me.   *25*

Fool. Her boat hath a leak,
        And she must not speak
        Why she dares not come over to thee.°

Edgar. The foul fiend haunts Poor Tom in the voice
  of a nightingale.° Hoppedance° cries in Tom's belly   30
  for two white herring.° Croak° not, black angel; I
  have no food for thee.

Kent. How do you, sir? Stand you not so amazed.°
  Will you lie down and rest upon the cushions?

Lear. I'll see their trial first. Bring in their evidence.   *35*
  [*To Edgar*] Thou, robèd man of justice, take
    thy place.
  [*To the Fool*] And thou, his yokefellow of equity,°
  Bench° by his side. [*To Kent*] You are o' th'
    commission;°
  Sit you too.

Edgar. Let us deal justly.   *40*

---

20 *arraign* bring to trial 20 *straight* straightaway 21 *justice* justicer,
judge 22 *sapient* wise 23 *he* i.e., a fiend 23-24 *Want'st . . . madam* (to
Goneril) i.e., do you want eyes to look at you during your trial?
The fiend serves that purpose 25 *bourn* brook (Edgar quotes from a
popular ballad) 26-28 *Her . . . thee* (the Fool parodies the ballad)
30 *nightingale* i.e., the Fool's singing 30 *Hoppedance* Hoberdidance
(another devil from Harsnett's *Declaration*) 31 *white herring* un-
smoked (? as against the black and sulfurous devil) 31 *Croak* rumble
(because his belly is empty) 33 *amazed* astonished 35 *evidence* the
evidence of witnesses against them 37 *yokefellow of equity* partner in
justice 38 *Bench* sit on the bench 38 *commission* those commissioned
as king's justices

Sleepest or wakest thou, jolly shepherd?
    Thy sheep be in the corn;°
And for one blast of thy minikin° mouth
    Thy sheep shall take no harm.°
45   Purr, the cat is gray.°

Lear. Arraign her first. 'Tis Goneril, I here take my
oath before this honorable assembly, she kicked
the poor King her father.

Fool. Come hither, mistress. Is your name Goneril?

50 *Lear.* She cannot deny it.

Fool. Cry you mercy, I took you for a joint stool.°

Lear. And here's another, whose warped looks
    proclaim
What store° her heart is made on. Stop her there!
Arms, arms, sword, fire! Corruption in the place!°
55 False justicer, why hast thou let her 'scape?

Edgar. Bless thy five wits!

Kent. O pity! Sir, where is the patience now
    That you so oft have boasted to retain?

Edgar. [*Aside*] My tears begin to take his part so
    much
60 They mar my counterfeiting.°

Lear. The little dogs and all,
    Tray, Blanch, and Sweetheart—see, they bark at
    me.

Edgar. Tom will throw his head at them. Avaunt, you
    curs.
    Be thy mouth or black or° white,

41-44 *Sleepest . . . harm* (probably quoted or adapted from an Elizabethan song) 42 *corn* wheat 43 *minikin* shrill 45 *gray* (devils were
thought to assume the shape of a gray cat) 51 *Cry . . . joint stool*
(proverbial and deliberately impudent apology for overlooking a person. A joint stool was a low stool made by a joiner, perhaps here a
stage property to represent Goneril and in line 52, Regan. "Joint stool"
can also suggest the judicial bench; hence Goneril may be identified
by the Fool, ironically, with those in power, who judge) 53 *store*
stuff 54 *Corruption . . . place* bribery in the court 60 *counterfeiting*
i.e., feigned madness 64 *or . . . or* either . . . or

Tooth that poisons if it bite;   65
Mastiff, greyhound, mongrel grim,
Hound or spaniel, brach° or lym,°
Or bobtail tike, or trundle-tail°—
Tom will make him weep and wail;
For, with throwing° thus my head,   70
Dogs leaped the hatch,° and all are fled.
Do, de, de, de. Sessa!° Come, march to wakes°
and fairs and market towns. Poor Tom, thy horn°
is dry.

Lear. Then let them anatomize Regan. See what breeds   75
about her heart.° Is there any cause in nature that
make° these hard hearts? [*To Edgar*] You, sir,
I entertain° for one of my hundred;° only I do not
like the fashion of your garments. You will say
they are Persian;° but let them be changed.   80

Kent. Now, good my lord, lie here and rest awhile.

Lear. Make no noise, make no noise; draw the
curtains.°
So, so. We'll go to supper i' th' morning.

Fool. And I'll go to bed at noon.°

Enter Gloucester.

Gloucester. Come hither, friend. Where is the King
my master?   85

Kent. Here, sir, but trouble him not; his wits are gone.

Gloucester. Good friend, I prithee take him in thy
arms.

---

67 *brach* bitch   67 *lym* bloodhound (from the liam or leash with
which he was led)   68 *bobtail . . . trundle-tail* short-tailed or long-
tailed cur   70 *throwing* jerking (as a hound lifts its head from the
ground, the scent having been lost)   71 *leaped the hatch* leaped over
the lower half of a divided door (i.e., left in a hurry)   72 *Sessa* be off
72 *wakes* feasts attending the dedication of a church   73 *horn* horn
bottle which the Bedlam used in begging a drink (Edgar is suggesting that he is unable to play his role any longer)   75-76 *Then . . .
heart* i.e., if the Bedlam's horn is dry, let Regan, whose heart has
become as hard as horn, be dissected   77 *make* (subjunctive)   78 *enter-
tain* engage   78 *hundred* i.e., Lear's hundred knights   80 *Persian*
gorgeous (ironically of Edgar's rags)   82 *curtains* (Lear imagines
himself in bed)   84 *And . . . noon* (the Fool's last words)

I have o'erheard a plot of death upon him.
There is a litter ready; lay him in't
And drive toward Dover, friend, where thou shalt
90   meet
Both welcome and protection. Take up thy master.
If thou shouldst dally half an hour, his life,
With thine and all that offer to defend him,
Stand in assurèd loss. Take up, take up,
95   And follow me, that will to some provision°
Give thee quick conduct.°

Kent.   Oppressèd nature sleeps.
This rest might yet have balmed thy broken
     sinews,°
Which, if convenience° will not allow,
Stand in hard cure.° [*To the Fool*] Come, help
     to bear thy master.
Thou must not stay behind.

100 *Gloucester.*   Come, come, away!
                              Exeunt [*all but Edgar*].

Edgar. When we our betters see bearing our woes,
We scarcely think our miseries our foes.°
Who alone suffers suffers most i' th' mind,
Leaving free° things and happy shows° behind;
105   But then the mind much sufferance° doth o'erskip
When grief hath mates, and bearing fellowship.°
How light and portable° my pain seems now,
When that which makes me bend makes the
     King bow.
He childed as I fathered. Tom, away.
110   Mark the high noises,° and thyself bewray°
When false opinion, whose wrong thoughts° defile
     thee,

---

95 *provision* maintenance   96 *conduct* direction   97 *balmed thy broken sinews* soothed thy racked nerves   98 *convenience* fortunate occasion   99 *Stand . . . cure* will be hard to cure   102 *our foes* enemies peculiar to ourselves   104 *free* carefree   104 *shows* scenes   105 *sufferance* suffering   106 *bearing fellowship* suffering has company   107 *portable* able to be supported or endured   110 *Mark the high noises* observe the rumors of strife among those in power   110 *bewray* reveal   111 *wrong thoughts* misconceptions

In thy just proof repeals and reconciles thee.°
What will hap more° tonight, safe 'scape the King!
Lurk,° lurk.   [*Exit.*]

Scene VII.   [*Gloucester's castle.*]

*Enter Cornwall, Regan, Goneril, Edmund, and
                    Servants.*

Cornwall. [*To Goneril*] Post speedily to my Lord
    your husband; show him this letter. The army of
    France is landed. [*To Servants*] Seek out the
    traitor Gloucester. [*Exeunt some of the Servants.*]

Regan. Hang him instantly.   5

Goneril. Pluck out his eyes.

Cornwall. Leave him to my displeasure. Edmund, keep
    you our sister company. The revenges we are
    bound° to take upon your traitorous father are not
    fit for your beholding. Advise the Duke where you   10
    are going, to a most festinate° preparation. We are
    bound to the like. Our posts° shall be swift and
    intelligent° betwixt us. Farewell, dear sister; fare-
    well, my Lord of Gloucester.°

                    Enter Oswald.

How now? Where's the King?   15

Oswald. My Lord of Gloucester hath conveyed him
    hence.

112 *In . . . thee* on the manifesting of your innocence recalls you
from outlawry and restores amity between you and your father
113 *What . . . more* whatever else happens 114 *Lurk* hide III.vii.
9 *bound* (1) forced (2) purposing to 11 *festinate* speedy 12 *posts*
messengers 13 *intelligent* full of information 14 *Lord of Gloucester*
i.e., Edmund, now elevated to the title

Some five or six and thirty of his knights,
Hot questrists° after him, met him at gate;
Who, with some other of the lords dependants,°
Are gone with him toward Dover, where they
20   boast
To have well-armèd friends.

Cornwall.   Get horses for your mistress.
                                        [*Exit Oswald.*]

Goneril. Farewell, sweet lord, and sister.

Cornwall. Edmund, farewell.
                            [*Exeunt Goneril and Edmund.*]

                    Go seek the traitor Gloucester,
Pinion him like a thief, bring him before us.
                            [*Exeunt other Servants.*]
25   Though well we may not pass upon° his life
Without the form of justice, yet our power
Shall do a court'sy to° our wrath, which men
May blame, but not control.

        Enter Gloucester, brought in by two or three.

                            Who's there, the traitor?

Regan. Ingrateful fox, 'tis he.

30 *Cornwall.* Bind fast his corky° arms.

Gloucester. What means your Graces? Good my
        friends, consider
You are my guests. Do me no foul play, friends.

Cornwall. Bind him, I say.

                                    [*Servants bind him.*]

Regan.   Hard, hard! O filthy traitor.

Gloucester. Unmerciful lady as you are, I'm none.

    Cornwall. To this chair bind him. Villain, thou shalt
85   find——

---

18 *questrists* searchers 19 *lords dependants* attendant lords (members of Lear's retinue) 25 *pass upon* pass judgment on 27 *do a
court'sy to* indulge 30 *corky* sapless (because old)

[*Regan plucks his beard.°*]

Gloucester. By the kind gods, 'tis mostly ignobly done
  To pluck me by the beard.

Regan. So white, and such a traitor?

Gloucester.   Naughty° lady,
  These hairs which thou dost ravish from my chin
  Will quicken° and accuse thee. I am your host.   *40*
  With robber's hands my hospitable favors°
  You should not ruffle° thus. What will you do?

Cornwall. Come, sir, what letters had you late° from
    France?

Regan. Be simple-answered,° for we know the truth.

Cornwall. And what confederacy have you with the
    traitors   *45*
  Late footed in the kingdom?

Regan. To whose hands you have sent the lunatic
    King:
  Speak.

Gloucester. I have a letter guessingly° set down,
  Which came from one that's of a neutral heart,
  And not from one opposed.

Cornwall.   Cunning.

Regan.   And false.   *50*

Cornwall. Where hast thou sent the King?

Gloucester. To Dover.

Regan. Wherefore to Dover? Wast thou not charged
    at peril°——

Cornwall. Wherefore to Dover? Let him answer that.

---

35 s.d. *plucks his beard* (a deadly insult)   38 *Naughty* wicked   40 *quicken* come to life   41 *hospitable favors* face of your host   42 *ruffle* tear at violently   43 *late* recently   44 *simple-answered* straightforward in answering   48 *guessingly* without certain knowledge   53 *charged at peril* ordered under penalty

Gloucester. I am tied to th' stake, and I must stand
55   the course.°

Regan. Wherefore to Dover?

Gloucester. Because I would not see thy cruel nails
         Pluck out his poor old eyes; nor thy fierce sister
60   In his anointed° flesh rash° boarish fangs.
         The sea, with such a storm as his bare head
         In hell-black night endured, would have buoyed° up
         And quenched the stellèd° fires.
         Yet, poor old heart, he holp° the heavens to rain.
         If wolves had at thy gate howled that dearn° time,
65   Thou shouldst have said, "Good porter, turn the
         key."°
         All cruels else subscribe.° But I shall see
         The wingèd° vengeance overtake such children.

Cornwall. See't shalt thou never. Fellows, hold the
         chair.
         Upon these eyes of thine I'll set my foot.

Gloucester. He that will think° to live till he be
70   old,
         Give me some help. —O cruel! O you gods!

Regan. One side will mock° another. Th' other too.

Cornwall. If you see vengeance——

First Servant.   Hold your hand, my lord!
         I have served you ever since I was a child;
75   But better service have I never done you
         Than now to bid you hold.

Regan.   How now, you dog?

First Servant. If you did wear a beard upon your chin,

---

⁵⁵ *course* coursing (in which a relay of dogs baits a bull or bear
tied in the pit)   ⁵⁹ *anointed* holy (because king)   ⁵⁹ *rash* strike with
the tusk, like a boar   ⁶¹ *buoyed* risen   ⁶² *stellèd* (1) fixed (as opposed to the planets or wandering stars)   (2) starry   ⁶³ *holp* helped
⁶⁴ *dearn* dread   ⁶⁵ *turn the key* i.e., unlock the gate   ⁶⁶ *All cruels else
subscribe* all cruel creatures but man are compassionate   ⁶⁷ *wingèd*
(1) heavenly   (2) swift   ⁷⁰ *will think* expects   ⁷² *mock* make ridiculous (because of the contrast)

I'd shake it° on this quarrel. What do you mean!°

Cornwall. My villain!°

                                         Draw and fight.

First Servant. Nay, then, come on, and take the
    chance of anger.   80

Regan. Give me thy sword. A peasant stand up thus?

    She takes a sword and runs at him behind,
            kills him.

First Servant. O, I am slain! my lord, you have one
    eye left
To see some mischief° on him. O!

Cornwall. Lest it see more, prevent it. Out, vile jelly.
    Where is thy luster now?   85

Gloucester. All dark and comfortless. Where's my son
    Edmund?
Edmund, enkindle all the sparks of nature°
To quit° this horrid act.

Regan.   Out, treacherous villain,
    Thou call'st on him that hates thee. It was he
That made the overture° of thy treasons to us;   90
Who is too good to pity thee.

Gloucester. O my follies! Then Edgar was abused.°
    Kind gods, forgive me that, and prosper him.

Regan. Go thrust him out at gates, and let him smell
    His way to Dover.   *Exit [one] with Gloucester.*
           How is't, my lord? How look you?°   95

Cornwall. I have received a hurt. Follow me, lady.
    Turn out that eyeless villain. Throw this slave
Upon the dunghill. Regan, I bleed apace.

---

78 *shake it* (an insult comparable to Regan's plucking of Gloucester's
beard) 78 *What . . . mean* i.e., what terrible thing are you doing
79 *villain* serf (with a suggestion of the modern meaning) 83 *mischief* injury 87 *enkindle . . . nature* fan your natural feeling into
flame 88 *quit* requite 90 *overture* disclosure 92 *abused* wronged
95 *How look you* how are you

Untimely comes this hurt. Give me your arm.

Exeunt.

100 *Second Servant.* I'll never care what wickedness I do,
    If this man come to good.

Third Servant.   If she live long,
    And in the end meet the old course of death,°
    Women will all turn monsters.

Second Servant. Let's follow the old Earl, and get the
    Bedlam
105 To lead him where he would. His roguish madness
    Allows itself to anything.°

Third Servant. Go thou. I'll fetch some flax and
    whites of eggs
    To apply to his bleeding face. Now heaven help
    him.   [*Exeunt severally.*]

---

102 *meet . . . death* die the customary death of old age   105-6 *His . . . anything* his lack of all self-control leaves him open to any suggestion

ACT IV

Scene I.   [*The heath.*]

Enter Edgar.

Edgar. Yet better thus, and known to be contemned,°
　　Than still contemned and flattered. To be worst,
　　The lowest and most dejected° thing of fortune,
　　Stands still in esperance,° lives not in fear:
　　The lamentable change is from the best,　　　　　5
　　The worst returns to laughter.° Welcome then,
　　Thou unsubstantial air that I embrace!
　　The wretch that thou hast blown unto the worst
　　Owes° nothing to thy blasts.

Enter Gloucester, led by an Old Man.

　　　　　　　　　　　But who comes here?
　　My father, poorly led?° World, world, O world!　　10
　　But that thy strange mutations make us hate thee,
　　Life would not yield to age.°

Old Man. O, my good lord, I have been your tenant,
　　and your father's tenant, these fourscore years.

Gloucester. Away, get thee away; good friend, be
　　gone:　　　　　　　　　　　　　　　　　　　15

IV.i. 1 *known to be contemned* conscious of being despised　3 *dejected*
abased　4 *esperance* hope　6 *returns to laughter* changes for the better
9 *Owes* is in debt for　10 *poorly led* (1) led like a poor man, with
only one attendant (2) led by a poor man　11-12 *But . . . age* we
should not agree to grow old and hence die, except for the hateful
mutability of life

Thy comforts° can do me no good at all;
Thee they may hurt.°

Old Man.   You cannot see your way.

Gloucester. I have no way and therefore want° no
          eyes;
    I stumbled when I saw. Full oft 'tis seen,
20 Our means secure us, and our mere defects
    Prove our commodities.° Oh, dear son Edgar,
    The food° of thy abusèd° father's wrath!
    Might I but live to see thee in° my touch,
    I'd say I had eyes again!

Old Man.   How now! Who's there?

Edgar. [*Aside*] O gods! Who is 't can say "I am at
25   the worst"?
    I am worse than e'er I was.

Old Man.   'Tis poor mad Tom.

Edgar. [*Aside*] And worse I may be yet: the worst
        is not
    So long as we can say "This is the worst."°

Old Man. Fellow, where goest?

Gloucester.   Is it a beggar-man?

30 *Old Man.* Madman and beggar too.

Gloucester. He has some reason,° else he could not
          beg.
    I' th' last night's storm I such a fellow saw,
    Which made me think a man a worm. My son
    Came then into my mind, and yet my mind
    Was then scarce friends with him. I have heard
35   more since.
    As flies to wanton° boys, are we to th' gods,

---

16 *comforts* ministrations **17** *hurt* injure **18** *want* require **20-21** *Our
. . . commodities* our resources make us overconfident, while our
afflictions make for our advantage **22** *food* i.e., the object on which
Gloucester's anger fed **22** *abusèd* deceived **23** *in* i.e., with, by means
of **27-28** *the . . . worst* so long as a man continues to suffer (i.e., is
still alive), even greater suffering may await him **31** *reason* faculty
of reasoning **36** *wanton* (1) playful (2) reckless

They kill us for their sport.

Edgar. [*Aside*]   How should this be?°
Bad is the trade that must play fool to sorrow,
Ang'ring° itself and others. Bless thee, master!

Gloucester. Is that the naked fellow?

Old Man.   Ay, my lord.   *40*

Gloucester. Then, prithee, get thee gone: if for my sake
Thou wilt o'ertake us hence a mile or twain
I' th' way toward Dover, do it for ancient° love,
And bring some covering for this naked soul,
Which I'll entreat to lead me.

Old Man.   Alack, sir, he is mad.   *45*

Gloucester. 'Tis the times' plague,° when madmen
lead the blind.
Do as I bid thee, or rather do thy pleasure;°
Above the rest,° be gone.

Old Man. I'll bring him the best 'parel° that I have,
Come on 't what will.   *Exit.*   *50*

Gloucester. Sirrah, naked fellow——

Edgar. Poor Tom's a-cold. [*Aside*] I cannot daub
it° further.

Gloucester. Come hither, fellow.

Edgar. [*Aside*] And yet I must. —Bless thy sweet
eyes, they bleed.   *55*

Gloucester. Know'st thou the way to Dover?

Edgar. Both stile and gate, horse-way and footpath.
Poor Tom hath been scared out of his good wits.
Bless thee, good man's son, from the foul fiend!
Five fiends have been in Poor Tom at once; of lust,   *60*

---

87 *How should this be* i.e., how can this horror be? 39 *Ang'ring*
offending 43 *ancient* (1) the love the Old Man feels, by virtue of
his long tenancy (2) the love that formerly obtained between master
and man 46 *times' plague* characteristic disorder of this time 47 *thy
pleasure* as you like 48 *the rest* all 49 *'parel* apparel 52-53 *daub it* lay
it on (figure from plastering mortar)

as Obidicut;° Hobbididence, prince of dumbness;° Mahu, of stealing; Modo, of murder; Flibbertigibbet, of mopping and mowing;° who since
possesses chambermaids and waiting-women. So,
65   bless thee, master!

Gloucester. Here, take this purse, thou whom the
      heavens' plagues
Have humbled to all strokes:° that I am wretched
Makes thee the happier. Heavens, deal so still!
Let the superfluous° and lust-dieted° man,
70   That slaves° your ordinance,° that will not see
Because he does not feel, feel your pow'r quickly;
So distribution should undo excess,°
And each man have enough. Dost thou know
      Dover?

Edgar. Ay, master.

Gloucester. There is a cliff whose high and bending°
75   head
Looks fearfully° in the confinèd deep:°
Bring me but to the very brim of it,
And I'll repair the misery thou dost bear
With something rich about me: from that place
I shall no leading need.

80 *Edgar.*   Give me thy arm:
      Poor Tom shall lead thee.   *Exeunt.*

---

61 *Obidicut* Hoberdicut, a devil (like the four that follow, from Harsnett's *Declaration*) 61-62 *dumbness* muteness (like the crimes and
afflictions in the next lines, the result of diabolic possession)
63 *mopping and mowing* grimacing and making faces 67 *humbled to
all strokes* brought so low as to bear anything humbly 69 *superfluous*
possessed of superfluities 69 *lust-dieted* whose lust is gratified (like
Gloucester's) 70 *slaves* (1) tramples, spurns like a slave (2) ?
tears, rends (Old English *slaefan*) 70 *ordinance* law 72 *So . . . excess*
then the man with too much wealth would distribute it among those
with too little 75 *bending* overhanging 76 *fearfully* occasioning fear
76 *confinèd deep* the sea, hemmed in below

Scene II.   [*Before the Duke of Albany's palace.*]

Enter Goneril and Edmund.

Goneril. Welcome, my lord: I marvel our mild husband
 Not met° us on the way.

     Enter Oswald.

       Now, where's your master?

Oswald. Madam, within; but never man so changed.
 I told him of the army that was landed:
 He smiled at it. I told him you were coming;   *5*
 His answer was, "The worse." Of Gloucester's treachery,
 And of the loyal service of his son
 When I informed him, then he called me sot,°
 And told me I had turned the wrong side out:
 What most he should dislike seems pleasant to him; *10*
 What like,° offensive.

Goneril. [*To Edmund*] Then shall you go no further.
 It is the cowish° terror of his spirit,
 That dares not undertake:° he'll not feel wrongs,
 Which tie him to an answer.° Our wishes on the way
 May prove effects.° Back, Edmund, to my brother; *15*
 Hasten his musters° and conduct his pow'rs.°

IV.ii. 2 *Not met* did not meet 8 *sot* fool 11 *What like* what he
should like 12 *cowish* cowardly 13 *undertake* venture 14 *tie him to
an answer* oblige him to retaliate 14-15 *Our . . . effects* our desires
(that you might be my husband), as we journeyed here, may be
fulfilled 16 *musters* collecting of troops 16 *conduct his pow'rs* lead
his army

I must change names° at home and give the
    distaff°
Into my husband's hands. This trusty servant
Shall pass between us: ere long you are like to hear,
20 If you dare venture in your own behalf,
A mistress's° command. Wear this; spare speech;

                    [*Giving a favor*]

Decline your head.° This kiss, if it durst speak,
Would stretch thy spirits up into the air:
Conceive,° and fare thee well.

Edmund. Yours in the ranks of death.

25 *Goneril.*   My most dear Gloucester!
                        Exit [Edmund].

O, the difference of man and man!
To thee a woman's services are due:
My fool usurps my body.°

Oswald.   Madam, here comes my lord.
                                Exit.

                Enter Albany.

Goneril. I have been worth the whistle.°

Albany.   O Goneril!
30 You are not worth the dust which the rude wind
Blows in your face. I fear your disposition:°
That nature which contemns° its origin
Cannot be bordered certain in itself;°
She that herself will sliver and disbranch°

---

17 *change names* i.e., exchange the name of "mistress" for that of
"master" 17 *distaff* spinning stick (wifely symbol) 21 *mistress's* lover's (and also, Albany having been disposed of, lady's or wife's)
22 *Decline your head* i.e., that Goneril may kiss him 24 *Conceive*
understand (with a sexual implication, that includes "stretch thy
spirits," 1. 23; and "death," 1. 25: "to die," meaning "to experience
sexual intercourse") 28 *My fool usurps body* my husband wrong-
fully enjoys me 29 *I . . . whistle* i.e., once you valued me (the
proverb is implied, "It is a poor dog that is not worth the whistling")
31 *disposition* nature 32 *contemns* despises 33 *bordered . . . itself*
kept within its normal bounds 34 *sliver and disbranch* cut off

From her material sap,° perforce must wither   35
And come to deadly use.°

Goneril. No more; the text° is foolish.

Albany. Wisdom and goodness to the vile seem vile:
  Filths savor but themselves.° What have you done?
  Tigers, not daughters, what have you performed?   40
  A father, and a gracious agèd man,
  Whose reverence even the head-lugged bear°
    would lick,
  Most barbarous, most degenerate, have you
    madded.°
  Could my good brother suffer you to do it?
  A man, a prince, by him so benefited!   45
  If that the heavens do not their visible spirits°
  Send quickly down to tame these vile offenses,
  It will come,
  Humanity must perforce prey on itself,
  Like monsters of the deep.

Goneril.   Milk-livered° man!   50
  That bear'st a cheek for blows, a head for wrongs;
  Who hast not in thy brows an eye discerning
  Thine honor from thy suffering;° that not know'st
  Fools do those villains pity who are punished
  Ere they have done their mischief.° Where's thy
    drum?   55
  France spreads his banners in our noiseless°
    land,
  With plumèd helm° thy state begins to threat,°

---

35 *material sap* essential and life-giving sustenance **36** *come to deadly use* i.e., be as a dead branch for the burning **37** *text* i.e., on which your sermon is based **39** *Filths savor but themselves* the filthy relish only the taste of filth **42** *head-lugged bear* bear-baited by the dogs, and hence enraged **43** *madded* made mad **46** *visible spirits* avenging spirits in material form **50** *Milk-livered* lily-livered (hence cowardly, the liver being regarded as the seat of courage) **52-53** *discerning . . . suffering* able to distinguish between insults that ought to be resented, and ordinary pain that is to be borne **54-55** *Fools . . . mischief* only fools are sorry for criminals whose intended criminality is prevented by punishment **56** *noiseless* i.e., the drum, signifying preparation for war, is silent **57** *helm* helmet **57** *thy . . . threat* France begins to threaten Albany's realm

Whilst thou, a moral° fool, sits still and cries
"Alack, why does he so?"

Albany.   See thyself, devil!
60   Proper° deformity seems not in the fiend
So horrid as in woman.

Goneril.   O vain fool!

Albany. Thou changèd and self-covered° thing,
for shame,
Be-monster not thy feature.° Were 't my fitness°
To let these hands obey my blood,°
65   They are apt enough to dislocate and tear
Thy flesh and bones: howe'er° thou art a fiend,
A woman's shape doth shield thee.

Goneril. Marry,° your manhood mew°——

Enter a Messenger.

Albany. What news?

Messenger. O, my good lord, the Duke of Cornwall's
70   dead,
Slain by his servant, going to° put out
The other eye of Gloucester.

Albany.   Gloucester's eyes!

Messenger. A servant that he bred,° thrilled with
remorse,°
Opposed against the act, bending his sword
75   To his great master, who thereat enraged
Flew on him, and amongst them felled° him dead,
But not without that harmful stroke which since

58 *moral* moralizing; but also with the implication that morality and
folly are one   60 *Proper* (1) natural (to a fiend) (2) fair-appearing
62 *changèd and self-covered* i.e., transformed, by the contorting of
her woman's face, on which appears the fiendish behavior she has
allowed herself. (Goneril has disguised nature by wickedness)   63 *Be-
monster not thy feature* do not change your appearance into a
fiend's   63 *my fitness* appropriate for me   64 *blood* passion   66 *howe'er*
but even if   68 *Marry* by the Virgin Mary   68 *your manhood mew*
(1) coop up or confine your (pretended) manhood (2) molt or shed
it, if that is what is supposed to "shield" me from you   71 *going to*
as he was about to   73 *bred* reared   73 *thrilled with remorse* pierced
by compassion   76 *amongst them felled* others assisting, they felled

Hath plucked him after.°

Albany.   This shows you are above,
You justicers,° that these our nether° crimes
So speedily can venge.° But, O poor Gloucester!   *80*
Lost he his other eye?

Messenger.   Both, both, my lord.
This letter, madam, craves° a speedy answer;
'Tis from your sister.

Goneril.   [*Aside*] One way I like this well;
But being widow, and my Gloucester with her,
May all the building in my fancy pluck   *85*
Upon my hateful life.° Another way,°
The news is not so tart.°—I'll read, and answer.
                                        Exit.

Albany. Where was his son when they did take his
    eyes?

Messenger. Come with my lady hither.

Albany.   He is not here.

Messenger. No, my good lord; I met him back° again. *90*

Albany. Knows he the wickedness?

Messenger. Ay, my good lord; 'twas he informed
    against him,
And quit the house on purpose, that their punish-
    ment
Might have the freer course.

Albany.   Gloucester, I live
To thank thee for the love thou showed'st the
    King,   *95*
And to revenge thine eyes. Come hither, friend:
Tell me what more thou know'st.   *Exeunt.*

---

78 *plucked him after* i.e., brought Cornwall to death with his servant   79 *justicers* judges   79 *nether* committed below (on earth)
80 *venge* avenge   82 *craves* demands   85-86 *May . . . life* these things
(1.84) may send my future hopes, my castles in air, crashing down
upon the hateful (married) life I lead now   86 *Another way* looked
at another way   87 *tart* sour   90 *back* going back

[Scene III.   *The French camp near Dover.*]

Enter Kent and a Gentleman.

Kent. Why the King of France is so suddenly gone
back, know you no reason?

Gentleman. Something he left imperfect in the
state,° which since his coming forth is thought of,
which imports° to the kingdom so much fear and
danger that his personal return was most required
and necessary.

Kent. Who hath he left behind him general?

Gentleman. The Marshal of France, Monsieur La Far.

Kent. Did your letters pierce° the queen to any dem-
onstration of grief?

Gentleman. Ay, sir; she took them, read them in my
presence,
And now and then an ample tear trilled° down
Her delicate cheek: it seemed she was a queen
Over her passion, who most rebel-like
Sought to be king o'er her.

Kent.   O, then it moved her.

Gentleman. Not to a rage: patience and sorrow
strove
Who should express her goodliest.° You have seen
Sunshine and rain at once: her smiles and tears
Were like a better way:° those happy smilets°
That played on her ripe lip seemed not to know
What guests were in her eyes, which parted thence

IV.iii. 3-4 *imperfect in the state* unsettled in his own kingdom 5 *im-
ports* portends 10 *pierce* impel 13 *trilled* trickled 18 *Who . . .
goodliest* which should give her the most becoming expression
20 *Were like a better way* i.e., improved on that spectacle 20 *smilets*
little smiles

As pearls from diamonds dropped. In brief,
Sorrow would be a rarity most belovèd,
If all could so become it.°

Kent.   Made she no verbal question?   25

Gentleman. Faith, once or twice she heaved° the name
    of "father"
Pantingly forth, as if it pressed her heart;
Cried "Sisters! Sisters! Shame of ladies! Sisters!
Kent! Father! Sisters! What, i' th' storm? i' th'
    night?
Let pity not be believed!"° There she shook   30
The holy water from her heavenly eyes,
And clamor moistened:° then away she started
To deal with grief alone.

Kent.   It is the stars,
The stars above us, govern our conditions;°
Else one self mate and make could not beget   35
Such different issues.° You spoke not with her
    since?

Gentleman. No.

Kent. Was this before the King returned?

Gentleman.   No, since.

Kent. Well, sir, the poor distressèd Lear's i' th'
    town;
Who sometime in his better tune° remembers   40
What we are come about, and by no means
Will yield to see his daughter.

Gentleman.   Why, good sir?

Kent. A sovereign° shame so elbows° him: his own
    unkindness

24-25 *Sorrow . . . it* sorrow would be a coveted jewel if it became
others as it does her   26 *heaved* expressed with difficulty   30 *Let pity
not be believed* let it not be believed for pity   32 *clamor moistened*
moistened clamor, i.e., mixed (and perhaps assuaged) her outcries
with tears   34 *govern our conditions* determine what we are
35-36 *Else . . . issues* otherwise the same husband and wife could
not produce such different children   40 *better tune* composed, less
jangled intervals   43 *sovereign* overpowering   43 *elbows* jogs his elbow
i.e., reminds him

That stripped her from his benediction, turned her
45 To foreign casualties,° gave her dear rights
To his dog-hearted daughters: these things sting
His mind so venomously that burning shame
Detains him from Cordelia.

Gentleman.   Alack, poor gentleman!

Kent. Of Albany's and Cornwall's powers you heard
not?

50 *Gentleman.* 'Tis so;° they are afoot.

Kent. Well, sir, I'll bring you to our master Lear,
And leave you to attend him: some dear cause°
Will in concealment wrap me up awhile;
When I am known aright, you shall not grieve
55 Lending me this acquaintance. I pray you, go
Along with me.   [*Exeunt.*]

[Scene IV.   *The same. A tent.*]

*Enter, with drum and colors, Cordelia, Doctor,
and Soldiers.*

Cordelia. Alack, 'tis he: why, he was met even now
As mad as the vexed sea; singing aloud;
Crowned with rank femiter and furrow-weeds,
With hardocks, hemlock, nettles, cuckoo-flow'rs,
5 Darnel,° and all the idle weeds that grow
In our sustaining corn.° A century° send forth;
Search every acre in the high-grown field,

---

45 *casualties* chances   50 *'Tis so* i.e., I have heard of them   52 *dear cause* important reason   IV.iv. 3-5 *femiter . . . Darnel: femiter* fumitory, whose leaves and juice are bitter; *furrow-weeds* weeds that grow in the furrow; or plowed land; *hardocks* ? hoar or white docks, burdocks, harlocks; *hemlock* a poison; *nettles* plants which sting and burn; *cuckoo-flow'rs* identified with a plant employed to remedy diseases of the brain; *Darnel* tares, noisome weeds   6 *sustaining corn* life-maintaining wheat   6 *century* ? sentry; troop of a hundred soldiers

And bring him to our eye [*Exit an Officer.*] What
   can man's wisdom°
In the restoring his bereavèd° sense?
He that helps him take all my outward° worth.   *10*

Doctor. There is means, madam:
   Our foster-nurse° of nature is repose,
The which he lacks: that to provoke° in him,
Are many simples operative,° whose power
Will close the eye of anguish.

Cordelia.   All blest secrets,   *15*
All you unpublished virtues° of the earth,
Spring with my tears! be aidant and remediate°
In the good man's distress! Seek, seek for him,
Lest his ungoverned rage dissolve the life
That wants the means to lead it.°

Enter Messenger.

Messenger.   News, madam;   *20*
The British pow'rs are marching hitherward.

Cordelia. 'Tis known before. Our preparation stands
In expectation of them. O dear father,
It is thy business that I go about;
Therefore° great France   *25*
My mourning and importuned° tears hath pitied.
No blown° ambition doth our arms incite,
But love, dear love, and our aged father's right:
Soon may I hear and see him!   *Exeunt.*

---

8 *What can man's wisdom* what can science accomplish   9 *bereavèd*
impaired   10 *outward* material   12 *foster-nurse* fostering nurse   13 *pro-*
voke induce   14 *simples operative* efficacious medicinal herbs   16 *un-*
published virtues i.e., secret remedial herbs   17 *remediate* remedial
20 *wants . . . it* i.e., lacks the reason to control the rage   25 *There-*
fore because of that   26 *importuned* importunate   27 *blown* puffed up

[Scene V.   *Gloucester's castle.*]

Enter Regan and Oswald.

Regan. But are my brother's pow'rs set forth?

Oswald.   Ay, madam.

Regan. Himself in person there?

Oswald.   Madam, with much ado:°
    Your sister is the better soldier.

Regan. Lord Edmund spake not with your lord at
        home?

5   *Oswald.* No, madam.

Regan. What might import° my sister's letter to him?

Oswald. I know not, lady.

Regan. Faith, he is posted° hence on serious matter.
    It was great ignorance,° Gloucester's eyes being
        out,
10   To let him live. Where he arrives he moves
    All hearts against us: Edmund, I think, is gone,
    In pity of his misery, to dispatch
    His nighted° life; moreover, to descry
    The strength o' th' enemy.

Oswald. I must needs after him, madam, with my
15   letter.

Regan. Our troops set forth tomorrow: stay with us;
    The ways are dangerous.

Oswald.   I may not, madam:
    My lady charged my duty° in this business.

IV.v. 2 *ado* bother and persuasion   6 *import* purport, carry as its
message   8 *is posted* has ridden speedily   9 *ignorance* folly   13 *nighted*
(1) darkened, because blinded (2) benighted   18 *charged my duty*
ordered me as a solemn duty

Regan. Why should she write to Edmund? Might not
   you
  Transport her purposes° by word? Belike,°   20
  Some things I know not what. I'll love thee much,
  Let me unseal the letter.

Oswald.   Madam, I had rather——

Regan. I know your lady does not love her husband;
  I am sure of that: and at her late° being here
  She gave strange eliads° and most speaking looks   25
  To noble Edmund. I know you are of her bosom.°

Oswald. I, madam?

Regan. I speak in understanding: y'are; I know 't:
  Therefore I do advise you, take this note:°
  My lord is dead; Edmund and I have talked;   30
  And more convenient° is he for my hand
  Than for your lady's: you may gather more.°
  If you do find him, pray you, give him this;°
  And when your mistress hears thus much from you,
  I pray, desire her call° her wisdom to her.   35
  So, fare you well.
  If you do chance to hear of that blind traitor,
  Preferment° falls on him that cuts him off.

Oswald. Would I could meet him, madam! I should
  show
  What party I do follow.

Regan.   Fare thee well.   40
                      Exeunt.

---

20 *Transport her purposes* convey her intentions 20 *Belike* probably
24 *late* recently 25 *eliads* amorous looks 26 *of her bosom* in her
confidence 29 *take this note* take note of this 31 *convenient* fitting
32 *gather more* surmise more yourself 33 *this* this advice 35 *call*
recall 38 *Preferment* promotion

[Scene VI. *Fields near Dover.*]

Enter Gloucester and Edgar.

Gloucester. When shall I come to th' top of that same
hill?
Edgar. You do climb up it now. Look, how we labor.
Gloucester. Methinks the ground is even.
Edgar. Horrible steep.
Hark, do you hear the sea?
Gloucester. No, truly.
5 *Edgar.* Why then your other senses grow imperfect
By your eyes' anguish.°
Gloucester. So may it be indeed.
Methinks thy voice is altered, and thou speak'st
In better phrase and matter than thou didst.
Edgar. Y'are much deceived: in nothing am I changed
But in my garments.
10 *Gloucester.* Methinks y'are better spoken.
Edgar. Come on, sir; here's the place: stand still. How
fearful
And dizzy 'tis to cast one's eyes so low!
The crows and choughs° that wing the midway air°
Show scarce so gross° as beetles. Half way down
15 Hangs one that gathers sampire,° dreadful trade!
Methinks he seems no bigger than his head.
The fishermen that walk upon the beach
Appear like mice; and yond tall anchoring° bark
Diminished to her cock;° her cock, a buoy

IV.vi. ⁶ *anguish* pain ¹³ *choughs* a kind of crow ¹³ *midway air* i.e.,
halfway down the cliff ¹⁴ *gross* large ¹⁵ *sampire* samphire, an aromatic
herb associated with Dover Cliffs ¹⁸ *anchoring* anchored ¹⁹ *cock* cock-
boat, a small boat usually towed behind the ship

    Almost too small for sight. The murmuring surge   *20*
That on th' unnumb'red idle pebble° chafes
Cannot be heard so high. I'll look no more,
Lest my brain turn and the deficient sight
Topple° down headlong.

Gloucester.   Set me where you stand.

Edgar. Give me your hand: you are now within a foot   *25*
Of th' extreme verge: for all beneath the moon
Would I not leap upright.°

Gloucester.   Let go my hand.
Here, friend, 's another purse; in it a jewel
Well worth a poor man's taking. Fairies° and gods
Prosper it with thee! Go thou further off;   *30*
Bid me farewell, and let me hear thee going.

Edgar. Now fare ye well, good sir.

Gloucester.   With all my heart.

Edgar. [*Aside*] Why I do trifle thus with his despair
Is done to cure it.°

Gloucester.   O you mighty gods!

                         He kneels.

This world I do renounce, and in your sights   *35*
Shake patiently my great affliction off:
If I could bear it longer and not fall
To quarrel° with your great opposeless° wills,
My snuff° and loathèd part of nature should
Burn itself out. If Edgar live, O bless him!   *40*
Now, fellow, fare thee well.

                         He falls.

Edgar.   Gone, sir, farewell.

---

21 *unnumb'red idle pebble* innumerable pebbles, moved to and fro
by the waves to no purpose 23-24 *the deficient sight/Topple* my failing
sight topple me 27 *upright* i.e., even up in the air, to say nothing
of forward, over the cliff 29 *Fairies* (who are supposed to guard
and multiply hidden treasure) 33-34 *Why . . . it* I play on his despair
in order to cure it 37-38 *fall/To quarrel with* rebel against 38 *oppose-
less* not to be, and not capable of being, opposed 39 *snuff* the gutter-
ing (and stinking) wick of a burnt-out candle

And yet I know not how° conceit° may rob
The treasury of life, when life itself
Yields to° the theft. Had he been where he thought,
By this had thought been past. Alive or dead?
Ho, you sir! friend! Hear you, sir! speak!
Thus might he pass° indeed: yet he revives.
What are you, sir?

Gloucester.   Away, and let me die.

Edgar. Hadst thou been aught but gossamer, feathers,
      air,
So many fathom down precipitating,°
Thou'dst shivered like an egg: but thou dost
      breathe;
Hast heavy substance; bleed'st not; speak'st; art
      sound.
Ten masts at each° make not the altitude
Which thou hast perpendicularly fell:
Thy life's° a miracle. Speak yet again.

Gloucester. But have I fall'n, or no?

Edgar. From the dread summit of this chalky bourn.°
Look up a-height;° the shrill-gorged° lark so far
Cannot be seen or heard: do but look up.

Gloucester. Alack, I have no eyes.
Is wretchedness deprived that benefit,
To end itself by death? 'Twas yet some comfort,
When misery could beguile° the tyrant's rage
And frustrate his proud will.

Edgar.   Give me your arm.
Up, so. How is 't? Feel you° your legs? You stand.

Gloucester. Too well, too well.

Edgar.   This is above all strangeness.
Upon the crown o' th' cliff, what thing was that

---

⁴²*how* but what   ⁴²*conceit* imagination   ⁴⁴*Yields .to* allows   ⁴⁷*pass*
die   ⁵⁰*precipitating* falling   ⁵³*at each* one on top of the other
⁵⁵*life's* survival   ⁵⁷*bourn* boundary   ⁵⁸*a-height* on high   ⁵⁸*gorged*
throated, voiced   ⁶³*beguile* cheat (i.e., by suicide)   ⁶⁵*Feel you* have
you any feeling in

Which parted from you?

Gloucester.   A poor unfortunate beggar.

Edgar. As I stood here below, methought his eyes
     Were two full moons; he had a thousand noses,   *70*
     Horns whelked° and waved like the enridgèd° sea:
     It was some fiend; therefore, thou happy father,°
     Think that the clearest° gods, who make them
          honors
     Of men's impossibilities,° have preserved thee.

Gloucester. I do remember now: henceforth I'll bear   *75*
     Affliction till it do cry out itself
     "Enough, enough," and die. That thing you speak
          of,
     I took it for a man; often 'twould say
     "The fiend, the fiend"——he led me to that place.

Edgar. Bear free° and patient thoughts.
          *Enter Lear [fantastically dressed with wild
                    flowers].*
                              But who comes here?   *80*
     The safer° sense will ne'er accommodate°
     His master thus.

Lear. No, they cannot touch me for coining;° I am
     the King himself.

Edgar. O thou side-piercing sight!   *85*

Lear. Nature's above art in that respect.° There's
     your press-money.° That fellow handles his bow

---

⁷¹ *whelked* twisted ⁷¹ *enridgèd* i.e., furrowed into waves ⁷² *happy
father* fortunate old man ⁷³ *clearest* purest ⁷³⁻⁷⁴ *who . . . impossi-
bilities* who cause themselves to be honored and revered by performing miracles of which men are incapable ⁸⁰ *free* i.e., emanci-
pated from grief and despair, which fetter the soul ⁸¹ *safer* sounder,
saner ⁸¹ *accommodate* dress, adorn ⁸³ *touch me for coining* arrest me
for minting coins (the king's prerogative) ⁸⁶ *Nature's . . . respect*
i.e., a born king is superior to legal (and hence artificial) inhibition.
There is also a glance here at the popular Renaissance debate, concerning the relative importance of nature (inspiration) and art (training) ⁸⁷ *press-money* (paid to conscripted soldiers)

like a crow-keeper;° draw me a clothier's yard.°
Look, look, a mouse! Peace, peace; this piece of
90 toasted cheese will do 't. There's my gauntlet;° I'll
prove it on° a giant. Bring up the brown bills.° O,
well flown,° bird! i' th' clout, i' th' clout:° hewgh!°
Give the word.°

Edgar. Sweet marjoram.°

95 *Lear.* Pass.

Gloucester. I know that voice.

Lear. Ha! Goneril, with a white beard! They flattered
me like a dog,° and told me I had white hairs
in my beard ere the black ones were there.° To
100 say "ay" and "no" to everything that I said! "Ay"
and "no" too was no good divinity.° When the
rain came to wet me once and the wind to make
me chatter; when the thunder would not peace at
my bidding; there I found 'em, there I smelt 'em
105 out. Go to, they are not men o' their words: they
told me I was everything; 'tis a lie, I am not ague-
proof.°

Gloucester. The trick° of that voice I do well remember: Is't not the king?

Lear.   Ay, every inch a king.
110 When I do stare, see how the subject quakes.
I pardon that man's life. What was thy cause?°

---

⁸⁸ *crow-keeper* a farmer scaring away crows ⁸⁸ *clothier's yard* (the
standard English arrow was a cloth-yard long. Here the injunction is
to draw the arrow back, like a powerful archer, a full yard to the ear)
⁹⁰ *gauntlet* armored glove, thrown down as a challenge ⁹¹ *prove it on*
maintain my challenge even against ⁹¹ *brown bills* halberds varnished
to prevent rust (here the reference is to the soldiers who carry them)
⁹⁶ *well flown* (falconer's cry; and perhaps a reference to the flight of
the arrow) ⁹² *clout* the target shot at ⁹² *hewgh* ? imitating the whizzing
of the arrow ⁹³ *word* password ⁹⁴ *Sweet marjoram* herb, used as a
remedy for brain disease ⁹⁸⁻⁹⁹ *I . . .
there* I was wise before I had even grown a beard ¹⁰¹ *no good divinity*
(bad theology, because contrary to the Biblical saying [II Corinthians
1:18], "Our word toward you was not yea and nay." See also James
5:12 "But let your yea be yea, and your nay, nay; lest ye fall into condemnation"; and Matthew 5:36-37) ¹⁰⁶⁻⁰⁷ *ague-proof* secure against
fever ¹⁰⁸ *trick* intonation ¹¹¹ *cause* offense

Adultery?
Thou shalt not die: die for adultery! No:
The wren goes to 't, and the small gilded fly
Does lecher° in my sight.   *115*
Let copulation thrive; for Gloucester's bastard son
Was kinder to his father than my daughters
Got° 'tween the lawful sheets.
To 't, luxury,° pell-mell! for I lack soldiers.°
Behold yond simp'ring dame,   *120*
Whose face between her forks presages snow,°
That minces° virtue and does shake the head
To hear of pleasure's name.°
The fitchew,° nor the soilèd° horse, goes to 't
With a more riotous appetite.   *125*
Down from the waist they are Centaurs,°
Though women all above:
But to the girdle° do the gods inherit,°
Beneath is all the fiend's.
There's hell, there's darkness, there is the
    sulphurous pit,   *130*
Burning, scalding, stench, consumption; fie, fie, fie!
pah, pah! Give me an ounce of civet;° good apothe-
cary, sweeten my imagination: there's money for thee.

Gloucester. O, let me kiss that hand!

Lear. Let me wipe it first; it smells of mortality.°   *135*

Gloucester. O ruined piece of nature! This great world
    Shall so wear out to nought.° Dost thou know me?

---

115 *lecher* copulate   118 *Got* begot   119 *luxury* lechery   119 *for . . .
soldiers* i.e., ? (1) whom copulation will supply (2) and am therefore powerless   121 *Whose . . . snow* whose cold demeanor seems to
promise chaste behavior ("forks": legs)   122 *minces* squeamishly pretends to   123 *pleasure's name* the very name of sexual pleasure
124 *fitchew* polecat (and slang for "prostitute")   124 *soilèd* put to
pasture, and hence wanton with feeding   126 *Centaurs* lustful creatures,
half man and half horse   128 *girdle* waist   128 *inherit* possess   132 *civet*
perfume   135 *mortality* (1) death (2) existence   136-37 *This . . . nought*
i.e., the universe (macrocosm) will decay to nothing in the same way
as the little world of man (microcosm)

Lear. I remember thine eyes well enough. Dost thou
squiny° at me? No, do thy worst, blind Cupid;° I'll
140 not love. Read thou this challenge;° mark but the
penning of it.

Gloucester. Were all thy letters suns, I could not see.

Edgar. I would not take° this from report: it is,
And my heart breaks at it.

145 *Lear.* Read.

Gloucester. What, with the case° of eyes?

Lear. O, ho, are you there with me?° No eyes in your
head, nor no money in your purse? Your eyes are
in a heavy case,° your purse in a light,° yet you
150 see how this world goes.

Gloucester. I see it feelingly.°

Lear. What, art mad? A man may see how this world
goes with no eyes. Look with thine ears: see how
yond justice rails upon yond simple° thief. Hark,
155 in thine ear: change places, and, handy-dandy,°
which is the justice, which is the thief? Thou hast
seen a farmer's dog bark at a beggar?

Gloucester. Ay, sir.

Lear. And the creature run from the cur? There thou
160 mightst behold the great image of authority:° a
dog's obeyed in office.°
Thou rascal beadle,° hold thy bloody hand!
Why dost thou lash that whore? Strip thy own
back;
Thou hotly lusts to use her in that kind°

---

139 *squiny* squint, look sideways, like a prostitute 139 *blind Cupid*
the sign hung before a brothel 140 *challenge* a reminiscence of
ll. 89-90 143 *take* believe 146 *case* empty sockets 147 *are . . . me* is
that what you tell me 149 *heavy case* sad plight (pun on l. 146)
149 *light* i.e., empty 151 *feelingly* (1) by touch (2) by feeling pain
(3) with emotion 154 *simple* common, of low estate 155 *handy-dandy*
i.e., choose, guess (after the children's game—"Handy-dandy, prickly
prandy"—of choosing the right hand) 160 *image of authority* symbol revealing the true meaning of authority 160-61 *a . . . office* i.e.,
whoever has power is obeyed 162 *beadle* parish constable 164 *kind*
i.e., sexual act

For which thou whip'st her. The usurer hangs the
   cozener.°   *165*
Through tattered clothes small vices do appear;
Robes and furred gowns° hide all. Plate sin with
   gold,
And the strong lance of justice hurtless° breaks;
Arm it in rags, a pygmy's straw does pierce it.
None does offend, none, I say, none; I'll able°
   'em: *170*
Take that° of me, my friend, who have the power
To seal th' accuser's lips. Get thee glass eyes,°
And, like a scurvy politician,° seem
To see the things thou dost not. Now, now, now,
   now.
Pull off my boots: harder, harder: so.   *175*

Edgar. O, matter and impertinency° mixed!
   Reason in madness!

Lear. If thou wilt weep my fortunes, take my eyes.
   I know thee well enough; thy name is Gloucester:
   Thou must be patient; we came crying hither: *180*
   Thou know'st, the first time that we smell the air
   We wawl and cry. I will preach to thee: mark.

Gloucester. Alack, alack the day!

Lear. When we are born, we cry that we are come
   To this great stage of fools. This'° a good block.° *185*

164-65 *The usurer . . . cozener* i.e., the powerful moneylender, in his
role as judge, puts to death the petty cheat 167 *Robes and furred
gowns* (worn by a judge) 168 *hurtless* i.e., without hurting the sinner
170 *able* vouch for 171 *that* (the immunity just conferred) (l. 170)
172 *glass eyes* spectacles 173 *scurvy politician* vile politic man
176 *matter and impertinency* sense and nonsense 185 *This'* this is
185 *block* (various meanings have been suggested, for example, the
stump of a tree, on which Lear is supposed to climb; a mounting-
block, which suggests "horse" l. 187; a hat [which Lear or another
must be made to wear], from the block on which a felt hat is mold-
ed, and which would suggest a "felt" l. 187. The proposal here is
that "block" be taken to denote the quintain, whose function is to bear
blows, "a mere lifeless block" [*As You Like It*, I.i.263], an object
shaped like a man and used for tilting practice. See also *Much Ado*,
II.i.246-7, "she misused me past the endurance of a block!" and, in
the same passage, the associated reference, "I stood like a man at
a mark [target]" [l. 253])

It were a delicate° stratagem, to shoe
A troop of horse with felt: I'll put 't in proof;°
And when I have stol'n upon these son-in-laws,
Then, kill, kill, kill, kill, kill, kill!

Enter a Gentleman [with Attendants].

190 *Gentleman.* O, here he is: lay hand upon him. Sir,
Your most dear daughter——

Lear. No rescue? What, a prisoner? I am even
The natural fool° of fortune. Use me well;
You shall have ransom. Let me have surgeons;
I am cut° to th' brains.

195 *Gentleman.*   You shall have anything.

Lear. No seconds?° all myself?
Why, this would make a man a man of salt,°
To use his eyes for garden water-pots,
Ay, and laying autumn's dust.

200 *Gentleman.* Good sir——

Lear. I will die bravely,° like a smug° bridegroom.°
What!
I will be jovial: come, come; I am a king;
Masters, know you that?

Gentleman. You are a royal one, and we obey you.

205 *Lear.* Then there's life in 't.° Come, and you get it,
you shall get it by running. Sa, sa, sa, sa.°

Exit [running; Attendants follow].

Gentleman. A sight most pitiful in the meanest wretch,
Past speaking of in a king! Thou hast one daughter
Who redeems nature from the general curse
210 Which twain have brought her to.°

---

186 *delicate* subtle   187 *put't in proof* test it   193 *natural fool* born
sport (with pun on "natural": "imbecile")   195 *cut* wounded   196 *seconds* supporters   197 *man of salt* i.e., all (salt) tears   201 *bravely* (1)
smartly attired (2) courageously   201 *smug* spick and span   201 *bridegroom* whose "brave" sexual feats are picked up in the pun on "die"
205 *there's life in't* there's still hope   206 *Sa . . . sa* hunting and
rallying cry; also an interjection of defiance   209-10 *general . . .
to* (1) universal condemnation which Goneril and Regan have made
for (2) damnation incurred by the original sin of Adam and Eve

Edgar. Hail, gentle° sir.

Gentleman.   Sir, speed° you: what's your will?

Edgar. Do you hear aught, sir, of a battle toward?°

Gentleman. Most sure and vulgar:° every one hears
    that,
  Which can distinguish sound.

Edgar.   But, by your favor,
  How near's the other army?   215

Gentleman. Near and on speedy foot; the main
    descry
  Stands on the hourly thought.°

Edgar.   I thank you, sir: that's all.

Gentleman. Though that the Queen on special cause
    is here,
  Her army is moved on.

Edgar.   I thank you, sir.

                     Exit [Gentleman].

Gloucester. You ever-gentle gods, take my breath
    from me;   220
  Let not my worser spirit° tempt me again
  To die before you please.

Edgar.   Well pray you, father.

Gloucester. Now, good sir, what are you?

Edgar. A most poor man, made tame° to fortune's
    blows;
  Who, by the art of known and feeling sorrows,°   225
  Am pregnant° to good pity. Give me your hand,
  I'll lead you to some biding.°

Gloucester.   Hearty thanks;

---

211 *gentle* noble   211 *speed* God speed   212 *toward* impending   213 *vulgar* common knowledge   216-17 *the . . . thought* we expect to see the
main body of the army any hour   221 *worser spirit* bad angel, evil
side of my nature   224 *tame* submissive   225 *art . . . sorrows* instruction of sorrows painfully experienced   226 *pregnant* disposed   227 *biding* place of refuge

The bounty and the benison° of heaven
To boot, and boot.°

Enter Oswald.

Oswald.   A proclaimed prize°! Most happy!°
That eyeless head of thine was first framed° flesh
To raise my fortunes. Thou old unhappy traitor,
Briefly thyself remember:° the sword is out
That must destroy thee.

Gloucester.   Now let thy friendly° hand
Put strength enough to 't.

[*Edgar interposes.*]

Oswald.   Wherefore, bold peasant,
Dar'st thou support a published° traitor? Hence!
Lest that th' infection of his fortune take
Like hold on thee. Let go his arm.

Edgar. Chill° not let go, zir, without vurther 'casion.°

Oswald. Let go, slave, or thou diest!

Edgar. Good gentleman, go your gait,° and let poor
volk° pass. And chud ha' bin zwaggered° out of my
life, 'twould not ha' bin zo long as 'tis by a vort-
night. Nay, come not near th' old man; keep out,
che vor' ye,° or I'se° try whether your costard°
or my ballow° be the harder: chill be plain with
you.

Oswald. Out, dunghill!

They fight.

---

²²⁸ *benison* blessing   ²²⁹ *To boot, and boot* also, and in the highest degree
²²⁹ *proclaimed prize* i.e., one with a price on his head   ²²⁹ *happy* fortunate (for Oswald)   ²³⁰ *framed* created   ²³² *thyself remember* i.e., pray,
think of your sins   ²³³ *friendly* i.e., because it offers the death Gloucester
covets   ²³⁵ *published* proclaimed   ²³⁸ *Chill . . .* (Edgar speaks in rustic
dialect)   ²³⁸ *Chill* I will   ²³⁸ *vurther 'casion* further occasion   ²⁴⁰ *gait*
way   ²⁴¹ *volk* folk   ²⁴¹ *And chud ha' bin zwaggered* if I could have been
swaggered   ²⁴⁴ *Che vor' ye* I warrant you   ²⁴⁴ *I'se* I shall   ²⁴⁴ *costard*
head (literally, "apple")   ²⁴⁵ *ballow* cudgel

Edgar. Chill pick your teeth,° zir: come; no matter
  vor your foins.°

  [*Oswald falls.*]

Oswald. Slave, thou hast slain me. Villain, take my   250
    purse:
  If ever thou wilt thrive, bury my body,
  And give the letters which thou find'st about° me
  To Edmund Earl of Gloucester; seek him out
  Upon the English party.° O, untimely death!
  Death!   255

  He dies.

Edgar. I know thee well. A serviceable° villain,
  As duteous° to the vices of thy mistress
  As badness would desire.

Gloucester.   What, is he dead?

Edgar. Sit you down, father; rest you.
  Let's see these pockets: the letters that he speaks
    of   260
  May be my friends. He's dead; I am only sorry
  He had no other deathsman.° Let us see:
  Leave,° gentle wax;° and, manners, blame us not:
  To know our enemies' minds, we rip their hearts;
  Their papers° is more lawful.   265

  Reads the letter.

  "Let our reciprocal vows be remembered. You
  have many opportunities to cut him off: if your
  will want not,° time and place will be fruitfully
  offered. There is nothing done, if he return the con-
  queror: then am I the prisoner, and his bed my   270
  jail; from the loathed warmth whereof deliver me,
  and supply the place for your labor.

  "Your—wife, so I would° say—affectionate

---

²⁴⁸ *Chill pick your teeth* I will knock your teeth out ²⁴⁹ *foins* thrusts
²⁵² *about* upon ²⁵⁴ *party* side ²⁵⁶ *serviceable* ready to be used ²⁵⁷ *du-
teous* obedient ²⁶² *deathsman* executioner ²⁶³ *Leave* by your leave
²⁶³ *wax* (with which the letter is sealed) ²⁶⁵ *Their papers* i.e., to rip
their papers ²⁶⁷⁻⁶⁸ *if . . . not* if your desire (and lust) be not lacking
²⁷³ *would* would like to

servant, and for you her own for venture,°
275   'Goneril.' "
O indistinguished space of woman's will!°
A plot upon her virtuous husband's life;
And the exchange° my brother! Here in the sands
Thee I'll rake up,° the post unsanctified°
280   Of murderous lechers; and in the mature° time,
With this ungracious paper° strike° the sight
Of the death-practiced° Duke: for him 'tis well
That of thy death and business I can tell.

Gloucester. The King is mad: how stiff° is my vile
      sense,°
285   That I stand up, and have ingenious° feeling
Of my huge sorrows! Better I were distract:°
So should my thoughts be severed from my griefs,
And woes by wrong imaginations° lose
The knowledge of themselves.
                              Drum afar off.

Edgar.   Give me your hand:
290   Far off, methinks, I hear the beaten drum.
Come, father, I'll bestow° you with a friend.
                              Exeunt.

Scene VII.   [*A tent in the French camp.*]

Enter Cordelia, Kent, Doctor, and Gentleman.

Cordelia. O thou good Kent, how shall I live and
      work,

---

²⁷⁴ *and . . . venture* i.e., and one who holds you her own for venturing (Edmund had earlier been promised union by Goneril, "If you dare venture in your own behalf," IV.ii.20).   ²⁷⁶ *indistinguished . . . will* unlimited range of woman's lust   ²⁷⁸ *exchange* substitute   ²⁷⁹ *rake up* cover up, bury   ²⁷⁹ *post unsanctified* unholy messenger   ²⁸⁰ *mature* ripe   ²⁸¹ *ungracious paper* wicked letter   ²⁸¹ *strike* blast   ²⁸² *death-practiced* whose death is plotted   ²⁸⁴ *stiff* unbending   ²⁸⁴ *vile sense* hateful capacity for feeling   ²⁸⁵ *ingenious* conscious   ²⁸⁶ *distract* distracted, mad   ²⁸⁸ *wrong imaginations* delusions   ²⁹¹ *bestow* lodge

To match thy goodness? My life will be too short,
And every measure fail me.

Kent. To be acknowledged, madam, is o'erpaid.
    All my reports go° with the modest truth,   *5*
    Nor more nor clipped,° but so.

Cordelia.   Be better suited:°
    These weeds° are memories° of those worser
      hours:
    I prithee, put them off.

Kent.   Pardon, dear madam;
    Yet to be known shortens my made intent:°
    My boon I make it,° that you know me not   *10*
    Till time and I think meet.°

Cordelia. Then be 't so, my good lord. [*To the Doctor.*] How does the King?

Doctor. Madam, sleeps still.

Cordelia. O you kind gods!
    Cure this great breach in his abusèd° nature.   *15*
    Th' untuned and jarring senses, O, wind up°
    Of this child-changèd° father.

Doctor.   So please your Majesty
    That we may wake the King: he hath slept long.

Cordelia. Be governed by your knowledge, and
      proceed
    I' th' sway of° your own will. Is he arrayed?   *20*

     Enter Lear in a chair carried by Servants.

IV.vii. 5 *go* conform 6 *clipped* curtailed 6 *suited* attired 7 *weeds*
clothes 7 *memories* reminders 9 *Yet . . . intent* to reveal myself just
yet interferes with the plan I have made 10 *My boon I make it* I ask
this reward 11 *meet* fitting 15 *abusèd* disturbed 16 *wind up* tune
17 *child-changèd* changed, deranged (and also, reduced to a child) by
the cruelty of his children 20 *I' th' sway of* according to

Gentleman. Ay, madam; in the heaviness of sleep
We put fresh garments on him.

Doctor. Be by, good madam, when we do awake him;
I doubt not of his temperance.°

Cordelia.   Very well.

Doctor. Please you, draw near. Louder the music
25   there!

Cordelia. O my dear father, restoration hang
Thy medicine on my lips, and let this kiss
Repair those violent harms that my two sisters
Have in thy reverence° made.

Kent.   Kind and dear Princess.

Cordelia. Had you not been their father, these white
30   flakes°
Did challenge° pity of them. Was this a face
To be opposed against the warring winds?
To stand against the deep dread-bolted° thunder?
In the most terrible and nimble stroke
Of quick, cross° lightning to watch—poor
35   perdu!°—
With this thin helm?° Mine enemy's dog,
Though he had bit me, should have stood that night
Against my fire; and wast thou fain,° poor father,
To hovel thee with swine and rogues° forlorn,
40 In short° and musty straw? Alack, alack!
'Tis wonder that thy life and wits at once
Had not concluded all.° He wakes; speak to him.

Doctor. Madam, do you; 'tis fittest.

---

24 *temperance* sanity **29** *reverence* revered person **30** *flakes* hairs (in long strands) **31** *challenge* claim **33** *deep dread-bolted* deep-voiced and furnished with the dreadful thunderbolt **35** *cross* zigzag **35** *perdu* (1) sentry in a forlorn position (2) lost one **36** *helm* helmet (his scanty hair) **38** *fain* pleased **39** *rogues* vagabonds **40** *short* (when straw is freshly cut, it is long, and suitable for bedding, given its flexibility and crispness. As it is used, it becomes musty, shreds into pieces, is "short." In contemporary Maine usage, "short manure" refers to dung mixed with straw that has been broken up; "long manure" to dung mixed with coarse new straw) **42** *concluded all* come to a complete end

Cordelia. How does my royal lord? How fares your
    Majesty?

Lear. You do me wrong to take me out o' th' grave: 45
    Thou art a soul in bliss; but I am bound
    Upon a wheel of fire,° that mine own tears
    Do scald like molten lead.

Cordelia.   Sir, do you know me?

Lear. You are a spirit, I know. Where did you die?

Cordelia. Still, still, far wide.°   50

Doctor. He's scarce awake: let him alone awhile.

Lear. Where have I been? Where am I? Fair daylight?
    I am mightily abused.° I should ev'n die with pity,
    To see another thus. I know not what to say.   55
    I will not swear these are my hands: let's see;
    I feel this pin prick. Would I were assured
    Of my condition.

Cordelia.   O, look upon me, sir,
    And hold your hand in benediction o'er me.
    You must not kneel.

Lear.   Pray, do not mock me:
    I am a very foolish fond° old man,   60
    Fourscore and upward, not an hour more nor less;
    And, to deal plainly,
    I fear I am not in my perfect mind.
    Methinks I should know you and know this man,
    Yet I am doubtful; for I am mainly° ignorant   65
    What place this is, and all the skill I have
    Remembers not these garments, nor I know not
    Where I did lodge last night. Do not laugh at me,
    For, as I am a man, I think this lady
    To be my child Cordelia.

Cordelia.   And so I am, I am.   70

Lear. Be your tears wet? Yes, faith. I pray, weep not.
    If you have poison for me, I will drink it.

---

⁴⁷ *wheel of fire* (torment associated by the Middle Ages with Hell,
where Lear thinks he is)   ⁵⁰ *wide* i.e., of the mark (of sanity)
⁵³ *abused* deluded   ⁶⁰ *fond* in dotage   ⁶⁵ *mainly* entirely

I know you do not love me; for your sisters
Have, as I do remember, done me wrong.
You have some cause, they have not.

75 *Cordelia.*   No cause, no cause.

Lear. Am I in France?

Kent.   In your own kingdom, sir.

Lear. Do not abuse° me.

Doctor. Be comforted, good madam: the great rage,°
    You see, is killed in him: and yet it is danger
80 To make him even o'er° the time he has lost.
    Desire him to go in; trouble him no more
    Till further settling.°

Cordelia. Will 't please your Highness walk?°

Lear. You must bear with me. Pray you now, forget
85 and forgive. I am old and foolish.

                    Exeunt. Mane[n]t° Kent and Gentleman.

Gentleman. Holds it true, sir, that the Duke of Corn-
    wall was so slain?

Kent. Most certain, sir.

Gentleman. Who is conductor of his people?

90 *Kent.* As 'tis said, the bastard son of Gloucester.

Gentleman. They say Edgar, his banished son, is with
    the Earl of Kent in Germany.

Kent. Report is changeable.° 'Tis time to look about;
    the powers° of the kingdom approach apace.

95 *Gentleman.* The arbitrement° is like to be bloody.
    Fare you well, sir.   [*Exit.*]

Kent. My point and period will be throughly
        wrought,°
    Or well or ill, as this day's battle's fought.

                                        Exit.

---

77 *abuse* deceive 78 *rage* frenzy 80 *even o'er* smooth over by filling
in; and hence, "recollect" 82 *settling* calming 83 *walk* (perhaps in
the sense of "withdraw") 85 s.d. *Mane[n]t* remain 93 *Report is
changeable* rumors are unreliable 94 *powers* armies 95 *arbitrement*
deciding encounter 97 *My . . . wrought* the aim and end, the close of
my life will be completely worked out

ACT V

Scene I.   [*The British camp near Dover.*]

Enter, with drum and colors, Edmund, Regan,
Gentlemen, and Soldiers.

Edmund. Know° of the Duke if his last purpose hold,°
   Or whether since he is advised° by aught
   To change the course: he's full of alteration
   And self-reproving: bring his constant pleasure.°

               [*To a Gentleman, who goes out.*]

Regan. Our sister's man is certainly miscarried.°   5

Edmund. 'Tis to be doubted,° madam.

Regan.   Now, sweet lord,
   You know the goodness I intend upon you:
   Tell me, but truly, but then speak the truth,
   Do you not love my sister?

Edmund.   In honored° love.

Regan. But have you never found my brother's way   *10*
   To the forfended° place?

Edmund.   That thought abuses° you.

V.i. 1 *Know* learn 1 *last purpose hold* most recent intention (to fight)
be maintained 2 *advised* induced 4 *constant pleasure* fixed (final)
decision 5 *miscarried* come to grief 6 *doubted* feared 9 *honored*
honorable 11 *forfended* forbidden 11 *abuses* (1) deceives (2) de-
means, is unworthy of

163

Regan. I am doubtful that you have been conjunct
   And bosomed with her, as far as we call hers.°

Edmund. No, by mine honor, madam.

15 *Regan.* I shall never endure her: dear my lord,
   Be not familiar with her.

Edmund.   Fear° me not.—
   She and the Duke her husband!

   *Enter, with drum and colors, Albany, Goneril
               [and] Soldiers.*

Goneril. [*Aside*] I had rather lose the battle than
   that sister
   Should loosen° him and me.

20 *Albany.* Our very loving sister, well be-met.°
   Sir, this I heard, the King is come to his daughter,
   With others whom the rigor of our state°
   Forced to cry out. Where I could not be honest,°
   I never yet was valiant: for this business,
25 It touches us, as° France invades our land,
   Not bolds the King, with others, whom, I fear,
   Most just and heavy causes make oppose.°

Edmund. Sir, you speak nobly.

Regan.   Why is this reasoned?°

Goneril. Combine together 'gainst the enemy;
30 For these domestic and particular broils°
   Are not the question° here.

Albany.   Let's then determine
   With th' ancient of war° on our proceeding.

Edmund. I shall attend you presently at your tent.

12-13 *I . . . hers* I fear that you have united with her intimately, in the
fullest possible way   16 *Fear* distrust   19 *loosen* separate   20 *be-met* met
22 *rigor . . . state* tyranny of our government   23 *honest* honorable
25 *touches us, as* concerns me, only in that   26-27 *Not . . . oppose* and
not in that France emboldens the King and others, who have been
led, by real and serious grievances, to take up arms against us
28 *reasoned* argued   30 *particular broils* private quarrels   31 *question*
issue   32 *th' ancient of war* experienced commanders

Regan. Sister, you'll go with us?°   35

Goneril. No.

Regan. 'Tis most convenient;° pray you, go with us.

Goneril. [*Aside*] O, ho, I know the riddle.°—I
     will go.

   Exeunt both the Armies. Enter Edgar [*disguised*].

Edgar. If e'er your Grace had speech with man so
     poor,
   Hear me one word.

Albany. [*To those going out*] I'll overtake you. [*To
     Edgar*] Speak.

         Exeunt [*all but Albany and Edgar*].

Edgar. Before you fight the battle, ope this letter.   40
   If you have victory, let the trumpet sound
   For° him that brought it: wretched though I seem,
   I can produce a champion that will prove°
   What is avouchèd° there. If you miscarry,   45
   Your business of° the world hath so an end,
   And machination° ceases. Fortune love you.

Albany. Stay till I have read the letter.

Edgar.   I was forbid it.
   When time shall serve, let but the herald cry,
   And I'll appear again.

Albany. Why, fare thee well: I will o'erlook° thy
     paper.   *Exit* [*Edgar*].   50

             Enter Edmund.

Edmund. The enemy's in view: draw up your powers.
   Here is the guess° of their true strength and
     forces
   By diligent discovery;° but your haste

---

84 *us* me (rather than Edmund)   36 *convenient* fitting, desirable   37 *riddle* real reason (for Regan's curious request)   41-42 *sound/For* summon   43 *prove* i.e., by trial of combat   44 *avouchèd* maintained   45 *of* in   46 *machination* plotting   50 *o'erlook* read over   52 *guess* estimate   53 *By diligent discovery* obtained by careful reconnoitering

  Is now urged on you.

Albany.   We will greet° the time. *Exit.*

55 *Edmund.* To both these sisters have I sworn my love;
  Each jealous° of the other, as the stung
  Are of the adder. Which of them shall I take?
  Both? One? Or neither? Neither can be enjoyed,
  If both remain alive: to take the widow
60 Exasperates, makes mad her sister Goneril;
  And hardly° shall I carry out my side,°
  Her husband being alive. Now then, we'll use
  His countenance° for the battle; which being done,
  Let her who would be rid of him devise
65 His speedy taking off. As for the mercy
  Which he intends to Lear and to Cordelia,
  The battle done, and they within our power,
  Shall never see his pardon; for my state
  Stands on me to defend, not to debate.° *Exit.*

Scene II. [*A field between the two camps.*]

Alarum° within. Enter, with drum and colors, Lear, Cordelia, and Soldiers, over the stage; and exeunt.

     Enter Edgar and Gloucester.

Edgar. Here, father,° take the shadow of this tree
  For your good host; pray that the right may thrive.
  If ever I return to you again,
  I'll bring you comfort.

Gloucester.   Grace go with you, sir.

            Exit [Edgar].

---

54 *greet* i.e., meet the demands of 56 *jealous* suspicious 61 *hardly* with difficulty 61 *carry . . . side* (1) satisfy my ambition (2) fulfill my bargain (with Goneril) 63 *countenance* authority 68-69 *for . . . debate* my position requires me to act, not to reason about right and wrong V.ii. s.d. *Alarum* a trumpet call to battle 1 *father* i.e., venerable old man (Edgar has not yet revealed his identity)

Alarum and retreat° within. [Re-]enter Edgar.

Edgar. Away, old man; give me thy hand; away!   *5*
     King Lear hath lost, he and his daughter ta'en:°
     Give me thy hand; come on.

Gloucester. No further, sir; a man may rot even here.

Edgar. What, in ill thoughts again? Men must endure
     Their going hence, even as their coming hither: *10*
     Ripeness° is all. Come on.

Gloucester.   And that's true too.
                               Exeunt.

Scene III.   [*The British camp near Dover.*]

*Enter, in conquest, with drum and colors, Ed-
mund; Lear and Cordelia, as prisoners; Soldiers,
Captain.*

Edmund. Some officers take them away: good guard,°
     Until their greater pleasures° first be known
     That are to censure° them.

Cordelia.   We are not the first
     Who with best meaning° have incurred the worst.
     For thee, oppressèd King, I am cast down;   *5*
     Myself could else out-frown false fortune's frown.
     Shall we not see these daughters and these sisters?

Lear. No, no, no, no! Come, let's away to prison:
     We two alone will sing like birds i' th' cage:
     When thou dost ask me blessing, I'll kneel down   *10*
     And ask of thee forgiveness: so we'll live,
     And pray, and sing, and tell old tales, and laugh

---

4 s.d. *retreat* (signaled by a trumpet)   6 *ta'en* captured   11 *Ripeness*
maturity, as of fruit that is ready to fall   V.iii.   1 *good guard* let there
be good guard   2 *their greater pleasures* the will of those in command,
the great ones   3 *censure* pass judgment on   4 *meaning* intentions

At gilded butterflies,° and hear poor rogues
Talk of court news; and we'll talk with them too,
15 Who loses and who wins, who's in, who's out;
And take upon's the mystery of things,
As if we were God's spies:° and we'll wear out,°
In a walled prison, packs and sects of great ones
That ebb and flow by th' moon.°

Edmund.   Take them away.

20 *Lear.* Upon such sacrifices, my Cordelia,
The gods themselves throw incense.° Have I caught
    thee?
He that parts us shall bring a brand from heaven,
And fire us hence like foxes.° Wipe thine eyes;
The good years° shall devour them,° flesh and fell,°
Ere they shall make us weep. We'll see 'em starved
25   first.
Come.   [*Exeunt Lear and Cordelia, guarded.*]

Edmund. Come hither, captain; hark.
Take thou this note: go follow them to prison:
One step I have advanced thee; if thou dost
30 As this instructs thee, thou dost make thy way
To noble fortunes: know thou this, that men
Are as the time is:° to be tender-minded
Does not become a sword:° thy great employment
Will not bear question;° either say thou'lt do 't,
Or thrive by other means.

35 *Captain.*   I'll do 't, my lord.

---

13 *gilded butterflies* i.e., gorgeously attired courtiers, fluttering after
nothing   16-17 *take . . . spies* profess to read the riddle of existence, as
if endowed with divine omniscience   17 *wear out* outlast   18-19 *packs
. . . moon* intriguing and partisan cliques of those in high station,
whose fortunes change every month   20-21 *Upon . . . incense* i.e., the
gods approve our renunciation of the world   22-23 *He . . . foxes* no human agency can separate us, but only divine interposition, as of a
heavenly torch parting us like foxes who are driven from their place of
refuge by fire and smoke   24 *good years* plague and pestilence ("unde-
fined malefic power or agency," *N.E.D.*)   24 *them* i.e., the enemies of
Lear and Cordelia   24 *fell* skin   32 *as the time is* i.e., absolutely determined by the exigencies of the moment   33 *become a sword* befit a soldier
34 *bear question* admit of discussion

Edmund. About it; and write happy° when th' hast
   done.
  Mark; I say, instantly, and carry it so°
  As I have set it down.

Captain. I cannot draw a cart, nor eat dried oats;
  If it be man's work, I'll do 't.   *Exit Captain.*   40

   *Flourish. Enter Albany, Goneril, Regan [another
           Captain, and] Soldiers.*

Albany. Sir, you have showed today your valiant
   strain,°
  And fortune led you well: you have the captives
  Who were the opposites of° this day's strife:
  I do require them of you, so to use them
  As we shall find their merits° and our safety   45
  May equally determine.

Edmund.   Sir, I thought it fit
  To send the old and miserable King
  To some retention and appointed guard;°
  Whose° age had charms in it, whose title more,
  To pluck the common bosom on his side,°   50
  And turn our impressed lances in our eyes°
  Which do command them. With him I sent the
   Queen:
  My reason all the same; and they are ready
  Tomorrow, or at further space,° t' appear
  Where you shall hold your session.° At this time   55
  We sweat and bleed: the friend hath lost his friend;
  And the best quarrels, in the heat, are cursed
  By those that feel their sharpness.°
  The question of Cordelia and her father

---

36 *write happy* style yourself fortunate   37 *carry it so* manage the affair
in exactly that manner (as if Cordelia had taken her own life)
41 *strain* (1) stock (2) character   43 *opposites of* opponents in   45 *merits*
deserts   48 *retention . . . guard* confinement under duly appointed
guard   49 *Whose* i.e., Lear's   50 *pluck . . . side* win the sympathy of
the people to himself   51 *turn . . . eyes* turn our conscripted lancers
against us   54 *further space* a later time   55 *session* trial   57-58 *the . . .
sharpness* the worthiest causes may be judged badly by those who have
been affected painfully by them, and whose passion has not yet cooled

Requires a fitter place.

60 *Albany.*   Sir, by your patience,
I hold you but a subject of° this war,
Not as a brother.

Regan.   That's as we list to grace° him.
Methinks our pleasure might have been demanded,
Ere you had spoke so far. He led our powers,
65 Bore the commission of my place and person;
The which immediacy may well stand up
And call itself your brother.°

Goneril.   Not so hot:
In his own grace he doth exalt himself
More than in your addition.°

Regan.   In my rights,
70 By me invested, he compeers° the best.

Goneril. That were the most,° if he should husband
    you.°

Regan. Jesters do oft prove prophets.

Goneril.   Holla, holla!
That eye that told you so looked but a-squint.°

Regan. Lady, I am not well; else I should answer
75 From a full-flowing stomach.° General,
Take thou my soldiers, prisoners, patrimony;°
Dispose of them, of me; the walls is thine:°
Witness the world, that I create thee here
My lord, and master.

Goneril.   Mean you to enjoy him?

80 *Albany.* The let-alone° lies not in your good will.

---

61 *subject of* subordinate in   62 *list to grace* wish to honor   65-67 *Bore
. . . brother* was authorized, as my deputy, to take command; his
present status, as my immediate representative, entitles him to be considered your equal   69 *your addition* honors you have bestowed on
him   70 *compeers* equals   71 *most* most complete investing in your
rights   71 *husband you* become your husband   73 *a-squint* cross-eyed
75 *From . . . stomach* angrily   76 *patrimony* inheritance   77 *walls is
thine* i.e., Regan's person, which Edmund has stormed and won
80 *let-alone* power to prevent

Edmund. Nor in thine, lord.

Albany.   Half-blooded° fellow, yes.

Regan. [*To Edmund*] Let the drum strike, and prove
    my title thine.°

Albany. Stay yet; hear reason. Edmund, I arrest thee
    On capital treason; and in thy attaint°
    This gilded serpent [*pointing to Goneril*]. For   85
      your claim, fair sister,
    I bar it in the interest of my wife.
    'Tis she is subcontracted° to this lord,
    And I, her husband, contradict your banes.°
    If you will marry, make your loves° to me;
    My Lady is bespoke.°   90

Goneril.   An interlude!°

Albany. Thou art armed, Gloucester: let the trumpet
    sound:
    If none appear to prove upon thy person
    Thy heinous, manifest, and many treasons,
    There is my pledge° [*throwing down a glove*]:
      I'll make° it on thy heart,
    Ere I taste bread, thou art in nothing less   95
    Than I have here proclaimed thee.

Regan.   Sick, O, sick!

Goneril. [*Aside*] If not, I'll ne'er trust medicine.°

Edmund. [*Throwing down a glove*] There's my
    exchange:° what in the world he is
    That names me traitor, villain-like he lies:°
    Call by the trumpet:° he that dares approach,   100

81 *Half-blooded* bastard, and so only half noble 82 *prove . . . thine*
prove by combat your entitlement to my rights 84 *in thy attaint* as a
sharer in the treason for which you are impeached 87 *subcontracted*
pledged by a contract which is called into question by the existence
of a previous contract (Goneril's marriage) 88 *contradict your banes*
forbid your announced intention to marry (by citing the precontract)
89 *loves* love-suits 90 *bespoke* already pledged 90 *interlude* play
94 *pledge* gage 94 *make* prove 97 *medicine* poison 98 *exchange* (technical term, denoting the glove Edmund throws down) 99 *villain-like he
lies* (the lie direct, a challenge to mortal combat) 100 *trumpet* trumpeter

On him, on you—who not?—I will maintain
My truth and honor firmly.

Albany. A herald, ho!

Edmund.   A herald, ho, a herald!

Albany. Trust to thy single virtue;° for thy soldiers,
105   All levied in my name, have in my name
Took their discharge.

Regan.   My sickness grows upon me.

Albany. She is not well; convey her to my tent.

                              [*Exit Regan, led.*]

                    Enter a Herald.

Come hither, herald. Let the trumpet sound—
And read out this.

110   *Captain.* Sound, trumpet!

                    A trumpet sounds.

Herald. (*Reads.*) "If any man of quality or degree°
within the lists° of the army will maintain upon Edmund, supposed Earl of Gloucester, that he is a
manifold traitor, let him appear by the third sound
115   of the trumpet: he is bold in his defense."

Edmund. Sound!

                    First trumpet.

Herald. Again!

                    Second trumpet.

Herald. Again!

                    Third trumpet.
          *Trumpet answers within. Enter Edgar, at the
          third sound, armed, a trumpet before him.°*

Albany. Ask him his purposes, why he appears
Upon this call o' th' trumpet.

120   *Herald.*   What are you?

---

104 *single virtue* unaided valor   111 *quality or degree* rank or position
112 *lists* rolls   118 s.d. *trumpet before him* trumpeter preceding him

Your name, your quality,° and why you answer
This present summons?

Edgar.   Know, my name is lost;
By treason's tooth bare-gnawn and canker-bit:°
Yet am I noble as the adversary
I come to cope.°

Albany.   Which is that adversary?   125

Edgar. What's he that speaks for Edmund, Earl of
     Gloucester?

Edmund. Himself: what say'st thou to him?

Edgar.   Draw thy sword,
That if my speech offend a noble heart,
Thy arm may do thee justice: here is mine.
Behold it is my privilege,   130
The privilege of mine honors,
My oath, and my profession.° I protest,
Maugre° thy strength, place, youth, and eminence,
Despite thy victor sword and fire-new° fortune,
Thy valor and thy heart,° thou art a traitor,   135
False to thy gods, thy brother, and thy father,
Conspirant° 'gainst this high illustrious prince,
And from th' extremest upward° of thy head
To the descent and dust below thy foot,°
A most toad-spotted traitor.° Say thou "No,"   140
This sword, this arm and my best spirits are bent°
To prove upon thy heart, whereto I speak,°
Thou liest.

Edmund.   In wisdom° I should ask thy name,
But since thy outside looks so fair and warlike,

---

121 *quality* rank   123 *canker-bit* eaten by the caterpillar   125 *cope* encounter   130-32 *it . . . profession* my knighthood entitles me to challenge you, and to have my challenge accepted   133 *Maugre* despite
134 *fire-new* fresh from the forge or mint   135 *heart* courage   137 *Con-
spirant* conspiring, a conspirator   138 *extremest upward* the very top
139 *the . . . foot* your lowest part (sole) and the dust beneath it
140 *toad-spotted traitor* spotted with treason (and hence venomous, as
the toad is allegedly marked with spots that exude venom)   141 *bent* directed   142 *whereto I speak* (Edgar speaks from the heart, and speaks
to the heart of Edmund)   143 *wisdom* prudence (since he is not obliged
to fight with one of lesser rank)

And that thy tongue some say° of breeding
145   breathes,
What safe and nicely° I might well delay°
By rule of knighthood, I disdain and spurn:
Back do I toss these treasons° to thy head;
With the hell-hated° lie o'erwhelm thy heart;
150   Which for they yet glance by and scarcely bruise,
This sword of mine shall give them instant way,
Where they shall rest for ever.° Trumpets, speak!

Alarums. [They] fight. [Edmund falls.]

Albany. Save° him, save him!

Goneril.   This is practice,° Gloucester:
By th' law of war thou wast not bound to answer
155   An unknown opposite;° thou art not vanquished,
But cozened and beguiled.

Albany.   Shut your mouth, dame,
Or with this paper shall I stop it. Hold, sir;°
Thou° worse than any name, read thine own evil.
No tearing, lady; I perceive you know it.

160 *Goneril.* Say, if I do, the laws are mine, not thine:
Who can arraign me for 't?

Albany.   Most monstrous! O!
Know'st thou this paper?

Goneril.   Ask me not what I know.

Exit.

Albany. Go after her; she's desperate; govern° her.

Edmund. What you have charged me with, that have
          I done;
165   And more, much more; the time will bring it out.
'Tis past, and so am I. But what art thou

---

145 *say* assay (i.e., touch, sign)   146 *safe and nicely* cautiously and
punctiliously   146 *delay* i.e., avoid   148 *treasons* accusations of treason
149 *hell-hated* hated like hell   150-52 *Which . . . ever* which accusations
of treason, since as yet they do no harm, even though I have hurled
them back, I now thrust upon you still more forcibly, with my sword,
so that they may remain with you permanently   153 *Save* spare
153 *practice* trickery   155 *opposite* opponent   157 *Hold, sir* (to Edmund:
"Just a moment!")   158 *Thou* (probably Goneril)   163 *govern* control

That hast this fortune on° me? If thou 'rt noble,
I do forgive thee.

Edgar.   Let's exchange charity.°
I am no less in blood° than thou art, Edmund;
If more,° the more th' hast wronged me.   **170**
My name is Edgar, and thy father's son.
The gods are just, and of our pleasant° vices
Make instruments to plague us:
The dark and vicious place° where thee he got°
Cost him his eyes.

Edmund.   Th' hast spoken right, 'tis true;   **175**
The wheel is come full circle; I am here.°

Albany. Methought thy very gait did prophesy°
A royal nobleness: I must embrace thee:
Let sorrow split my heart, if ever I
Did hate thee or thy father!

Edgar.   Worthy° Prince, I know 't.   **180**

Albany. Where have you hid yourself?
How have you known the miseries of your father?

Edgar. By nursing them, my lord. List a brief tale;
And when 'tis told, O, that my heart would burst!
The bloody proclamation to escape°   **185**
That followed me so near—O, our lives' sweetness,
That we the pain of death would hourly die
Rather than die at once!°—taught me to shift
Into a madman's rags, t' assume a semblance
That very dogs disdained: and in this habit°   **190**
Met I my father with his bleeding rings,°
Their precious stones new lost; became his guide,
Led him, begged for him, saved him from despair;

---

167 *fortune on* victory over   168 *charity* forgiveness and love   169 *blood*
lineage   170 *If more* if I am more noble (since legitimate)   172 *of our
pleasant* out of our pleasurable   174 *place* i.e., the adulterous bed
174 *got* begot   176 *Wheel . . . here* i.e., Fortune's wheel, on which
Edmund ascended, has now, in its downward turning, deposited him
at the bottom, whence he began   177 *gait did prophesy* carriage did
promise   180 *Worthy* honorable   185 *to escape* (my wish) to escape the
sentence of death   186-88 *O . . . once* how sweet is life, that we choose
to suffer death every hour rather than make an end at once   190 *habit*
attire   191 *rings* sockets

Never—O fault!—revealed myself unto him,
195 Until some half-hour past, when I was armed,
    Not sure, though hoping, of this good success,
    I asked his blessing, and from first to last
    Told him our pilgrimage.° But his flawed° heart—
    Alack, too weak the conflict to support—
200 'Twixt two extremes of passion, joy and grief,
    Burst smilingly.

Edmund.   This speech of yours hath moved me,
    And shall perchance do good: but speak you on;
    You look as you had something more to say.

Albany. If there be more, more woeful, hold it in;
205 For I am almost ready to dissolve,°
    Hearing of this.

Edgar.   This would have seemed a period°
    To such as love not sorrow; but another,
    To amplify too much, would make much more,
    And top extremity.°
210 Whilst I was big in clamor,° came there in a man,
    Who, having seen me in my worst estate,°
    Shunned my abhorred° society; but then, finding
    Who 'twas that so endured, with his strong arms
    He fastened on my neck, and bellowed out
215 As he'd burst heaven; threw him on my father;
    Told the most piteous tale of Lear and him
    That ever ear received: which in recounting
    His grief grew puissant,° and the strings of life
    Began to crack: twice then the trumpets sounded,
    And there I left him tranced.°

220 *Albany.*   But who was this?

Edgar. Kent, sir, the banished Kent; who in disguise
    Followed his enemy° king, and did him service
    Improper for a slave.

---

198 *our pilgrimage* of our (purgatorial) journey   198 *flawed* cracked
205 *dissolve* i.e., into tears   206 *period* limit   207-09 *but . . . extremity*
just one woe more, described too fully, would go beyond the extreme
limit   210 *big in clamor* loud in lamentation   211 *estate* condition
212 *abhorred* abhorrent   218 *puissant* overmastering   220 *tranced* insensi-
ble   222 *enemy* hostile

Enter a Gentleman, with a bloody knife.

Gentleman. Help, help, O, help!

Edgar.   What kind of help?

Albany.   Speak, man.

Edgar. What means this bloody knife?

Gentleman.   'Tis hot, it smokes;°   225
It came even from the heart of—O, she's dead!

Albany. Who dead? Speak, man.

Gentleman. Your lady, sir, your lady: and her sister
By her is poisoned; she confesses it.

Edmund. I was contracted° to them both: all three   230
Now marry° in an instant.

Edgar.   Here comes Kent.

Albany. Produce the bodies, be they alive or dead.

                          [Exit Gentleman.]

This judgment of the heavens, that makes us tremble,
Touches us not with pity.

                 Enter Kent.

               O, is this he?
The time will not allow the compliment°   235
Which very manners° urges.

Kent.   I am come
To bid my king and master aye° good night:
Is he not here?

Albany.   Great thing of° us forgot!
Speak, Edmund, where's the King? and where's Cordelia?
Seest thou this object,° Kent?   240

The bodies of Goneril and Regan are brought in.

Kent. Alack, why thus?

---

225 *smokes* steams   230 *contracted* betrothed   231 *marry* i.e., unite in death   235 *compliment* ceremony   236 *very manners* ordinary civility 237 *aye* forever   238 *thing of* matter by   240 *object* sight (the bodies of Goneril and Regan)

Edmund.   Yet° Edmund was beloved:
   The one the other poisoned for my sake,
   And after slew herself.

Albany. Even so. Cover their faces.

245 *Edmund.* I pant for life:° some good I mean to do,
   Despite of mine own nature. Quickly send,
   Be brief in it, to th' castle; for my writ°
   Is on the life of Lear and on Cordelia:
   Nay, send in time.

Albany.   Run, run, O, run!

250 *Edgar.* To who, my lord? Who has the office?° Send
   Thy token of reprieve.°

Edmund. Well thought on: take my sword,
   Give it the captain.

Edgar.   Haste thee, for thy life.

                                   [*Exit Messenger.*]

Edmund. He hath commission from thy wife and me
255   To hang Cordelia in the prison, and
   To lay the blame upon her own despair,
   That she fordid° herself.

Albany. The gods defend her! Bear him hence awhile.

                                   [*Edmund is borne off.*]

   *Enter Lear, with Cordelia in his arms [Gentle-
   man, and others following].*

Lear. Howl, howl, howl, howl! O, you are men of
   stones:
260   Had I your tongues and eyes, I'd use them so
   That heaven's vault should crack. She's gone for
   ever.
   I know when one is dead and when one lives;
   She's dead as earth. Lend me a looking-glass;
   If that her breath will mist or stain the stone,°
   Why, then she lives.

---

241 *Yet* in spite of all 245 *pant for life* gasp for breath 247 *writ* command (ordering the execution) 250 *office* commission 251 *token of reprieve* sign that they are reprieved 257 *fordid* destroyed 264 *stone* i.e., the surface of the crystal looking glass

Kent.   Is this the promised end?°

Edgar. Or image° of that horror?

Albany.   Fall and cease.°

Lear. This feather stirs; she lives. If it be so,
It is a chance which does redeem° all sorrows
That ever I have felt.

Kent.   O my good master.

Lear. Prithee, away.

Edgar.   'Tis noble Kent, your friend.   270

Lear. A plague upon you, murderers, traitors all!
I might have saved her; now she's gone for ever.
Cordelia, Cordelia, stay a little. Ha,
What is 't thou say'st? Her voice was ever soft,
Gentle and low, an excellent thing in woman.   275
I killed the slave that was a-hanging thee.

Gentleman. 'Tis true, my lords, he did.

Lear.   Did I not, fellow?
I have seen the day, with my good biting falchion°
I would have made them skip: I am old now,
And these same crosses° spoil me.° Who are you?   280
Mine eyes are not o' th' best: I'll tell you straight.°

Kent. If Fortune brag of two° she loved and hated,
One of them we behold.

Lear. This is a dull sight.° Are you not Kent?

Kent.   The same,
Your servant Kent. Where is your servant Caius?°   285

Lear. He's a good fellow, I can tell you that;
He'll strike, and quickly too: he's dead and rotten.

Kent. No, my good lord; I am the very man.

---

265 *promised end* Doomsday   266 *image* exact likeness   266 *Fall and cease* i.e., let the heavens fall, and all things finish   268 *redeem* make good   278 *falchion* small curved sword   280 *crosses* troubles   280 *spoil me* i.e., my prowess as a swordsman   281 *tell you straight* recognize you straightway   282 *two* i.e., Lear, and some hypothetical second, who is also a prime example of Fortune's inconstancy ("loved and hated")   284 *dull sight* (1) melancholy spectacle (2) faulty eyesight (Lear's own, clouded by weeping)   285 *Caius* (Kent's name, in disguise)

Lear. I'll see that straight.°

290 *Kent.* That from your first of difference and decay°
     Have followed your sad steps.

Lear.   You are welcome hither.

Kent. Nor no man else:° all's cheerless, dark and
     deadly.
     Your eldest daughters have fordone° themselves,
     And desperately° are dead.

Lear.   Ay, so I think.

295 *Albany.* He knows not what he says, and vain is it
     That we present us to him.

Edgar.   Very bootless.°

               Enter a Messenger.

Messenger. Edmund is dead, my lord.

Albany.   That's but a trifle here.
     You lords and noble friends, know our intent.
     What comfort to this great decay may come°
300 Shall be applied. For us, we° will resign,
     During the life of this old majesty,
     To him our absolute power: [*To Edgar and Kent*]
     you, to your rights;
     With boot,° and such addition° as your honors
     Have more than merited. All friends shall taste
305 The wages of their virtue, and all foes
     The cup of their deservings. O, see, see!

Lear. And my poor fool° is hanged: no, no, no
     life?
     Why should a dog, a horse, a rat, have life,

---

289 *see that straight* attend to that in a moment   290 *your . . . decay*
beginning of your decline in fortune   292 *Nor no man else* no, I am
not welcome, nor is anyone else   293 *fordone* destroyed   294 *desperately* in despair   296 *bootless* fruitless   299 *What . . . come* whatever
aid may present itself to this great ruined man   300 *us, we* (the royal
"we")   303 *boot* good measure   303 *addition* additional titles and rights
307 *fool* Cordelia ("fool" being a term of endearment. But it is perfectly possible to take the word as referring also to the Fool)

And thou no breath at all? Thou'lt come no more,
Never, never, never, never, never.   *310*
Pray you, undo this button.° Thank you, sir.
Do you see this? Look on her. Look, her lips,
Look there, look there.

He dies.

Edgar.   He faints. My lord, my lord!

Kent. Break, heart; I prithee, break.

Edgar.   Look up, my lord.

Kent. Vex not his ghost:° O, let him pass! He hates
    him   *315*
That would upon the rack° of this tough world
Stretch him out longer.°

Edgar.   He is gone indeed.

Kent. The wonder is he hath endured so long:
He but usurped° his life.

Albany. Bear them from hence. Our present business   *320*
Is general woe. [*To Kent and Edgar*] Friends of
    my soul, you twain,
Rule in this realm and the gored state sustain.

Kent. I have a journey, sir, shortly to go;
My master calls me, I must not say no.

Edgar. The weight of this sad time we must obey,°   *325*
Speak what we feel, not what we ought to say.
The oldest hath borne most: we that are young
Shall never see so much, nor live so long.

Exeunt, with a dead march.

FINIS

---

³¹¹ *undo this button* i.e., to ease the suffocation Lear feels   ³¹⁵ *Vex
. . . ghost* do not trouble his departing spirit   ³¹⁶ *rack* instrument of
torture, stretching the victim's joints to dislocation   ³¹⁷ *longer* (1) in
time (2) in bodily length   ³¹⁹ *usurped* possessed beyond the allotted
term   ³²⁵ *obey* submit to

Textual Note

The earliest extant version of Shakespeare's *King Lear* is the First Quarto of 1608. This premier edition is known as the Pied Bull Quarto, after the sign which hung before the establishment of the printer. The title page reads as follows: "M. William Shak-speare: / HIS / True Chronicle Historie of the life and / death of King Lear and his three / Daughters. / *With the vnfortunate life of* Edgar, *sonne* / and heire to the Earle of Gloster, and his / sullen and assumed humor of / Tom of Bedlam: / *As it was played before the Kings Maiestie at Whitehall vpon* / S. Stephans *night in Christmas Hollidayes.* / By his Maiesties seruants playing vsually at the Gloabe / on the Bancke-side. / LONDON, / Printed for *Nathaniel Butter,* and are to be sold at his shop in *Pauls* / Church-yard at the signe of the Pide Bull neere / S^t. *Austin's* Gate. 1608." Twelve copies of the First Quarto survive. They are, however, in ten different states, because proofreading, and hence correcting, took place as the play was being printed. The instances (167 in all) in which these copies of Q1 differ one from another have been enumerated by contemporary scholarship.[1]

In 1619 appeared the Second Quarto, known as the N. Butter Quarto, and falsely dated in the same year as the first (the title page reads: "Printed for Nathaniel Butter. 1608"). The source of Q2 was apparently a copy of Q1 in which a number of sheets had been corrected.

Four years later *King Lear* was reprinted once more, this time in the first collection of Shakespeare's works, the First Folio of 1623. The source of the Folio text seems to have been, again, a corrected copy of Q1. The corrections in this copy, however, do not duplicate those in

---

[1] W. W. Greg, *The Variants in the First Quarto of "King Lear,"* London, 1940 (for 1939).

the presumptive source of Q2, but are at once more and less extensive. In some cases the Quarto which lies behind the Folio offers corrections not found in the source of Q2. In other cases, corrections incorporated in the course of Q2 are not included in the source of F1. The Folio text, moreover, omits some 300 lines found in the Quarto, and thus leads to the supposition that the copy used in preparing the Folio had been collated with the prompt book—a shorter, acting version of the play—in the possession of Shakespeare's company. The Folio text would seem, then, to stand in close relation to Shakespeare's play as it was actually performed. On the other hand, the Folio does include some 100 lines not found in the Quarto.

Given the great discrepancies between Q and F, and given the greatness of *King Lear,* it is worth spending a bit more time in reviewing opinions concerning the relationship of the two versions. Until fairly recently, the orthodox view was that Q1 was based on a version put together by some actors who relied on their imperfect memories of a performance, which means that they often garbled lines. The orthodox view of the text in the Folio held that although it continued some of Q's errors, it corrected many errors and added important material. The printer used a copy of Q, but for some passages he also used the playhouse's promptbook, a manuscript that was based on Shakespeare's manuscript. The cuts in F were cuts made in production. But other views are possible: for instance, some additions in F can be seen not as the restoration of Shakespeare's material but as inauthentic material found in the playhouse manuscript. How did such material enter into the manuscript? When the Globe burned in 1613, presumably the promptbook was lost, and the company had to construct a new one, probably without Shakespeare's help, since Shakespeare had retired to Stratford around 1611. Perhaps the most forceful new view of the texts is presented in *The Division of the Kingdom: Shakespeare's Two Versions of "King Lear"* (1983), edited by Gary Taylor and Michael Warren. This collection of essays by eleven scholars argues that Q is more or less the play as Shakespeare wrote it in 1605–06, and that F—with its additions and reassignment of some speeches—is based on a promptbook which represents Shakespeare's own reshaping of the play, perhaps around 1610–11. There is, however, at least one great difficulty with this theory: Even if we grant that F represents a revision, how can we be certain that Shakespeare was the reviser? The authors of *The Division of the Kingdom* argue that the omissions in F improve the play, but it is hard, for instance, to see F's omission of the mock trial scene in III.vi. as an improvement, even though one writer in the book assures us that this omission "strengthens the dramatic structure."

The present text of *King Lear* relies chiefly on the Folio, but it turns to the Quarto when the Folio is guilty of an obvious misprinting, or when it omits pertinent material found in the Quarto, or when its version seems to the editor so inferior to the Quarto version as to demand precedence for the latter, or when an emendation, even though perhaps unnecessary (like Edwards' "top th' legitimate"), has been canonized by use and wont.

In the preparation of this text, the spelling of Folio and Quarto has been modernized; punctuation and capitalization have been altered, when alteration seemed suitable; character designations have been expanded or clarified (F "Cor." become "Cordelia," F "Bastard" and "Steward" become "Edmund" and "Oswald"); contractions not affecting pronunciation have been eliminated (F "banish'd" becomes "banished"); necessary quotation marks (as in the reading of a letter) have been supplied; as have diacritical marks whenever a syllable that is normally unemphasized must be stressed (as in "oppressèd"). These changes are not recorded.

All other departures from the Folio appearing in this text are recorded here in italic type. Unless specifically noted, these departures derive in every case from the First Quarto [Q]. If some other source is levied on, such as the Second Quarto [Q2] or Second Folio [F2] or the conjecture of an editor (for example, [Theobald]), that source is given, within brackets, immediately after the reading. There follows next, in roman type, the Folio reading which has been superseded. If an editor's emendation has been preferred to both Folio and Quarto readings, the emendation, with its provenance, is followed by the Folio and Quarto readings it replaces.

Stage directions are not given lineation. Reference to them in these notes is determined, therefore, by the line of text they follow. If a stage direction occurs at the beginning of a scene, reference is to the line of text it precedes. On occasion, the stage direction in the present text represents a conflation of Folio and Quarto. In that case, both Folio and Quarto readings are set down in the notes. Stage directions and notations of place, printed within brackets, are, unless otherwise noted, substantially from the Globe edition. The list of Dramatis Personae, first given by Rowe, is taken also from the Globe edition.

I.i. *Act I. Scene 1* Actus Primus. Scena Prima 5 *equalities* qualities 34 s.d. *Sound . . . Attendants* Sennet. Enter King Lear, Cornwall, Albany, Gonerill, Regan, Cordelia, and attendants [F] Sound a Sennet, Enter one bearing a Coronet, then Lear, then the Dukes of Albany, and Cornwall, next Gonerill, Regan, Cordelia, with followers [Q] 70 *speak* [F omits] 98 *loved me. I* loved me 99 *Return* I return 106 *To love my father all* [F omits] 112 *mysteries* [F2] miseries [F] mistress [Q] 157 *as a pawn* as pawn 158 *nor* nere [i.e., "ne'er"] 165 *the* thy 172 *sentence* sentences 176 *diseases* disasters 190 *Gloucester* Cor[delia] 208 *on* in 216 *best object* object 227 *well* will 235 *Better thou* Better thou hadst 250 *respects of fortune* respect and Fortunes 268 s.d. *Lear . . . Attendants* [Capell] Exit Lear and Burgundy [Q] 283 *shame them derides* with shame derides 291 *hath not been* hath been 299-300 *ingrafted* ingraffed 306 *let's hit* let us sit

I.ii. *Scene II* Scena Secunda 21 *top th'* [Edwards] to' th' [F] tooth' [Q] 103-05 *Edmund . . . earth* [F omits] 142 *Fut* [F omits] 144 *Edgar* [F omits] 145 *and pat* [Steevens] Pat [F] and out [Q] 156-64 *as . . . come* [F omits] 165 *Why, the* The 178 *brother* [F omits] 185 *Go armed* [F omits] 191 s.d. *Exit Edgar* Exit

I.iii. *Scene III* Scena Tertia 17-21 *Not . . . abused* [F omits] 25-26 *I would . . . speak* [F omits] 27 *Go, prepare* prepare

I.iv. *Scene IV* Scena Quarta 1 *well* will 51 *daughter* Daughters 100 *Fool* my Boy 115 *Lady the Brach* [Steevens] the

Lady Brach [F] Ladie oth'e brach [Q]   144-59 *That . . . snatching* [F omits]   158 *on't* [Q2] [F omits] an't [Q]   158 *ladies* [Q corrected] [F omits] lodes [Q uncorrected]   167 *crown* Crownes   182 *fools* Foole   195 *Methinks* [F omits]   222 *it had* it's had   225 *Come, Sir* [F omits]   234 *or his* his   237-41 *I . . . father* [F omits]   264 *O . . . come* [F omits]   298 *the cause* more of it   311 *Yea . . . this* [F omits]   350 *You are* [F2] Your are [F] Y'are [Q]   350 *attasked for* [Q corrected: "attaskt"] at task for [F] alapt [Q uncorrected]

I.v. *Scene V* Scena Quinta   1 s.d. *Enter . . . Fool* [Q2] Enter Lear, Kent, Gentleman, and Foole   17 *Why . . . boy* What can'st tell Boy

II.i. *Act II. Scene I* Actus Secundus. Scena Prima   21 s.d. *Enter Edgar* [placed by Theobald] [F prints after l. 20]   55 *But* And   72 *I should* should I   73 *ay* [F omits]   80 *I . . . him* [F omits]   80 s.d. *Tucket within* [placed by Malone] [F prints after l. 79]   81 *why* wher   89 *strange news* strangenesse

II.ii. *Scene II* Scena Secunda   23 *clamorous* [Q corrected] clamours [F] clamarous [Q uncorrected]   44 s.d. *Enter . . . drawn* Enter Bastard, Cornewall, Regan, Gloster, Servants [F] Enter Edmund with his rapier drawne, Gloster the Duke and Dutchesse [Q]   77 *too t'*   80 *Renege* Revenge   81 *gale* gall   110 *flick'ring* [Pope: "flickering"] flicking [F] flitkering [Q]   125 *dread* dead   132 *respect* respects   141 s.d. *Stocks brought out* [placed by Dyce] [F prints after l. 139] [Q omits]   143-47 *His . . . with* [F omits]   145 *contemnèd'st* [Capell] [F omits] contaned [Q uncorrected] temnest [Q corrected]   153 *For . . . legs* [F omits]   154 *Come . . . away* [F assigns to Cornwall]   154 *my good Lord* my Lord   154 s.d. *Exeunt . . . Kent* Exit [F] [Q omits]   155 *Duke's* Duke   176 s.d. *Sleeps* [F omits]

II.iii. *Scene III* [Steevens] [F, Q omit]   4 *unusual* unusall   15 *mortified bare arms* mortified Armes   18 *sheepcotes* Sheeps-Cotes

II.iv.1 s.d. *Scene IV* [Steevens] [F, Q omit]   2 *messenger* Messengers   6 *thy* ahy   9 *man's* man   18-19 *No . . . have* [F omits]   30 *panting* painting   33 *whose* those   61 *the* the the the   75 *have* hause   86 s.d. *Enter . . . Gloucester* [F prints after l. 84]   130 *mother's* Mother   167 *her pride* [F omits]   183 s.d. *Enter Oswald* [placed by Dyce] [F and Q print after l. 181]   185 *fickle* fickly   188 s.d. *Enter Goneril* [placed by Johnson] [F and Q print after l. 186]   282 s.d. *Storm and tempest* [F prints after l. 283] [Q omits]   285 s.d. *Exeunt . . . Fool* [Q2] Exeunt [F] Exeunt Lear, Leister, Kent, and Foole [Q]   294 s.d. *Enter Gloucester* [F and Q print after l. 293]

III.i. *Act III. Scene 1* Actus Tertius. Scena Prima 7-14 *tears
. . . all* [F omits] 30-42 *But . . . you* [F omits]

III.ii. *Scene II* Scena Secunda 3 *drowned* drown 71 *That* And
78 *True . . . boy* True boy

III.iii. *Scene III* Scaena Tertia

III.iv. *Scene IV* Scena Quarta 7 *skin: so* [Rowe] skinso [F] skin, so
[Q] 10 *thy* they 27 s.d. *Exit* [placed by Johnson] [F prints after
1. 26] [Q omits] 38 s.d. *Enter Fool* [Duthie] Enter Edgar, and
Foole [F, which prints after 1. 36] [Q omits] 44 s.d. *Enter Edgar*
Enter Edgar, and Foole [F, which prints after 1. 36] [Q omits] 46
blows . . . wind blow the windes 47 *thy cold bed* thy bed 52
ford Sword 57 *Bless* Blisse 58 *Bless* blisse 63 *What, has* Ha's
91 *deeply* deerely 101 *sessa* [Malone] Sesey [F] caese [Q] cease
[Q2] 116 s.d. *Enter . . . torch* [F prints after 1. 111] Enter
Gloster [Q, which prints after 1. 116] 117 *foul fiend Flibbertigibbet* foule Flibbertigibbet 118 *till . . . cock* at first Cocke 138
hath had hath

III.v. *Scene V* Scena Quinta 13 *his* this 26 *dearer* deere

III.vi. *Scene VI* Scena Sexta 5 s.d. *Exit* [placed by Capell] [F
prints after 1. 3] 17-55 *The . . . 'scape* [F omits] 22 *Now*
[Q2] [F omits] no [Q] 25 *bourn* [Capell] [F omits] broome [Q]
34 *cushions* [F omits] cushings [Q] 47 *she kicked* [Q2] [F omits]
kicked [Q] 53 *made on* [Capell] [F omits] made an [Q] 67
lym [Hanmer] Hym [F] him [Q] 68 *tike, or trundle* tight, or
Trouble 72 *Sessal* [Malone] sese [F] [Q omits] 84 s.d. *Enter
Gloucester* [placed by Capell] [F prints after 1. 80] 97-100 *Oppressèd . . . behind* [F omits] 101-14 *When . . . lurk* [F omits]

III.vii. *Scene VII* Scena Septima 21 s.d. *Exit Oswald* [Staunton]
[F and Q omit] 23 s.d. *Exeunt . . . Edmund* [Staunton] [F
(Exit) and Q (Exit Gon. and Bast.) print after 1. 22] 28 s.d.
Enter . . . three [Q, which prints after "traitor"] Enter Gloucester,
and Servants [F, which prints as here after "control"] 59 *rash*
sticke 64 *dearn* sterne 79 s.d. *Draw and fight* [F omits] 81
s.d. *She . . . him* Killes him [F] Shee . . . behind [Q] 100-108
I'll . . . him [F omits] 100 *Second Servant* [Capell] [F omits]
Servant [Q] 101 *Third Servant* [Capell] [F omits] 2 Servant
[Q] 104 *Second Servant* [Capell] [F omits] 1 Ser. [Q] 105
roguish [Q2] [Q omits] 107 *Third Servant* [Capell] [F omits]
2 Ser. [Q] 108 s.d. *Exeunt severally* [F omits] Exit [Q]

IV.i. *Act IV Scene 1* Actus Quartus. Scena Prima 9 s.d. *led by
an Old Man* [Q, which prints after 1. 12] and an Old man [F,
which places after 1. 9, as here] 41 *Then, prithee, get thee gone*
Get thee away 60-65 *Five . . . master* [F omits] 62-63 *Flibber-*

tigibbet [Pope] Stiberdigebit [Q] 63 *mopping and mowing* [Theobald] Mobing, & Mohing [Q]

IV. ii. *Scene II* Scena Secunda 1 s.d. *Enter Goneril and Edmund*
Enter Gonerill, Bastard, and Steward 2 s.d. [after "way"] *Enter
Oswald* [placed by Theobald] [Q prints after "master," 1.2] [F
omits] 25 s.d. *Exit Edmund* [placed by Rowe] Exit [F, which
prints after "death"] [Q omits] 28 s.d. *Exit* [F omits] Exit Stew.
[Q] 31-50 *I . . . deep* [F omits] 32 *its* ith [Q] 45 *benefited*
[Q corrected] beniflicted [Q uncorrected] 47 *these* [Jennens; Heath
conj.] the [Q uncorrected] this [Q corrected] 49 *Humanity* [Q corrected] Humanly [Q uncorrected] 53-59 *that . . . so* [F omits] 56
noiseless [Q corrected] noystles [Q uncorrected] 57 *thy state
begins to threat* [Jennens] thy slayer begin threats [Q uncorrected]
thy state begins thereat [Q corrected] thy slaier begins threats
[Q2] 58 *Whilst* [Q corrected] Whil's [Q uncorrected] 62-69
Thou . . . news [F omits] 65 *dislocate* [Q3] dislecate [Qq.1,2]
68 *mew* [Q corrected] now [Q uncorrected] 68 s.d. *Enter a
Messenger* [F prints after 1. 61] Enter a Gentleman [Q, which
prints after 1. 69; and Q2, which prints after 1. 68, as here] 75
thereat enraged threat-enrag'd 79 *justicers* [Q corrected] Iustices
[F, Q] 87 s.d. *Exit* [F omits]

IV.iii. *Scene III* Scena Tertia [for Scene IV] 1 s.d. *Enter . . .
Gentleman* [F omits the entire scene] 12 *sir* [Theobald] say 17
strove [Pope] streme 21 *seemed* [Pope: "seem'd"] seeme 30
believed [Q2] beleeft 32 *moistened* [Capell] moystened her
56 *Exeunt* [Pope] Exit

IV.iv. *Scene IV* [Pope] Scena Tertia [F] [Q omits] 1 s.d. *Cordelia, Doctor, and Soldiers* Cordelia, Gentlemen, and Souldiours
[F] Cordelia, Doctor and others [Q] 3 *femiter* Fenitar 6 *century* Centery 18 *distress* desires 28 *right* Rite

IV.v. *Scene V* [Pope] Scena Quarta [F] [Q omits] 39 *meet him*
meet

IV.vi. *Scene VI* [Pope] Scena Quinta [Q omits] 17 *walk* walk'd
34 s.d. *He kneels* [F omits] 41 s.d. *He falls* [F omits] 71
whelked wealk'd 71 *enridgèd* enraged 83 *coining* crying 97
had white had the white 166 *Through* Thorough *small* great
167 *Plate sin* [Theobald] Place sinnes [Q omits] 199 *Ay . . .
dust* [F omits] 200 *Good sir* [Q2] [F and Q omit] 206 s.d.
Exit . . . follow Exit [F] Exit King running [Q] 208 *one* a
244 *I'se* [Johnson: "Ise"] ice [F] ile [Q] 247 s.d. *They fight*
[F omits] 255 s.d. *He dies* [F omits] 274 *and . . . venture*
[Q reads "Venter"] [F omits] [This line, from the First Quarto,
is almost universally omitted from editions of the play] 276

indistinguished indinguish'd 289 s.d. *Drum afar off* [F prints after l. 287] A drum a farre off [Q, which prints as here]

IV.vii. *Scene VII* Scena Septima 1 s.d. *Enter . . . Gentleman* Enter Cordelia, Kent, and Gentleman [F] Enter Cordelia, Kent, and Doctor [Q] 24 *doubt not* doubt 24-25 *Very . . . there* [F omits] 32 *warring* iarring 33-36 *To . . . helm* [F omits] 79-80 *and . . . lost* [F omits] 85 s.d. *Exeunt . . . Gentleman* Exeunt 86-98 *Holds . . . fought* [F omits]

V.i. *Act V Scene I* Actus Quintus. Scena Prima 11-13 *That . . . hers* [F omits] 16 *Fear me not* Feare not 18-19 *I . . . me* [F omits] 23-28 *Where . . . nobly* [F omits] 33 *I . . . tent* [F omits] 36 *pray you* pray 39 s.d. *To those going out* [F and Q omit] *To Edgar* [F and Q omit] *Exeunt* [placed by Cambridge edition] [Q prints after "word," l. 39] [F omits] 46 *love* loues 50 s.d. *Exit* [placed by Dyce] [F and Q print after l. 49]

V.ii. *Scene II* Scena Secunda

V.iii. *Scene III* Scena Tertia 13 *hear poor rogues* heere (poore Rogues) [reference in F is to Lear and Cordelia] 26 s.d. *Exeunt . . . guarded* Exit [F] [Q omits] 39-40 *I . . . do't* [F omits] 40 s.d. *Exit Captain* [F prints after 1.38] [Q omits] 48 *and appointed guard* [F and Q omit] 55-60 *At . . . place* [F omits] 56 *We* [Q corrected, and Q2] mee [Q] 58 *sharpness* [Q corrected, and Q2] sharpes [Q] 84 *attaint* arrest 85 *sister* Sisters 98 *he is* hes 103 *Edmund . . . ho, a herald* [F omits] 108 s.d. *Enter a Herald* [placed by Hanmer] [F prints after l. 102] [Q omits] 110 *Sound, trumpet* [F omits] 110 s.d. *A trumpet sounds* [F prints after l. 109] [Q omits] trumpet [F2] Tumpet 116 *Sound* [F omits] 116 s.d. *First trumpet* [F prints after l. 115] [Q omits] 118 s.d. *Enter . . . him* Enter Edgar armed [F] Enter Edgar at the third sound, a trumpet before him [Q] 137 *illustrious* illustirous 145 *some say* (some say) 152 s.d. *fight* Fights [F, which prints after l. 153, "him"] [Q omits] 162 *Ask . . . know* [F gives to Edmund] 162 s.d. *Exit* [placed here by Q: "Exit. Gonorill"] [F prints after l. 161, "for't"] 206-23 *This . . . slave* [F omits] 215 *him* [Theobald] me [Q] [F omits] 223 s.d. *Enter . . . knife* Enter a Gentleman [F] Enter one with a bloudie knife [Q] 234 s.d. *Enter Kent* [placed by Q2] [F prints after l. 231, "Kent"] [Q prints after "allow" in l. 235] 240 s.d. *The . . . in* Gonerill and Regans bodies brought out [F, which prints after l. 232] 253 s.d. *Exit Messenger* [Theobald] [F and Q omit] 259 *Howl, howl, howl, howl* Howle, howle, howle *you are* your are 279 *them* him 291 *You are* [Q2] Your are [F] You'r [Q] 296 s.d. *Enter a Messenger* [F, which prints after "him"] Enter Captaine [Q, placed as here]

The Date and Source of *King Lear*

King Lear was probably written between 1603 and 1606. The evidence is as follows. Under the date of November 26, 1607, the printers Nathaniel Butter and John Busby entered the play in the Stationers' Register, thereby asserting their right to print it. That right was exercised in the following year, with the appearance of the First Quarto of 1608. The title page of that quarto (Q1) announces a performance of the play as having taken place before the King on St. Stephen's Night (December 26) in the Christmas holidays. The entry in the Stationers' Register (1607), since it refers to the Court performance as occurring on "Christmas Last," fixes the date of that performance as December 26, 1606. This date is therefore the *terminus ad quem* for the composition of the play. The earliest date, that of 1603, is more difficult to establish. Probably it is fixed by the entry in the Stationers' Register, on March 16, 1603, of Samuel Harsnett's *Declaration of Egregious Popishe Impostures*. Harsnett's work, a treatise on diabolism and an attack on the Jesuits, was written in 1602–03. It is utilized by Shakespeare in his play, chiefly for the names of the demons who lurk about Poor Tom. Assume—and it is reasonable to do so—that Shakespeare did not have access to Harsnett's *Declaration* before the date of publication, and 1603 becomes the *terminus a quo* for the writing of *King Lear*.

Astrological reference furnishes another clue. Gloucester, citing as portentous "These late eclipses in the sun and moon" (I. ii. 112), is commonly thought to be speaking of a contemporary event. There were in fact eclipses in 1601 and, more pertinently, in September (the moon) and October (the sun) of 1605. It has been suggested, moreover, that a publication of 1606, telling of "The Earth's and Moone's late and horrible obscurations," lies directly behind Gloucester's superstitious mutterings. The pamphlet in question, translated from the High Dutch and edited by the almanac writer Edward Gresham, is entitled *Strange fearful & true news which happened at Carlstadt, in the Kingdome of Croatia.* Its preface is dated February 11, 1606.

Finally, there is the re-emergence, in the period just before the first recorded performance of Shakespeare's play, of the older dramatic version of his story, *The True Chronicle History of King Leir.* Though this play was probably written about 1590, and was on the boards in 1594, it was published and perhaps acted again in 1605: on May 8, 1605, it is entered in the Stationers' Register. Presumably Shakespeare used the edition appearing in that year, in writing his own play.

The publication, then, of the old chronicle history in 1605, the notable eclipses occurring in the fall of the same year, and the appearance of Gresham's pamphlet early in 1606 seem to point to the winter of 1605–06 as the period in which Shakespeare wrote *King Lear.*

The ultimate source of the play is an ancient folk tale existing in many versions. It first appears as literature in the twelfth-century *Historia Regum Britanniae* (ii, 11-15), by Geoffrey of Monmouth. Throughout the Middle Ages and on into the Renaissance, the Lear story retained its popularity, appearing in some fifty different accounts. Shakespeare was familiar with it from the retelling in what is perhaps his most important source book, the second edition (1587) of *The Chronicles of England, Scotlande, and Irelande* by Raphael Holinshed, first compiled in 1577. From Edmund Spenser, in *The Faerie Queene* (1590), Shakespeare derived the name of Cordelia in its present form, and also the detail of her death by hanging (II. x. 27-32). Other suggestions were furnished by John Higgins, in *A Mirror for Magistrates* (1574), that immensely popular collection of stories of the falls of princes; and of course, by *The True Chronicle History of King Leir and his three daughters*. John Marston, in *The Malcontent* (1604), dramatizes a feigned suicide (4.3) that seems to parallel Gloucester's, at the Cliffs of Dover (IV. vi). The author of *The London Prodigal* (1605), a play once attributed to Shakespeare and performed by his company, anticipates the rustic dialogue affected by Edgar in his combat with Oswald (IV. vi). As previously noted, Harsnett and, possibly, Gresham were also of use to Shakespeare. So, in less tangible ways, was his great French contemporary, Montaigne, whose *Essais* were translated into English by John Florio in 1603. Numerous words and passages in Florio's translation (which Shakespeare may have read in manuscript) are echoed in *King Lear*. More impressive, however, is the impact on Shakespeare of Montaigne's skeptical thought, as expressed particularly in the *Apology for Raymond Sebonde*.

None of these sources of *Lear* includes the analogous story of Gloucester and his two sons. That story Shakespeare adapted from Sir Philip Sidney's account of the unhappy King of Paphlagonia, in his famous romantic narrative *Arcadia* (ii, 10), written early in the 1580's but not published until 1590. The tying of the subplot to the old and sufficiently horrid tale of King Lear and his daughters has, of course, the effect of engrossing the horror, until the audience is almost persuaded that ferocious cruelty is not so much an aberration as the norm. Certainly, if Lear is childed as Edgar is fathered it is no longer possible to see as merely sensational or idiosyncratic the evil that Shakespeare anatomizes in the play. Earlier writers, handling one or the other story, allow of that view. Shakespeare, in fusing the two stories, is at pains to controvert it. What is more, he darkens consistently, in manipulating his sources, whatever dark suggestion is latent in them. In the old *Leir,* in Holinshed, in Spenser, in the *Mirror for Magistrates,* the travails of the King are intermitted at last. Vice is punished and virtue rewarded: Cordelia triumphs over her wicked sisters; her father, restored to the throne, dies at the apogee, and in peace. It is true that, in some sources, Cordelia ends a suicide. But that is an irrelevant epilogue: the chief business of the tale is happily resolved.

It is left to Shakespeare to cancel that happy resolution. He is the first to educe tragedy from what is essentially a melodramatic romance. The madness of Lear is altogether his own contribution. So is the pathetic figure of the Fool. So is the murder of Cordelia, that cruelest stroke of all, which is made to fall just as the good are preparing to taste the wages of their virtue. Some sense of Shakespeare's lack of ruth, of his invention, and not least, of his tact may be gathered from a perusal of the source material on which he worked.

Selections from Raphael Holinshed
The Chronicles of England, Scotland, and Ireland

Leir the son of Baldud was admitted ruler over the Britains, in the year of the world 3105, at what time Joas reigned in Juda. This Leir was a prince of right noble demeanor, governing his land and subjects in great wealth. He made the town of Caerleir now called Leicester, which standeth upon the river of Sore. It is written that he had by his wife three daughters without other issue, whose names were Gonorilla, Regan, and Cordeilla, which daughters he greatly loved, but specially Cordeilla the youngest far above the two elder. When this Leir therefore was come to great years, & began to wax unwieldy through age, he thought to understand the affections of his daughters towards him, and prefer her whom he best loved, to the succession over the kingdom. Whereupon he first asked Gonorilla the eldest, how well she loved him: who calling her gods to record, protested that she loved him more than her own life, which by right and reason should be most dear unto her. With which answer the father, being well pleased, turned to the second, and demanded of her how well she loved him: who answered (confirming her sayings with great oaths) that she loved him more than tongue could express, and far above all other creatures of the world.

Then called he his youngest daughter Cordeilla before him, and asked of her what account she made of him, unto whom she made this answer as followeth: "Knowing the great love and fatherly zeal that you have always borne towards me (for the which I may not answer you otherwise than I think, and as my conscience leadeth me) I protest unto you, that I have loved you ever, and will continually (while I live) love you as my natural father. And if you would more understand of the love that I bear you, ascertain yourself, that so much as you have, so much you are worth, and so much I love you, and no more." The father being nothing content with this answer, married his two eldest daughters, the one unto Henninus, the duke of Cornwall, and the other unto Maglanus, the duke of Albania, betwixt whom he willed and ordained that his land should be divided after his death, and the one half thereof immediately should be assigned to them in hand: but for the third daughter Cordeilla he reserved nothing.

Nevertheless it fortuned that one of the princes of Gallia (which now is called France), whose name was Aganippus, hearing of the beauty, womanhood, and good conditions of the said Cordeilla, desired to have her in marriage, and sent over to her father, requiring that he might have her to wife; to whom answer was made, that he might have his daughter, but as for any dower he could have none, for all was promised and assured to her other sisters already. Aganippus notwithstanding this answer of denial to receive anything by way of dower with Cordeilla, took her to wife, only moved thereto (I say) for respect of her person and amiable virtues. This Aganippus was one of the twelve kings that ruled Gallia in those days, as in British history it is recorded. But to proceed.

After that Leir was fallen into age, the two dukes that had married his two eldest daughters, thinking it long ere the government of the land did come to their hands, arose against him in armor, and reft from him the governance of the land, upon conditions to be continued for term of life: by the which he was put to his portion, that is, to live after a rate assigned to him for the maintenance of his estate, which in process of time was diminished as well by Maglanus as by Henninus. But the greatest grief that Leir took was to see the unkindness of his daughters, which seemed to think that all was too much which their father had, the same being never so little: in so much that going from the one to the other, he was brought to that misery, that scarcely they would allow him one servant to wait upon him.

In the end, such was the unkindness, or (as I may say) the unnaturalness which he found in his two daughters, notwithstanding their fair and pleasant words uttered in time past, that being constrained of necessity, he fled the land, & sailed into Gallia, there to seek some comfort of his youngest daughter Cordeilla, whom beforetime he hated. The lady Cordeilla hearing that he was arrived in poor estate, she first sent to him privily a certain sum of money to apparel himself withal, and to retain a certain number of servants that might attend upon him in honorable wise, as appertained to the estate which he had borne: and then so accompanied, she appointed him to come to the court, which he did, and was so joyfully, honorably, and lovingly received, both by his son-in-law Aganippus, and also by his daughter Cordeilla, that his heart was greatly comforted: for he was no less honored, than if he had been king of the whole country himself.

Now when he had informed his son-in-law and his daughter in what sort he had been used by his other daughters, Aganippus caused a mighty army to be put in a readiness, and likewise a great navy of ships to be rigged, to pass over into Britain with Leir his father-in-law, to see him again restored to his kingdom. It was accorded, that Cordeilla should also go with him to take possession of the land, the which he promised to leave unto her, as the rightful inheritor after his decease, notwithstanding any former grant made to her sisters or to their husbands in any manner of wise.

Hereupon, when this army and navy of ships were ready, Leir and his daughter Cordeilla with her husband took the sea, and arriving in Britain, fought with their enemies, and discomfited them in battle, in the which Maglanus and Henninus were slain; and then was Leir restored to his kingdom, which he ruled after this by the space of two years, and then died, forty years after he first began to reign.

Sir Philip Sidney from *Arcadia*

The pitiful state, and story of the Paphlagonian unkind King, and his kind son, first related by the son, then by the blind father.

It was in the kingdom of Galacia, the season being (as in the depth of winter) very cold, and as then suddenly grown to so extreme and foul a storm, that never any winter (I think) brought forth a fouler child: so that the Princes were even compelled by the hail, that the pride of the wind blew into their faces, to seek some shrouding place within a certain hollow rock offering it unto them, they made it their shield against the tempest's fury. And so staying there, till the violence thereof was passed, they heard the speech of a couple, who not perceiving them (being hid within that rude canopy) held a strange and pitiful disputation which made them step out; yet in such sort, as they might see unseen. There they perceived an aged man, and a young, scarcely come to the age of a man, both poorly arrayed, extremely weatherbeaten; the old man blind, the young man leading him:

and yet through all those miseries, in both these seemed to appear a kind of nobleness, not suitable to that affliction. But the first words they heard were these of the old man. Well Leonatus (said he) since I cannot persuade thee to lead me to that which should end my grief, & thy trouble, let me now entreat thee to leave me: fear not, my misery cannot be greater than it is, & nothing doth become me but misery; fear not the danger of my blind steps. I cannot fall worse than I am. And do not, I pray thee, do not obstinately continue to infect thee with my wretchedness. But fly, fly from this region, only worthy of me. Dear father (answered he) do not take away from me the only remnant of my happiness: while I have power to do you service, I am not wholly miserable. Ah my son (said he, and with that he groaned, as if sorrow strove to break his heart), how evil fits it me to have such a son, and how much doth thy kindness upbraid my wickedness? These doleful speeches, and some others to like purpose (well showing they had not been borne to the fortune they were in), moved the Princes to go out unto them, and ask the younger what they were? Sirs (answered he, with a good grace, and made the more agreeable by a certain noble kind of piteousness) I see well you are strangers, that know not our misery so well here known, that no man dare know, but that we must be miserable. Indeed our state is such, as though nothing is so needful unto us as pity, yet nothing is more dangerous unto us, than to make ourselves so known as may stir pity. But your presence promiseth, that cruelty shall not overrun hate. And if it did, in truth our state is sunk below the degree of fear.

This old man (whom I lead) was lately rightful Prince of this country of Paphlagonia, by the hard-hearted ungratefulness of a son of his, deprived, not only of his kingdom (whereof no foreign forces were ever able to spoil him) but of his sight, the riches which Nature grants to the poorest creatures. Whereby, & by other his unnatural dealings, he hath been driven to such grief, as even now he would have had me to have led him to the top of this rock, thence to cast himself headlong to death:

and so would have made me (who received my life of him) to be the worker of his destruction. But noble Gentlemen (said he) if either of you have a father, and feel what dutiful affection is engraffed in a son's heart, let me entreat you to convey this afflicted Prince to some place of rest & security. Amongst your worthy acts it shall be none of the least, that a King, of such might and fame, and so unjustly oppressed, is in any sort by you relieved.

But before they could make him answer, his father began to speak, Ah my son (said he) how evil an historian are you, that leave out the chief knot of all the discourse? my wickedness, my wickedness. And if thou doest it to spare my ears, (the only sense now left me proper for knowledge) assure thy self thou dost mistake me. And I take witness of that sun which you see (with that he cast up his blind eyes, as if he would hunt for light), and wish myself in worse case than I do wish myself, which is as evil as may be, if I speak untruly; that nothing is so welcome to my thoughts, as the publishing of my shame. Therefore know you Gentlemen (to whom from my heart I wish that it may not prove ominous foretoken of misfortune to have met with such a miser as I am) that whatsoever my son (O God, that truth binds me to reproach him with the name of my son) hath said, is true. But besides those truths this also is true, that having had in lawful marriage, of a mother fit to bear royal children, this son (such one as partly you see, and better shall know by my short declaration) and so enjoyed the expectations in the world of him, till he was grown to justify their expectations (so as I needed envy no father for the chief comfort of mortality, to leave another oneself after me) I was carried by a bastard son of mine (if at least I be bound to believe the words of that base woman my concubine, his mother) first to mislike, then to hate, lastly to destroy, to do my best to destroy, this son (I think you think) undeserving destruction. What ways he used to bring me to it, if I should tell you, I should tediously trouble you with as much poisonous hypocrisy, desperate fraud, smooth malice, hidden ambition, & smiling envy, as in any living person could be harbored. But I list it not, no remembrance, (no, of naughtiness) delights me, but mine own; & me thinks, the accusing his trains might in some manner excuse my fault, which certainly I loathe to do. But the conclusion is, that I gave order to some servants of mine, whom I thought as apt for such charities as myself, to lead him out into a forest, & there to kill him.

But those thieves (better natured to my son than myself) spared his life, letting him go, to learn to live poorly: which he did, giving himself to be a private soldier, in a country hereby. But as he was ready to be greatly advanced for some noble pieces of service which he did, he heard news of me: who (drunk in my affection to that unlawful and unnatural son of mine) suffered myself so to be governed by him, that all favors and punishments passed by him, all offices, and places of importance, distributed to his favorites; so that ere I was aware, I had left myself nothing but the name of a King: which he shortly weary of too, with many indignities (if anything may be called an indignity, which was laid upon me) threw me out of my seat, and put out my eyes; and then (proud in his tyranny) let me go, neither imprisoning, nor killing me: but rather delighting to make me feel my misery; misery indeed, if ever there were any: full of wretchedness, fuller of disgrace, and fullest of guiltiness. And as he came to the crown by so unjust means, as unjustly he kept it, by force of stranger soldiers in citadels, the nests of tyranny, & murderers of liberty; disarming all his own countrymen, that no man durst show himself a well-willer of mine: to say the truth (I think) few of them being so (considering my cruel folly to my good son, and foolish kindness to my unkind bastard): but if there were any who fell to pity of so great a fall, and had yet any sparks of unstained duty left in them towards me, yet durst they not show it, scarcely with giving me alms at their doors; which yet was the only sustenance of my distressed life, nobody daring to show so much charity, as to lend me a hand to guide my dark steps: Till this son of mine (God knows, worthy of a more virtuous, and more fortunate father) forgetting

my abominable wrongs, not recking danger, & neglecting
the present good way he was in doing himself good, came
hither to do this kind office you see him perform towards me, to my unspeakable grief; not only because his
kindness is a glass even to my blind eyes, of my naughtiness, but that above all griefs, it grieves me he should
desperately adventure the loss of his soul-deserving life
for mine, that yet owe more to fortune for my deserts,
as if he would carry mud in a chest of crystal. For well I
know, he that now reigneth, how much soever (and with
good reason) he despiseth me, of all men despised; yet
he will not let slip any advantage to make away him,
whose just title (ennobled by courage and goodness)
may one day shake the seat of a never secure tyranny.
And for this cause I craved of him to lead me to the top
of this rock, indeed I must confess, with meaning to free
him from so serpentine a companion as I am. But he finding what I purposed only therein since he was born,
showed himself disobedient unto me. And now Gentlemen, you have the true story, which I pray you publish
to the world, that my mischievous proceedings may be
the glory of his filial piety, the only reward now left for
so great a merit. And if it may be, let me obtain that of
you, which my son denies me: for never was there more
pity in saving any, than in ending me; both because
therein my agonies shall end, and so shall you preserve
this excellent young man, who else willfully follows his
own ruin.

The matter in itself lamentable, lamentably expressed
by the old Prince (which needed not take to himself
the gestures of pity, since his face could not put off the
marks thereof) greatly moved the two Princes to compassion, which could not stay in such hearts as theirs
without seeking remedy. But by and by the occasion was
presented: for Plexirtus (so was the bastard called) came
thither with forty horse, only of purpose to murder this
brother; of whose coming he had soon advertisement,
and thought no eyes of sufficient credit in such a matter, but his own; and therefore came himself to be
actor, and spectator. And as soon as he came, not

regarding the weak (as he thought) guard of but two
men, commanded some of his followers to set their hands
to his, in the killing of Leonatus. But the young Prince
(though not otherwise armed but with a sword) how
falsely soever he was dealt with by others, would not betray himself: but bravely drawing it out, made the death
of the first that assaulted him, warn his fellows to come
more warily after him. But then Pyrocles and Musidorus
were quickly become parties (so just a defense deserving as much as old friendship) and so did behave them
among that company (more injurious, than valiant) that
many of them lost their lives for their wicked master.

Yet perhaps had the number of them at last prevailed,
if the King of Pontus (lately by them made so) had not
come unlooked for to their succor. Who (having had a
dream which had fixed his imagination vehemently upon
some great danger, presently to follow those two Princes
whom he most dearly loved) was come in all haste, following as well as he could their track with a hundred
horses in that country, which he thought (considering
who then reigned) a fit place enough to make the stage
of any tragedy.

But then the match had been so ill made for Plexirtus,
that his ill-led life, & worse-gotten honor should have
tumbled together to destruction; had there not come in
Tydeus & Telenor, with forty or fifty in their suit, to the
defense of Plexirtus. These two were brothers, of the
noblest house of that country, brought up from their
infancy with Plexirtus: men of such prowess, as not to
know fear in themselves, and yet to teach it others that
should deal with them: for they had often made their
lives triumph over most terrible dangers; never dismayed
and ever fortunate; and truly no more settled in their
valor, than disposed to goodness and justice, if either
they had lighted on a better friend, or could have
learned to make friendship a child, and not the father of
virtue. But bringing up (rather than choice) having first
knit their minds unto him, (indeed crafty enough, either to hide his faults, or never to show them, but
when they might pay home) they willingly held out the

course, rather to satisfy him, than all the world; and rather to be good friends, than good men: so as though they did not like the evil he did, yet they liked him that did the evil; and though not councilors of the offense, yet protectors of the offender. Now they having heard of this sudden going out, with so small a company, in a country full of evil-wishing minds toward him (though they knew not the cause) followed him; till they found him in such case as they were to venture their lives, or else he to lose his: which they did with such force of mind and body, that truly I may justly say, Pyrocles & Musidorus had never till then found any, that could make them so well repeat their hardest lesson in the feats of arms. And briefly so they did, that if they overcame not; yet were they not overcome, but carried away that ungrateful master of theirs to a place of security; howsoever the Princes labored to the contrary. But this matter being thus far begun, it became not the constancy of the Princes so to leave it; but in all haste making forces both in Pontus and Phrygia, they had in few days, left him but only that one strong place where he was. For fear having been the only knot that had fastened his people unto him, that once untied by a greater force, they all scattered from him; like so many birds, whose cage had been broken.

In which season the blind King (having in the chief city of his realm, set the crown upon his son Leonatus' head) with many tears (both of joy and sorrow) setting forth to the whole people, his own fault & his son's virtue, after he had kissed him, and forced his son to accept honor of him (as of his new-become subject) even in a moment died, as it should seem: his heart broken with unkindness & affliction, stretched so far beyond his limits with this excess of comfort, as it was able no longer to keep safe his royal spirits. But the new King (having no less lovingly performed all duties to him dead, than alive) pursued on the siege of his unnatural brother, as much for the revenge of his father, as for the establishing of his own quiet. In which siege truly I cannot but acknowledge the prowess of those two brothers, than whom the

Princes never found in all their travel two men of greater ability to perform, nor of abler skill for conduct.

But Plexirtus finding, that if nothing else, famine would at last bring him to destruction, thought better by humbleness to creep, where by pride he could not march. For certainly so had nature formed him, & the exercise of craft conformed him to all turnings of sleights, that though no man had less goodness in his soul than he, no man could better find the places whence arguments might grow of goodness to another: though no man felt less pity, no man could tell better how to stir pity: no man more impudent to deny, where proofs were not manifest; no man more ready to confess with a repenting manner of aggravating his own evil, where denial would but make the fault fouler. Now he took this way, that having gotten a passport for one (that pretended he would put Plexirtus alive into his hands) to speak with the King his brother, he himself (though much against the minds of the valiant brothers, who rather wished to die in brave defense) with a rope about his neck, barefooted, came to offer himself to the discretion of Leonatus. Where what submission he used, how cunningly in making greater the fault he made the faultiness the less, how artificially he could set out the torments of his own conscience, with the burdensome cumber he had found of his ambitious desires, how finely seeming to desire nothing but death, as ashamed to live, he begged life, in the refusing it, I am not cunning enough to be able to express: but so fell out of it, that though at first sight Leonatus saw him with no other eye, than as the murderer of his father; & anger already began to paint revenge in many colors, ere long he had not only gotten pity, but pardon, and if not an excuse of the fault past, yet an opinion of future amendment: while the poor villains (chief ministers of his wickedness, now betrayed by the author thereof) were delivered to many cruel sorts of death; he so handling it, that it rather seemed, he had rather come into the defense of an unremediable mischief already committed, than that they had done it at first by his consent.

from *The True Chronicle History of King Leir*

Scene XXIV

Enter the Gallian King and Queen, and Mum-
ford, with a basket, disguised like country folk.

King. This tedious journey all on foot, sweet Love,
Cannot be pleasing to your tender joints,
Which ne'er were used to these toilsome walks.

Cordella. I never in my life took more delight
In any journey, than I do in this:
It did me good, when as we hapt to light
Amongst the merry crew of country folk,
To see what industry and pains they took,
To win them commendations 'mongst their friends.
Lord, how they labor to bestir themselves,
And in their quirks to go beyond the moon,
And so take on them with such antic fits,
That one would think they were beside their wits!
Come away, Roger, with your basket.

Mumford. Soft, Dame, here comes a couple of old
        youths,
I must needs make myself fat with jesting at them.

Cordella. Nay, prithy do not, they do seem to be
Men much o'ergone with grief and misery.
Let's stand aside, and harken what they say.

        [*Enter Leir and Perillus very faintly.*]

Leir. Ah, my Perillus, now I see we both
Shall end our days in this unfruitful soil.
Oh, I do faint for want of sustenance:
And thou, I know, in little better case.
No gentle tree affords one taste of fruit,
To comfort us, until we meet with men:
No lucky path conducts our luckless steps
Unto a place where any comfort dwells.
Sweet rest betide unto our happy souls;
For here I see our bodies must have end.

Perillus. Ah, my dear Lord, how doth my heart
    lament,
  To see you brought to this extremity!
  O, if you love me, as you do profess,
  Or ever thought well of me in my life,
           [*He strips up his arm.*]
  Feed on this flesh, whose veins are not so dry
  But there is virtue left to comfort you.
  O, feed on this, if this will do you good,
  I'll smile for joy, to see you suck my blood.

Leir. I am no Cannibal, that I should delight
  To slake my hungry jaws with human flesh:
  I am no devil, or ten times worse than so,
  To suck the blood of such a peerless friend.
  O, do not think that I respect my life
  So dearly, as I do thy loyal love.
  Ah, Britain, I shall never see thee more,
  That hast unkindly banishèd thy King:
  And yet thou dost not make me to complain,
  But they which were more near to me than thou.

Cordella. What do I hear? this lamentable voice,
  Me thinks, ere now I oftentimes have heard.

Leir. Ah, Gonorill, was half my kingdom's gift
  The cause that thou didst seek to have my life?
  Ah, cruel Ragan, did I give thee all,
  And all could not suffice without my blood?
  Ah, poor Cordella, did I give thee nought,
  Nor never shall be able for to give?
  O, let me warn all ages that ensueth,
  How they trust flattery, and reject the truth.
  Well, unkind girls, I here forgive you both,
  Yet the just heavens will hardly do the like;
  And only crave forgiveness at the end
  Of good Cordella, and of thee, my friend;
  Of God, whose maiesty I have offended,
  By my transgression many thousand ways:
  Of her, dear heart, whom I for no occasion
  Turned out of all, through flatterers' persuasion:
  Of thee, kind friend, who but for me, I know,

Hadst never come unto this place of woe.

Cordella. Alack, that ever I should live to see
My noble father in this misery.

King. Sweet Love, reveal not what thou art as yet,
Until we know the ground of all this ill.

Cordella. O, but some meat, some meat: do you not
see,
How near they are to death for want of food?

Perillus. Lord, which didst help thy servants at their
need.
Or now or never send us help with speed.
Oh comfort, comfort! yonder is a banquet,
And men and women, my Lord: be of good cheer;
For I see comfort coming very near.
O my Lord, a banquet, and men and women!

Leir. O, let kind pity mollify their hearts,
That they may help us in our great extremes.

Perillus. God save you, friends; & if this blessèd
banquet
Affordeth any food or sustenance,
Even for his sake that saved us all from death,
Vouchsafe to save us from the grip of famine.

[*She bringeth him to the table.*]

Cordella. Here father, sit and eat, here sit and drink:
And would it were far better for your sakes.

Perillus takes Leir by the hand to the table.

Perillus. I'll give you thanks anon: my friend doth
faint,
And needeth present comfort.

[*Leir drinks.*]

Mumford. I warrant, he ne'er stays to say grace:
O, there's no sauce to a good stomach.

Perillus. The blessed God of heaven hath thought upon
us.

Leir. The thanks be his, and these kind courteous
folk,
By whose humanity we are preserved.

They eat hungrily, Leir drinks.

Cordella. And may that draught be unto him, as was
That which old Eson drank, which did renew
His withered age, and made him young again.
And may that meat be unto him, as was
That which Elias ate, in strength whereof
He walkèd forty days, and never fainted.
Shall I conceal me longer from my father?
Or shall I manifest myself to him?

King. Forbear a while, until his strength return,
Lest being overjoyed with seeing thee,
His poor weak senses should forsake their office,
And so our cause of joy be turned to sorrow.

Perillus. What cheer, my Lord? how do you feel
yourself?

Leir. Me thinks, I never ate such savory meat:
It is as pleasant as the blessed manna,
That rained from heaven amongst the Israelites:
It hath recalled my spirits home again,
And made me fresh, as erst I was before.
But how shall we congratulate their kindness?

Perillus. In faith, I know not how sufficiently;
But the best mean that I can think on, is this:
I'll offer them my doublet in requital;
For we have nothing else to spare.

Leir. Nay, stay, Perillus, for they shall have mine.

Perillus. Pardon, my Lord, I swear they shall have
mine.

Perillus proffers his doublet: they will not take it.

Leir. Ah, who would think such kindness should
remain
Among such strange and unacquainted men:
And that such hate should harbor in the breast
Of those, which have occasion to be best?

Cordella. Ah, good old father, tell to me thy grief,
I'll sorrow with thee, if not add relief.

Leir. Ah, good young daughter, I may call thee so;
For thou art like a daughter I did owe.

Cordella. Do you not owe her still? what, is she dead?

Leir. No, God forbid: but all my interest's gone,
By showing myself too much unnatural:
So have I lost the title of a father,
And may be called a stranger to her rather.

Cordella. Your title's good still; for 'tis always known,
A man may do as him list with his own.
But have you but one daughter then in all?

Leir. Yes, I have more by two, than would I had.

Cordella. O, say not so, but rather see the end:
They that are bad, may have the grace to mend:
But how have they offended you so much?

Leir. If from the first I should relate the cause,
'Twould make a heart of adamant to weep;
And thou, poor soule, kindhearted as thou art,
Dost weep already, ere I do begin.

Cordella. For God's love tell it, and when you have
done,
I'll tell the reason why I weep so soon.

Leir. Then know this first, I am a Briton born,
And had three daughters by one loving wife;
And though I say it, of beauty they were sped;
Especially the youngest of the three,
For her perfections hardly matched could be:
On these I doted with a jealous love,
And thought to try which of them loved me best,
By asking them, which would do most for me?
The first and second flattered me with words,
And vowed they loved me better than their lives:
The youngest said, she loved me as a child
Might do: her answer I esteemed most vile,
And presently in an outrageous mood,
I turned her from me to go sink or swim:
And all I had, even to the very clothes,
I gave in dowry with the other two:
And she that best deserved the greatest share,
I gave her nothing, but disgrace and care.
Now mark the sequel: When I had done thus,

I sojourned in my eldest daughter's house,
Where for a time I was entreated well,
And lived in state sufficing my content:
But every day her kindness did grow cold,
Which I with patience put up well enough,
And seemed not to see the things I saw:
But at the last she grew so far incensed
With moody fury, and with causeless hate,
That in most vile and contumelious terms,
She bade me pack, and harbor somewhere else.
Then was I fain for refuge to repair
Unto my other daughter for relief,
Who gave me pleasing and most courteous words;
But in her actions showed herself so sore,
As never any daughter did before:
She prayed me in a morning out betime,
To go to a thicket two miles from the court,
Pointing that there she would come talk with me:
There she had set a shag-haired murdering wretch,
To massacre my honest friend and me.
Then judge yourself, although my tale be brief,
If ever man had greater cause of grief.

King. Nor never like impiety was done,
Since the creation of the world begun.

Leir. And now I am constrained to seek relief
Of her, to whom I have been so unkind;
Whose censure, if it do award me death,
I must confess she pays me but my due:
But if she show a loving daughter's part,
It comes of God and her, not my desert.

Cordella. No doubt she will, I dare be sworn she will.

Leir. How know you that, not knowing what she is?

Cordella. Myself a father have a great way hence,
Used me as ill as ever you did her;
Yet, that his reverend age I once might see,
I'd creep along, to meet him on my knee.

Leir. O, no men's children are unkind but mine.

Cordella. Condemn not all, because of other's crime:

But look, dear father, look, behold and see
Thy loving daughter speaketh unto thee.

[*She kneels.*]

Leir. O, stand thou up, it is my part to kneel,
And ask forgiveness for my former faults.

[*He kneels.*]

Cordella. O, if you wish I should enjoy my breath,
Dear father rise, or I receive my death.

[*He riseth.*]

Leir. Then I will rise, to satisfy your mind,
But kneel again, till pardon be resigned.

[*He kneels.*]

Cordella. I pardon you: the word beseems not me:
But I do say so, for to ease your knee.
You gave me life, you were the cause that I
Am what I am, who else had never been.

Leir. But you gave life to me and to my friend,
Whose days had else, had an untimely end.

Cordella. You brought me up, when as I was but
young,
And far unable for to help myself.

Leir. I cast thee forth, when as thou wast but young,
And far unable for to help thyself.

Cordella. God, world and nature say I do you wrong,
That can endure to see you kneel so long.

King. Let me break off this loving controversy,
Which doth rejoice my very soul to see.
Good father, rise, she is your loving daughter,

[*He riseth.*]

And honors you with as respective duty.
As if you were the monarch of the world.

Cordella. But I will never rise from off my knee,
Until I have your blessing, and your pardon
Of all my faults committed any way,
From my first birth unto this present day.

Leir. The blessing, which the God of Abraham gave

Unto the tribe of Juda, light on thee,
And multiply thy days, that thou mayst see
Thy children's children prosper after thee.
Thy faults, which are just none that I do know,
God pardon on high, and I forgive below.

[She riseth.]

Cordella. Now is my heart at quiet, and doth leap
Within my breast, for joy of this good hap:
And now (dear father) welcome to our court,
And welcome (kind Perillus) unto me,
Mirror of virtue and true honesty.

Leir. O, he hath been the kindest friend to me,
That ever man had in adversity.

Perillus. My tongue doth fail, to say what heart
    doth think,
I am so ravished with exceeding joy.

King. All you have spoke: now let me speak my mind,
And in few words much matter here conclude:

[He kneels.]

If ere my heart do harbor any joy,
Or true content repose within my breast,
Till I have rooted out this viperous sect,
And repossessed my father of his crown,
Let me be counted for the perjuredest man,
That ever spoke word since the world began.

[Rise.]

Mumford. Let me pray too, that never prayed before;

[Mumford kneels.]

If ere I resalute the British earth,
(As [ere't be long] I do presume I shall)
And do return from thence without my wench,
Let me gelded from my recompense.

[Rise.]

King. Come, let's to arms for to redress this wrong:
Till I am there, me thinks, the time seems long.

[Exeunt.]

Commentaries

Samuel Johnson.

From "Preface to Shakespeare" and "King Lear"

PREFACE TO SHAKESPEARE

Nothing can please many, and please long, but just representations of general nature. Particular manners can be known to few, and therefore few only can judge how nearly they are copied. The irregular combinations of fanciful invention may delight awhile, by that novelty of which the common satiety of life sends us all in quest; but the pleasures of sudden wonder are soon exhausted, and the mind can only repose on the stability of truth.

Shakespeare is above all writers, at least above all modern writers, the poet of nature; the poet that holds up to his readers a faithful mirror of manners and of life. His characters are not modified by the customs of particular places, unpracticed by the rest of the world; by the peculiarities of studies or professions, which can operate but upon small numbers; or by the accidents of transient fashions or temporary opinions: they are the genuine progeny of common humanity, such as the world will always supply, and observation will always find. His persons act and speak by the influence of those general passions and principles by which all minds are agitated, and the whole system of life is continued in motion. In the writings of other poets a character is too often an individual; in those of Shakespeare it is commonly a species.

It is from this wide extension of design that so much instruction is derived. It is this which fills the plays of

From *The Plays of William Shakespeare*, London, 1765.

Shakespeare with practical axioms and domestic wisdom. It was said of Euripides, that every verse was a precept; and it may be said of Shakespeare, that from his works may be collected a system of civil and economical prudence. Yet his real power is not shown in the splendor of particular passages, but by the progress of his fable, and, the tenor of his dialogue; and he that tries to recommend him by select quotations, will succeed like the pedant in *Hierocles,* who, when he offered his house to sale, carried a brick in his pocket as a specimen. . . .

Other dramatists can only gain attention by hyperbolical or aggravated characters, by fabulous and unexampled excellence or depravity, as the writers of barbarous romances invigorated the reader by a giant and a dwarf; and he that should form his expectations of human affairs from the play, or from the tale, would be equally deceived. Shakespeare has no heroes; his scenes are occupied only by men, who act and speak as the reader thinks that he should himself have spoken or acted on the same occasion: Even where the agency is supernatural the dialogue is level with life. Other writers disguise the most natural passions and most frequent incidents; so that he who contemplates them in the book will not know them in the world: Shakespeare approximates the remote, and familiarizes the wonderful; the event which he represents will not happen, but if it were possible, its effects would be probably such as he has assigned; and it may be said, that he has not only shown human nature as it acts in real exigencies, but as it would be found in trials, to which it cannot be exposed.

This therefore is the praise of Shakespeare, that his drama is the mirror of life; that he who has mazed his imagination, in following the phantoms which other writers raise up before him, may here be cured of his delirious ecstasies, by reading human sentiments in human language; by scenes from which a hermit may estimate the transactions of the world, and a confessor predict the progress of the passions. . . .

The censure which he has incurred by mixing comic

and tragic scenes, as it extends to all his works, deserves more consideration. Let the fact be first stated, and then examined.

Shakespeare's plays are not in the rigorous and critical sense either tragedies or comedies, but compositions of a distinct kind; exhibiting the real state of sublunary nature, which partakes of good and evil, joy and sorrow, mingled with endless variety of proportion and innumerable modes of combination; and expressing the course of the world, in which the loss of one is the gain of another; in which, at the same time, the reveler is hasting to his wine, and the mourner burying his friend; in which the malignity of one is sometimes defeated by the frolic of another; and many mischiefs and many benefits are done and hindered without design.

Out of this chaos of mingled purposes and casualties the ancient poets, according to the laws which custom had prescribed, selected some the crimes of men, and some their absurdities; some the momentous vicissitudes of life, and some the lighter occurrences; some the terrors of distress, and some the gaieties of prosperity. Thus rose the two modes of imitation, known by the names of *tragedy* and *comedy*, compositions intended to promote different ends by contrary means, and considered as so little allied, that I do not recollect among the Greeks or Romans a single writer who attempted both.

Shakespeare has united the powers of exciting laughter and sorrow not only in one mind but in one composition. Almost all his plays are divided between serious and ludicrous characters, and, in the successive evolutions of the design, sometimes produce seriousness and sorrow, and sometimes levity and laughter.

That this is a practice contrary to the rules of criticism will be readily allowed; but there is always an appeal open from criticism to nature. The end of writing is to instruct; the end of poetry is to instruct by pleasing. That the mingled drama may convey all the instruction of tragedy or comedy cannot be denied, because it includes both in its alternations of exhibition, and approaches nearer than either to the appearance of life, by showing how great machinations and slender designs may promote or obviate one another, and the high and the low cooperate in the general system by unavoidable concatenation.

It is objected, that by this change of scenes the passions are interrupted in their progression, and that the principal event, being not advanced by a due gradation of preparatory incidents, wants at last the power to move, which constitutes the perfection of dramatic poetry. This reasoning is so specious, that it is received as true even by those who in daily experience feel it to be false. The interchanges of mingled scenes seldom fail to produce the intended vicissitudes of passion. Fiction cannot move so much, but that the attention may be easily transferred; and though it must be allowed that pleasing melancholy be sometimes interrupted by unwelcome levity, yet let it be considered likewise, that melancholy is often not pleasing, and that the disturbance of one man may be the relief of another; that different auditors have different habitudes; and that, upon the whole, all pleasure consists in variety. . . .

Shakespeare engaged in dramatic poetry with the world open before him; the rules of the ancients were yet known to few; the public judgment was unformed; he had no example of such fame as might force him upon imitation, nor critics of such authority as might restrain his extravagance: He therefore indulged his natural disposition, and his disposition, as Rymer has remarked, led him to comedy. In tragedy he often writes with great appearance of toil and study, what is written at last with little felicity; but in his comic scenes, he seems to produce without labor, what no labor can improve. In tragedy he is always struggling after some occasion to be comic, but in comedy he seems to repose, or to luxuriate, as in a mode of thinking congenial to his nature. In his tragic scenes there is always something wanting, but his comedy often surpasses expectation or desire. His comedy pleases by the thoughts and the language, and his tragedy for the greater part by incident and action. His tragedy seems to be skill, his comedy to be instinct.

The force of his comic scenes has suffered little diminution from the changes made by a century and a half, in manners or in words. As his personages act upon principles arising from genuine passion, very little modified by particular forms, their pleasures and vexations are communicable to all times and to all places; they are natural, and therefore durable; the adventitious peculiarities of personal habits are only superficial dyes, bright and pleasing for a little while, yet soon fading to a dim tinct, without any remains of former luster; but the discriminations of true passion are the colors of nature; they pervade the whole mass, and can only perish with the body that exhibits them. The accidental compositions of heterogeneous modes are dissolved by the chance which combined them; but the uniform simplicity of primitive qualities neither admits increase, nor suffers decay. The sand heaped by one flood is scattered by another, but the rock always continues in its place. The stream of time, which is continually washing the dissoluble fabrics of other poets, passes without injury by the adamant of Shakespeare.

If there be, what I believe there is, in every nation, a style which never becomes obsolete, a certain mode of phraseology so consonant and congenial to the analogy and principles of its respective language as to remain settled and unaltered; this style is probably to be sought in the common intercourse of life, among those who speak only to be understood, without ambition of elegance. The polite are always catching modish innovations, and the learned depart from established forms of speech, in hope of finding or making better; those who wish for distinction forsake the vulgar, when the vulgar is right; but there is a conversation above grossness and below refinement, where propriety resides, and where this poet seems to have gathered his comic dialogue. He is therefore more agreeable to the ears of the present age than any other author equally remote, and among his other excellencies deserves to be studied as one of the original masters of our language. . . .

Shakespeare with his excellencies has likewise faults, and faults sufficient to obscure and overwhelm any other merit. I shall show them in the proportion in which they appear to me, without envious malignity or superstitious veneration. No question can be more innocently discussed than a dead poet's pretensions to renown; and little regard is due to that bigotry which sets candor higher than truth.

His first defect is that to which may be imputed most of the evil in books or in men. He sacrifices virtue to convenience, and is so much more careful to please than to instruct, that he seems to write without any moral purpose. From his writings indeed a system of social duty may be selected, for he that thinks reasonably must think morally; but his precepts and axioms drop casually from him; he makes no just distribution of good or evil, nor is always careful to show in the virtuous a disapprobation of the wicked; he carries his persons indifferently through right and wrong, and at the close dismisses them without further care, and leaves their examples to operate by chance. This fault the barbarity of his age cannot extenuate; for it is always a writer's duty to make the world better, and justice is a virtue independent on time or place.

The plots are often so loosely formed, that a very slight consideration may improve them, and so carelessly pursued, that he seems not always fully to comprehend his own design. He omits opportunities of instructing or delighting which the train of his story seems to force upon him, and apparently rejects those exhibitions which would be more affecting, for the sake of those which are more easy.

It may be observed, that in many of his plays the latter part is evidently neglected. When he found himself near the end of his work, and, in view of his reward, he shortened the labor, to snatch the profit. He therefore remits his efforts where he should most vigorously exert them, and his catastrophe is improbably produced or imperfectly represented.

He had no regard to distinction of time or place, but

gives to one age or nation, without scruple, the customs, institutions, and opinions of another, at the expense not only of likelihood, but of possibility. . . .

In tragedy his performance seems constantly to be worse, as his labor is more. The effusions of passion which exigence forces out are for the most part striking and energetic; but whenever he solicits his invention, or strains his faculties, the offspring of his throes is tumor, meanness, tediousness, and obscurity.

In narration he affects a disproportionate pomp of diction and a wearisome train of circumlocution, and tells the incident imperfectly in many words, which might have been more plainly delivered in few. Narration in dramatic poetry is naturally tedious, as it is unanimated and inactive, and obstructs the progress of the action; it should therefore always be rapid, and enlivened by frequent interruption. Shakespeare found it an encumbrance, and instead of lightening it by brevity, endeavored to recommend it by dignity and splendor.

His declamations or set speeches are commonly cold and weak, for his power was the power of nature; when he endeavored, like other tragic writers, to catch opportunities of amplification, and instead of inquiring what the occasion demanded, to show how much his stores of knowledge could supply, he seldom escapes without the pity or resentment of his reader.

It is incident to him to be now and then entangled with an unwieldy sentiment, which he cannot well express, and will not reject; he struggles with it a while, and if it continues stubborn, comprises it in words such as occur, and leaves it to be disentangled and evolved by those who have more leisure to bestow upon it.

Not that always where the language is intricate the thought is subtle, or the image always great where the line is bulky; the equality of words to things is very often neglected, and trivial sentiments and vulgar ideas disappoint the attention, to which they are recommended by sonorous epithets and swelling figures.

But the admirers of this great poet have never less

reason to indulge their hopes of supreme excellence, than when he seems fully resolved to sink them in dejection, and mollify them with tender emotions by the fall of greatness, the danger of innocence, or the crosses of love. He is not long soft and pathetic without some idle conceit, or contemptible equivocation. He no sooner begins to move, than he counteracts himself; and terror and pity, as they are rising in the mind, are checked and blasted by sudden frigidity.

A quibble is to Shakespeare, what luminous vapors are to the traveler; he follows it at all adventures, it is sure to lead him out of his way, and sure to engulf him in the mire. It has some malignant power over his mind, and its fascinations are irresistible. Whatever be the dignity or profundity of his disquisition, whether he be enlarging knowledge or exalting affection, whether he be amusing attention with incidents, or enchaining it in suspense, let but a quibble spring up before him, and he leaves his work unfinished. A quibble is the golden apple for which he will always turn aside from his career, or stoop from his elevation. A quibble, poor and barren as it is, gave him such delight, that he was content to purchase it, by the sacrifice of reason, propriety and truth. A quibble was to him the fatal Cleopatra for which he lost the world, and was content to lose it.

It will be thought strange, that, in enumerating the defects of this writer, I have not yet mentioned his neglect of the unities; his violation of those laws which have been instituted and established by the joint authority of poets and critics.

For his other deviations from the art of writing I resign him to critical justice, without making any other demand in his favor, than that which must be indulged to all human excellence; that his virtues be rated with his failings: But, from the censure which this irregularity may bring upon him, I shall, with due reverence to that learning which I must oppose, adventure to try how I can defend him.

His histories, being neither tragedies nor comedies, are not subject to any of their laws; nothing more is necessary to all the praise which they expect, than that the changes of action be so prepared as to be understood, that the incidents be various and affecting, and the characters consistent, natural and distinct. No other unity is intended, and therefore none is to be sought.

In his other works he has well enough preserved the unity of action. He has not, indeed, an intrigue regularly perplexed and regularly unraveled; he does not endeavor to hide his design only to discover it, for this is seldom the order of real events, and Shakespeare is the poet of nature: But his plan has commonly what Aristotle requires, a beginning, a middle, and an end; one event is concatenated with another, and the conclusion follows by easy consequence. There are perhaps some incidents that might be spared, as in other poets there is much talk that only fills up time upon the stage; but the general system makes gradual advances, and the end of the play is the end of expectation.

To the unities of time and place he has shown no regard, and perhaps a nearer view of the principles on which they stand will diminish their value, and withdraw from them the veneration which, from the time of Corneille, they have very generally received by discovering that they have given more trouble to the poet, than pleasure to the auditor.

The necessity of observing the unities of time and place arises from the supposed necessity of making the drama credible. The critics hold it impossible, that an action of months or years can be possibly believed to pass in three hours; or that the spectator can suppose himself to sit in the theater, while ambassadors go and return between distant kings, while armies are levied and towns besieged, while an exile wanders and returns, or till he whom they saw courting his mistress, shall lament the untimely fall of his son. The mind revolts from evident falsehood, and fiction loses its force when it departs from the resemblance of reality.

From the narrow limitation of time necessarily arises the contraction of place. The spectator, who knows that he saw the first act at Alexandria, cannot suppose that he sees the next at Rome, at a distance to which not the dragons of Medea could, in so short a time, have transported him; he knows with certainty that he has not changed his place; and he knows that place cannot change itself; that what was a house cannot become a plain; that what was Thebes can never be Persepolis.

Such is the triumphant language with which a critic exults over the misery of an irregular poet, and exults commonly without resistance or reply. It is time therefore to tell him, by the authority of Shakespeare, that he assumes, as an unquestionable principle, a position, which, while his breath is forming it into words, his understanding pronounces to be false. . . .

There is no reason why a mind thus wandering in ecstasy should count the clock, or why an hour should not be a century in that calenture of the brains that can make the stage a field.

The truth is, that the spectators are always in their senses, and know, from the first act to the last, that the stage is only a stage, and that the players are only players. They came to hear a certain number of lines recited with just gesture and elegant modulation. The lines relate to some action, and an action must be in some place; but the different actions that complete a story may be in places very remote from each other. . . .

Time is, of all modes of existence, most obsequious to the imagination; a lapse of years is as easily conceived as a passage of hours. In contemplation we easily contract the time of real actions, and therefore willingly permit it to be contracted when we only see their imitation.

It will be asked, how the drama moves, if it is not credited. It is credited with all the credit due to a drama. It is credited, whenever it moves, as a just picture of a real original; as representing to the auditor what he would himself feel, if he were to do or suffer what is there feigned to be suffered or to be done. The reflection that strikes the heart is not, that the evils before us are real evils, but that they are evils to which we ourselves may be exposed. If there be any fallacy, it is not that we fancy the players, but that we fancy ourselves unhappy for a moment; but we rather lament the possibility than suppose the presence of misery, as a mother weeps over her babe, when she remembers that death may take it from her. The delight of tragedy proceeds from our consciousness of fiction; if we thought murders and treasons real, they would please no more. . . .

[Shakespeare's] plots, whether historical or fabulous, are always crowded with incidents, by which the attention of a rude people was more easily caught than by sentiment or argumentation; and such is the power of the marvelous even over those who despise it, that every man finds his mind more strongly seized by the tragedies of Shakespeare than of any other writer; others please us by particular speeches, but he always makes us anxious for the event, and has perhaps excelled all but Homer in securing the first purpose of a writer, by exciting restless and unquenchable curiosity and compelling him that reads his work to read it through.

The shows and bustle with which his plays abound have the same original. As knowledge advances, pleasure passes from the eye to the ear, but returns, as it declines, from the ear to the eye. Those to whom our author's labors were exhibited had more skill in pomps or processions than in poetical language, and perhaps wanted some visible and discriminated events, as comments on the dialogue. He knew how he should most please; and whether his practice is more agreeable to nature, or whether his example has prejudiced the nation, we still find that on our stage something must be done as well as said, and inactive declamation is very coldly heard, however musical or elegant, passionate or sublime. . . .

KING LEAR

The Tragedy of *Lear* is deservedly celebrated among the dramas of Shakespeare. There is perhaps no play which keeps the attention so strongly fixed; which so much agitates our passions and interests our curiosity. The artful involutions of distinct interests, the striking opposition of contrary characters, the sudden changes of fortune, and the quick succession of events, fill the mind with a perpetual tumult of indignation, pity, and hope. There is no scene which does not contribute to the aggravation of the distress or conduct of the action, and scarce a line which does not conduce to the progress of the scene. So powerful is the current of the poet's imagination, that the mind, which once ventures within it, is hurried irresistibly along.

On the seeming improbability of Lear's conduct, it may be observed that he is represented according to histories at that time vulgarly received as true. And perhaps if we turn our thoughts upon the barbarity and ignorance of the age to which this story is referred, it will appear not so unlikely as while we estimate Lear's manners by our own. Such preference of one daughter to another, or resignation of dominion on such conditions, would be yet credible, if told of a petty prince of Guinea or Madagascar. Shakespeare, indeed, by the mention of his Earls and Dukes, has given us the idea of times more civilized, and of life regulated by softer manners; and the truth is, that though he so nicely discriminates, and so minutely describes the characters of men, he commonly neglects and confounds the characters of ages, by mingling customs ancient and modern, English and foreign.

My learned friend Mr. Warton, who has in the *Adventurer* very minutely criticized this play, remarks, that the instances of cruelty are too savage and shocking, and that the intervention of Edmund destroys the simplicity of the story. These objections may, I think, be answered, by repeating, that the cruelty of the daughters is an historical fact, to which the poet has added little, having only drawn it into a series by dialogue and action. But I am not able to apologize with equal plausibility for the extrusion of Gloucester's eyes, which seems an act too horrid to be endured in dramatic exhibition, and such as must always compel the mind to relieve its distress by incredulity. Yet let it be remembered that our author well knew what would please the audience for which he wrote.

The injury done by Edmund to the simplicity of the action is abundantly recompensed by the addition of variety, by the art with which he is made to cooperate with the chief design, and the opportunity which he gives the poet of combining perfidy with perfidy, and connecting the wicked son with the wicked daughters, to impress this important moral, that villainy is never at a stop, that crimes lead to crimes, and at last terminate in ruin.

But though this moral be incidentally enforced, Shakespeare has suffered the virtue of Cordelia to perish in a just cause, contrary to the natural ideas of justice, to the hope of the reader, and, what is yet more strange, to the faith of chronicles. Yet this conduct is justified by the Spectator, who blames Tate for giving Cordelia success and happiness in his alteration, and declares, that, in his opinion, *the tragedy has lost half its beauty*. Dennis has remarked, whether justly or not, that, to secure the favorable reception of *Cato, the town was poisoned with much false and abominable criticism,* and that endeavors had been used to discredit and decry poetical justice. A play in which the wicked prosper, and the virtuous miscarry, may doubtless be good, because it is a just representation of the common events of human life: but since all reasonable beings naturally love justice, I cannot easily be persuaded, that the observation of justice makes a play worse; or, that if other excellencies are equal, the audience will not always rise better pleased from the final triumph of persecuted virtue.

In the present case the public has decided. Cordelia, from the time of Tate, has always retired with victory and felicity. And, if my sensations could add anything to the general suffrage, I might relate, that I was many years ago shocked by Cordelia's death, that I know not whether I ever endured to read again the last scenes of the play till I undertook to revise them as an editor.

A. C. Bradley

From *Shakespearean Tragedy*

. . . [The] chief value [of the double action in *King Lear*] is not merely dramatic. It lies in the fact—in Shakespeare without a parallel—that the subplot simply repeats the theme of the main story. Here, as there, we see an old man "with a white beard." He, like Lear, is affectionate, unsuspicious, foolish, and self-willed. He, too, wrongs deeply a child who loves him not less for the wrong. He, too, meets with monstrous ingratitude from the child whom he favors, and is tortured and driven to death. This repetition does not simply double the pain with which the tragedy is witnessed: it startles and terrifies by suggesting that the folly of Lear and the ingratitude of his daughters are no accidents or merely individual aberrations, but that in that dark cold world some fateful malignant influence is abroad, turning the hearts of the fathers against their children and of the children against their fathers, smiting the earth with a curse, so that the brother gives the brother to death and the father the son, blinding the eyes, maddening the brain, freezing the springs of pity, numbing all powers except the nerves of anguish and the dull lust of life.

Hence too, as well as from other sources, comes that feeling which haunts us in *King Lear,* as though we

From *Shakespearean Tragedy* by A. C. Bradley. London: Macmillan & Co., Ltd., 1904. Reprinted by permission of Macmillan & Co., Ltd. (London), St Martin's Press, Inc. (New York), and the Macmillan Company of Canada, Ltd.

were witnessing something universal—a conflict not so much of particular persons as of the powers of good and evil in the world. And the treatment of many of the characters confirms this feeling. Considered simply as psychological studies few of them, surely, are of the highest interest. Fine and subtle touches could not be absent from a work of Shakespeare's maturity; but, with the possible exception of Lear himself, no one of the characters strikes us as psychologically a *wonderful* creation, like Hamlet or Iago or even Macbeth; one or two seem even to be somewhat faint and thin. And, what is more significant, it is not quite natural to us to regard them from this point of view at all. Rather we observe a most unusual circumstance. If Lear, Gloster and Albany are set apart, the rest fall into two distinct groups, which are strongly, even violently, contrasted: Cordelia, Kent, Edgar, the Fool on one side, Goneril, Regan, Edmund, Cornwall, Oswald on the other. These characters are in various degrees individualized, most of them completely so; but still in each group there is a quality common to all the members, or one spirit breathing through them all. Here we have unselfish and devoted love, there hard self-seeking. On both sides, further, the common quality takes an extreme form; the love is incapable of being chilled by injury, the selfishness of being softened by pity; and, it may be added, this tendency to extremes is found again in the characters of Lear and Gloster, and is the main source of the accusations of improbability directed against their conduct at certain points. Hence the members of each group tend to appear, at least in part, as varieties of one species; the radical differences of the two species are emphasized in broad hard strokes; and the two are set in conflict, almost as if Shakespeare, like Empedocles, were regarding Love and Hate as the two ultimate forces of the universe.

The presence in *King Lear* of so large a number of characters in whom love or self-seeking is so extreme, has another effect. They do not merely inspire in us emotions of unusual strength, but they also stir the intellect to wonder and speculation. How can there be such men and women? we ask ourselves. How comes it that humanity can take such absolutely opposite forms? And, in particular, to what omission of elements which should be present in human nature, or, if there is no omission, to what distortion of these elements is it due that such beings as some of these come to exist? This is a question which Iago (and perhaps no previous creation of Shakespeare's) forces us to ask, but in *King Lear* it is provoked again and again. And more, it seems to us that the author himself is asking this question: "Then let them anatomize Regan, see what breeds about her heart. Is there any cause in nature that makes these hard hearts?" —the strain of thought which appears here seems to be present in some degree throughout the play. We seem to trace the tendency which, a few years later, produced Ariel and Caliban, the tendency of imagination to analyze and abstract, to decompose human nature into its constituent factors, and then to construct beings in whom one or more of these factors is absent or atrophied or only incipient. This, of course, is a tendency which produces symbols, allegories, personifications of qualities and abstract ideas; and we are accustomed to think it quite foreign to Shakespeare's genius, which was in the highest degree concrete. No doubt in the main we are right here; but it is hazardous to set limits to that genius. The Sonnets, if nothing else, may show us how easy it was to Shakespeare's mind to move in a world of "Platonic" ideas; and, while it would be going too far to suggest that he was employing conscious symbolism or allegory in *King Lear,* it does appear to disclose a mode of imagination not so very far removed from the mode with which, we must remember, Shakespeare was perfectly familiar in Morality plays and in the *Fairy Queen.*

This same tendency shows itself in *King Lear* in other forms. To it is due the idea of monstrosity—of beings, actions, states of mind, which appear not only abnormal but absolutely contrary to nature; an idea, which, of course, is common enough in Shakespeare, but appears with unusual frequency in *King Lear,* for instance in the lines:

> Ingratitude, thou marble-hearted fiend,
> More hideous when thou show'st thee in a child
> Than the sea-monster!

or in the exclamation,

>   Filial ingratitude!
> Is it not as this mouth should tear this hand
> For lifting food to't?

It appears in another shape in that most vivid passage where Albany, as he looks at the face which had be-witched him, now distorted with dreadful passions, sud-denly sees it in a new light and exclaims in horror:

> Thou changed and self-cover'd thing, for shame,
> Bemonster not thy feature. Were't my fitness
> To let these hands obey my blood,
> They are apt enough to dislocate and tear
> Thy flesh and bones: howe'er thou art a fiend,
> A woman's shape doth shield thee.

It appears once more in that exclamation of Kent's, as he listens to the description of Cordelia's grief:

>   It is the stars,
> The stars above us, govern our conditions;
> Else one self mate and mate could not beget
> Such different issues.

(This is not the only sign that Shakespeare had been musing over heredity, and wondering how it comes about that the composition of two strains of blood or two parent souls can produce such astonishingly different products.)

This mode of thought is responsible, lastly, for a very striking characteristic of *King Lear*—one in which it has no parallel except *Timon*—the incessant references to the

lower animals and man's likeness to them. These references are scattered broadcast through the whole play
as though Shakespeare's mind were so busy with the
subject that he could hardly write a page without some
allusion to it. The dog, the horse, the cow, the sheep, the
hog, the lion, the bear, the wolf, the fox, the monkey,
the polecat, the civet cat, the pelican, the owl, the crow,
the chough, the wren, the fly, the butterfly, the rat, the
mouse, the frog, the tadpole, the wall newt, the water
newt, the worm—I am sure I cannot have completed the
list, and some of them are mentioned again and again.
Often, of course, and especially in the talk of Edgar as
the Bedlam, they have no symbolical meaning; but not seldom, even in his talk, they are expressly referred to for
their typical qualities—"hog in sloth, fox in stealth, wolf
in greediness, dog in madness, lion in prey," "The fitchew
nor the soiled horse goes to't with a more riotous appetite." Sometimes a person in the drama is compared,
openly or implicitly, with one of them. Goneril is a kite:
her ingratitude has a serpent's tooth: she has struck her
father most serpentlike upon the very heart: her visage
is wolfish: she has tied sharp-toothed unkindness like a
vulture on her father's breast: for her husband she is a
gilded serpent: to Gloster her cruelty seems to have the
fangs of a boar. She and Regan are dog-hearted: they
are tigers, not daughters: each is an adder to the other:
the flesh of each is covered with the fell of a beast.
Oswald is a mongrel, and the son and heir of a mongrel: ducking to everyone in power, he is a wag-tail:
white with fear, he is a goose. Gloster, for Regan, is an
ingrateful fox: Albany, for his wife, has a cowish spirit
and is milk-liver'd: when Edgar as the Bedlam first appeared to Lear he made him think a man a worm. As
we read, the souls of all the beasts in turn seem to us
to have entered the bodies of these mortals; horrible in
their venom, savagery, lust, deceitfulness, sloth, cruelty,
filthiness; miserable in their feebleness, nakedness, defenselessness, blindness; and man, "consider him well,"
is even what they are. Shakespeare, to whom the idea of
the transmigration of souls was familiar and had once

been material for jest,[1] seems to have been brooding on humanity, in the light of it. It is remarkable, and somewhat sad, that he seems to find none of man's better qualities in the world of the brutes (though he might well have found the prototype of the selfless love of Kent and Cordelia in the dog whom he so habitually maligns); but he seems to have been asking himself whether that which he loathes in man may not be due to some strange wrenching of this frame of things, through which the lower animal souls have found a lodgment in human forms, and there found—to the horror and confusion of the thinking mind—brains to forge, tongues to speak, and hands to act, enormities which no mere brute can conceive or execute. He shows us in *King Lear* these terrible forces bursting into monstrous life and flinging themselves upon those human beings who are weak and defenseless, partly from old age, but partly because they *are* human and lack the dreadful undivided energy of the beast. And the only comfort he might seem to hold out to us is the prospect that at least this bestial race, strong only where it is vile, cannot endure: though stars and gods are powerless, or careless, or empty dreams, yet there must be an end of this horrible world:

[1] *E.g.* in *As You Like It*, III. ii. 187, "I was never so berhymed since Pythagoras' time, that I was an Irish rat, which I can hardly remember"; *Twelfth Night*, IV. ii. 55, "*Clown*. What is the opinion of Pythagoras concerning wild fowl? *Mal*. That the soul of our grandam might haply inhabit a bird. *Clown*. What thinkest thou of his opinion? *Mal*. I think nobly of the soul, and no way approve his opinion," etc. But earlier comes a passage which reminds us of *King Lear*, *Merchant of Venice*, IV. i. 128:

> O be thou damn'd, inexecrable dog!
> And for thy life let justice be accused.
> Thou almost makest me waver in my faith
> To hold opinion with Pythagoras,
> That souls of animals infuse themselves
> Into the trunks of men: thy currish spirit
> Govern'd a wolf, who, hang'd for human slaughter,
> Even from the gallows did his fell soul fleet,
> And, whilst thou lay'st in thy unhallow'd dam,
> Infused itself in thee; for thy desires
> Are wolvish, bloody, starv'd and ravenous.

It will come;
Humanity must perforce prey on itself
Like monsters of the deep.

The influence of all this on imagination as we read *King Lear* is very great; and it combines with other influences to convey to us, not in the form of distinct ideas but in the manner proper to poetry, the wider or universal significance of the spectacle presented to the inward eye. But the effect of theatrical exhibition is precisely the reverse. There the poetic atmosphere is dissipated; the meaning of the very words which create it passes half-realized; in obedience to the tyranny of the eye we conceive the characters as mere particular men and women; and all that mass of vague suggestion, if it enters the mind at all, appears in the shape of an allegory which we immediately reject. A similar conflict between imagination and sense will be found if we consider the dramatic center of the whole tragedy, the Storm-scenes. The temptation of Othello and the scene of Duncan's murder may lose upon the stage, but they do not lose their essence, and they gain as well as lose. The Storm-scenes in *King Lear* gain nothing and their very essence is destroyed. It is comparatively a small thing that the theatrical storm, not to drown the dialogue, must be silent whenever a human being wishes to speak, and is wretchedly inferior to many a storm we have witnessed. Nor is it simply that, as Lamb observed, the corporal presence of Lear, "an old man tottering about the stage with a walking-stick," disturbs and depresses that sense of the greatness of his mind which fills the imagination. There is a further reason, which is not expressed, but still emerges, in these words of Lamb's: "the explosions of his passion are terrible as a volcano: they are storms turning up and disclosing to the bottom that sea, his mind, with all its vast riches." Yes, "they are *storms*." For imagination, that is to say, the explosions of Lear's passion, and the bursts of rain and thunder, are not, what for the senses they must be, two things, but manifestations of one thing. It is the powers of the tormented

soul that we hear and see in the "groans of roaring wind
and rain" and the "sheets of fire"; and they that, at intervals almost more overwhelming, sink back into darkness and silence. Nor yet is even this all; but, as those
incessant references to wolf and tiger made us see humanity "reeling back into the beast" and ravening against
itself, so in the storm we seem to see Nature herself
convulsed by the same horrible passions; the "common
mother,"

> Whose womb immeasurable and infinite breast
> Teems and feeds all,

turning on her children, to complete the ruin they have
wrought upon themselves. Surely something not less, but
much more, than these helpless words convey, is what
comes to us in these astounding scenes; and if, translated thus into the language of prose, it becomes confused and inconsistent, the reason is simply that it itself
is poetry, and such poetry as cannot be transferred to the
space behind the footlights, but has its being only in
imagination. Here then is Shakespeare at his very greatest, but not the mere dramatist Shakespeare.

And now we may say this also of the catastrophe,
which we found questionable from the strictly dramatic
point of view. Its purpose is not merely dramatic. This
sudden blow out of the darkness, which seems so far
from inevitable, and which strikes down our reviving
hopes for the victims of so much cruelty, seems now
only what we might have expected in a world so wild
and monstrous. It is as if Shakespeare said to us: "Did
you think weakness and innocence have any chance
here? Were you beginning to dream that? I will show you
it is not so."

I come to a last point. As we contemplate this world,
the question presses on us, What can be the ultimate
power that moves it, that excites this gigantic war and
waste, or, perhaps, that suffers them and overrules them?
And in *King Lear* this question is not left to *us* to ask,
it is raised by the characters themselves. References to

religious or irreligious beliefs and feelings are more frequent than is usual in Shakespeare's tragedies, as frequent perhaps as in his final plays. He introduces characteristic differences in the language of the different persons about fortune or the stars or the gods, and shows how the question, What rules the world? is forced upon their minds. They answer it in their turn: Kent, for instance:

> It is the stars,
> The stars above us, govern our condition:

Edmund:

> Thou, nature, art my goddess; to thy law
> My services are bound:

and again,

> This is the excellent foppery of the world, that, when we are sick in fortune—often the surfeit of our own behavior—we make guilty of our disasters the sun, the moon and the stars; as if we were villains by necessity, fools by heavenly compulsion, . . . and all that we are evil in by a divine thrusting on:

Gloster:

> As flies to wanton boys are we to the gods;
> They kill us for their sport;

Edgar:

> Think that the clearest gods, who make them honours
> Of men's impossibilities, have preserved thee.

Here we have four distinct theories of the nature of the ruling power. And besides this, in such of the characters as have any belief in gods who love good and hate evil, the spectacle of triumphant injustice or cruelty provokes questionings like those of Job, or else the thought, often repeated, of divine retribution. To Lear at one moment the storm seems the messenger of heaven:

> Let the great gods,
> That keep this dreadful pother o'er our heads,
> Find out their enemies now. Tremble, thou wretch,
> That hast within thee undivulged crimes. . . .

At another moment those habitual miseries of the poor,
of which he has taken too little account, seem to him to
accuse the gods of injustice:

> Take physic, pomp;
> Expose thyself to feel what wretches feel,
> That thou mayst shake the superflux to them
> And show the heavens more just;

and Gloster has almost the same thought (IV. i. 67 ff.).
Gloster again, thinking of the cruelty of Lear's daughters,
breaks out,

> but I shall see
> The winged vengeance overtake such children.

The servants who have witnessed the blinding of Gloster
by Cornwall and Regan, cannot believe that cruelty so
atrocious will pass unpunished. One cries,

> I'll never care what wickedness I do,
> If this man come to good;

and another,

> if she live long,
> And in the end meet the old course of death,
> Women will all turn monsters.

Albany greets the news of Cornwall's death with the
exclamation,

> This shows you are above,
> You justicers, that these our nether crimes
> So speedily can venge;

and the news of the deaths of the sisters with the words,

> This judgment of the heavens, that makes us tremble,
> Touches us not with pity.

Edgar, speaking to Edmund of their father, declares

> The gods are just, and of our pleasant vices
> Make instruments to plague us,

and Edmund himself assents. Almost throughout the latter half of the drama we note in most of the better characters a preoccupation with the question of the ultimate power, and a passionate need to explain by reference to it what otherwise would drive them to despair. And the influence of this preoccupation and need joins with other influences in affecting the imagination, and in causing it to receive from *King Lear* an impression which is at least as near of kin to the *Divine Comedy* as to *Othello*.

For Dante that which is recorded in the *Divine Comedy* was the justice and love of God. What did *King Lear* record for Shakespeare? Something, it would seem, very different. This is certainly the most terrible picture that Shakespeare painted of the world. In no other of his tragedies does humanity appear more pitiably infirm or more hopelessly bad. What is Iago's malignity against an envied stranger compared with the cruelty of the son of Gloster and the daughters of Lear? What are the sufferings of a strong man like Othello to those of helpless age? Much too that we have already observed—the repetition of the main theme in that of the underplot, the comparisons of man with the most wretched and the most horrible of the beasts, the impression of Nature's hostility to him, the irony of the unexpected catastrophe—these, with much else, seem even to indicate an intention to show things at their worst, and to return the sternest of replies to that question of the ultimate power and those appeals for retribution. Is it an accident, for example, that Lear's first appeal to something beyond the earth,

> O heavens,
> If you do love old men, if your sweet sway
> Allow obedience, if yourselves are old,
> Make it your cause:

is immediately answered by the iron voices of his daughters, raising by turns the conditions on which they will give him a humiliating harborage; or that his second appeal, heart-rending in its piteousness,

> You see me here, you gods, a poor old man,
> As full of grief as age; wretched in both:

is immediately answered from the heavens by the sound of the breaking storm? Albany and Edgar may moralize on the divine justice as they will, but how, in the face of all that we see, shall we believe that they speak Shakespeare's mind? Is not his mind rather expressed in the bitter contrast between their faith and the events we witness, or in the scornful rebuke of those who take upon them the mystery of things as if they were God's spies? Is it not Shakespeare's judgment on his kind that we hear in Lear's appeal,

> And thou, all-shaking thunder,
> Smite flat the thick rotundity o' the world!
> Crack nature's moulds, all germens spill at once,
> That make ingrateful man!

and Shakespeare's judgment on the worth of existence that we hear in Lear's agonized cry, "No, no, no life!"?

Beyond doubt, I think, some such feelings as these possess us, and, if we follow Shakespeare, ought to possess us, from time to time as we read *King Lear*. And some readers will go further and maintain that this is also the ultimate and total impression left by the tragedy. *King Lear* has been held to be profoundly "pessimistic" in the full meaning of that word—the record of a time when contempt and loathing for his kind had overmastered the poet's soul, and in despair he pronounced man's life to be simply hateful and hideous. And if we exclude the biographical part of this view, the rest may claim some support even from the greatest of Shakespearean critics since the days of Coleridge, Hazlitt and Lamb. Mr. Swinburne, after observing that *King Lear* is "by far the most Aeschylean" of Shakespeare's works, proceeds thus:

"But in one main point it differs radically from the work and the spirit of Aeschylus. Its fatalism is of a darker and harder nature. To Prometheus the fetters of the lord and enemy of mankind were bitter; upon Orestes the hand of heaven was laid too heavily to bear; yet in the not utterly infinite or everlasting distance we see beyond them the promise of the morning on which mystery and justice shall be made one; when righteousness and omnipotence at last shall kiss each other. But on the horizon of Shakespeare's tragic fatalism we see no such twilight of atonement, such pledge of reconciliation as this. Requital, redemption, amends, equity, explanation, pity and mercy, are words without a meaning here.

> As flies to wanton boys are we to the gods;
> They kill us for their sport.

Here is no need of the Eumenides, children of Night everlasting; for here is very Night herself.

"The words just cited are not casual or episodical; they strike the keynote of the whole poem, lay the keystone of the whole arch of thought. There is no contest of conflicting forces, no judgment so much as by casting of lots: far less is there any light of heavenly harmony or of heavenly wisdom, of Apollo or Athene from above. We have heard much and often from theologians of the light of revelation: and some such thing indeed we find in Aeschylus; but the darkness of revelation is here." [2]

2 *A Study of Shakespeare,* (1880) pp. 171, 172.

It is hard to refuse assent to these eloquent words, for they express in the language of a poet what we feel at times in reading *King Lear* but cannot express. But do they represent the total and final impression produced by the play? If they do, this impression, so far as the substance of the drama is concerned (and nothing else is in question here), must, it would seem, be one composed almost wholly of painful feelings—utter depression, or indignant rebellion, or appalled despair. And that would surely be strange. For *King Lear* is admittedly one of the world's greatest poems, and yet there is surely no other of these poems which produces on the whole this effect, and we regard it as a very serious flaw in any considerable work of art that this should be its ultimate effect. So that Mr. Swinburne's description, if taken as final, and any description of *King Lear* as "pessimistic" in the proper sense of that word, would imply a criticism which is not intended, and which would make it difficult to leave the work in the position almost universally assigned to it.

But in fact these descriptions, like most of the remarks made on *King Lear* in the present lecture, emphasize only certain aspects of the play and certain elements in the total impression; and in that impression the effect of these aspects, though far from being lost, is modified by that of others. I do not mean that the final effect resembles that of the *Divine Comedy* or the *Oresteia*: how should it, when the first of these can be called by its author a "Comedy," and when the second, ending (as doubtless the *Prometheus* trilogy also ended) with a solution, is not in the Shakespearean sense a tragedy at all? Nor do I mean that *King Lear* contains a revelation of righteous omnipotence or heavenly harmony, or even a promise of the reconciliation of mystery and justice. But then, as we saw, neither do Shakespeare's other tragedies contain these things. Any theological interpretation of the world on the author's part is excluded from them, and their effect would be disordered or destroyed equally by the ideas of righteous or of unrighteous omnipotence. Nor, in reading them, do we think of "justice" or "equity" in the sense of a strict requital or such an adjustment of merit and prosperity as our moral sense is said to demand; and there never was vainer labor than that of critics who try to make out that the persons in these dramas meet with "justice" or their "deserts." But, on the other hand, man is not represented in these tragedies as the mere plaything of a blind or capricious power, suffering woes which have no relation to his character and actions; nor is the world represented as given over to darkness. And in these respects *King Lear,* though the most terrible of these works, does not differ in essence from the rest. Its keynote is surely to be heard neither in the words wrung from Gloster in his anguish, nor in Edgar's words "the gods are just." Its final and total result is one in which pity and terror, carried perhaps to the extreme limits of art, are so blended with a sense of law and beauty that we feel at last, not depression and much less despair, but a consciousness of greatness in pain, and of solemnity in the mystery we cannot fathom. . . .

But there is another aspect of Lear's story, the influence of which modifies, in a way quite different and more peculiar to this tragedy, the impressions called pessimistic and even this impression of law. There is nothing more noble and beautiful in literature than Shakespeare's exposition of the effect of suffering in reviving the greatness and eliciting the sweetness of Lear's nature. The occasional recurrence, during his madness, of autocratic impatience or of desire for revenge serves only to heighten this effect, and the moments when his insanity becomes merely infinitely piteous do not weaken it. The old King who in pleading with his daughters feels so intensely his own humiliation and their horrible ingratitude, and who yet, at fourscore and upward, constrains himself to practice a self-control and patience so many years disused; who out of old affection for his Fool, and in repentance for his injustice to the Fool's beloved mistress, tolerates incessant and cutting reminders of his own folly and wrong; in whom the rage of the storm awakes a power and a poetic grandeur surpassing

even that of Othello's anguish; who comes in his affliction
to think of others first, and to seek, in tender solici-
tude for his poor boy, the shelter he scorns for his own
bare head; who learns to feel and to pray for the
miserable and houseless poor, to discern the falseness
of flattery and the brutality of authority, and to pierce
below the differences of rank and raiment to the common humanity beneath; whose sight is so purged by
scalding tears that it sees at last how power and place
and all things in the world are vanity except love; who
tastes in his last hours the extremes both of love's rap-
ture and of its agony, but could never, if he lived on or
lived again, care a jot for aught beside—there is no figure, surely, in the world of poetry at once so grand,
so pathetic, and so beautiful as his. Well, but Lear owes
the whole of this to those sufferings which made us
doubt whether life were not simply evil, and men like the
flies which wanton boys torture for their sport. Should
we not be at least as near the truth if we called this
poem *The Redemption of King Lear,* and declared that the
business of "the gods" with him was neither to torment
him, nor to teach him a "noble anger," but to lead him
to attain through apparently hopeless failure the very
end and aim of life? One can believe that Shakespeare
had been tempted at times to feel misanthropy and
despair, but it is quite impossible that he can have been
mastered by such feelings at the time when he produced this conception. . . .

. . . Lear's insanity, which destroys the coherence, also
reduces the poetry of his imagination. What it stimu-
lates is that power of moral perception and reflection
which had already been quickened by his sufferings. This,
however partial and however disconnectedly used, first
appears, quite soon after the insanity has declared itself,
in the idea that the naked beggar represents truth and
reality, in contrast with those conventions, flatteries, and
corruptions of the great world, by which Lear has so
long been deceived and will never be deceived again. . . .

. . . *King Lear* . . . is the tragedy in which evil is shown
in the greatest abundance; and the evil characters are

peculiarly repellent from their hard savagery, and because so little good is mingled with their evil. The effect is therefore more startling than elsewhere; it is even appalling. But in substance it is the same as elsewhere. . . .

On the one hand we see a world which generates terrible evil in profusion. Further, the beings in whom this evil appears at its strongest are able, to a certain extent, to thrive. They are not unhappy, and they have power to spread misery and destruction around them. All this is undeniable fact.

On the other hand this evil is *merely* destructive: it founds nothing, and seems capable of existing only on foundations laid by its opposite. It is also self-destructive. . . . These . . . are undeniable facts; and, in face of them, it seems odd to describe *King Lear* as "a play in which the wicked prosper" (Johnson).

Thus the world in which evil appears seems to be at heart unfriendly to it. And this impression is confirmed by the fact that the convulsion of this world is due to evil, mainly in the worst forms here considered, partly in the milder forms which we call the errors or defects of the better characters. Good, in the widest sense, seems thus to be the principle of life and health in the world; evil, at least in these worst forms, to be a poison. The world reacts against it violently, and, in the struggle to expel it, is driven to devastate itself.

If we ask why the world should generate that which convulses and wastes it, the tragedy gives no answer, and we are trying to go beyond tragedy in seeking one. But the world, in this tragic picture, *is* convulsed by evil, and rejects it.

. . . I might almost say that the "moral" of *King Lear* is presented in the irony of this collocation:

> *Albany.* The gods defend her!
> *Enter Lear with Cordelia dead in his arms.*

The "gods," it seems, do *not* show their approval by "defending" their own from adversity or death, or by giving them power and prosperity. These, on the contrary, are worthless, or worse; it is not on them, but on the renunciation of them, that the gods throw incense. They breed lust, pride, hardness of heart, the insolence of office, cruelty, scorn, hypocrisy, contention, war, murder, self-destruction. The whole story beats this indictment of prosperity into the brain. Lear's great speeches in his madness proclaim it like the curses of Timon on life and man. But here, as in *Timon,* the poor and humble are, almost without exception, sound and sweet at heart, faithful and pitiful. And here adversity, to the blessed in spirit, is blessed. It wins fragrance from the crushed flower. It melts in aged hearts sympathies which prosperity had frozen. It purges the soul's sight by blinding that of the eyes.[3] Throughout that stupendous Third Act the good are seen growing better through suffering, and the bad worse through success. The warm castle is a room in hell, the storm-swept heath a sanctuary. The judgment of this world is a lie; its goods, which we covet, corrupt us; its ills, which break our bodies, set our souls free;

> Our means secure us, and our mere defects
> Prove our commodities.

Let us renounce the world, hate it, and lose it gladly. The only real thing in it is the soul, with its courage, patience, devotion. And nothing outward can touch that.

This, if we like to use the word, is Shakespeare's "pessimism" in *King Lear*. . . .

---

[3] "I stumbled when I saw," says Gloster.

Harley Granville-Barker

From *Prefaces to Shakespeare*

THE MAIN LINES OF CONSTRUCTION

King Lear, alone among the great tragedies, adds to its plot a subplot fully developed. And it suffers somewhat under the burden. After a few preliminary lines—Shakespeare had come to prefer this to the grand opening, and in this instance they are made introductory to plot and subplot too—we have a full and almost formal statement of the play's main theme and a show of the characters that are to develop it, followed by a scene which sets out the subplot as fully. The two scenes together form a sort of double dramatic prologue; and they might, by modern custom, count as a first act, for after them falls the only clearly indicated time-division in the play. The Folio, however, adds the quarrel with Goneril before an act-pause is allowed: then—whatever its authority, but according to its usual plan—sets out four more acts, the second allotted to the parallel quarrel with Regan, the third to the climax of the main theme; the fourth we may call a picture of the wreck of both Lear and Gloucester, and in it subplot and main plot are blended, and the fifth act is given to the final and rather complex catastrophe. This division, then, has thus much dramatic validity, and a producer may legitimately choose to abide by it. On the other hand, one may contend, the play's action flows unchecked throughout (but for the one check which does not coincide with the .act-division of the Folio). Still it is not to be supposed that a Jacobean

Reprinted from *Prefaces to Shakespeare*, I, by Harley Granville-Barker. Reprinted by permission of Princeton University Press. Copyright 1946 by Princeton University Press.

audience did, or a modern audience would, sit through a performance without pause. Yet again, it does not follow that the Folio's act-divisions were observed as intervals in which the audience dispersed and by which the continuity of dramatic effect was altogether broken. A producer must, I think, exercise his own judgment. There may be something to be said for more "breathing-spaces," but I should myself incline to one definite interval only, to fall after Act III. . . .

The scene in which Lear divides his kingdom is a magnificent statement of a magnificent theme. It has a proper formality, and there is a certain megalithic grandeur about it, Lear dominating it, that we associate with Greek tragedy. Its probabilities are neither here nor there. A dramatist may postulate any situation he has the means to interpret, if he will abide by the logic of it after.[1] The producer should observe and even see stressed the scene's characteristics; Lear's two or three passages of such an eloquence as we rather expect at a play's climax than its opening, the strength of such single lines as

> The bow is bent and drawn, make from the shaft

with its hammering monosyllables; and the hard-bitten

> Nothing: I have sworn; I am firm

together with the loosening of the tension in changes to rhymed couplets, and the final drop into prose by that businesslike couple, Goneril and Regan. Then follows, with a lift into lively verse for a start, as a contrast and as the right medium for Edmund's sanguine conceit, the

---

[1] Later, on p. 313 of his volume, Barker says: "We must not . . . [moreover], appraise either . . . [Gloucester's initial] simplicity or Edgar's . . . with detachment—for by that light, no human being, it would seem, between infancy and dotage, could be so gullible. Shakespeare asks us to allow him the fact of the deception, even as we have allowed him Lear's partition of the kingdom. It is his starting point, the dramatist's let's pretend, which is as essential to the beginning of a play as a "let it be granted" to a proposition of Euclid. And, within bounds, the degree of pretence makes surprisingly little difference. It is what the assumption will commit him to that counts."

development of the Gloucester theme. Shakespeare does this at his ease, allows himself diversion and time. He has now both the plot of the ungrateful daughters and the subplot of the treacherous son under way.

But the phenomenon for which Shakespeareans learn to look has not yet occurred, that inexplicable "springing to life"—a springing, it almost seems, into a life of its own—of character or theme. Very soon it does occur; Lear's entrance, disburdened from the care of state, is its natural signal. On his throne, rightly enough, he showed formal and self-contained. Now he springs away; and now the whole play in its relation to him takes on a liveliness and variety; nor will the energy be checked or weakened, or, if checked, only that the next stroke may be intenser, till the climax is past, till his riven and exhausted nature is granted the oblivion of sleep. This is the master movement of the play, which enshrines the very soul of the play—and in the acting, as I have suggested, there should be no break allowed. To read and give full imaginative value to those fifteen hundred lines at a stretch is certainly exhausting; if they were written at one stretch of inspiration the marvel is that Shakespeare, with his Lear, did not collapse under the strain, yet the exactions of his performance he tempers with all his skill. Lear is surrounded by characters, which each in a different way take a share of the burden from him. Kent, the Fool, and Edgar as Poor Tom are a complement of dramatic strength; and the interweaving of the scenes concerning Oswald, Edmund, and Gloucester saves the actor's energy for the scenes of the rejection and the storm.

As the Lear theme expanded under his hand Shakespeare had begun, and perforce, to economize his treatment of the Gloucester-Edgar-Edmund story. Edgar himself is indeed dismissed from the second scene upon no more allowance of speech than

> I'm sure on't, not a word.

—with which the best of actors may find it hard to make his presence felt; and at our one view of him before he had been left negative enough. Edmund is then brought

rapidly into relation with the main plot, and the blending
of main plot and subplot begins. Edgar also is drawn into
Lear's orbit; and, for the time, to the complete sacrifice
of his own interests in the play. "Poor Tom" is in effect
an embodiment of Lear's frenzy, the disguise no part of
Edgar's own development.

As we have seen, while Act III is at the height of its
argument, Shakespeare is careful to keep alive the lower-
pitched theme of Edmund's treachery, his new turn to
the betrayal of his father. He affords it two scenes, of
twenty-five lines each, wedged between the three dominant scenes of the storm and Lear's refuge from it. They
are sufficient and no more for their own purpose; in their
sordidness they stand as valuable contrast to the spiritual
exaltation of the others. The supreme moment for Lear
himself, the turning point, therefore, of the play's main
theme, is reached in the second of the three storm-scenes,
when the proud old king kneels humbly and alone in his
wretchedness to pray. This is the argument's absolute
height; and from now on we may feel (as far as Lear is
concerned) the tension relax, through the first grim passage of his madness, slackening still through the fantastic
scene of the arraignment of the joint-stools before that
queer bench of justices, to the moment of his falling
asleep and his conveyance away—his conveyance, we find
it to be, out of the main stream of the play's action.
Shakespeare then deals the dreadful blow to Gloucester.
The very violence and horror of this finds its dramatic
justification in the need to match in another sort—
since he could not hope to match it in spiritual inten-
sity—the catastrophe to Lear. And now we may imagine
him, if we please, stopping to consider where he was.
Anticlimax, after this, is all but inevitable. Let the producer take careful note how Shakespeare sets out to avoid
the worst dangers of it.

Had the play been written upon the single subject of
Lear and his daughters, we should now be in sight of its
end. But the wealth of material Shakespeare has posited
asks for use, and his own imagination, we may suppose,

is still teeming. But by the very nature of the material (save Cordelia) left for development the rest of the play must be pitched in a lower key. Shakespeare marshals the action by which the wheel of Gloucester's weakness and Edmund's treachery is brought full circle with extraordinary skill and even more extraordinary economy. Yet for all this, except in a fine flash or two, the thing stays by comparison pedestrian. He is only on the wing again when Lear and Cordelia are his concern; in the scenes of their reconciliation and of the detached tragedy of Lear's death with the dead Cordelia in his arms, as in the still more detached and—as far as the mere march of the action is concerned—wholly unjustifiable scene of Lear mad and fantastically crowned with wild flowers. We must add, though, to the inspired passages the immediately preceding fantasy of Gloucester's imaginary suicide, an apt offset to the realistic horror of his blinding, and occasion for some inimitable verse. The chief fact to face, then, is that for the rest of the play, the best will be incidental and not a necessary part of the story. The producer therefore must give his own best attention to Albany, Goneril, and Regan and their close-packed contests, and to the nice means by which Edgar is shaped into a hero; and in general must see that this purposeful disciplined necessary stuff is given fullness and, as far as may be, spontaneity of life in its interpretation. If he will take care of this the marvelous moments will tend to take care of him.

Shakespeare strengthens the action at once with the fresh interest of the Edmund-Goneril-Regan intrigue, daring as it is to launch into this with the short time left him for its development and resolving. He is, indeed, driven to heroic compressions, to implications, effects by "business," action "off," almost to "love-making by reference only." Goneril's first approach to Edmund (or his to her; but we may credit the lady, I think, with the throwing of the handkerchief) is only clearly marked out for the actors by Regan's reference to it five scenes later, when she tells us that at Goneril's

> late being here
> She gave strange oeilliads and most speaking looks
> To noble Edmund.

(Regan credits her with what, if we prefer our Shakespeare modernized, we might literally translate into "giving the glad eye.") But this silent business of the earlier
scene is important and must be duly marked if the ar-
rival of the two together and Edmund's turning back to
avoid meeting Albany, the "mild husband," is to
have its full effect. For the first and last of their spoken
love-making, excellently characteristic as it is, consists of
Goneril's

> Our wishes on the way
> May prove effects. . . .
>   This trusty servant
> Shall pass between us: ere long you are like to hear,
> If you dare venture in your own behalf,
> A mistress's command. Wear this; spare speech;
> Decline your head: this kiss, if it durst speak,
> Would stretch thy spirits up into the air.
> Conceive, and fare thee well.

and Edmund's ("Spare speech," indeed!)

> Yours in the ranks of death!

—all spoken in Oswald's presence too. It is, of course, not
only excellent but sufficient. The regal impudency of the
woman, the falsely chivalrous flourish of the man's response—pages of dialogue might not tell us more of their
relations; and, of these relations, is there much more
that is dramatically worth knowing? The point for the
producer is that no jot of such a constricted dramatic opportunity must be missed.

For the whole working-out of this lower issue of the
play the same warning stands true; an exact and un-
blurred value must be given to each significant thing.
The interaction of circumstance and character is close-
knit and complex, but it is clear. Keep it clear and it can
be made effective to any audience that will listen,
and is not distracted from listening. Let us underline this

last phrase and now make the warning twofold. In working out a theme so full of incident and of contending characters Shakespeare allows for no distraction of attention at all, certainly not for the breaking of continuity which the constant shifting of realistically localized scenery must involve. The action, moreover, of these later scenes is exceptionally dependent upon to-ings and fro-ings. Given continuity of performance and no more insistence upon whereabouts than the action itself will indicate, the impression produced by the constant busy movement into our sight and out again of purposeful, passionate or distracted figures, is in itself of great dramatic value, and most congruous to the plot and counterplot of the play's ending. The order for Lear's and Cordelia's murder, the quarrel over Edmund's precedence, Albany's sudden self-assertion, Regan's sickness, Edgar's appearance, the fight, his discovery of himself, Goneril's discomfiture, the telling of Kent's secret, Regan's and Goneril's death, the alarm to save Lear and Cordelia—Shakespeare, by the Folio text, gets all this into less than two hundred lines, with a fair amount of rhetoric and incidental narrative besides. He needs no more, though bareness does nearly turn to banality sometimes. But unless we can be held in an unrelaxed grip we may not submit to the spell.

He has kept a technical master stroke for his ending:

Enter Lear with Cordelia in his arms.

There should be a long, still pause, while Lear passes slowly in with his burden, while they all stand respectful as of old to his majesty. We may have wondered a little that Shakespeare should be content to let Cordelia pass from the play as casually as she seems to in the earlier scene. But this is the last of her, not that. Dumb and dead, she that was never apt of speech—what fitter finish for her could there be? What fitter ending to the history of the two of them, which began for us with Lear on his throne, conscious of all eyes on him, while she shamed and angered him by her silence? The same company are here, or all but the same, and they await his pleasure. Even Regan and Goneril are here to pay him a ghastly homage. But he knows none of them—save for a blurred moment Kent whom he banished—none but Cordelia. And again he reproaches her silence; for

> Her voice was ever soft,
> Gentle and low, an excellent thing in woman.

Then his heart breaks. . . .

THE CHARACTERS AND THEIR INTERPLAY
LEAR

But it is upon Lear's own progress that all now centers, upon his passing from that royal defiance of the storm to the welcomed shelter of the hovel. He passes by the road of patience:

> No, I will be the pattern of all patience;
> I will say nothing,

of—be it noted—a thankfulness that he is at last simply

> a man
> More sinn'd against than sinning . . .

to the humility of

> My wits begin to turn.
> Come on, my boy. How dost, my boy? Art cold?
> I am cold myself. Where is this straw, my fellow?
> The art of our necessities is strange
> That can make vile things precious. Come, your
>   hovel . . .

and, a little later yet, mind and body still further strained towards breaking point, to the gentle dignity, when Kent would make way for him—to the more than kingly dignity of

> Prithee, go in thyself: seek thine own ease.
> This tempest will not give me leave to ponder
> On things would hurt me more. But I'll go in:
> In, boy; go first.

Now comes the crowning touch of all:

> I'll pray, and then I'll sleep.

In the night's bleak exposure he kneels down, like a child at bedtime, to pray.

> Poor naked wretches, wheresoe'er you are,
> That bide the pelting of this pitiless storm,
> How shall your houseless heads and unfed sides,
> Your loop'd and window'd raggedness, defend you
> From seasons such as these? O, I have ta'en
> Too little care of this! Take physic, pomp;
> Expose thyself to feel what wretches feel,
> That thou mayst shake the superflux to them,
> And show the heavens more just.

To this heaven of the spirit has he come, the Lear of unbridled power and pride. And how many dramatists, could they have achieved so much, would have been content to leave him here! Those who like their drama rounded and trim might approve of such a finish, which would leave us a play more compassable in performance no doubt. But the wind of a harsher doctrine is blowing through Shakespeare. Criticism, as we have seen, is apt to fix upon the episode of the storm as the height of his attempt and the point of his dramatic defeat; but it is this storm of the mind here beginning upon which he expends skill and imagination most recklessly till inspiration has had its will of him; and the drama of desperate vision ensuing it is hard indeed for actors to reduce to the positive medium of their art—without reducing it to ridicule. The three coming scenes of Lear's madness show us Shakespeare's art at its boldest. They pass beyond the needs of the plot, they belong to a larger synthesis. Yet the means they employ are simple enough; of a kind of absolute simplicity, indeed.

The boldest and simplest is the provision of Poor Tom, that living instance of all rejection. Here, under our eyes, is Lear's new vision of himself.

What! have his daughters brought him to this pass?
Could'st thou save nothing? Did'st thou give them all?

Side by side stand the noble old man, and the naked,
scarce human wretch.

Is man no more than this? Consider him well. Thou
owest the worm no silk, the beast no hide, the sheep
no wool, the cat no perfume. Ha! here's three on's
are sophisticated; thou art the thing itself; unaccommodated man is no more but such a poor, bare,
forked animal as thou art. Off, off, you lendings!
Come; unbutton here.

Here is a volume of argument epitomized as only drama
can epitomize it, flashed on us by word and action combined. And into this, one might add, has Shakespeare
metamorphosed the didactics of those old Moralities
which were the infancy of his art.

What! hath your grace no better company?

gasps poor Gloucester, bewailing at once the King's
wrongs and his own, as he offers shelter from the storm.
But Lear, calmness itself now, will only pace up and
down, arm in arm with this refuse of humanity:—nor
will he seek shelter without him. So they reach the outhouse, all of his own castle that Gloucester dare offer.
What a group! Kent, sturdy and thrifty of words; Gloucester, tremulous; the bedraggled and exhausted Fool;
and Lear, magnificently courteous and deliberate, keeping
close company with his gibbering fellow-man.

They are in shelter. Lear is silent; till the Fool—himself never overfitted, we may suppose, in body or mind for
the rough and tumble of the world—rallies, as if to cele-
brate their safety, to a semblance of his old task. Edgar,
for his own safety's sake, must play Poor Tom to the
life now. Kent has his eyes on his master, watching him
—at what new fantastic trick? The old king is setting two
joint-stools side by side; they are Regan and Goneril, and
the Fool and the beggar are to pass judgment upon them.

The lunatic mummery of the trial comes near to something we might call pure drama—as one speaks of pure mathematics or pure music—since it cannot be rendered into other terms than its own. Its effect depends upon the combination of the sound and meaning of the words and the sight of it being brought to bear as a whole directly upon our sensibility. The sound of the dialogue matters almost more than its meaning. Poor Tom and the Fool chant antiphonally; Kent's deep and kindly tones tell against the higher, agonized, weakening voice of Lear. But the chief significance is in the show. Where Lear, such a short while since, sat in his majesty, there sit the Fool and the outcast, with Kent whom he banished beside them; and he, witless, musters his failing strength to beg justice upon a joint-stool. Was better justice done, the picture ironically asks, when he presided in majesty and sanity and power?

But what, as far as Lear is concerned, is to follow? You cannot continue the development of a character in terms of lunacy—in darkness, illuminated by whatever brilliant flashes of lightning. Nor can a madman well dominate a play's action. From this moment Lear no longer is a motive force; and the needs of the story— the absolute needs of the character—would be fulfilled if, from this exhausted sleep upon the poor bed in the outhouse, he only woke to find Cordelia at his side. But Shakespeare contrives another scene of madness for him, and one which lifts the play's argument to a yet rarer height. It is delayed; and the sense of redundancy is avoided partly by keeping Lear from the stage altogether for a while, a short scene interposed sufficiently reminding us of him.

His reappearance is preluded—with what consonance! —by the fantastically imaginative episode of Gloucester's fall from the cliff. There also is Edgar, the aura of Poor Tom about him still. Suddenly Lear breaks in upon them. The larger dramatic value of the ensuing scene can hardly be overrated. For in it, in this encounter between mad Lear and blind Gloucester, the sensual man robbed of his eyes, and the despot, the light of his mind put out, Shakespeare's sublimation of the two old stories is consummated. No moral is preached to us. It is presented as it was when king and beggar fraternized in the storm and beggar and Fool were set on the bench of justice, and we are primarily to feel the significance. Yet this does not lack interpretation; less explicit than when Lear, still sane, could read the lesson of the storm, clearer than was the commentary on the mock trial. It is Edgar here that sets us an example of sympathetic listening. His asides enforce it, and the last one:

> O! matter and impertinency mixed,
> Reason in madness!

will reproach us if we have not understood. The train of fancies fired by the first sight of Gloucester, with its tragically comic

> Ha! Goneril with a white beard!

(Goneril, disguised, pursuing him still!) asks little gloss.

> They flattered me like a dog. . . . To say 'Ay' and 'No' to everything I said! . . . When the rain came to wet me once and the wind to make me chatter, when the thunder would not peace at my bidding, there I found 'em, there I smelt 'em out. Go to, they are not men o' their words; they told me I was everything; 'tis a lie, I am not ague-proof.

Gloucester's dutiful

> Is't not the king?

begins to transform him in those mad eyes. And madness sees a Gloucester there that sanity had known and ignored.

> I pardon that man's life: What was thy cause?
> Adultery?
> Thou shalt not die: die for adultery! No:
> The wren goes to't, and the small gilded fly

Does lecher in my sight.
Let copulation thrive; for Gloucester's bastard son
Was kinder to his father than my daughters
Got 'tween the lawful sheets.

Gloucester knows better; but how protest so to the mere erratic voice? Besides which there is only the kindly stranger-peasant near. A slight unconscious turn of the sightless eyes toward him, a simple gesture—unseen—in response from Edgar, patiently biding his time, will illuminate the irony and the pathos.

Does the mad mind pass logically from this to some uncanny prevision of the ripening of new evil in Regan and Goneril? Had it in its sanity secretly surmised what lay beneath the moral surface of their lives, so ready to emerge?

Behold yon simpering dame
Whose face between her forks presageth snow;
That minces virtue and does shake the head
To hear of pleasure's name;
The fitchew, nor the soiled horse, goes to't
With a more riotous appetite.

But a man—so lunatic logic runs—must free himself from the tyrannies of the flesh if he is to see the world clearly:

Give me an ounce of civet, good apothecary, to sweeten my imagination.

And then a blind man may see the truth of it, so he tells the ruined Gloucester:

Look with thine ears: see how yond justice rails upon yond simple thief. Hark in thine ear: change places, and, handy-dandy, which is the justice, which is the thief? Thou hast seen a farmer's dog bark at a beggar? . . . And the creature run from the cur? There thou might'st behold the great image of authority; a dog's obeyed in office.

It is the picture of the mock trial given words. But with a difference! There is no cry now for vengeance on the wicked. For what are we that we should smite them?

> Thou rascal beadle, hold thy bloody hand!
> Why dost thou lash that whore? Strip thine own back;
> That hotly lust'st to use her in that kind
> For which thou whip'st her. The usurer hangs the
>   cozener.
> Through tattered clothes small vices do appear;
> Robes and furr'd gowns hide all. Plate sin with gold,
> And the strong lance of justice hurtless breaks;
> Arm it in rags, a pigmy's straw doth pierce it.

Shakespeare has led Lear to compassion for sin as well as suffering, has led him mad to where he could not hope to lead him sane—to where sound common sense will hardly let us follow him:

> None does offend, none, I say, none.

To a deep compassion for mankind itself.

> I know thee well enough; thy name is Gloucester;
> Thou must be patient; we came crying hither:
> Thou know'st the first time that we smell the air
> We wawl and cry. I will preach to thee: mark. . . .
> When we are born, we cry that we are come
> To this great stage of fools.

This afterpart of Lear's madness may be redundant, then, to the strict action of the play, but to its larger issues it is most germane. It is perhaps no part of the play that Shakespeare set out to write. The play that he found himself writing would be how much the poorer without it!

The simple perfection of the scene that restores Lear to Cordelia one can leave unsullied by comment. What need of any? Let the producer only note that there is reason in the Folio's stage direction:

> *Enter Lear in a chair carried by servants.*

For when he comes to himself it is to find that he is royally attired and as if seated on his throne again. It is from this throne that he totters to kneel at Cordelia's feet. Note, too, the pain of his response to Kent's

> In your own kingdom, sir.
> Do not abuse me.

Finally, Lear must pass from the scene with all the ceremony due to royalty; not mothered—please!—by Cordelia.

Cordelia found again and again lost, what is left for Lear but to die? But for her loss, however, his own death might seem to us an arbitrary stroke; since the old Lear, we may say, is already dead. Shakespeare, moreover, has transported him beyond all worldly issues. This is, perhaps, why the action of the battle which will seemingly defeat his fortunes is minimized. What does defeat matter to him—or even victory? It is certainly the key to the meaning of the scene which follows. Cordelia, who would "out-frown false fortune's frown," is ready to face her sisters and to shame them—were there a chance of it!—with the sight of her father's wrongs. But Lear himself has no interest in anything of the sort.

> No, no, no, no! Come, let's away to prison.
> We two alone will sing like birds i' the cage:
> When thou dost ask me blessing, I'll kneel down,
> And ask of thee forgiveness: so we'll live,
> And pray, and sing, and tell old tales, and laugh
> At gilded butterflies, and hear poor rogues
> Talk of court news. . . .

He has passed beyond care for revenge or success, beyond even the questioning of rights and wrongs. Better indeed to be oppressed, if so you can be safe from contention. Prison will bring him freedom.

> Upon such sacrifices, my Cordelia,
> The gods themselves throw incense. Have I caught
> thee?

He that parts us shall bring a brand from heaven
And fire us hence like foxes. Wipe thine eyes;
The good years shall devour them, flesh and fell,
Ere they shall make us weep: we'll see 'em starve
    first.

Lear's death, upon one ground or another, is artisti-
cally inevitable. Try to imagine his survival; no further
argument will be needed. The death of Cordelia has been
condemned as a wanton outrage upon our feelings and
so as an aesthetic blot upon the play. But the dramatic
mind that was working to the tune of

As flies to wanton boys are we to the gods;
They kill us for their sport,

was not likely to be swayed by sentiment. The tragic
truth about life, to the Shakespeare that wrote *King Lear*,
included its capricious cruelty. And what meeter sacrifice
to this than Cordelia? Besides, as we have seen, he must
provide this new Lear with a tragic determinant, since
"the great rage . . . is kill'd in him," which precipitated
catastrophe for the old Lear. And what but Cordelia's
loss would suffice?

We have already set Lear's last scene in comparison
with his first; it will be worth while to note a little more
particularly the likeness and the difference. The same
commanding figure; he bears the body of Cordelia as
lightly as ever he carried robe, crown and scepter before.
All he has undergone has not so bated his colossal
strength but that he could kill her murderer with his bare
hands.

I kill'd the slave that was a-hanging thee.
'Tis true, my lords, he did,

says the officer in answer to their amazed looks. Albany,
Edgar, Kent and the rest stand silent and intent around
him; Regan and Goneril are there, silent too. He stands,
with the limp body close clasped, glaring blankly at them

for a moment. When speech is torn from him, in place of
the old kingly rhetoric we have only the horrible, half
human

> Howl, howl, howl, howl!

Who these are, for all their dignity and martial splendor,
for all the respect they show him, he neither knows nor
cares. They are men of stone and murderous traitors;
though, after a little, through the mist of his suffering,
comes a word for Kent. All his world, of power and passion and will, and the wider world of thought over which
his mind in its ecstasy had ranged, is narrowed now to
Cordelia; and she is dead in his arms.

Here is the clue to the scene; this terrible concentra-
tion upon the dead, and upon the unconquerable fact of
death. This thing was Cordelia; she was alive, she is
dead. Here is human tragedy brought to its simplest
terms, fit ending to a tragic play that has seemed to out-
leap human experience. From power of intellect and will,
from the imaginative sweep of madness, Shakespeare
brings Lear to this; to no moralizing nor high thoughts,
but just to

> She's gone for ever.
> I know when one is dead and when one lives;
> She's dead as earth. Lend me a looking-glass;
> If that her breath will mist or stain the stone,
> Why, then she lives.

Lacking a glass, he catches at a floating feather. That
stirs on her lips; a last mockery. Kent kneels by him to
share his grief. Then to the bystanders comes the news of
Edmund's death; the business of life goes forward, as it
will, and draws attention from him for a moment. But
what does he heed? When they turn back to him he has
her broken body in his arms again.

Harry Levin

The Heights and the Depths: A Scene from *King Lear*

Speaking of depths and heights, I hope that my title has not provoked a wider curiosity than can be sharply focused by my subtitle. I shall not be talking about the periods of Shakespeare's development, or looking for his autobiography in his dramaturgy, or assuming—with Edward Dowden and others—that he wrote his tragedies out of some private grief and later, when he felt mellower, turned back to comedies. The moods and changes that continue to interest us today are not those which we attribute to the artist in person, but those which we experience through his art. Its characteristic transitions from splendor to torment, from *O altitudo* to *de profundis,* seem to accord with a basic principle of tragic vicissitude. What I propose to discuss, in some contextual detail, is one extremely specific illustration of that principle, a text often cited but seldom re-examined, probably because our modes of stagecraft have strategically changed.

"Gain Shakespeare's effects by Shakespeare's means when you can." Such was the sound advice of Granville-Barker for the modern interpretation of Shakespeare. However, there are times when the theatrical interpreter

From *More Talking of Shakespeare,* ed. John Garrett. New York: Theatre Arts Books; London: Longmans, Green & Company, Ltd., 1959. Reprinted by permission of Longmans, Green & Company, Ltd.

cannot use Shakespearean means, even though the academic interpreter may know how a certain Shakespearean effect was accomplished. We cannot cast a boy as Cleopatra, though Shakespeare did; very few actresses are up to the part in our time, even after a long and respectable career in the theatre. Shakespeare would never have been able to spread his drama of *Antony and Cleopatra* through forty-two scenes, crossing and recrossing the Mediterranean, had he been forced to compress it within a proscenium, relying upon a succession of backdrops or a revolving stage. Working within an adaptable but permanent structure—mainly a forestage flanked by adequate exits or entrances, backed by some sort of curtained area and an upper balcony—Shakespeare achieved unlimited effects by limited means.

These were primarily verbal. To one with his gift for turning words into pictures, the absence of scenery was a stimulus to the pictorial imagination. Hence Shakespeare did his own scene-painting, verbally. "This castle hath a pleasant seat," says Duncan, praising the air; and Banquo goes on to enlarge our mental picture of Glamis Castle with his lyrical speech about the temple-haunting martlet, the pendent bed, and the heaven's breath. This delicate imagery has the quality of repose in painting, or so Sir Joshua Reynolds has commented. Repose indeed! for here the gentle Duncan will all too soon be taking his last repose; before morning that heavenly courtyard will be all the drunken porter fancies, when he envisages it as a gateway to hell; and we shall have been transported, as it were, from the heights to the depths.

Shakespeare used no programs, and does not seem to have put much faith in locality-boards.

> Alack! the night comes on, and the bleak winds
> Do sorely ruffle,

says Gloucester, thereby setting the time and place at the end of the Second Act of *King Lear*:

for many miles about
There's scarce a bush.

And with a clatter of doors being closed and shutters
banged, the clanging of gates and other sound effects
which are actually verbal, the stage is set—that vastest
and barest of stages—for the storm scenes of Act III,
which alternate between the indoors and the open air,
and gain the effect of wind and rain by means of the old
King's efforts to outscorn them. Granville-Barker's preface to *King Lear* is a practical refutation of A. C. Bradley's influential and paradoxical argument that, though it
may be Shakespeare's greatest achievement, it is too huge
for the stage. This, in turn, was a philosophical rationali-
zation of Charles Lamb's opinion that performance was un-
bearable. Now Lamb was more of a theatergoer than
Bradley, but he could only have witnessed the play in
productions which were cruelly cut and badly adulterated.
He therefore concluded that the spectacle of an old man,
tottering about in a storm with a stick, could only be
painful or disgusting.

Other critics have recoiled more strongly from that
terrifying scene where Gloucester's eyes are put out
coram populo, not behind the scenes as in *Oedipus Rex,*
but in full view of the audience and in complete violation
of classical decorum. It is a deliberate and definitive
breach, a more flagrant gesture of indecorum than the
Elizabethan intermixture of hornpipes with funerals, or
the abasement of kings to the level of clowns in the
companionship of Lear and his Fool. Yet even that hor-
rendous act has a certain propriety as a literal climax to a
whole train of metaphors involving eyesight and suggesting moral perception, the lack of which is so fatal for
Gloucester and Lear. None so blind as those who have
eyes and see not. Their eyes may be open, but—like those
of Lady Macbeth in her sleepwalking scene—their sense is
shut. This visual metaphor is generalized into *hybris,* the
pride that goes before a tragic fall, with the self-denuncia-
tion of Antony:

But when we in our viciousness grow hard—
O misery on't!—the wise gods seel our eyes;
In our own filth drop our clear judgments; make us
Adore our errors; laugh at's while we strut
To our confusion.

When we become too intimately involved in the tragic experience, we tend to feel pain and disgust as Lamb did, rather than pity and fear. *Catharsis,* if it clears the mind through those classic emotions, does so by placing the object at an aesthetic distance from the spectator. He must, of course, apprehend it through sympathy, empathy, or some sort of identification with it. But he also achieves a sense of perspective through his detachment from it. Recent dramatic theory would stress this latter stage, which Bertolt Brecht terms "estrangement," as the most important aspect of the emotional process. But long ago Lucretius evoked the intellectual pleasure of looking out on troubled waters when one was safe ashore, of looking down on the violent conflicts of men from the heights of philosophy. Tragedy presents such knowledge, not in philosophic abstraction but in concrete exemplification. Thus, though it cries to us out of the depths, it offers us a way of temporarily detaching ourselves from the human predicament, and rising above those situations in which it has vicariously involved us.

The example for which I should like to claim your particular attention is neither the pitiful involvement of Lear in the storm nor the terrible blinding of Gloucester. It is a subsequent and incidental episode, the sixth scene of Act IV, a curiously didactic scene best known for its purple passage describing Dover Cliff. How near we really come to Dover Cliff is a moot question, as I shall try to show in my attempt to recover an unique effect which could only have been attained through Shakespearean means. Elsewhere in drama it has certain precedents and analogies, but none of them comes very close to the matter at hand. In the *Plutus* of Aristophanes, the others threaten to throw the blind god over a precipice, and the threat is averted when he reveals his name. In

the repertory of Japanese Kabuki, the dance-drama
Shakkyo concerns an old lion who pushes a young one
off a cliff as a kind of test: by climbing back, the cub
proves his manhood—or, rather, his lionhood.

That would seem to be the normal relationship between the two generations, father and son. Shakespeare
reverses it, when Edmund accuses Edgar of maintaining
that "the father should be as ward to the son." The ac-
cusation will come true ironically, when the disguised
Edgar leads the blinded Gloucester. "In this play," Dame
Edith Sitwell has aptly observed, "we see the upheaval of
all Nature, the reversal of all histories." Tragedy always
seems to hinge upon a reversal, or peripety. Here a
peripety is the starting point, when the King reverses his
traditional role by stepping down from the throne. As
the tragedy broadens, moving out of the realm of history into the sphere of nature, it sets off a series of
further reversals. The antagonism between crabbed age
and flaming youth, always a latent tension in Shakespeare's plays, breaks into overt conflict in *King Lear*. It
was implicit in classical comedy, to be sure, and terribly
explicit in the dire prophecy of Matthew: "And brother
shall deliver up brother to death, and the father his child:
and children shall rise up against parents, and cause them
to be put to death."

This abrogation of the most fundamental commitments,
straining family ties beyond endurance and turning simple
affections into complex hatreds, is still a major source of
power in literature. Filial ingratitude is an obsessive
theme with Proust, just as parricide is with Dostoevsky.
Like the sons of old Karamazov, Edgar and Edmund in-
carnate the good and evil of their father's character.
Science, natural philosophy, "the wisdom of nature can
reason it thus and thus, yet nature finds itself scourged
by the sequent effects," the superstitious Gloucester la-
ments at the outset, anxious to blame his fate upon the
stars. The worst of the many symptoms of upheaval that
he enumerates is "the bond cracked between son and
father." In Gloucester's own case, it is "son against
father," though he suspects the wrong son as it turns out.

In the King's case, it is "father against child," and Gloucester underlines the parallel. Shakespeare never made bolder use of the double plot than when he matched the dynastic struggle of the main plot with its domestic counterpart, the Gloucester underplot. To take a *donnée* so exceptional, to hit upon so unheard-of a set of circumstances and double them, was to call the entire moral order into question, as A. W. Schlegel pointed out.

The story in outline harks back, far beyond the old play that Shakespeare adapted, through chronicle and legend, to the mounds of British prehistory and the fens of Druidical myth. But Shakespeare, shrewd folklorist that he was, found the same archetype at work in the most fashionable book of romantic fiction among his contemporaries, Sir Philip Sidney's *Arcadia*. Two heroes of that romance, in the course of their princely adventures, had encountered the blind King of Paphlagonia begging his dutiful son to lead him to headlong death from the top of a rock because, as he put it, "I cannot fall worse than I am." From the doleful speeches of father and son, it emerged that a bastard son and brother had betrayed them both through his "unnatural dealings"—a protesting phrase which Gloucester echoes at the moment when the two plots first come together in the play. The interpolated narrative ends in a battle and a reinstatement, with the blind King dying joyfully and the rightful heir forgiving his perfidious half-brother.

Sidney devotes a single chapter to this minor encounter; yet he tells us it is "worthy to be remembered for the unused examples therein, as well of true natural goodness, as of wretched ungratefulnesse." Edgar and Edmund, then, are exemplary figures, models of filial conduct, for better and worse. The worse of the two has an obvious dramatic advantage. It is always easier to portray an effectual villain than a young man of simple-minded good will. Some of Milton's critics have sympathized more with his Satan than with his Son of God. Yet the title page of the First Quarto leaves no doubt as to who, after Lear himself, is the male protagonist: who is, so to speak, the *jeune premier*. It reads in part: "With the unfortunate life of Edgar, sonne and heire to the Earle of Gloster, and his sullen and assumed humor of Tom of Bedlam." Instead of remaining just a nice young man, rather pallid and timid, Edgar is allowed to rival Shakespeare's dynamic villains by assuming a dangerous and colorful role.

Edmund has played his part from the beginning, though he already looks toward a denouement of some sort when he summons Edgar from hiding: "and pat he comes, like the catastrophe of the old comedy." Even while Edmund is soliloquizing, he is rehearsing his initial interview with his half-brother, and the notes he sings—*mi contra fa*—significantly form the forbidden interval known as *diabolus in musica*. His own "cue," as it happens, will become Edgar's: "a sigh like Tom o' Bedlam." But Edgar, at this point, is no less credulous than their father. With Gloucester he falls into Edmund's trap, is suspected of parricidal intentions, and proscribed as an outlaw. In his fugitive soliloquy, he determines

> To take the basest and most poorest shape
> That ever penury, in contempt of man,
> Brought near to beast.

He will disguise himself, paradoxically, by taking off his clothes and exposing himself to the elements. "With presented nakedness," when we next see him, he will be attempting to

> outface
> The winds and persecutions of the sky.

And Edgar seems to anticipate the storm, even as Lear seems to conjure it up with his imprecations of blast and fog.

As Edgar goes on to describe the role of Poor Tom, we can understand why it made him so popular on the Elizabethan stage. But, though it is quasi-comic, we can scarcely regard it as comic relief; rather, with its vagrant grotesquerie, it intensifies the tragic pathos. Those Bedlam beggars were harmless madmen released from their lunatic asylum, the notorious Hospital of St. Mary's of Bethlehem in London. Wandering aimlessly about the countryside, with their teeth chattering from exposure and their bare flesh lacerated by self-torture, they besought the stranger's alms with their prayers or curses. Edgar not only dresses the part; he fills it in with apt charms and exorcisms and brilliant bits of histrionic improvisation. He even seems to have worked up the names of devils from a current theological pamphlet: Turleygod, Flibbertigibbet, Frateretto, the last a likely name for a diabolical brother. Not the least of many ironies is that this innocent youth must pretend to be the victim of demonic possession, haunted by the foul fiend in many shapes—albeit these demons, on naturalistic inspection, are merely vermin.

Dramatic tradition gave Tom of Bedlam a forerunner in the person of Diccon the Bedlam, the Vice or mischief-maker in the crude old Cambridge comedy of *Gammer Gurton's Needle*. Edgar, too, will play the Vice in his later manipulations, when he intervenes on behalf of Gloucester. Meanwhile he acts as an object lesson for Lear. The extent of Lear's reversal may be grasped by contrasting the first scene of Act I with the last in Act II. In the former the bidding goes up, as Goneril and Regan bid for the kingdom with their large speeches of love. In the latter the haggling goes down, as the daughters cut down the retinue of their father. An hundred, fifty, five-and-twenty knights. "Ten, or five." "What need one?" By that time we are ready to move on with Lear from the court, the world of superfluity, to the heath, the world of necessity—from the heights toward the depths. His retort in farewell is the first of his speeches on need and its opposite, luxury, especially luxurious clothing and the difference it makes between the sophisticated courtier and the basest beggar, between man's life and beast's.

When Lear has exposed himself to the pinch of necessity, when he has felt the storm and first expressed a new insight into the houseless lives of naked wretches, it is then that the ragged Edgar appears as the personi-

fication of abject poverty and misery. "Is man no more
than this?" the King demands, striving to emulate Tom
by removing his own regal garments. "Unaccommodated
man"—the naked wretch in the state of nature—"is no
more but such a poor, bare, forked animal as thou
art." Commentators have told us how richly the prose
of this passage is interlarded with primitivistic specula-
tions from Montaigne, whom Shakespeare knew so well
through Florio's translation, and who had inspired so
much of Hamlet's self-questioning. Lear has his own version
of Hamlet's exclamation, "What a piece of work is a man!"
Unaccommodate him, banish him from the commodities
of the court, take away the trappings of civilization,
complete his exposure to the elements. What is there left
to differentiate him from all the other animals, by whose
sharpened fangs we feel increasingly surrounded? Will he
be naturally good, as Rousseau would argue? Or is he
inherently evil, as Hobbes would have it, a wolf to his fellow man?

The Machiavellian bastard, Gloucester's natural son Edmund, dedicates himself to the goddess Nature, as he ruth-
lessly envisions her; while, through his cruel machinations,
Edgar is placed in such a false position that their
father calls his legitimate son an "unnatural villain." On
the other hand, Edgar stands closer to nature; Lear
hails him as a natural philosopher, who should be able to
answer his questions concerning "the cause of thunder"
and the other mysteries of the cosmos. This affinity,
based on the fact that Edgar is Lear's godson, is confirmed by their respective plights, as Edgar keenly real-
izes: "He childed as I father'd!" As the pair enter the
hovel together, Edgar's snatches of balladry and fairy
tale transform it into a legendary dark tower, where a
young squire is undergoing a ritual of knightly initiation
while nameless giants objurgate: "Fie, foh, and fum."
Edgar is more of a spectator than a feature of the
spectacle in the ensuing scene, summing it up in the
sententious understatement that "grief hath mates" or
misery loves company.

This is the hallucinatory arraignment, where his own

half-hearted pretence meets Lear's actual madness, accompanied by the half-witted folly of the natural fool with his one pathetic joke: the rain rains every day for those who are excluded from the sunshine of royal favor. The only person present who can speak sanely, Kent in his servant guise of Caius, counsels patience. Edgar is so moved at times that his tears interfere with his impersonation, "mar" his "counterfeiting." Gloucester, whom Edgar has welcomed as a squinting fiend, re-enters to terminate the scene by ordering that the King be conveyed on a litter to Dover. Thereafter, in his master's absence, he becomes the scapegoat. What follows is the scene of his sacrifice, upon which there is no temptation to dwell, except for pointing out that this reversal—despite its extreme brutality—is humanely mitigated by a recognition. Peripety, according to Aristotle, is most effective when it coincides with such a recognition, *anagnorisis*.

When Cornwall inquires "Where is thy lustre now?", Gloucester responds, "All dark and comfortless." Then, when the malicious Regan apprises him of Edmund's villainy, he suddenly recognizes that Edgar is innocent. Thus, at the very moment of blinding, Gloucester sees how blind he has been all along. "I stumbled when I saw," he will live to say. Now, in the absence of eyesight, he will be guided by a kind of ethical illumination. One of the servants, an old man, suggests that the "roguish madness" of "the Bedlam" would qualify him to be Gloucester's guide. Their conjunction is brought about in the first scene of Act IV. Kent has previously consoled himself with the thought that he could fall no lower than the stocks, and that any turn of Fortune's wheel would mean a rise in the world for him. Similarly, Edgar *solus* now views himself as "The lowest and most dejected thing of fortune," whose condition any change would improve. But alas, he speaks too soon. The sight of his bleeding father is worse than anything he has met so far.

"The worst is not," Edgar thereupon reflects, "so long as we can say, 'This is the worst.'" This may be re-

garded as Shakespeare's variation on the tragic theme of
Sophocles, "Call no man happy until he is dead," or the
cry from the depths when Job curses the light and gropes
in the dark. Gloucester, in spite of his infirmity, half-
recognizes Edgar as that thing between a madman and
a beggar which makes him "think man a worm," but also
made him think of his son. And it is at this significant
juncture that Gloucester voices his pessimistic view of the
human condition:

> As flies to wanton boys, are we to the gods;
> They kill us for their sport.

The world-view that opens up is as hopeless as Hardy's,
governed by nothing more serene or secure than crass
casualty and blind chance. It seems proper to Gloucester that a madman should lead a blind man, so long as
he knows the way to Dover Cliff. "From that place,"
he declares with grim succinctness, "I shall no leading
need." In his desperation, faced with what seems to be
the pointless hostility of the universe, what can he do
but dispatch his own "nighted life"? That is the last resort
of Stoicism; and Shakespeare, in his Roman plays, consistently treats suicide as an honorable mode of death. In
his tragedies with a Christian background, his attitude is
shaded with disapproval, and he cites God's canon against
self-slaughter.

King Lear is supposed to take place in prehistoric Britain, and to be roughly contemporaneous with the ancient
Kings of Judea. Shakespeare has taken pains to have
his characters invoke "the gods" in the plural and swear
by conspicuously pagan divinities. But Edgar, that Good
Samaritan with his faith, humility, and charity, seems to
be *anima naturaliter christiana.* Curiously enough, in the
original legend, where Lear regains his crown and Cordelia is dethroned again after his death, she ends by com-
mitting suicide in prison. It is her ghost which arises to
retell the family history and point the moral in the standard Elizabethan collection of poetic case-histories,
falls of princes or sad stories of the deaths of kings, the

Mirror for Magistrates. There the usual reversal, the change of fortune from prosperity to adversity, from the heights to the depths, is presented as a warning to those who are highly placed, lest they be precipitated.

> From greatest haps, that worldly wightes atchieue:
> To more distresse then any wretche aliue.

So Cordelia's monologue concludes. Comparably the first play performed before Queen Elizabeth, *Gorboduc,* one of whose collaborators was co-author of the *Mirror for Magistrates,* warned the queenly magistrate against the division of her realm and even foreshadowed *King Lear* in introducing a dissension between rival Dukes of Cornwall and Albany.

Downfall was the formula for tragedy that Shakespeare inherited and elaborated, not only in plot and characterization but in language and staging as well. The dying fall is its traditional posture. Its vicissitudes, such as the ups and downs of Richard II's reign, lend their thematic pattern to his tragedy, wherein his fall is a comedown literally as well as figuratively. Aloft, on the upper stage, the imagined walls of Flint Castle, Richard compares himself to Phaeton; descending to the lower stage, he condescends to pun about the "base court." Descent is even more desperate in *King John*, where Prince Arthur is killed in escaping from the Castle of Angiers. Elevation as the basis of a godlike overview is dramatized at those moments when Prospero is *"on the top,"* apparently looking down from the musicians' gallery. Antony, coming down from his vantage-point after the battle or hoisted up to Cleopatra's Monument in death, acts out the movement of his destiny. The danger of high places, the tragic vertigo, is vividly brought home in Horatio's fear lest Hamlet topple off some dreadful summit, "That beetles o'er his base into the sea." And that is all we need to know in order to establish the certainty that Shakespeare never visited Denmark, which is as conspicuous for its summits as Bohemia is for its sea-coasts.

But we must turn back to Dover Cliff. "Wherefore to

Dover?" Three times Gloucester is asked this question
by his torturers. Lear was there, of course; and Lear was
there because the French Army was there, though the
King of France had discreetly withdrawn so that his rescue party would not be mistaken for a foreign invasion. There the gleaming white cliffs, greeting the traveler
on his return from the continent, mark a perpetual bourn.
"Within these breakwaters English is spoken," writes
W. H. Auden,

> without
> Is the immense improbable atlas.

Nature in Lear, he has been chastened to learn, "is on
the very verge/ Of her confine." Just as the tempest in
his mind, in the "little world of man" or microcosm, is
a reverberation of the macrocosm, the disturbance of
outer nature; so now Gloucester, led by Edgar, has
reached the "extreme verge," the edge of the precipice.
It is like the thin line between life and death, between the
known and the unknown, that lies before Tolstoy's heroes
in *War and Peace*.

Here Edgar, the assumed madman, addresses his charge,
the blind man—and remember that we are just as blind
as Gloucester. Theatrical convention prescribes that we
accept whatever is said on the subject of immediate place
as the setting. We may grow slightly suspicious, when
Gloucester fails to notice the slant of the ground or
the sound of the sea; and we join him in remarking an
alteration of tone, since Poor Tom has shifted to blank
verse and soon embarks on his topographical passage.

> How fearful
> And dizzy 'tis to cast one's eyes so low!

His downward glance proceeds to the half-way point,
where it encounters the samphire-gatherer at his precarious business of picking the herb of Saint-Pierre from
the rocks. Thence to the beach, where the fishermen look
like mice, the birds like insects, the ships like their

boats, and the buoys are invisible. Everything suffers a diminution in scale. "I'll look no more," vows Edgar at the end of fifteen lines,

> Lest my brain turn, and the deficient sight

—a relevant phrase, "deficient sight," which universalizes the blindness of Gloucester while commenting on the trepidation of heights—

> I'll look no more,
> Lest my brain turn, and the deficient sight
> Topple down headlong.

This may strike the average reader or hearer with a distant, dizzying, vertiginous impact; Addison remarked that it could hardly be read without producing giddiness; but Dr. Johnson refused to be impressed. A precipice in the mind, he argued, should be "one great and dreadful image of irresistible destruction." Here we were too readily diverted by "the observation of particulars." Clearly, Johnson's criterion was the neo-classical grudge against concreteness that prompted him to inveigh against numbering the streaks of the tulip. In Boswell's account, he went even further when he discussed Edgar's speech with Garrick and others: "It should be all precipice—all vacuum. The crows impede your fall." It was the same Miltonic taste that emended Macbeth's "blanket of the dark" to "blank height." Yet Lessing finds Shakespeare's description superior to Milton's lines where the angels scan the "vast immeasurable abyss" of chaos. In *Paradise Lost* the declension is out of scale, Lessing asserted; the distance traversed is too vast to be fathomable in human dimensions. To jump to the beach from a cliff as high as ten masts is breath-taking danger, whereas a limitless precipitation through the void is mere astronomy. That vista may be even less thrilling today, as traffic increases in outer space.

The sense of immediacy and the sense of remoteness, the sensation of being up here one moment and down there a few seconds later, together with all the other sensations heightened by the hazards of the plunge, these feelings are concentrated into our identification with Gloucester and our prospective detachment from him. He is presumably standing at the brink as he lets go Edgar's hand, rewarding him and bidding him farewell. Whereupon Edgar, in a cryptic aside, gives us our first hint that the situation is not precisely what Gloucester believes it to be:

> Why I do trifle thus with his despair
> Is done to cure it.

From this announcement, at least, it is clear that Edgar has a stratagem for saving Gloucester; but, on a non-representational stage, it would still be difficult to foresee how the rescue might be effected. On a proscenium stage, the whole situation would be impossible; for, depending on realistic scenery, we should be fully aware whether Gloucester was or was not at the top of a hill. The best that nineteenth-century staging could do was to cut the passage heavily, letting Edgar catch Gloucester as he lurches forward into a faint, and quickly shifting to the next phase of the scene with the entrance of Lear. Meanwhile the audience would not be undergoing any throes of suspense, since the scenic arrangements would have indicated that Gloucester was perfectly safe. On occasions, the Dover Cliffs have been painted upon the backdrop; it was to be inferred that Edgar had taken Gloucester directly to the beach, where he should not have had any trouble in hearing the waves.

"He falls," according to the stage direction, which editors have embellished but not improved. Most of them add *"forward"*; some add *"and swoons."* He falls, at all events, but not far. Not so far as from the upper stage, I should guess, inasmuch as Romeo needed a rope and—lacking one—Prince Arthur lost his life. There may be a single step or a simple platform; or, again, the business may be enough—enough for Edgar to play his trick upon Gloucester and to lay bare the trick that Shakespeare

has played upon ourselves, his audience. Gloucester, having gone through the motions of an ineffectual jump, lies on the ground; Edgar, assuming another character, now rushes up to revive him; and both are changed men. In complementary verses, breathless with polysyllabics, Edgar describes how Gloucester has fallen perpendicularly from a vast altitude and somehow survived: "Thy life's a miracle." Vainly, but not without irony, he exhorts him: "Look up a-height." And in contrast to all the *hybris,* the giddy exaltation of looking down from the heights, we seem to have plunged into the depths and to have touched bottom; we can fall no lower.

This is the nadir; the worst is over; we seem to be looking up; and the situation is framed by larger perspectives. "As I stood here below methought," begins Edgar, as if he were recounting a dream, a bad dream which ends with Tom of Bedlam turning into a fiend and flying away. Edgar's portrayal of his departing self is an exorcism, leaving innocence no longer possessed by guilt. Just as Gloucester utters his cry of despair—comparing the gods to boys and ourselves to flies—on his first encounter with mad Tom, so with Tom's departure Edgar voices his answering affirmation:

> Think that the clearest gods, who make them honors
> Of men's impossibilities, have preserv'd thee.

Providence must be at work, after all; and if we discern the workings of cosmic design in our personal destinies, then no man has a right to take his life; he must bear the slings and arrows of fortune, however outrageous they seem. To the Stoic argument for suicide Edgar would oppose the Christian attitude, in words which reverberate from the Gospel of Luke: "The things which are impossible with men are possible with God." Since our eyes have been opened, we are bound to bear witness that Edgar himself has been fully responsible for the stratagem he now attributes to divine intervention. His intentions were kindly, where Edmund's have been malign; but he has deceived their father quite

as much with his imaginary fall as Edmund earlier did
with his forged letter. "Let's see," said Gloucester,
snatching at that device, "come; if it be nothing, I shall
not need spectacles." He saw; he stumbled; and, now that
he is sightless, he is rescued by the victim of the letter.
Edgar has proved to be as good a stage manager as Edmund, and in a better cause. Yet, unless his presence in
the vicinity is the result of stage management on the part
of the gods—unless it is providential, that is to say, rather
than coincidental—we must admit that his miracle is
more truly a pious fraud; and we must conclude that the
gods help those who help themselves, or else those who
are so fortunate as to be helped by their fellow men.

Man stands on his own feet in *King Lear*. There is no
supernatural soliciting; there are no ghosts or witches
or oracles; and the only demons are those which Edgar
imagines while enacting his demonic role. Man takes his
questionings directly to nature. Perhaps the ultimate
meaning of Gloucester's fall is its symbolic gesture of ex-
piation, re-enacting his own original sin, as well as the
fall of man and his consequent progression toward self-
knowledge. Other agonists have undergone it under widely
differing conditions: Herman Melville narrates it, in
his *White-Jacket*, as a fall from the yardarm of a ship at
sea. Because he could not bear his great affliction without cursing the gods, Gloucester has attempted to shake it
off "patiently." But Edgar's moral, which completes the
exercise, redefines patience as the ability to bear one's
sufferings, to face and endure them in calm of mind:
"Bear free and patient thoughts."

Patience has been the greatest need of the King. He has
resolved to be "the pattern of all patience"; whereupon
he has run the gamut of passions, from rage through
hysteria to delirium and finally lunacy. It is as an escaping lunatic, grotesquely decked with weeds, that he is confronted by Edgar and Gloucester at this strategic moment
of the play; and it may well be the shock of this reunion
that has obscured the significance of their foregoing scene.
From the interchange it would appear that, if Lear
stands for reason in madness, Gloucester may stand for

vision in blindness. When Lear asks if he sees how the
world goes, Gloucester replies: "I see it feelingly." His
groping pun is heavily fraught with shame and remorse
for the figure he has earlier cut: "the superfluous and
lust-dieted man . . . that will not see/Because he does
not feel." This parallels the insight that Lear has acquired on the heath: "to feel what wretches feel."
Gloucester has immediately recognized Lear's voice; Lear
rounds out the recognition scene by naming Gloucester
and preaching, "Thou must be patient."

Lear is unquestionably the *persona patiens,* as Coleridge insisted; he is the agonizing figure of this passion
play where all the characters suffer. Having committed his
rash action, he suffers for it on and on, until he is
justified in regarding himself as "a man/More sinn'd
against than sinning." Edmund is the main agent, in
Coleridge's estimation; certainly, he is most active in pull-
ing the strings at the outset. "The younger rises when the
old doth fall." But the defeated opportunist concedes that,
with its last revolution, his wheel comes full circle.
Edgar, his polar rival, is passive at first; he suffers, then
he acts; and it is his suffering that prepares him for action. When Gloucester thanks and blesses him for his
anonymous aid, he characterizes himself as

A most poor man, made tame to fortune's blows;
Who, by the art of known and feeling sorrows,
Am pregnant to good pity.

As such, he is the right instrument for conveying a sense
of fellow-feeling, both to Lear in the hovel on the heath
and to Gloucester at Dover Cliff.

It is a cruel world where the honest Kent must go in-
cognito, and where the once-naïve Edgar has to run
through a protean repertory of roles. After the disap-
pearance of Tom of Bedlam, he is more simply a neutral
benefactor, the Good Samaritan. But when he protects
Gloucester from Oswald's attack and is called "bold peasant" by the courtier, he adapts himself to that appellation by replying in a rustic dialect. He disposes of

Oswald, thereby saving the life that Gloucester would have thrown away. But he cannot disclose his identity before he has made his appearance as a nameless champion; and even this last masquerade is preceded by another one, that of the messenger delivering the challenge. However, the battle must precede the tournament. *Drums afar off* have terminated the Cliff Scene. They grow louder when the French forces, flying Cordelia's colors, march to meet the British. While the engagement is taking place off-stage, we await the outcome with Gloucester under a tree.

Hard upon the heels of retreating soldiers, Edgar reports the defeat and capture of Lear and Cordelia, and Gloucester reverts to his former mood of self-pity. Why should he let himself be led any farther? "A man may rot even here." But just as growth yields to decay, so decay fosters growth, in the biological cycle. What is important, fulfillment, is a matter of timing. Man must reconcile himself to the fact that nature will take its course. Edgar, picking up Gloucester's negative image, transposes it into the most positive statement of the play:

> Men must endure
> Their going hence, even as their coming hither;
> Ripeness is all.

Edgar's aphorism can be traced back to Montaigne's essay, "That to philosophize is to learn how to die." Such was the end of knowledge for the tragic playwright, as well as for the skeptical philosopher. It is rather more than a coincidence that the same sentiment is expressed, though not imaged, at the same point in *Hamlet*: "The readiness is all." The manner of one's death and the moment of it were ultimate concerns to the Elizabethans.

By averting the suicide and nursing his father's miseries, Edgar has saved him from despair. Could he but live to see his son in his touch, Gloucester has feelingly vowed, "I'd say I had eyes again." We do not witness the recognition scene wherein this yearning is fulfilled at last.

But in the final scene, when the explanations come out,
Edgar relates the circumstances of Gloucester's happy
death, " 'Twixt two extremes of passion, joy and grief."
These mixed emotions match the smiles and tears with
which Cordelia has received the news of her father: "Sunshine and rain at once." Edmund, sincerely moved by his
brother's report, resolves to do some good; but retro-
spective narration prolongs the delay, and his one hu-
mane impulse is thwarted; the reprieve of Cordelia
comes too late. When the brothers fought and were rec-
onciled, Edgar pronounced upon his brother and father
in apocryphal terms:

> The gods are just, and of our pleasant vices
> Make instruments to plague us.

Edmund's existence is at once the consequence of, and
the retribution for, Gloucester's sin.

> The dark and vicious place where thee he got
> Cost him his eyes.

Where the inequities of this world have made Gloucester and Lear more and more doubtful as to the justice
of heaven, Edgar is wholeheartedly its exponent. Albany, too, can point to the death of Cornwall, fatally
wounded in the very act of torturing Gloucester, as an
indication that the guilty are punished here below. But
so are the innocent. So is Cordelia; and this, more than
anything else, I suspect, is why critics have flinched at
the notion of performing the play. There is a grim
sort of poetic justice in the scene where the King refuses
to accept her death; and his own demise, just after-
wards, is a deliverance for him. But audiences have fre-
quently shared his and Gloucester's unwillingness to bear
an unhappy ending patiently; the chronicle-history
ended happily; while the adaptation by Nahum Tate, which
all but replaced Shakespeare's tragedy for a hundred and
fifty years, managed to marry off Cordelia to Edgar,
who thanks the King with these concluding lines:

> Thy bright example shall convince the World
> (Whatever Storms of Fortune are decreed)
> That Truth and Vertue shall at last succeed.

Shakespeare's Edgar repeats to the dying Lear his optimistic counsel to Gloucester: "Look up, my lord." But he cannot contrive another miracle. The problem of evil is unresolved at the conclusion, though the prevailing catastrophe is accepted. It is, as Kent says, a presentiment of doomsday, "the promis'd end." Edgar, rather than Albany, speaks the final speech in the Folio. Well might he proclaim a farewell to dissembling and a renewal of sincerity. It is high time to "Speak what we feel, not what we ought to say." And, in his terminal couplet, our deficient sight is contrasted with the insight painfully achieved through old age:

> The oldest hath borne most: we that are young,
> Shall never see so much, nor live so long.

We leave him looking across the straits, listening to the cadence of human misery in the ebb and flow of the tides, and catching that eternal note of sadness which Sophocles heard long ago and which Matthew Arnold caught in his poem, "Dover Beach." As with Oedipus, blind and dying at Colonus, so with Gloucester at Dover. In each case, the passion of a patriarch has met with compassion on the part of a filial survivor, be it Edgar or Antigone. But it is Goethe who puts his finger on the archetype in that relationship: *"Ein alter Mann ist stets ein König Lear."* May I translate freely, in order to keep the rhyme?

> An aged man is always like King Lear.
> Effort and struggle long have passed him by;
> And love and leadership are pledged elsewhere;
> And youth must work out its own destiny.
> Come on, old fellow, come along with me.

Maynard Mack

From *King Lear in Our Time*

I turn now to a closer scrutiny of the play. In the remarks that follow I shall address myself primarily to three
topics, which I believe to be both interesting in themselves
and well suited to bring before us other qualities of this
tragedy which stir the twentieth-century imagination. The
first topic is the externality of Shakespeare's treatment of
action in *King Lear*; the second is the profoundly social
orientation of the world in which he has placed this action;
and the third is what I take to be the play's dominant
tragic theme, summed up best in Lear's words to Gloucester in Dover fields: "We came crying hither."

As we watch it in the theatre, the action of *King Lear*
comes to us first of all as an experience of violence and
pain. No other Shakespearean tragedy, not even *Titus*,
contains more levels of raw ferocity, physical as well as
moral. In the action, the exquisite cruelties of Goneril and
Regan to their father are capped by Gloucester's blinding
onstage, and this in turn by the wanton indignity of Cordelia's murder. In the language, as Miss Caroline Spurgeon
has pointed out, allusions to violence multiply and ac-
cumulate into a pervasive image as of "a human body in
anguished movement—tugged, wrenched, beaten, pierced,
stung, scourged, dislocated, flayed, gashed, scalded, tortured, and finally broken on the rack."[1]

From *King Lear in Our Time*, by Maynard Mack, © 1965 The Regents
of the University of California. Used by permission of the University of
California Press, Berkeley, California.
1 *Shakespeare's Iterative Imagery* (1935), p. 342.

Miss Spurgeon's comment tends to formulate the play in terms of passiveness and suffering. But the whole truth is not seen unless it is formulated also in terms of agency and aggression. If the *Lear* world is exceptionally anguished, it is chiefly because it is exceptionally contentious. Tempers in *King Lear* heat so fast that some critics are content to see in it simply a tragedy of wrath. Unquestionably, it does contain a remarkable number of remarkably passionate collisions. Lear facing Cordelia, and Kent facing Lear, in the opening scene; Lear confronting Goneril at her house with his terrifying curse; Kent tangling with Oswald outside Gloucester's castle; Cornwall run through by his own servant, who warns Regan that if she had a beard he'd "shake it on this quarrel"; Edgar and Edmund simulating a scuffle in the first act, and later, in the last act, hurling charge and countercharge in the scene of their duel; the old king himself defying the storm: these are only the more vivid instances of a pattern of pugnacity which pervades this tragedy from beginning to end, shrilling the voices that come to us from the stage and coloring their language even in the tenderest scenes. The pattern gives rise to at least one locution which in frequency of occurrence is peculiar to *King Lear*—to "outface the winds and persecutions of the sky," to "outscorn the to-and-fro contending wind and rain," to "outjest his heart-struck injuries," to "outfrown false Fortune's frown." And it appears as a motif even in that pitiful scene at Dover, where the old king, at first alone, throws down his glove before an imaginary opponent—"There's my gauntlet, I'll prove it on a giant"—and, afterward, when the blind Gloucester enters, defies him, too: "No, do thy worst, blind Cupid, I'll not love." So powerful is this vein of belligerence in the linguistic texture of the play that pity itself is made, in Cordelia's words, something that her father's white hair must "challenge." Even "had you not been their father," she says in an apostrophe to the sleeping king, referring to the suffering he has been caused by his other daughters, "these white flakes did challenge pity of them."

It goes without saying that in a world of such contenti-

ousness most of the *dramatis personae* will be outrageous-
ly self-assured. The contrast with the situation in *Hamlet*,
in this respect, is striking and instructive. There, as I have
argued in another place, the prevailing mood tends to be
interrogative.[2] Doubt is real in *Hamlet*, and omnipresent.
Minds, even villainous minds, are inquiet and uncertain.
Action does not come readily to anyone exept Laertes and
Fortinbras, who are themselves easily deflected by the
stratagems of the king, and there is accordingly much emphasis on the fragility of the human will. All this is
changed in *King Lear*. Its mood, I would suggest (if it
may be caught in a single word at all), is imperative. The
play asks questions, to be sure, as *Hamlet* does, and far
more painful questions because they are so like a child's,
so simple and unmediated by the compromises to which
much experience usually impels us: "Is man no more than
this?" "Is there any cause in nature that makes these hard
hearts?" "Why should a dog, a horse, a rat have life And
thou no breath at all?" Such questionings in *King Lear*
stick deep, like Macbeth's fears in Banquo.

Yet it is not, I think, the play's questions that establish
its distinctive coloring onstage. (Some of its questions we
shall return to later.) It is rather its commands, its invoca-
tions and appeals that have the quality of commands, its
flat-footed defiances and refusals: "Come not between the
dragon and his wrath." "You nimble lightnings, dart your
blinding flames into her scornful eyes!" "Blow, winds, and
crack your cheeks! rage! blow!" "Thou shalt not die; die
for adultery, no!" "A plague upon you, murderers, traitors, all! I might have sav'd her . . ." In the psychological
climate that forms round a protagonist like this, there is
little room for doubt, as we may see from both Lear's and
Goneril's scorn of Albany. No villain's mind is inquiet.
Action comes as naturally as breathing and twice as quick.
And, what is particularly unlike the situation in the earlier
tragedies, the hero's destiny is self-made. Lear does not
inherit his predicament like Hamlet; he is not duped by
an antagonist like Othello. He walks into disaster head on.

2 "The World of Hamlet," *The Yale Review*, XLI (1952), 502-523.

This difference is of the first importance. *King Lear*, to follow R. W. Chambers in applying Keats's memorable phrase, is a vale of soul-making,[3] where to all appearances the will is agonizingly free. As if to force the point on our attention, almost every character in the play, including such humble figures as Cornwall's servant and the old tenant who befriends Gloucester, is impelled soon or late to take some sort of stand—to show, in Oswald's words, "what party I do follow." One cannot but be struck by how much positioning and repositioning of this kind the play contains. Lear at first takes up his position with Goneril and Regan, France and Kent take theirs with Cordelia, Albany takes his with Goneril, and Gloucester (back at his own house), with Cornwall and Regan. But then all reposition. Kent elects to come back as his master's humblest servant. The Fool elects to stay with the great wheel, even though it runs downhill. Lear elects to become a comrade of the wolf and owl rather than return to his elder daughters. Gloucester likewise has second thoughts and comes to Lear's rescue, gaining his sight though he loses his eyes. Albany, too, has second thoughts, and lives, he says, only to revenge those eyes. In the actions of the old king himself, the taking of yet a third position is possibly implied. For after the battle, when Cordelia asks, "Shall we not see these daughters and these sisters?" Lear replies (with the vehemence characteristic of him even in defeat), "No, no, no, no!" and goes on to build, in his famous following lines, that world entirely free of pugnacity and contentiousness in which he and Cordelia will dwell: "We two alone will sing like birds i' th' cage."

Movements of the will, then, have a featured place in *King Lear*. But what is more characteristic of the play than their number is the fact that no one of them is ever exhibited to us in its inward origins or evolution. Instead of scenes recording the genesis or gestation of an action— scenes of introspection or persuasion or temptation like those which occupy the heart of the drama in *Hamlet*,

[3] *King Lear* (W. P. Ker Memorial Lecture), p. 48.

Othello, and *Macbeth*—*King Lear* offers us the moment at which will converts into its outward expressions of action and consequence; and this fact, I suspect, helps account for the special kind of painfulness that the play always communicates to its audiences. In *King Lear* we are not permitted to experience violence as an externalization of a psychological drama which has priority in both time and significance, and which therefore partly palliates the violence when it comes. This is how we do experience, I think, Hamlet's vindictiveness to his mother, Macbeth's massacres, Othello's murder: the act in the outer world is relieved of at least part of its savagery by our understanding of the inner act behind it. The violences in *King Lear* are thrust upon us quite otherwise—with the shock that comes from evil which has nowhere been inwardly accounted for, and which, from what looks like a studiedly uninward point of view on the playwright's part, must remain unaccountable, to characters and audience alike: "Is there any cause in nature that makes these hard hearts?"

The relatively slight attention given in *King Lear* to the psychological processes that ordinarily precede and determine human action suggests that here we are meant to look for meaning in a different quarter from that in which we find it in the earlier tragedies. In *Hamlet*, Shakespeare had explored action in its aspect of dilemma. Whether or not we accept the traditional notion that Hamlet is a man who cannot make up his mind, his problem is clearly conditioned by the unsatisfactory nature of the alternatives he faces. Any action involves him in a kind of guilt, the more so because he feels an already existing corruption in himself and in his surroundings which contaminates all action at the source. "Virtue cannot so inoculate our old stock but we shall relish of it." Hence the focus of the play is on those processes of consciousness that can explain and justify suspension of the will. In *Othello*, by contrast, Shakespeare seems to be exploring action in its aspect of error. Othello faces two ways of understanding love: Iago's and Desdemona's—which is almost to say, in the play's terms, two systems of valuing and two ways of being—but we are left in no doubt that one of the ways is wrong. Even if we take Iago and Desdemona, as some critics do, to be dramatic emblems of conflicting aspects in Othello's own nature, the play remains a tragedy of error, not a tragedy of dilemma. "The pity of it, Iago" is that Othello makes the wrong choice when the right one is open to him and keeps clamoring to be known for what it is even to the very moment of the murder. The playwright's focus in this play is therefore on the corruptions of mind by which a man may be led into error, and he surrounds Iago and Desdemona with such overtones of damnation and salvation as ultimately must attend any genuine option between evil and good.

King Lear, as I see it, confronts the perplexity and mystery of human action at a later point. Choice remains in the forefront of the argument, but its psychic antecedents have been so effectively shrunk down in this primitivized world that action seems to spring directly out of the bedrock of personality. We feel sure no imaginable psychological process could make Kent other than loyal, Goneril other than cruel, Edgar other than "a brother noble." Such characters, as we saw earlier, are qualities as well as persons: their acts have consequences but little history. The meaning of action here, therefore, appears to lie rather in effects than in antecedents, and particularly in its capacity, as with Lear's in the opening scene, to generate energies that will hurl themselves in unforeseen and unforeseeable reverberations of disorder from end to end of the world.

The elements of that opening scene are worth pausing over, because they seem to have been selected to bring before us precisely such an impression of unpredictable effects lying coiled and waiting in an apparently innocuous posture of affairs. The atmosphere of the first episode in the scene, as many a commentator has remarked, is casual, urbane, even relaxed. In the amenities exchanged by Kent and Gloucester, Shakespeare allows no hint to penetrate of Gloucester's later agitation about "these late eclipses," or about the folly of a king's abdicating his responsibilities and dividing up his power. We are momentarily lulled into a security that is not immediately broken even when the court assembles and Lear informs us that he will shake off all business and "unburthen'd crawl toward death." I suspect we are invited to sense, as Lear speaks, that this is a kingdom too deeply swaddled in forms of all kinds—too comfortable and secure in its "robes and furr'd gowns"; in its rituals of authority and deference (of which we have just heard and witnessed samples as Gloucester is dispatched offstage, the map demanded, and a "fast intent" and "constant will" thrust on our notice by the king's imperious personality); and in its childish charades, like the one about to be enacted when the daughters speak. Possibly we are invited to sense, too, that this is in some sort an emblematic kingdom—almost a paradigm of hierarchy and rule, as indeed the scene before us seems to be suggesting, with its wide display of ranks in both family and state. Yet perhaps too schematized, too regular—a place where complex realities have been too much reduced to formulas, as they are on a map: as they are on that visible map, for instance, on which Lear three times lays his finger in this scene ("as if he were marking the land itself," says Granville-Barker), while he describes with an obvious pride its tidy catalogue of "shadowy forests" and "champains," "plenteous rivers and wide-skirted meads." Can it be that here, as on that map, is a realm where everything is presumed to have been charted, where all boundaries are believed known, including those of nature and human nature; but where no account has been taken of the heath which lies in all countries and in all men and women just beyond the boundaries they think they know?

However this may be, into this emblematic, almost dream-like situation erupts the mysterious thrust of psychic energy that we call a choice, an act; and the waiting coil of consequences leaps into threatening life, bringing with it, as every act considered absolutely must, the inscrutable where we had supposed all was clear, the unexpected though we thought we had envisaged all contingencies and could never be surprised. Perhaps it is to help us see this that the consequences in the play are made so spectacular. The first consequence is Lear's totally unlooked-for redistribution of his kingdom into two parts instead of three, and his rejection of Cordelia. The second is his totally unlooked-for banishment of his most trusted friend and counselor. The third is the equally unlooked-for rescue of his now beggared child to be the Queen of France; and what the unlooked-for fourth and fifth will be, we already guess from the agreement between Goneril and Regan, as the scene ends, that something must be done, "and i' th' heat." Thereafter the play seems to illustrate, with an almost diagrammatic relentlessness and thoroughness, the unforeseen potentials that lie waiting to be hatched from a single choice and act: nakedness issues out of opulence, madness out of sanity and reason out of madness, blindness out of seeing and insight out of blindness, salvation out of ruin. The pattern of the unexpected is so completely worked out, in fact, that, as we noticed in the preceding chapter, it appears to embrace even such minor devices of the plot as the fact that Edmund, his fortune made by two letters, is undone by a third.

Meantime, as we look back over the first scene, we may wonder whether the gist of the whole matter has not been placed before us, in the play's own emblematic terms, by Gloucester, Kent, and Edmund in that brief conversation with which the tragedy begins. This conversation touches on two actions, we now observe, each loaded with menacing possibilities, but treated with a casualness at this point that resembles Lear's in opening his trial of love. The first action alluded to is the old king's action in dividing his kingdom, the dire effects of which we are almost instantly to see. The other action is Gloucester's action in begetting a bastard son, and the dire effects of this will also speedily be known. What is particularly striking, however, is that in the latter instance the principal effect is already on the stage before us, though its nature is undisclosed, in the person of the bastard son himself. Edmund, like other "consequences," looks tolerable enough till revealed in full: "I cannot wish the fault undone, the issue of it being so proper," says Kent, meaning by proper "handsome"; yet there is a further dimension of meaning in the word that we will only later understand, when Edgar relates the darkness of Edmund to the darkness wherein he was got and the darkness he has brought to his father's eyes. Like other consequences, too, Edmund looks to be predictable and manageable—in advance. "He hath been out nine years," says Gloucester, who has never had any trouble holding consequences at arm's length before, "and away he shall again." Had Shakespeare reflected on the problem consciously—and it would be rash, I think, to be entirely sure he did not—he could hardly have chosen a more vivid way of giving dramatic substance to the unpredictable relationships of act and consequence than by this confrontation of a father with his unknown natural son— or to the idea of consequences come home to roost, than by this quiet youthful figure, studying "deserving" as he prophetically calls it, while he waits upon his elders.

In *King Lear* then, I believe it is fair to say, the inscrutability of the energies that the human will has power to release is one of Shakespeare's paramount interests. By the inevitable laws of drama, this power receives a degree of emphasis in all his plays, especially the tragedies. The difference in *King Lear* is that it is assigned the whole canvas. The crucial option, which elsewhere comes toward the middle of the plot, is here presented at the very outset. Once taken, everything that happens after is made to seem, in some sense, to have been set in motion by it, not excluding Gloucester's recapitulation of it in the subplot. Significantly, too, the act that creates the crisis, the act on which Shakespeare focuses our dramatic attention, is not (like Lear's abdication) one which could have been expected to germinate into such a harvest of disaster. The old king's longing for public testimony of affection seems in itself a harmless folly: it is not an outrage, not a crime, only a foolish whim. No more could Cordelia's death have been expected to follow from her truthfulness or Gloucester's salvation to be encompassed by a son whom he disowns and seeks to kill.

All this, one is driven to conclude, is part of Shakespeare's point. In the action he creates for Lear, the act of choice is cut loose not simply from the ties that normally bind it to prior psychic causes, but from the ties that usually limit its workings to commensurate effects. In this respect the bent of the play is mythic: it abandons verisimilitude to find out truth, like the story of Oedipus; or like the *Rime of the Ancient Mariner*, with which, in fact, it has interesting affinities. Both works are intensely emblematic. Both treat of crime and punishment and reconciliation in poetic, not realistic, terms. In both the fall is sudden and unaccountable, the penalty enormous and patently exemplary. The willful act of the mariner in shooting down the albatross has a nightmarish inscrutability like Lear's angry rejection of the daughter he loves best; springs from a similar upsurge of egoistic willfulness; hurls itself against what was until that moment a natural "bond," and shatters the universe. Nor do the analogies end with this. When the mariner shoots the albatross, the dark forces inside him that prompted his deed project themselves and become the landscape, so to speak, in which he suffers his own nature: it is his own alienation, his own waste land of terror and sterility that he meets. Something similar takes place in Shakespeare's play. Lear, too, as we saw earlier, suffers his own nature, encounters his own heath, his own storm, his own nakedness and defenselessness, and by this experience, like the mariner, is made another man.

Linda Bamber

The Woman Reader in *King Lear*

When adults show children how to read a map, they
say, "Here is *your* street (or state or nation)," and the
habit of finding ourselves on the map persists when we are
grown up. When travelers return with pictures of Cairo or
Barcelona, they say, "That's the hotel we stayed in, there,"
as if it explained the picture. If a work of fiction is a map
of its own world, the first question we ask of it is, "Where
am *I* in here?" or "Who is like me?" This question is un-
sophisticated but important, because it shapes our most
basic responses. Only when we have answered it do we
know whom to love and hate and what to hope for.

For women the problem of locating ourselves in literature is complicated by the fact that so much of the literature of the past is written by men. Who is "like me" when
the character offered as a version of the self is a man?
When I began to read the great literature of the past I
never thought to ask this question. My (excellent) teach-
ers were almost all men, and I read stories and poems
and plays by men without noticing the difference. In the
end you could say I imprinted to a different species. I
thought I was a man, just as Tarzan thought he was an
ape. Of course, I also knew I wasn't. But my responses to
literature were confused by an identity problem generated
for me by literature itself.

In *King Lear*, the character who is "like me" is of
course King Lear. Lear is passionate, articulate, capable
of growth, capable of catastrophic error, important to himself and to everyone else in the play. He claims he is
"more sinned against than sinning," and that's how I feel,

too. But King Lear is a man while I am a woman. When I identify with him, an important part of my identity, my femininity, is homeless. If the *King Lear* world is organized around a man, what is the status of women in it? Are women important in this world, or are they (fictionally) second-class citizens? If I can find satisfactory answers to these questions I am free to identify with Lear as much as I can; otherwise, identifying with Lear means denigrating a part of myself.

The best solution would be finding an alternative, female home in the play. Is there a woman character who represents us as well as Lear himself? If so, we could breathe a sigh of relief and simply graph the play as an ellipse (which has two focal points) instead of a circle. But authors—women as well as men—tend to represent "us" much more fully in characters of their own sex than in characters of the opposite sex, and Shakespeare is no exception. In *King Lear* the women are either more or less than human. Goneril and Regan are too bad to live, much less to represent us, and Cordelia is perfect. The evil sisters present no temptations to the woman reader, but it is worth dealing in some detail with the problems of identifying with perfection.

Cordelia is never selfish or aggressive; when she hurts her father it is only because she is separate from him, not because of a failure of love:

> Good my lord,
> You have begot me, bred me, loved me. I
> Return those duties back as are right fit,
> Obey you, love you and most honor you.
> Why have my sisters husbands, if they say
> They love you all? Haply, when I shall wed,
> That lord whose hand must take my plight shall carry
> Half my love with him, half my care and duty.
> Sure I shall never marry like my sisters,
> To love my father all. (I.i.97–106)

This is the only moment in the play in which Cordelia asserts herself, and even here she is not so much asserting herself as mediating between the claims of her father and the claims of her future husband. Her characteristic gestures are of selfless love. No matter how well I think of myself, I would never go so far as to say that she is "like me."

Cordelia's perfection is maintained in this play by her silence. First she refuses to speak the self-serving language of flattery; next she listens in silence when her father disinherits her. "The barbarous Scythian," he tells her,

> Or he that makes his generation messes
> To gorge his appetite, shall to my bosom
> Be as well neighbored, pitied, and relieved,
> As thou my sometime daughter. (I.i.118–122)

The next voice to speak is not Cordelia's but Kent's. It is Kent who protests the injustice and craziness of Lear's behavior, Kent who is angry and blunt in Cordelia's defense:

> Be Kent unmannerly
> When Lear is mad. What wouldst thou do, old man?
> Think'st thou that duty shall have dread to speak
> When power to flattery bows? To plainness honor's bound
> When majesty falls to folly. (I.i.147–151)

Why is it Kent who speaks aggressively to Lear rather than Cordelia? Possibly because in the world of *King Lear* an angry woman risks losing our sympathy, even when anger is so clearly required that another character must be enlisted to supply it. Nor is it only anger that Cordelia notably fails to express. Later in the play, when she receives the news of Lear's misery, she feels a great deal but says very little. The whole description of her behavior turns Cordelia into a kind of icon of grief, precious as a jewel but inarticulate. She controls her emotions, reigns "queen / Over her passion," cries a few silent tears, which part from her eyes "as pearls from diamonds." "Made she no verbal question?" Kent asks the Gentleman, who replies,

> Faith, once or twice she heaved the name of "father"
> Pantingly forth, as if it pressed her heart;
> Cried, "Sisters! Sisters! Shame of ladies! Sisters!
> Kent! Father! Sisters What, i' th' storm? i' th' night?
> Let pity not be believed" There she shook
> The holy water from her heavenly eyes,
> And clamor moistened: then away she started
> To deal with grief alone. (IV.iii.26–33)

Cordelia's inarticulateness, the fewness and brokenness of her words at times of great emotion, is her glory. Lear's glory, by contrast, is to express his feelings fully, variously, and without restraint. The price of Cordelia's perfection seems to be her renunciation of language, and in the medium of poetic drama, this is a heavy price to pay. Cordelia may be as valuable, even as lovable as Lear, but there is simply not enough of her to balance the enormous pull of our sympathy to him. She doesn't represent me because often she isn't even there.

There is no single woman character, then, who represents me in the play. But if we group the three sisters together and call them something like "the feminine" or "the Other" (as opposed to Lear, who represents "the Self"), we can find a kind of rough sexual justice in *King Lear*. Women are important here not as I am important to myself but as the outside world is important to me. They are like the rock on which the hero is broken and remade; they are the thing outside the Self that cannot be controlled and cannot be renounced. "The Other" is equal to the tragic hero as the second term in a dialectic is equal to the first. Women play the role of "the Other" not only in *King Lear* but in all Shakespeare's plays. In all four genres—comedy, history, tragedy, and romance—the nature of the feminine reflects the nature of the world outside the Self. Before returning to *King Lear* it is worth pausing to consider how this works.

In the comedies, the world outside us is manifestly reliable and orderly, a source of pleasure rather than a threat —and so is the nature of the feminine. In *As They Liked It*, Alfred Harbage has made a statistical survey of Shakespeare's characters, dividing them by groups into good and bad. The highest percentage of good characters in any group is the percentage of good women in the comedies: 96 percent good, 4 percent bad. The possibility of betrayal in this world is very slight. The women will not betray the men, the comic world will not betray its central characters, the playwright will not betray our expectations of a happy ending. The world of Shakespearean comedy is fundamentally safe and its women are fundamentally good. We are free in this world to play, to court danger in sport. Sometimes it seems as though the games have gotten out of hand: Oberon's cruel love games in *A Midsummer Night's Dream*, Shylock's murderous bond in *The Merchant of Venice*, and Orsino's threat to Cesario's life in *Twelfth Night*—all these give us some bad moments. But an invisible hand unravels everything and we enjoy the thrill of danger without its deadly consequences. Similarly, the women problem is raised only to be dismissed. We are titillated with reminders that women might be unfaithful; the cuckoldry jokes of *Much Ado About Nothing* and Portia's ring trick in *The Merchant of Venice* remind us of what could happen. But it never does. The women are as transparently faithful as the plot is transparently comic. We are always on our way to the happy ending, to marriage, to the love of good women.

In the romances, the world is a much more serious place—not, as in the tragedies, because it may betray us—but because it may be lost altogether. The protagonist of a Shakespearean romance loses his whole world; Pericles, Leontes, and Prospero live for a time in the absence of everything they care for. But although the world may be lost, it may also be found; and of course the most obvious property of the feminine in this genre is also its tendency to come and go. It is notable that in *The Winter's Tale* the two male characters who disappear from Sicilia, Mamillus and Antigonous, disappear for good. It is the women characters, Perdita and Hermione, who return. In Shakespearean romance, the feminine is infinitely valuable, capable of being utterly lost but capable also of miraculous self-renewal. Again, the nature of the feminine is congruent with the nature of the world outside the Self.

The feminine in the history plays is more difficult to characterize briefly than it is in the comedies and romances; perhaps it is best described as unproblematic. The feminine Other may be unambiguously hated, as Joan is in *1 Henry VI;* cheerfully courted, as Katherine is in *Henry V*; or cleverly used to further a career, as Queen Elizabeth is in *Richard III*. But whatever role she plays, she never offers any metaphysical complications, never raises issues of identity for the masculine Self. Emotions toward women are unconfused; the feminine Other does not call the masculine Self into question. Similarly, the world outside the Self in the histories is simple compared to the world of the tragedies. Because it is almost wholly a political world, it, too, offers few metaphysical or psychological problems. The world divides up smartly into friends and enemies; everyone is playing the same game, however nastily. In tragedy, by contrast, the world becomes murkier, the masculine-historical enterprise loses its centrality, friends and enemies become hard to distinguish from each other, and the feminine becomes a problem.

In Shakespearean tragedy, the world outside the Self seems to thicken. It becomes hard to make out. It is not necessarily evil, although it *may* be evil; in any case, it causes so much suffering that it will at certain moments at least *appear* evil. It is a world that is separate from us who inhabit it; it will not yield to our desires and fantasies no matter how desperately we need it to do so. This means that in tragedy, recognition—*anagnorisis*, the banishing of ignorance—is a major goal. We question the tragic universe to discover its laws, since they are what we must live by. The worlds of comedy and romance, by contrast, are shaped by our hearts' desires; and in history, we are busily remaking the world to suit ourselves.

The feminine in the tragedies can be similarly defined in terms of evil, obduracy, and the problem of *anagnorisis*. First of all, women in the tragedies constitute the *single* group in which Harbage finds more bad than good: 58 percent bad and only 42 percent good. Like the world outside the Self, the feminine causes suffering, appears evil, and may actually *be* evil. And like the world outside the Self, women in the tragedies are notably separate from us, governed by their own laws whether their natures are good or evil. The hero can only recognize them for what they are or fail to do so. The effort to control them is useless; neither the feminine Other nor the world outside the Self is within our power in Shakespeare's tragedy.

The idea of a congruence between women and the world can be taken even further. In *King Lear*, as in *Othello*, the world outside the hero is starkly divided between good and evil, and so are the principal women characters—Goneril, Regan, Cordelia, and Desdemona. In *Hamlet* and *Antony and Cleopatra*, by contrast, the outside world is a mixture of good and bad; it is hard to tell manly strength from mindless ambition, and restraint may be confused with weakness. The women in these two plays are similarly a confusing mixture of good and evil, and finally may be neither. We never know the extent of Gertrude's guilt, or whether Cleopatra, if offered better terms, would have sold out to Caesar. But we know all along that Desdemona and Cordelia are perfectly good and Goneril and Regan vile beasts. In *Lear* and *Othello*, kindness and constancy are to be found in their purest forms, as are their opposites, cruelty and malice.

It is time to return to my original question. Am I content with the role played in *King Lear* by the wandering portion of my identity, the part I cannot invest in King Lear? On the whole, I think I should be. For one thing, I am flattered to think that I may be capable of such thrilling modulations between good and evil as exist in the world of *King Lear*. It makes me interesting to myself. Identifying with the intensely problematic world outside the hero gives me another way of participating in the major questions of the play, questions about the violent extremes we find within ourselves and in our experience. More importantly, I am content to identify with the world outside the hero because the dialectic between King Lear and the outside world is what creates the satisfactions of tragedy. It is when Lear cannot get what he wants from the outside world that *he* becomes interesting. We do not really want the tragic world to yield to the hero's desires; we want to see what happens to him when his suffering cracks him open, and he goes out on the heath to become something new. There, thanks to the resistance offered by the tragic world, we are in the presence of exciting possibilities. The hero may triumph over his losses; naked, he may be more splendid than he appeared when he was clothed. Or, like Coriolanus, the hero of one of the Roman plays, he may collapse. Both the risk and the possibility of Shakespearean tragedy depend on the Otherness of the tragic universe to the masculine Self. In identifying with the world outside the hero, I am identifying with something as powerful in creating the drama as the hero himself.

What is the nature of the resistance offered by the feminine Other in *King Lear*? On the one hand, it is a matter of malice: Goneril and Regan are selfish beasts who wish their father ill. On the other hand, it is a matter of pure separateness. Cordelia, as we have seen, is guilty of nothing but being a separate person from her father, of having her own social role to play. In many ways the resistance Cordelia offers is more interesting. Cordelia simply resists Lear's claim to be the sun around which everything revolves. The mere presence of another inviolable person is enough to shatter Lear's identity. The tragic hero wants to be the only star in the sky.

The feminine Other creates drama by resisting the hero, but also by being endlessly desirable to him. The desire of the hero for women and the world keeps him both alive and vulnerable; it keeps open the possibility of both suffering and fulfillment. A comparison between Lear and Gloucester will illustrate the point. Gloucester, who has sons instead of daughters, loses his capacity for desire and with it both his vulnerability to his experience and his chance of happiness. He tries to kill himself, is rescued by Edgar, feels suicidal again when he witnesses Lear's madness, urges Oswald to kill him, and finally is parked by Edgar in "the shadow of this tree." "A man may rot even here" (V.ii.8), he tells Edgar when Edgar returns. Since

Edgar and Gloucester are in the middle of a battle there is no time for an elaborate response. "Men must endure / Their going hence, even as their coming hither," Edgar tells his father briefly. "Ripeness is all. Come on." Gloucester gets up and plods on. "And that's true, too," he says. Nothing makes much difference to him anymore. Lear, by contrast, dies upon a wish. "Do you see this?" he asks urgently, bent over the dead Cordelia's head. "Look on her," he cries, tortured by hope. "Look, her lips, / Look there, look there." Lear's feelings stay alive to the end of the play.

As many people have noticed, there is a sexual component to Lear's desire for his daughters. When Lear is hurt by Goneril and Regan, he denounces them as if he were their lover, not their father:

> The fitchew, nor the soiled horse, goes to 't
> With a more riotous appetite.
> Down from the waist they are Centaurs,
> Though women all above:
> But to the girdle do the gods inherit,
> Beneath is all the fiend's.
> There's hell, there's darkness, there is the sulphurous pit,
> Burning, scalding, stench, consumption, fie, fie, fie!
>
> (IV.vi.124–131)

Why does Lear blast women for their sexual appetites rather than for their cruelty? Goneril and Regan are in fact unfaithful wives, but Lear doesn't know that, and anyway they haven't betrayed *him* sexually. But in Shakespeare's mind any wound that really matters is felt as a sexual wound. Sexual vulnerability, like sexual desire, is archetypal for Shakespeare. Lear's connection to his daughters is like a sexual connection in that it keeps sending him back for more. Finally Gloucester has had enough of life itself, but Lear can always think of something else to want from his daughters. First he wants flattery, then revenge, then recognition, kindness, forgiveness, companionship—whatever he can get. Beaten and cornered by his

enemies, he comes up with yet another fantasy of being
sustained by his daughter's love:

> Come, let's away to prison,
> We two alone will sing like birds i'th'cage:
> When thou dost ask me blessing I'll kneel down
> And ask of thee forgiveness: so we'll live,
> And pray, and sing, and tell old tales, and laugh
> At gilded butterflies, and hear poor rogues
> Talk of court news; and we'll talk with them too,
> Who loses and who wins, who's in, who's out;
> And take upon's the mystery of things,
> As if we were God's spies. (V.iii.8–17)

Lear is sometimes taken to task for this speech. It shows,
according to a certain school of literary criticism, that
Lear still hasn't learned his lesson, still thinks his desires
are all-important, still can't face reality. But is it a tragic
hero's job to learn his lesson, or is it his job to stay alive
and kicking to the end of the play? Gloucester learns his
lesson, but who cares what happens to him? Only Edgar.
We lose interest in Gloucester when *he* loses interest in
the world.

　　Women in *King Lear* are congruent with the tie that
binds us to life itself. As the feminine Other, women are
inviolably separate from the masculine Self, and they are
as active and aggressive in creating the plot as the hero
himself. Taken together, the three sisters range from one
end to the other on the scale of human moral behavior;
and if the feminine is, as so often in fiction by men, schizo-
phrenically split up into good and evil, it must be admitted
that so is everything else in the play. Edgar and Edmund
are almost as deeply divided as Cordelia and her sisters. It
is a play *about* extremes—of wealth and poverty, wisdom
and folly, heights and depths. As individual characters the
women in this play are very partial portraits; but as com-
ponents of the feminine Other they do add up. Only when
I refuse the role of Other altogether, only when nothing
will satisfy but a female version of the Self, do I refuse to
shelter the female portion of my identity with Shakespeare's women. At that point, if I'm smart, I take a break
from Shakespeare and pick up *Middlemarch*.

Suggested References

The number of possible references is vast and grows alarmingly. (The *Shakespeare Quarterly* devotes one issue each year to a list of the previous year's work, and *Shakespeare Survey*—an annual publication—includes a substantial review of recent scholarship, as well as an occasional essay surveying a few decades of scholarship on a chosen topic.) Though no works are indispensable, those listed below have been found especially helpful.

1. Shakespeare's Times

Byrne, M. St. Clare. *Elizabethan Life in Town and Country.* Rev. ed. New York: Barnes & Noble, 1961. Chapters on manners, beliefs, education, etc., with illustrations.

Joseph, B. L. *Shakespeare's Eden: The Commonwealth of England, 1558–1629.* New York: Barnes & Noble, 1971. An account of the social, political, economic, and cultural life of England.

Schoenbaum, S. *Shakespeare: The Globe and the World.* New York: Oxford University Press, 1979. A readable, handsomely illustrated book on the world of the Elizabethans.

Shakespeare's England. 2 vols. London: Oxford University Press. 1916. A large collection of scholarly essays on a wide variety of topics (e.g. astrology, costume, gardening, horsemanship), with special attention to Shakespeare's references to these topics.

Stone, Laurence. *The Crisis of the Aristocracy, 1558–1641,* abridged edition. London: Oxford University Press, 1967.

2. Shakespeare

Barnet, Sylvan. *A Short Guide to Shakespeare.* New York: Harcourt Brace Jovanovich, 1974. An introduction to all of the works and to the dramatic traditions behind them.

Bentley. Gerald E. *Shakespeare: A Biographical Handbook.* New Haven, Conn.: Yale University Press, 1961. The facts

about Shakespeare, with virtually no conjecture inter-
mingled.

Bush, Geoffrey. *Shakespeare and the Natural Condition.*
Cambridge, Mass.: Harvard University Press, 1956. A
short, sensitive account of Shakespeare's view of "Nature,"
touching most of the works.

Chambers, E. K. *William Shakespeare: A Study of Facts and
Problems.* 2 vols. London: Oxford University Press, 1930.
An invaluable, detailed reference work; not for the casual
reader.

Chute, Marchette. *Shakespeare of London.* New York: Dutton, 1949. A readable biography fused with portraits of
Stratford and London life.

Clemen, Wolfgang H. *The Development of Shakespeare's
Imagery.* Cambridge, Mass.: Harvard University Press,
1951. (Originally published in German, 1936.) A temperate
account of a subject often abused.

Granville-Barker, Harley. *Prefaces to Shakespeare.* 2 vols.
Princeton, N.J.: Princeton University Press, 1946–47. Essays on ten plays by a scholarly man of the theater.

Harbage, Alfred. *As They Liked It.* New York: Macmillan,
1947. A long, sensitive essay on Shakespeare, morality, and
the audience's expectations.

Kernan, Alvin B., ed. *Modern Shakespearean Criticism: Essays on Style, Dramaturgy, and the Major Plays.* New
York: Harcourt Brace Jovanovich, 1970. A collection of
major formalist criticism.

————. "The Plays and the Playwrights." In *The Revels History of Drama in English,* general editors Clifford Leech
and T. W. Craik. Vol. III. London: Methuen, 1975. A
book-length essay surveying Elizabethan drama with substantial discussions of Shakespeare's plays.

Schoenbaum, S. *Shakespeare's Lives.* Oxford: Clarendon
Press, 1970. A review of the evidence, and an examination
of many biographies, including those by Baconians and
other heretics.

————. *William Shakespeare: A Compact Documentary Life.*
New York: Oxford University Press, 1977. A readable
presentation of all that the documents tell us about Shakespeare.

Traversi, D. A. *An Approach to Shakespeare.* 3rd rev. ed. 2
vols. New York: Doubleday, 1968–69. An analysis of the

plays, beginning with words, images, and themes rather than with characters.

Van Doren, Mark. *Shakespeare*. New York: Holt, 1939. Brief, perceptive readings of all of the plays.

3. Shakespeare's Theater

Beckerman, Bernard. *Shakespeare at the Globe, 1599–1609*. New York: Macmillan, 1962. On the playhouse and on Elizabethan dramaturgy, acting, and staging.

Chambers, E. K. *The Elizabethan Stage*. 4 vols. New York: Oxford University Press, 1945. A major reference work on theaters, theatrical companies, and staging at court.

Cook, Ann Jennalie. *The Privileged Playgoers of Shakespeare's London, 1576–1642*. Princeton, N.J.: Princeton University Press, 1981. Sees Shakespeare's audience as more middle-class and more intellectual than Harbage (below) does.

Gurr, Andrew. *The Shakespearean Stage: 1579–1642*. 2d edition. Cambridge: Cambridge University Press, 1980. On the acting companies, the actors, the playhouses, the stages, and the audiences.

Harbage, Alfred. *Shakespeare's Audience*. New York: Columbia University Press, 1941. A study of the size and nature of the theatrical public, emphasizing its representativeness.

Hodges, C. Walter. *The Globe Restored*. London: Ernest Benn, 1953. A well-illustrated and readable attempt to reconstruct the Globe Theater.

Hosley, Richard. "The Playhouses." In *The Revels History of Drama in English*, general editors Clifford Leech and T. W. Craik. Vol. III. London: Methuen, 1975. An essay of one hundred pages on the physical aspects of the playhouses.

Kernodle, George R. *From Art to Theatre: Form and Convention in the Renaissance*. Chicago: University of Chicago Press, 1944. Pioneering and stimulating work on the symbolic and cultural meanings of theater construction.

Nagler, A. M. *Shakespeare's Stage*. Trans. Ralph Manheim. New Haven, Conn.: Yale University Press, 1958. A very brief introduction to the physical aspects of the playhouse.

Slater, Ann Pasternak. *Shakespeare the Director*. Totowa, N.J.: Barnes and Noble, 1982. An analysis of theatrical effects (e.g., kissing, kneeling) in stage directions and dialogue.

Thomson, Peter. *Shakespeare's Theatre*. London: Routledge and Kegan Paul, 1983. A discussion of how plays were staged in Shakespeare's time.

4. Miscellaneous Reference Works

Abbott, E. A. *A Shakespearean Grammar*. New Edition. New York: Macmillan, 1877. An examination of differences between Elizabethan and modern grammar.

Bevington, David. *Shakespeare*. Arlington Heights, Ill.: A. H. M. Publishing, 1978. A short guide to hundreds of important writings on the works.

Bullough, Geoffrey. *Narrative and Dramatic Sources of Shakespeare*. 8 vols. New York: Columbia University Press, 1957–75. A collection of many of the books Shakespeare drew upon, with judicious comments.

Campbell, Oscar James, and Edward G. Quinn. *The Reader's Encyclopedia of Shakespeare*. New York: Crowell, 1966. More than 2,600 entries, from a few sentences to a few pages, on everything related to Shakespeare.

Greg, W. W. *The Shakespeare First Folio*. New York: Oxford University Press, 1955. A detailed yet readable history of the first collection (1623) of Shakespeare's plays.

Kökeritz, Helge. *Shakespeare's Names*. New Haven, Conn.: Yale University Press, 1959. A guide to the pronunciation of some 1,800 names appearing in Shakespeare.

——. *Shakespeare's Pronunciation*. New Haven, Conn.: Yale University Press, 1953. Contains much information about puns and rhymes.

Muir, Kenneth. *The Sources of Shakespeare's Plays*. New Haven, Conn.: Yale University Press, 1978. An account of Shakespeare's use of his reading.

The Norton Facsimile: The First Folio of Shakespeare. Prepared by Charlton Hinman. New York: Norton, 1968. A handsome and accurate facsimile of the first collection (1623) of Shakespeare's plays.

Onions, C. T. *A Shakespeare Glossary*. 2d ed., rev., with enlarged addenda. London: Oxford University Press, 1953. Definitions of words (or senses of words) now obsolete.

Partridge, Eric. *Shakespeare's Bawdy*. Rev. ed. New York: Dutton, 1955. A glossary of bawdy words and phrases.

Shakespeare Quarterly. See headnote to Suggested References.

Shakespeare Survey. See headnote to Suggested References.

Shakespeare's Plays in Quarto. A Facsimile Edition. Ed. Michael J. B. Allen and Kenneth Muir. Berkeley, Calif.: University of California Press, 1981. A book of nine hundred pages, containing facsimiles of twenty-two of the quarto editions of Shakespeare's plays. An invaluable complement to *The Norton Facsimile. The First Folio of Shakespeare* (see above).

Smith, Gordon Ross. *A Classified Shakespeare Bibliography 1936–1958.* University Park, Pa.: Pennsylvania State University Press, 1963. A list of some 20,000 items on Shakespeare.

Spevack, Marvin. *The Harvard Concordance to Shakespeare.* Cambridge, Mass.: Harvard University Press, 1973. An index to Shakespeare's words.

Wells, Stanley, ed. *Shakespeare: Select Bibliographies.* London: Oxford University Press, 1973. Seventeen essays surveying scholarship and criticism of Shakespeare's life, work, and theater.

5. King Lear

Blaney, Peter W. M. *The Texts of "King Lear" and Their Origins.* Cambridge: Cambridge University Press, 1982.

Bradley, A. C. *Shakespearean Tragedy.* London: Macmillan, 1904. Part of the material on *King Lear* is reprinted above.

Colie, Rosalie, and F. T. Flahiff, eds. *Some Facets of "King Lear."* Toronto: University of Toronto Press, 1974.

Elton, William. *"King Lear" and the Gods.* San Marino, Calif.: Huntington Library, 1966.

Fraser, Russell A. *Shakespeare's Poetics in Relation to "King Lear."* London: Routledge and Kegan Paul, 1962.

Goldberg, S. L. *An Essay on "King Lear."* Cambridge: Cambridge University Press, 1974.

Granville-Barker, Harley. *Prefaces to Shakespeare.* 2 vols. Princeton, N.J.: Princeton University Press, 1946–47. Part of the material on *King Lear* is reprinted above.

Heilman, Robert. *This Great Stage: Image and Structure in "King Lear."* Baton Rouge, La.: Louisiana State University Press, 1948.

Kernan, Alvin B. *The Playwright as Magician.* New Haven, Conn.: Yale University Press, 1979.

Knight, G. Wilson. *The Wheel of Fire.* New York and London: Oxford University Press, 1930.

Lamb, Charles. "On Shakespeare's Tragedies" (1880), *The Complete Works in Prose and Verse of Charles Lamb.* London: Chatto and Windus, 1875.

Mack, Maynard. *King Lear in Our Time.* Berkeley, Calif.: University of California Press, 1965. Part of the material is reprinted above.

Muir, Kenneth, ed. *Shakespeare Survey,* 33 (1980).

Nicoll, Allardyce, ed. *Shakespeare Survey,* 13 (1960).

Novy, Marianne. *Love's Argument: Gender Relations in Shakespeare.* Chapel Hill, N.C.: University of North Carolina Press, 1984.

Rosen, William. *Shakespeare and the Craft of Tragedy.* Cambridge, Mass.: Harvard University Press, 1960.

Taylor, Gary, and Michael Warren, eds. *The Division of the Kingdoms: Shakespeare's Two Versions of "King Lear."* Oxford: Clarendon Press, 1983.

WORLD DRAMA

☐ **THE IMPORTANCE OF BEING EARNEST AND OTHER PLAYS by Oscar Wilde.** Introduction by Sylvan Barnet. Also included are *Lady Windermere's Fan,* and *Salomé.* (520734—$2.75)*

☐ **TARTUFFE and OTHER PLAYS by Molière.** Translated, with an Introduction by Donald M. Fame. Includes *The Ridiculous Précieuses, The School for Husbands, The School for Wives, Don Juan, The Versailles Impromptu,* and *The Critique of The School for Wives.* (520114—$3.50)*

☐ **CHEKHOV: THE MAJOR PLAYS by Anton Chekhov.** *Ivanov, The Sea Gull, Uncle Vanya, The Three Sisters* and *The Cherry Orchard.* New translation by Ann Dunnigan. Foreword by Robert Brustein. (517679—$2.95)

☐ **IBSEN: FOUR MAJOR PLAYS, Volume I, by Henrik Ibsen.** *The Master Builder, A Doll's House, Hedda Gabler,* and *The Wild Duck.* New translation with Foreword by Rolf Fjelde. (519396—$2.50)*

☐ **IBSEN: FOUR MAJOR PLAYS, Volume II, by Henrik Ibsen.** *Ghosts, An Enemy of the People, The Lady from the Sea,* and *John Gabriel Borkman.* New translation by Rolf Fjelde. (516559—$2.50)

☐ **PLAYS by George Bernard Shaw,** Introduction by Eric Bentley. *Man and Superman, Candida, Arms and the Man,* and *Mrs. Warren's Profession.* (517865—$3.95)†

☐ **PYGMALION and MY FAIR LADY.** George Bernard Shaw's brilliant romantic play and the internationally acclaimed musical adaptation by Alan Jay Lerner, together in one special edition. (519264—$2.95)*

  *Price slightly higher in Canada
  †Not available in Canada

**Buy them at your local
bookstore or use coupon
on next page for ordering.**

By the year 2000, 2 out of 3 Americans could be illiterate.

It's true.

Today, 75 million adults...about one American in three, can't read adequately. And by the year 2000, U.S. News & World Report envisions an America with a literacy rate of only 30%.

Before that America comes to be, you can stop it...by joining the fight against illiteracy today.

Call the Coalition for Literacy at toll-free **1-800-228-8813** and volunteer.

Volunteer Against Illiteracy. The only degree you need is a degree of caring.